Withdrawn/ABCL

Praise for Keri Arthur
Winner of the *Romantic Times* 2008 Reviewers' Choice Awards for Career Achievement in Urban Fantasy

"One of the best urban fantasy authors in print today."
—Darque Reviews

"You'll be hooked."   —*USA Today*

Darkness Splintered

"Readers will be swept up in a whirlwind of action that doesn't let up."   —*RT Book Reviews*

"There is plenty of action, suspense, danger, and romance at every turn of the page.... I have enjoyed watching Risa grow and adapt to her situation. I really can't wait to see how everything ends."   —Urban Fantasy Investigations

"This story has a way of [getting] into your mind to the extent where you are trying to sleep and then find yourself picking up the book again even though it's already four a.m."   —Night Owl Reviews

"The pace doesn't seem to let up even for a second.... Each time I pick up a [Dark Angels] book, Risa's grown a little more, become a little stronger, and is in deeper shit."
—The Book Swarm

"Urban fantasy at its best! Arthur captures readers and catapults them into a world that is both authentic and explosive.... This book is a must read."   —Readaholics Anonymous

"The biggest indicator of [being] a phenomenal author is ... writ[ing] book after book that keeps the reader coming back for more, and this surely fits Keri Arthur.... [She] should be on every urban fantasy lover's autobuy list, which she proves yet again with this fabulous showing in *Darkness Splintered*. An absolute must read!"
—A Book Obsession

continued ...

"So much is going on, but it never feels rushed. . . . Arthur really knows what she's doing and *Darkness Splintered* just might be the best in the series!"   —Under the Covers

"Captivating and hard to put down."
                                        —Happily Ever After-Reads

Darkness Unmasked

"Another compelling web of action, intrigue, mystery, and suspense! . . . The outside world simply disappears when I have a Dark Angels book in hand. . . . While a lot of series start to lag at the five-book mark, somehow I feel like this thrill ride is just getting started. . . . These books have everything you want in a perfectly written urban fantasy."
                                        —Literal Addiction

"Awesome. . . . A lot of series start to go stale after multiple installments, but that just isn't the case here."
                                        —A Book Obsession

"This is another gripping read in a series that I can't get enough of."   —Happily Ever After-Reads

"A well-written, thrilling urban fantasy."
                                        —All Things Urban Fantasy

Darkness Hunts

"[A] kick-ass heroine. . . . I'm enjoying this series more and more with each book."   —Happily Ever After-Reads

"Another thrilling installment in the Dark Angels series. . . . I am definitely looking forward to the next book."
                                        —All Things Urban Fantasy

"An absolute thrilling ride from start to finish!"
                                        —A Book Obsession

"I am a huge fan of this Dark Angels series . . . a must read for urban fantasy readers."   —Book Savvy Babe

"This series is awesome. . . . I absolutely cannot wait to read the next in the series."   —AwesomeSauce Book Club

"I cannot imagine anyone not loving this series!"
                                        —Urban Fantasy Investigations

"Chock-full of revelations, nonstop action, and a true MUST read for fans . . . a page-turner that will have readers on the edge of their seats."   —Nocturne Romance Reads

Darkness Devours

"Prepare for intense action and sexual attraction to take center stage. . . . Arthur writes stellar action scenes. . . . I absolutely cannot wait to read what happens next in this indomitable story. *Darkness Devours* is bloody good with its provocative heroine and killer plotline."

—Joyfully Reviewed

"An intricate and thrilling urban fantasy filled with sensuality, violence, and imagination . . . mesmerizing."

—Night Owl Reviews

Darkness Rising

"You will fall hard for [Keri Arthur's] Dark Angels series."   —Coffee Time Romance & More

"A highly imaginative world with memorable characters . . . everything a fan of romance and urban fantasy would enjoy. There is a cosmopolitan mix of supernatural creatures: werewolves, vampires, and witches . . . an exciting new series!"   —Night Owl Reviews

Darkness Unbound

"Keri Arthur has blown me away again. Her worlds are so complex and 'real.' . . . Risa makes readers fall in love with her. . . . I highly recommend Arthur's books."—*USA Today*

"Must read! I love, love, love it! Arthur's . . . kick-ass action and indelible heroine left me enraptured. Risa Jones is . . . one of a kind; she is the next generation's paranormal superheroine!"   —Joyfully Reviewed

Full Moon Rising

"Keri Arthur skillfully mixes her suspenseful plot with heady romance. . . . Sexy vampires, randy werewolves, and unabashed, unapologetic, joyful sex—you've gotta love it. Smart, sexy, and well conceived."   —Kim Harrison

"Deliciously sexy . . . [it] pulls you in and won't let go. Keri Arthur knows how to thrill! Buckle up and get ready for a wild, cool ride!"   —Shana Abé

Also by Keri Arthur

The Dark Angels Series
Darkness Unbound
Darkness Rising
Darkness Devours
Darkness Hunts
Darkness Unmasked
Darkness Splintered

The Souls of Fire Series
Fireborn

Withdrawn/ABCL

DARKNESS FALLS

A DARK ANGELS NOVEL

KERI ARTHUR

3907504760565l

A SIGNET BOOK

SIGNET
Published by the Penguin Group
Penguin Group (USA) LLC, 375 Hudson Street,
New York, New York 10014

Ⓟ

USA | Canada | UK | Ireland | Australia | New Zealand | India | South Africa | China
penguin.com
A Penguin Random House Company

First published by Signet, an imprint of New American Library,
a division of Penguin Group (USA) LLC

First Printing, December 2014

Copyright © Keri Arthur, 2014
Penguin supports copyright. Copyright fuels creativity, encourages diverse voices,
promotes free speech, and creates a vibrant culture. Thank you for buying an
authorized edition of this book and for complying with copyright laws by not
reproducing, scanning, or distributing any part of it in any form without permission. You are supporting writers and allowing Penguin to continue to publish
books for every reader.

Ⓟ REGISTERED TRADEMARK—MARCA REGISTRADA

ISBN 978-0-451-41960-6

Printed in the United States of America
10   9   8   7   6   5   4   3   2   1

PUBLISHER'S NOTE
This is a work of fiction. Names, characters, places, and incidents either are the
product of the author's imagination or are used fictitiously, and any resemblance
to actual persons, living or dead, business establishments, events, or locales is
entirely coincidental.

If you purchased this book without a cover you should be aware that this book
is stolen property. It was reported as "unsold and destroyed" to the publisher and
neither the author nor the publisher has received any payment for this "stripped
book."

I'd like to thank my lovely editor, Danielle Perez; copy editor Eileen Chetti for making sense of my Aussie English; publicist Nita Basu for getting the word out; and the fabulous Tony Mauro for the cover art.

A special thanks to those whose support I couldn't survive without: my agent, Miriam Kriss; my crit buddies and best friends, Robyn, Mel, Chris, Carolyn, and Freya; and my lovely daughter, Kasey.

Chapter 1

The Raziq were coming.

The energy of their approach was very distant, but it blasted heat and thunder across my senses and sent me reeling. But even worse was the sheer and utter depth of rage that accompanied that distant wave. I'd known they ⸱ld be angry that we'd deceived them, but this . . . This as murderous.

Up until now, the Raziq had used minor demons to kidnap me whenever they'd wanted to talk to me—although *their* version of talk generally involved some kind of torture. This time, however, there would be no talking. There would be only death and destruction.

And they would take out everyone—and everything—around us in the process.

It was a horrendous prospect given that we were still at the Brindle, a place that not only held aeons of witch knowledge but was also home to at least two dozen witches.

I reached for my sword. Even though we couldn't fight in this place of peace, I still felt safer with Amaya's weight in my hand. But she wasn't there. Just for an instant, panic surged; then I realized I'd left her behind, among the ruins of our home. In the aftermath of my father's destruction, I'd been desperate to see whether Mirri—who'd been under a death sentence, thanks to Father's magic—had by some miracle survived, and I hadn't given Amaya a second thought.

"We cannot stay here." The familiar masculine tones broke through the fear that had been holding me captive.

My gaze met Azriel's. He wasn't only my guardian but my lover, the father of my child, and the being I was now linked to forever in both life *and* afterlife. When I died, I would become what he was—a Mijai, a reaper warrior tasked not only with protecting the gates to heaven and hell, but also with hunting down the demons who broke through hell's gate to cause havoc here on Earth.

Of course, reapers weren't actually flesh beings— although they could certainly attain that form whenever they wished—but rather beings made of energy who lived on the gray fields, the area that divided Earth from heaven and hell. While I *was* part werewolf and therefore flesh, I was also part Aedh. The Aedh were energy beings who at one time lived on the fields as the reapers had, and also had been the traditional guardians of the gates. My father had been one of the Raziq—a group of rebel Aedh who were responsible for both the destruction of the Aedh and the creation of the three keys to the gates— and he was also the reason the keys were currently lost.

Or rather, only one key was still lost. I'd found the first two, but both had been stolen from under my nose by the dark sorceress who'd subsequently opened two of hell's three gates.

Things hadn't quite gone according to plan for her when she'd opened the second one, however, because she'd been captured by demons and dragged into the pits of hell. I was keeping everything crossed that that was *exactly* where she'd remain, but given the way luck had been treating us of late, it was an even-money bet she wouldn't.

"Risa," Azriel repeated when I didn't immediately answer him. "We *must* not stay here."

"I know."

But where the hell were we going to go that was safe

from the wrath of the Raziq? There *was* nowhere safe. Maybe not even hell itself—not that I particularly wanted to go *there*.

I briefly closed my eyes and tried to control the panic surging through me. And yet that approaching wave of anger filled every recess of my mind, making thought, let alone calm, near impossible. If they got hold of me ... My skin crawled.

It took a moment to register that my skin *was* actually crawling. Or at least part of it was. I glanced down. The wingless, serpentlike dragon tattoo on my left forearm was on the move, twisting around like a wild thing trapped. Anger gleamed in its dark eyes and its scales glowed a rich, vibrant lilac in the half-light of the room.

Of course, it wasn't an ordinary tattoo. It was a Dušan, a creature of magic that had been designed to protect me when I walked the fields. It was a gift from my father, and one of the few decent things he'd actually done for me since this whole key saga had begun.

Unfortunately, the Dušan was of little use here on Earth. It shouldn't even have been able to move on this plane, let alone partially disengage from my skin, as it had in the past.

"What's wrong now?"

I glanced at Ilianna—my best friend, flatmate, and a powerful witch in her own right. Her warm tones were rich with concern, and not without reason. After all, she'd only *just* managed to save the life of her mate, Mirri, from my father's foul magic, and here I was again, threatening not only Mirri's life but Ilianna's, her mom's, and those of everyone else who currently stood within the walls of this place. Because not even the magic of the Brindle, as powerful as it was, would stop the Raziq. It had been designed to protect the witches from the evil of *this* world. It was never meant to be a defense against what came from the gray fields.

"The Raziq hunt us." Azriel's reply was flat. Matter-of-fact. Yet his anger reverberated through every inch of my being, as fierce as anything I could feel from the Raziq. But it wasn't just anger; it was anticipation, and *that* was possibly scarier. He drew his sword and met my gaze. If the ominous black-blue fire that flickered down the sides of Valdis—which was the name of the demon locked within the metal of his sword, and who imbued it with a life and power of its own—was anything to go by, she was as ready to fight as her master. As ready as Amaya would have been had she been here. "We need to leave. *Now.*"

Ilianna frowned. "Then go home—"

"We can't," I cut in. "Home's gone."

It had been blown to smithereens when I'd thrust Amaya's black steel into my father's flesh and had allowed her to consume him. It was an action I didn't regret, not after everything the bastard had done.

"Yes," Ilianna replied. "But the wards your father gave us should still be active. I placed a spell on them that prevents anything or anyone other than us from moving them."

"Even from what basically resembled a bomb blast?"

She hesitated. "*That* I can't guarantee."

"A half guarantee is better than nothing." Azriel's gaze met mine again. "If they *aren't* active, then we stand and fight. The Raziq still need you, no matter how furious they might currently be."

Yes, but they didn't need *him*. And they would destroy him if they could. Still, what other choice did we have? No matter where we went, either here or on the gray fields, others would pay the price. I hesitated. "Will the Brindle's magic react if we transport out from within its walls?"

"Normally, yes," Kiandra, the Brindle's head witch, replied. She stood near Mirri and Zaira, Ilianna's mom, her gaze bright and all too knowing in the shadowed room. "But given the events of the last few days, I have woven specific exceptions into our barriers."

"Thanks." We were going to need them. I swallowed, then stepped toward Azriel.

"Call me," Ilianna said. "Let me know you're okay."

I didn't reply. I couldn't. Azriel's energy had already ripped through us, swiftly transporting us across the fields. We reappeared in the blackened ruins of the home I'd once shared with Ilianna and Tao—although to call them ruins was something of a misnomer. "Ruins" implied there was some form of basic structure left. There was nothing here. No walls, no ceiling, not even a basement. Just a big black hole that had once held a building we'd all loved.

I stepped away from Azriel and glanced up. The sky was filled with stars, and I wondered whether an entire day had passed us by. So much had happened over the past few days that I'd lost track.

Time appeared. The familiar, somewhat harsh tone that ran through my thoughts was heavy with displeasure. *Alone should not be.*

Sorry. I felt vaguely absurd for even issuing an apology. I mean, when it was all said and done, Amaya was a *sword.* But somewhere in the past few days, she had become more a friend than merely a means of protection.

I picked my way through the rubble and found her half-wedged into the blackened soil. I pulled her free and definitely felt a whole lot safer. Though it wasn't as if Amaya or Azriel—or anyone else, for that damn matter—could save me if the Raziq really *had* decided enough was enough.

"The Raziq have split," Azriel commented.

Confusion—and a deepening sense of dread—ran through me. "Meaning what?"

The ferocity that roiled through the connection between us gave his blue eyes an icy edge. "Half of them chase us here. The rest continue toward the Brindle."

"Oh fuck!"

"They plan to demonstrate the cost of misdirection, and there is nothing we can do to prevent it." His expression hardened, and I hadn't thought *that* was possible. "And before you say it, I will *not* let you endanger yourself for them."

"And I will *not* stand here and let others pay the price for decisions I've made!"

"We have no other choice—"

"There's *always* a fucking choice, Azriel. Standing here while others die in my place is *not* one of them."

"Making a stand at the Brindle will *not* alter the fate of the Brindle."

"Don't you think I know that?" I thrust a hand through my hair and began to pace. There *had* to be an answer. Had to be some way to protect the Brindle and everyone within her without either Azriel or me having to make a stand. Damn it, if only Ilianna had had the time to create more protection stones . . . The thought stuttered to a halt. "Oh my god, the protection stones."

Azriel frowned. "They are still active. I can feel their presence."

"Exactly!" I swung around to face him. "You need to get them to the Brindle. It's the only chance they have against the Raziq."

"I will not—"

"For god's sake, stop arguing and just do as I ask!"

He crossed his arms and glared at me. His expression was so fierce my insides quaked, even though I knew he would never, ever hurt me.

"My task is to protect you. No one else. You. I cannot and *will* not leave you unprotected, especially not *now*."

Not when there is life and love yet to be explored between us. Not when you carry our child. The words spun through my thoughts, as fierce as his expression and yet filled with such passion that my heart damn near melted. I walked back to him and touched his arm. His skin twitched, but the muscles underneath were like steel. My warrior was ready for battle.

"I know it goes against every instinct, Azriel, but I couldn't live with myself if anyone at the Brindle died because of me."

"And I would not want to live without you. There *is* nowhere that is safe from the wrath of the Raziq."

"Maybe not—" I hesitated, suddenly remembering what he'd said about the Aedh temples and the remnants of the priests who still haunted that place. They weren't ghosts, as such—more echoes of the beings they'd once been—but they were nevertheless damn dangerous. I'd briefly encountered one of them when I'd been chasing the sorceress to hell's gate, and it had left me in no doubt that he could destroy me without a second's hesitation.

"*That* is not a true option," Azriel said, obviously following my thoughts. "And there is certainly no guarantee that the priests will even acknowledge you again, let alone provide any sort of assistance."

"That's a chance I'm willing to take." And it was certainly a better option than letting the Brindle pay the cost for my deceit. "Those who haunt that place weren't aware of the Raziq's duplicity, Azriel, but I think they might be now. And you're the one who told me that if they decide you're an intruder, they can cause great harm."

"But the Raziq were once priests—"

"*And* they're also the reason the Aedh no longer exist to guard the gates," I cut in. "This might be the only way both of us are going to survive a confrontation with the Raziq, and we *have* to take it."

He stared at me for several heartbeats, then swore viciously. Not in my language, in his. I blinked at the realization that I'd understood it, but I let it slide. Right now it didn't matter a damn how or when *that* had happened. All that did matter was surviving the next few minutes.

Because the Raziq were getting nearer. They'd breached the barrier between the fields and Earth and were closing in even as we stood here. I suspected the only reason they hadn't yet confronted us was simply that we had moved. But that wouldn't help the Brindle.

Azriel sheathed his sword, then caught my hand and tugged me toward him. "If we're going to do this, then we do it somewhere where your body is going to be safe while you're on the fields."

"Not the Brindle—"

"No."

The word was barely out of his mouth when his energy ripped through us again. We appeared in a room that was dark but not unoccupied. The scents in the air told me exactly where we were—Aunt Riley's. She was the very last person I wanted to endanger in *any* way. I wasn't actually blood related to Riley, but after my mom's death, she and her pack were the only family I had left.

But before I could make any objection about being there, she said, "I'm gathering there's a good reason behind your sudden appearance in our bedroom at this ungodly hour."

Her tone was wry, and she didn't sound the slightest bit sleepy. But then, she'd once been not only a guardian, but one of their best. I guess old habits—like sleeping light—die hard.

"The Aedh hunt us." Azriel's voice was tight. He didn't like doing this any more than I did, though I suspected our reasons were very different. "I need you to keep Risa's body safe while she's on the gray fields."

And with that, he kissed me—fiercely but all too briefly—then disappeared. Leaving me reeling, battling for breath, and more frightened than I'd ever been. Because I was about to face the wrath of the Raziq alone, even if for only a few minutes.

Not alone, Amaya grumbled. *Here am.*

Yes, she was. But even a demon sword with a thirst for bloodshed might not be enough to counter the fury I could feel in the Raziq.

And why the hell could I even feel that? Had it something to do with whatever Malin—the woman in charge of the Raziq and my father's pissed-off ex—had done to me that time she'd tortured me? I didn't know, because Malin had also erased my knowledge of the procedure to prevent my father from figuring out what she'd done. But with him dead, maybe it was time to find out.

"Risa?" This time it was Riley's mate, Quinn, who spoke.

He was the reason Azriel had brought me here. While Riley may once have been a guardian, Quinn was a whole lot more. He was a vampire who'd once been a Cazador—who were basically the high vampire council's elite hit squad—and was also what I was: a half-breed Aedh. One who'd undergone priest's training. If there was anyone here on Earth who could stand against the wrath of the Raziq for more than a second, it would be him.

I swallowed heavily, but it didn't do a whole lot to ease the dryness in my throat. What I was about to do was the very last thing I'd *ever* wanted to do, but the reality was I'd been left with little other choice.

"There's no time to explain," I said. "I have to get onto the fields immediately. People will die if I don't."

"Then do it." Quinn climbed out of bed and walked to the wardrobes that lined one wall of their bedroom. "No one will get past us."

I hoped he was right, but it wasn't like I was going to be around to find out. I sat cross-legged on the thick, cushiony carpet, saw Quinn open a door and reach for the weapons within, then closed my eyes and took a deep breath.

As I released it, I released awareness of everything around me, concentrating on nothing more than slowing the frantic beat of my heart so I could free my psyche, my soul—or whatever else people liked to call it—from the constraints of my flesh. *That* was what the Raziq were following—not my flesh, but my spirit. I hoped they would follow me onto the fields and not wreak hell on the two people I cared about most in this world.

As the awareness of everything around me began to fade, warmth throbbed at my neck—a sign that the charm Ilianna had given me when we'd both still been teenagers was at work, protecting me as my psyche pulled free and stepped onto the gray fields. Here the real world was little more than a shadow, a place where those things that could not be seen on the living plane became visible. It was also the land between life and death, a place through which souls journeyed to whatever gateway was their next destination, be it heaven or hell.

But it was far from uninhabited. The reapers lived here, and so did the Raziq who remained.

And right now it was a dangerous place for me to be. The Raziq could move far faster here than I could. My only hope was reaching the Aedh temples that surrounded and protected the gates.

I turned and ran. The Dušan immediately exploded from my arm, her energy flowing through me as her serpentine form gained flesh and shape, became real and solid. She swirled around me, the wind of her body buffeting mine as her sharp ebony gaze scanned the fields around us. Looking for trouble. Looking to fight.

I had to wonder whether even she would have any hope against the Raziq. Because they were coming. The thunder of their approach shook the very air around us.

Fear surged, and it lent me the strength to go faster. But running seemed a hideously slow method of movement, even if everything around me was little more than a blur. I wished I could transport myself to the temples instantaneously, as Azriel had in the past, but I wasn't yet of this world, even if I was destined to become a Mijai upon death.

The Dušan's movements were becoming more and more frantic. I swore and reached for every ounce of energy I had left, until it felt as if I were flying through the fields of gray.

But even when I reached the temples, I felt no safer. This place was as ghostly and surreal as the rest of the fields, but it was also a place filled with impossible shapes, high, soaring arches, and honeycombed domes sitting atop floating towers. Yet it no longer felt as empty as it had the first time I'd come here. There was an awareness—an anger—here now, and it filled the temple grounds with a watchful energy that stung my skin and sent chills through my being.

I stopped in the expanse of emptiness that divided the temple buildings from the simply adorned gates to heaven and hell. The Dušan surged around me, her movements sharp, agitated. I tightened my grip on Amaya as I turned to face the oncoming Raziq. Amaya began to hiss in expectation, the noise jarring against the watchful silence. But none of the priestly remnants appeared or spoke. I had no doubt they were aware of my presence, but it seemed that, for now, they were content to watch.

Leaving me hoping like *hell* that I hadn't been wrong, that they *would* interfere if the Raziq got too violent.

But it wasn't like I had any other choice now, anyway. They were here.

Electricity surged, dark and violent. Without warning, both the Dušan and I were flung backward. I hit vaporous ground that felt as hard as anything on Earth and tumbled into the wall of a building that stood impossibly on a point.

Amaya was screaming, the Dušan was screaming, and their joint fury echoed both through my brain and across the fields. The Dušan surged upward, briefly disappearing into grayness before she dove into the midst of the Raziq, snapping and tearing at the beings I couldn't see, could only feel. A second later, she was sent tumbling again.

If they could do that to a Dušan, what hope did I have?

Amaya screamed again. She wanted to rend, to tear, to consume, but there were far too many of them. We didn't stand a chance ... and yet, I couldn't give up—not without a fight. Not this time.

I pushed to my feet, raised Amaya, and spit, "Do your worst, Malin. But you might want to remember you still need me to find that last key. And if you kill me, I become Mijai and beyond even *your* reach. Not something you'd want, I'd guess."

For a moment, there was no response; then that dark energy surged again. I swore and dove out of the way, and the dark energy hit the building that loomed above me. Its ghostly, gleaming sides rippled, the waves small at first but gaining in depth as they rolled upward, until the whole building quivered and shook and the thick, heavy top began to crumble and fall. I scrambled out of the way only to feel another bolt arrowing toward me. I swore and went left, but this time I wasn't quite fast enough. The energy sizzled past my legs, wrapping them in heat, until it felt as if my flesh were melting from my bones.

A scream tore up my throat, but I clamped down on it hard, and it came out little more than a hiss. I wasn't flesh; I was energy. *This* was nothing more than mind games.

Mind games that felt painfully real.

Damn it, no! If I was going to go down, then I sure as hell was going to take some of these bastards with me.

Amaya, do your worst. And with that, I flung her as hard as I could into the seething mass of energy that was the Raziq. They scattered, as I knew they would, but Amaya arced around, her sides spitting lilac flames that splayed out like burning bullets. Whether they hit any targets, I have no idea, because I wasn't about to hang around waiting for another bolt to hit me. I scrambled to my feet and ran to the right of the Raziq. Amaya surged through their midst, still spitting her bullets as she returned to me. The minute she thumped into my hand, I swung her with every ounce of strength and anger within me. Steel connected with energy and the resulting explosion was brief but fierce and would have knocked me off my feet had it not been for my grip on my sword. Amaya wasn't going anywhere; she had a soul to devour, and devour she did. It took barely a heartbeat, but that was time enough for the rest of the Raziq to rally. Again that dark energy swept across the silent watchfulness of the temple's fields, but this time the invisible blow was broader, cutting the possibility of diving out of its path.

Amaya, shield! I dropped to one knee and held Amaya in front of me. Lilac fire instantly flared out from the tip of her blade and formed a circle that encased me completely.

And just in time.

The dark energy hit the barrier, and with enough force that it pushed me backward several feet. Amaya screamed in fury, her shield burning and bubbling where the Raziq's energy flayed her. She held firm, but I had to wonder for how long. Not very, I suspected.

Damn it, where were the remnants? The Raziq were the reason we were all in this mess—they were the reason the priests were dead. Did they not realize that? Did

they not want to avenge that? I knew Aedh were supposedly emotionless beings, but they were not above pride
and they certainly weren't above anger. Surely the priests
had to feel *something* about their demise.

But what if they didn't know or care?

Maybe it was time to remind them of their duty to
protect the gates.

"Killing me won't solve your current problem, Malin."
I had to shout to be heard above both Amaya's screech-
ing and the thunderous impact of the dark energy against
her shield. I had no idea where the Dušan was, but she
was still very much active if her bellows were anything
to go by. "As long as there's one key left, you—as an
Aedh priest—cannot be free from the responsibility of
caring for the gates. If you so desperately want to close
the gates permanently and therefore end your servitude
to them, then you're better off trying to sweet-talk me."

"Sweet-talk?" The voice was feminine and decidedly
pleasant. There was none of the malevolence I could feel
in the dark energy, yet it nevertheless sent chills down
my spine. Malin could charm the pants off a spider even
as she dissected it piece by tiny piece. She'd dissected me
once. That time, at least, she'd put me back whole, though
not entirely the same. And while Azriel certainly knew
what she'd done to me, he wasn't saying anything. This
time, however, I suspected she would not be so generous.
"You defy us at every turn, you do not take our threats
seriously, and you expect us to simply accept your games
of misdirection? Since when did insanity become a
thread in your being?"

"I'm guessing it happened the day you lot entered my
life." It probably wasn't the wisest thing to say, but hey,
what the hell? It wasn't like she could get any angrier.
Although the fresh burst of energy that hit Amaya's
shield very much suggested I was wrong. And the fact

that *she* was no longer screaming was an ominous sign her strength was weakening.

Is, she muttered. If there was one thing my sword hated, it was admitting she wasn't all-powerful. *Yours must draw soon.*

Her drawing on my strength was the very last thing *I* wanted right now, but again, until Malin and the rest of the Raziq calmed down a tad, it wasn't like we had another choice.

Presuming, of course, they *would* calm down.

"And insanity aside," I continued, "it doesn't alter the fact you still need me to find the final key."

"Not if we've now decided it would be better to destroy both the gates that are opened and the one that is not."

My body went cold. If they did *that*, then heaven help us all. Hell would be unleashed both on the fields and on Earth, and I very much suspected neither world would survive.

But would the fates and the priestly remnants allow that?

Their continuing silence—at least when it came to the Raziq—very much suggested they might.

"The mere fact you make such a threat shows just how far the Raziq have fallen." Azriel's voice cut across the noise and the anger that filled the temple grounds as cleanly as sunshine through rain. Relief made my arms shake, and tears stung my eyes. I blinked them away furiously. It wasn't over yet. Not by a long shot. It was still him and me against all of them.

"You no longer deserve the name of priests," he continued, voice ominously flat. "And you certainly no longer have the umbrella of protection such a title endows."

"Do *not* make idle threats, Mijai." Any pretense of civility had finally been stripped from Malin's voice. It was evil personified; nothing more, nothing less. "We both know you would not dare to violate the sanctity of this place."

"Not without the permission of the fates," he agreed. "And *that* we now have."

With those words lingering ominously in the air, he appeared.

And he wasn't alone.

Chapter 2

Azriel stood on the far side of the massed Raziq, his casual stance belying the fury in his eyes and the fierceness of his grip on Valdis. In this ghostly, gray-clad world, he shone with a light that was intense and golden, and it cut through the shadows as brightly as the sun.

Behind him stood another eight Mijai. All of them were battle scarred—some more so than even Azriel—and all of them radiated a savage desire to fight. But then, the Raziq were the reason so many of them had those scars. The sorceress may have opened hell's gates—thereby allowing so many demons to breach the remaining barrier—but it was the Raziq who'd made the keys that had enabled her to do it.

If what Azriel had said was true—and he wasn't given to lies or exaggeration—then for the first time in a *very* long time, the powers that be had given the Mijai permission to do something more than merely hunt down the escapees from hell. They'd given them the power to deal with the very people who'd *caused* this mess in the first place.

Which—considering they hadn't stopped what had basically amounted to the genocide of the Aedh—was one big damn step. And one that showed just how tenuous the current situation was to both the gray fields and Earth.

But there was another, more personal, benefit to Azriel's sudden appearance—it had drawn Malin's attention away from me, and *that* meant the thick beam of energy no longer assaulted Amaya's shield.

Drop can? Amaya asked.

I hesitated, my gaze flickering to the turgid mass of energy that was the rest of the Raziq. They seemed to have gathered behind Malin, and none of them appeared to be paying any particular attention to me—although it was a little hard to be certain given that they were all concealed from my sight. Still, with the shield sucking strength from both Amaya *and* me, it was better to err on the side of caution and use it only when absolutely necessary.

Besides, while I didn't doubt either the fighting skills or the determination of the reapers, they were still outnumbered two to one. I needed to keep as much strength on hand as I could, because once the attention of the Raziq was no longer held by the reapers, some of those "spare" Raziq would undoubtedly come after me.

I took a deep breath that really did little to bolster my courage, then said, *Yeah, do it.*

The lilac flames retreated instantly. I waited, tension rippling through every particle, ready to flee the instant anything *remotely* resembling an attack headed my way.

Nothing happened. I didn't relax, however. Just because they weren't attacking didn't mean they soon wouldn't.

"We both know the fates would never sanctify such an action." Contempt filled Malin's tone. "This place is sacred. They hold no jurisdiction here."

"They have *always* held jurisdiction here." Azriel's voice was flat, unemotional. But his need to kill—to avenge not so much what Malin and her crew had done in relation to the keys as what they'd done to *me*—was so strong I could almost taste it. Yet he held it in check, and I had no idea why if he had the fates' permission to deal with the Raziq.

Because, he said, *the fates would prefer* not *to shed*

*blood in this place. She is right in that it is sacred. There-
fore, the Raziq have one chance to walk away. As much as
I hope—pray—they do not, I will not gainsay the will of
the fates. Not when I now have so much more at risk.*

Meaning me. God, why the hell had it taken me so
damn long to realize what I'd been searching so long for
had been right in front of me the whole time? Why had
I wasted so much time being afraid and not trusting instinct and emotion when it came to him?

That is a question I have often asked myself. Though
his mental tones were touched by wry amusement, there
was no evidence of it in his voice as he added, "The fates
have not seen the necessity of interfering until now, Malin. But your actions endanger us all."

"My actions will free *us*. And that is all that matters."

"As ever, you do not see the bigger picture. You are
too bound by your own dreams and desires."

He made a slight motion with his hand, and the dark
energy covering the Raziq trembled and quivered, as if
assaulted by a very great force. Then, with little fanfare,
it faded, and the Raziq were finally revealed.

It was the first time I'd actually seen them, and they
were—like most Aedh—almost terrifyingly beautiful to
behold. The ten men were uniformly tall, with broad shoulders, muscular physiques, and faces that were as close to
perfection as creation ever got. The nine women had the
bodies of Amazons and the faces of angels, and they all
had golden hair that glowed as fiercely as the wings on
their backs in the diffused light of the fields. Their eyes—
which varied from lilac, like mine, to vibrant blues or the
richest of greens—were so filled with power it was almost
impossible to meet their gaze for any great length of time.
But there was little in the way of life or warmth in their
expressions. All that could be seen was either remote con-
descension or utter contempt or—in Malin's case—outright
animosity and hate.

For an unemotional being, she sure did seem to be displaying a whole lot of emotion.

Malin laughed. The bitter sound echoed uneasily across the temple's grounds. "And I suppose *that* little demonstration is meant to cower us?"

Azriel's answering smile was cold. Ferocious. "It was meant as nothing more than it was—an unveiling of evil."

"Reaper, I grow bored of you."

And with that, she attacked. Not Azriel. Me.

I swore and dove out of the way, but the bolt was too fast, my reaction—and Amaya's—too slow. The energy hit with all the force of a hammer. It pinned me, flayed me, *ate* at me, until it felt as if there were thousands upon thousands of tiny maggots boring into my skin.

I screamed, but the sound was lost to Amaya's screech of fury—a sound that was accompanied by a more masculine roar. The energy flaying me abruptly cut off, even as energy flared from Amaya's sides and encased me in a protective shield of lilac. I didn't immediately move; it was all I could do to drag in air, to *not* scream in pain as Malin's energy continued its munching even as it dissipated.

Up! Amaya's screech was as painful as those fading remnants. *Move must!*

I forced my eyes open, saw five Raziq barreling toward me, and swore—though the words came out little more than a harsh scrape of sound. Beyond the five, in an incandescent cloud that sizzled and cracked with such force that it shook the surreal buildings and burned the air, Azriel and his reapers fought the other thirteen Raziq.

Malin was nowhere to be seen.

Runs. Amaya's mental tones were scathing. *Coward much.*

Malin didn't strike me as a coward. If she was running, then she was running *to* something rather than from us.

I had a bad feeling I needed to stop her from reaching whatever it was she was running for. But before I could do that, I had to deal with the Raziq coming at me.

I pushed to my feet, my breathing harsh and sweat trickling down my spine. I might not be flesh in this world, but my energy form seemed to react in the exact same way. Maybe it was simply a form of muscle memory—my being reacting in the only way it knew how.

Drop the shield, I said. *We can't risk the constant pull at our strength.*

Stronger we should be, she muttered, as the purple haze of energy retreated.

Yes, we should, but to get stronger I needed time to relax and regroup—and *that* wasn't going to happen anytime soon. Not until I dealt with the Raziq and the keys.

Even then, there was no guarantee of a long and happy life, simply because I still had to find the sorceress, and I was still left with Madeline Hunter. And she, in many ways, was the worst of the lot. She wasn't only one of the leaders of the high vampire council *and* the head honcho of the Directorate, but also—quite literally—a monster wearing human flesh who apparently had a direct line of communication to the god she worshipped.

She was also, unfortunately, a monster I worked for.

But Hunter was a problem for another day. I had to survive *this* one before I started worrying about anything— or anyone—else.

Count to three, then move sharply left, I said, then raised Amaya and flung her hard.

The approaching Raziq scattered left and right, as I figured they might. Amaya jagged left and flames shot from her sides. They swiftly ensnared one of the Raziq, bringing him down even as they cocooned him. He writhed, screamed, fought, all to little effect. Amaya chuckled, the sound triumphant as she consumed her prey.

Bolts of energy shot toward me. I ran, swerving

around to the right, the bolts nipping at my heels. Sparks spun around me, fierce and bright in the gray.

Amaya arrowed around and slapped back into my palm. I raised her above my head and leapt high, twisting in midair and slashing wildly at the nearest Aedh as I flew over him. I hit the ethereal ground, rolled to my feet, and spun around, my sword held at the ready. The Aedh I'd struck had stopped. *Completely* stopped. He wasn't moving, wasn't reacting. Wasn't doing *anything*.

Then light began to gleam from the top of his head, a sliver of brightness that gradually lengthened, growing ever wider as it crept down his neck and then his spine, until he was no longer whole but two separate halves.

We'd split him asunder.

Deserved more, Amaya commented, her mental tones indignant as the two halves of the Aedh began to disintegrate. *Consume should have.*

Even you can't eat them all.

Bet can.

I snorted, then jumped sideways as several more bolts of energy came at me. I threw Amaya to scatter them again, then ran like hell, my gaze sweeping across the temple's grounds. I spotted Azriel and relief filled me. He was still standing, still fighting, though his torso bore several wounds that gleamed with ruddy fire. Others had obviously not been so lucky. The reaper numbers were down to six, but the Raziq had suffered greater losses—only eight now stood. Though that meant the odds were more even, it certainly didn't ease the tension curling through me. It wasn't over yet—not by a long shot. As long as even one of them lived, neither of our worlds would be safe.

Amaya thudded back into my grip, heavier than before. She'd obviously consumed another Aedh. The back of my neck crawled with awareness. I swung around, Amaya raised high. Bright steel met energy, and the resulting explosion sent me tumbling backward.

I was still rolling when a rope of energy hit me, winding itself around me, then pinning me in place. I couldn't move, couldn't raise Amaya. She hissed and shot flames out from her sides; they crawled across the line of energy holding me captive, spitting and sizzling as she battled to free us both.

It wasn't going to be soon enough. The remaining two Raziq of the original five who'd been sent after me were coming. Not only could I see them, but I could feel their determination to make me pay—suffer—before they bent me to their will. And I knew that once again they intended to unravel the threads of my being—only this time, when they put me back together, they would ensure I could do nothing other than obey them. Fear bloomed, thick and fast, its taste so bitter that bile rose in my throat and threatened to choke me. I swore and struggled against the bonds holding me captive, desperate to get free.

Two serpentine forms—one winged, one not—shot out of the ether. Azriel's headed for the two Raziq, while mine swept me up, rope and all, and carried me away from the battlefield and out of immediate danger.

The Dušan will take you to Malin, Azriel said. *She is up to no good.*

Malin is more than I can handle alone, Azriel.

Perhaps, he agreed, *but rest assured she will not find you so easy to kill now—not after inserting her own DNA within you.*

When the hell did she do that?

When she tore you— The rest of the sentence was ended by a grunt. Pain flickered down the mental lines, and I knew he'd been wounded again.

Damn it, Azriel, you need—

To finish what I started here, he cut in, tone fierce. *As much as I might wish otherwise, I have been tasked with ending the Raziq. I cannot—dare not—do otherwise.*

I glanced down. My Dušan wasn't taking me to the gates—which was where I'd half expected Malin to be—but rather over the external temple buildings and into the inner sanctum. It was a place that would have rejected my presence—and probably killed me outright—if not for the bracelet I now wore. It was black string twined with a silverish thread, and it had an almost ghostly glow. My father had given it to me to chase the sorceress, and its presence on my wrist was the only reason I had access to both his private quarters and the more sacred areas of this place.

I guess that was *two* good things he'd done for me.

Malin's a Raziq, I commented. *And you have permission to deal with them.*

But she *is not mine to end—the fates were clear on that, if nothing else.*

The fates, as usual, were being *damned* unhelpful. I took a deep breath, trying to calm the fear that sat like a stone in the middle of my being. Damn it, I didn't want our child to grow up without his father!

He won't. I am injured, but nowhere near expiry.

Well, make sure you stay that way! The bright structures below were less impossibly shaped than before, yet even more ethereal. There was no sign of Malin, however. *But what has Malin inserting her DNA in me got to do with it being less likely that she can kill me?*

You are now a creation of three races—werewolf, Aedh, and reaper. It gives you strength and power not only in your world and mine, but here, in the one place Malin thinks she has no equal.

I frowned. *But I can't do what she—*

You can, he cut in again, *if you apply yourself and* believe. *She may have had aeons to understand and use the power of this place, but she is no longer the more powerful.*

And what of the remnants? Will they help me if you happen to be wrong and it all goes to hell in a handbasket?

The remnants have not yet intervened because they have had no need to. But they assisted you the last time you were here and they will do so again, if you actually call. They can no more ignore you than I can.

I snorted. *That remark can be taken two ways, reaper.*

And both would be true. There was a brief edge of amusement in his mental tones. *Now, go. I must concentrate.*

The mental line shut down, but I could nevertheless feel his presence; it was a soft buzz of electricity that would flare to life the minute either of us wished it.

The Dušan began spiraling down. Soon we were gliding through canyons that were deep but not shadowed, thanks to the incandescence of the sturdy buildings that soared high above us.

Eventually, the Dušan slithered to a halt at the base of a building that was egg shaped and had a lustrous pearl-like sheen. The sheer force of energy radiating off it made my soul shiver in fear. This place, whatever the fuck it was, was both ancient *and* powerful. More powerful than anything or anyone I'd ever come across—even the gates to heaven and hell themselves.

The Dušan raked a claw through my body, cutting the cords that bound me without hurting me. I scrambled to my feet as the bindings fell away, then raised Amaya. She was hissing like a banshee, and the sound echoed uneasily across the silence.

Have said before, calling banshee an insult, she muttered. *Am better.*

Yeah, you are, I agreed. *Sorry.*

She preened at that, and her noise died down to a background scratch. I scanned the building from left to right, but the surface appeared unbroken by either windows or doors. There had to be some way of getting in, though. After all, the Dušan had been following Malin's trail and this was where we'd stopped.

With little in the way of options, I stepped forward and pressed a hand against the building's luminous side. Warmth pulsed under my fingertips. It felt like a heartbeat, and instinct suggested this place was oddly alive and aware. I shivered and hoped like hell this was one of those occasions when instinct was wrong.

As the pulsing got stronger, light began to flare softly across the building's warm surface. Ripples of energy rolled away from my touch, growing ever stronger, until the whole building seemed to shimmer. Then a black crack appeared to the right of my fingertips. It bloomed rapidly across the surface, until it had formed an inky stain the size of a basketball.

In, Amaya said. *Hunt we must.*

I'm not going to fit—

Will, she cut in. *Believe.*

Azriel had urged the same thing, but it was kinda hard to do when the world kept sending you into a tailspin. But again, it wasn't like I had a lot of other choices, not if I wanted to stop Malin from doing whatever she intended to do inside this place.

I gripped Amaya tighter, closed my eyes, and imagined myself arrowing through that circle.

Energy tingled through me; then there was a brief sense of movement. I opened my eyes and saw darkness. Complete and utter darkness. Not even Amaya's flames were able to break the depressing weight of it. But I could feel her warmth in my hand, and that was at least some comfort.

I glanced over my shoulder and noticed that the

Dušan was still outside, her serpentine form flowing back and forth across the entrance hole I'd created, her agitation evident in every lilac inch.

No come, Amaya said. *Outside must stay.*

"Well, that's damned inconvenient," I muttered, although it wasn't entirely surprising. The Dušan hadn't been able to enter my father's quarters, either. "Any idea where the hell we're supposed to go in this ink?"

Something, Amaya said. *Hides.*

My grip on her tightened. *Is it Malin?*

Tell not, she said. *Black heavy.*

Where?

Left. Find will.

Yeah, I thought grimly, but will it be us finding her, or her finding us? And how the hell was I supposed to fight in this goddamn ink?

You will tell me if I'm about to crash into something, won't you? I said, and flowed forward cautiously.

Something suspiciously like a chuckle ran across the rear of my thoughts, although she didn't actually answer. I held her out in front of me, so that if I *did* run into something, she'd at least hit it first. We moved through the ink for what seemed like hours, but maybe that was a side effect of having absolutely no sensory input, and no clue as to what might lie underneath night's cloak.

Here, Amaya said eventually. *Stop.*

I did so and once again scanned the blackness around us. I still had no sense of anything or anyone . . . and yet, there was an oddly different feel to the air here. It felt . . . anticipatory.

Damn it, I needed to see!

Then lift, Amaya said.

Lift what? I took a step forward. Movement stirred the ink, and it wasn't mine.

The dark.

I took several more steps forward. Again there was an

answering echo of movement, and a deep, oddly unclean energy began to stir around us. It stung my being, the sensation unpleasant. *I can't lift this, Amaya.*

Try can, she muttered, displeasure heavy in her mental tones.

I took a deep breath and released it slowly. Azriel might have implied that I could use the power of this place *if* I applied myself and believed, but the whole trouble with *that* was the fact that I had no idea where to begin.

In mind, Amaya said. *Will do.*

Meaning all I had to do was imagine? That sounded entirely too easy, especially considering absolutely nothing else on this goddamn quest had been. But I resolutely closed my eyes and imagined the ink was nothing more than a suffocating fog. Then I pictured a breeze coming through and scattering that fog, revealing what lay underneath. I fixed the image firmly in mind, put as much belief into it as I possibly could, and literally *willed* it to happen.

For several heartbeats, nothing did. Then a strong breeze began to play through my particles and there was an odd sort of shift, as if the whole place had somehow moved. I opened my eyes and saw darkness.

But it wasn't the ink of before.

There were shadows out there now—some humanoid, some reptilian or animal, and some that bore striking similarities to the Aedh. And there were all sorts of flora, round spheres that resembled planets in miniature, and many other things that had absolutely no resemblance to anything I'd ever seen before. It was almost as if this place was some sort of monument to all the things that lived and breathed, as well as all those that didn't.

Creation's reference library, perhaps?

But why in the hell would Malin come here?

"To destroy creation, of course," came the amused reply. "Or, at least, the part of it that references the temples and the gates."

I swung around, my fingers automatically tightening against Amaya's hilt. Malin strolled out from behind some kind of stone crustacean, her golden wings little more than gossamer wisps in this place and her body even less defined. But the malevolence that oozed from her being played across the shadows and made it hard to breathe.

You don't need to breathe here, I reminded myself fiercely. *You are energy, and of this place now.*

Malin laughed, the sound cutting. "You can never be of this place, little Risa. Do not believe the reaper's lies, because they will get you killed." She paused, and I had an odd sense that she was smiling—a cool, cold, cruel smile—even if I couldn't see it. "Of course, it is not likely you are going to survive this encounter anyway."

"One of us certainly won't," I replied evenly. "But then, it's not actually me you have to fear, Malin. It's the remnants."

She was still moving toward me, her pace even, measured. As if she had all the time in the world and absolutely nothing to fear.

I frowned. Something wasn't right . . . I swung around and raised Amaya. She connected with something solid and sparks flew, briefly highlighting the long length of blade that had almost chopped me in two. Amaya's flames crawled down its length, but there was nothing and no one holding the other end. Nothing but darkness itself. Amaya hissed, the sound of displeasure.

Cannot eat, she muttered. *Of this place.*

Of this place? The thought died as awareness surged. I shifted sideways sharply, felt the air recoil as a fist the size of a car smashed down on the spot I'd been standing in a second before.

A *fist.* Fucking hell, she was bringing the things that were held in this place to *life.*

"The remnants cannot hurt me," she said. This time, her voice was coming from the left, even though her shadowy form still approached from directly ahead. "They dare not. Not in this place."

I flung Amaya at the Malin I could see, then closed my eyes and imagined myself standing behind the one I couldn't. There was a brief snap of movement; then malevolence hit me like a punch to the gut and it was all I could do not to exhale in pain. I clenched my fist and swung, as hard as I could. Felt the burn of electricity across particle fingertips as I connected with something—or someone. Heard her grunt before the sense of malice was abruptly ripped away.

I'd hit her. I'd actually *hit* her. And if I could do that, then I sure as hell could do more.

I opened my hand, felt Amaya thud into it, then imagined myself standing behind Malin again. This time, however, she was ready for me. Shadowed lightning arced toward me, the heat of it so fierce every particle burned. I flung out a hand, imagined a shield, and there was one. The lightning hit it and bounced back to its source. Malin swore and disappeared into the shadows again.

Behind!

Fear surged. I jumped high, flipped around, and swung Amaya as hard as I could. Black steel connected with bloody red and sparks flew, bright fireflies in which I briefly glimpsed Malin's eyes.

And saw only madness.

She would destroy this place, destroy two worlds, and even all creation itself, if that was what it took to achieve her goal of freedom. I couldn't fight that. No one could. No one but the remnants, perhaps.

But given that *they* were conspicuously absent, I had to at least try.

Malin disappeared again. I imagined myself standing to her right and swung Amaya. Once again, red steel con-

nected with black. Malin's cool smile briefly flashed, and
her sword became two, then three, then four and more,
each one linking to the next via a fiery thread. I swore and
ran backward, attempting to get away from the rapidly
multiplying web of metal. Felt the sharp caress of air behind me. I dove away, but not quickly enough. Energy
smashed into my particles and knocked me aside, where
it pinned me, bored into me, ate at me. A scream tore up
my throat, but I bit down on it hard. If she could multiply
her weapons, then I damn well could, too.

But nothing happened.

Can't, Amaya said. *Am unique.*

"Well, fuck," I muttered, and imagined instead a fist
smashing down on the source of the energy. There was a
sharp whoosh of air; then the dark surface underneath
me shook as something heavy hit not too far away. The
energy gnawing at my particles abruptly ceased, but not
the swords. They came at me, a thick rush of red that
reminded me of a bloody river. I hoped like hell it wasn't
an omen, that it wasn't *my* blood that would soon be
running like a river in this place.

I imagined myself away from them, but the net of
swords flung themselves at me, cutting off any avenue of
escape and surrounding me in a web of needle-sharp
steel. Again I tried to transport myself elsewhere, but
when I opened my eyes, all I saw was the gleam of swords
as their points began to slowly inch toward me.

Amaya, shield.

Flames flared from her steel, hissing and spitting
against the duller red of the other swords, but they had
little effect. I swore again and slashed at them. Shards of
steel went flying, but for every one we shattered, two took
its place.

Laughter rolled around me, a bitter, contemptuous
sound. "You will die, dear Risa, as your father deserved
to die. Slowly, and in great pain." She briefly appeared

out of the gloom. "The swords will suck you dry, then spit your remnants into the endless ether; there will be no rebirth, no becoming a reaper, nothing but darkness and the knowledge that you failed."

With that, she disappeared again. Steel slid into my foot. I swore, jerked away from its touch, and slashed down on the other weapon. Steel went flying, but once again, two more weapons took its place. More steel slid into my particles, their touch heated, foul. Desperation surged. Damn it, there had to be a way out of this! But the swords had me pinned on all sides . . . all sides but one, I realized suddenly.

I imagined a hole opening up underneath me, and a heartbeat later I was dropping down—fast. High above, steel glimmered, but they weren't following. They simply continued their slow press inward.

Relief shuddered through me, but I wasn't entirely sure why, given I still had a psycho bitch to stop. I imagined running after her, closing in on her, and suddenly I was. I raised Amaya and flung her. She made no sound as she cut through the shadows, but Malin nevertheless sensed her. She made a motion with her hand and a net of sliver wrapped itself around my sword and stopped her dead. Amaya screamed, the sound echoing both in my head and through the shadows.

Hurts, she wailed. *Burns!*

I swore and grabbed her as I ran past. Imagining her net free didn't work, so I picked it away as best I could as she alternated between cursing and screaming—both in pain and for blood.

Malin was still running ahead of us. I frowned, suddenly wondering why she was actually doing that. I mean, why not simply imagine herself where it was that she wanted to be? Had Azriel somehow restricted her movements when he'd torn her concealing net away?

Movement, to my left. Before I could react, I was sent

flying. I sailed through the air and splattered against something cold and solid, then slid in a heap to its base. For several seconds I couldn't do anything, couldn't hear anything. My head was ringing, there were stars doing a merry dance all around me, and the darkness seemed to be moving.

I blinked. The darkness *was* moving.

I cursed and flung myself out of the way, but that shadowed, obelisk form somehow grabbed me, and once again I was sailing though the air. This time I crashed into metal, and the resulting clang was a clarion sound that cut through the darkness and stirred to life something out there in the shadows.

Up, up! Amaya screamed. *Move must!*

I tried. I couldn't. My particles were burning and I just didn't have the energy. I closed my eyes and imagined myself away from the obelisk. Felt an answering sense of movement, but it was neither fast nor far.

I twisted around, saw the giant obelisk with arms thundering toward me, and forced myself forward, as fast as I could. It still wasn't enough. Not only was the thing behind me catching me, but Malin had come out of the canyons and was heading toward a single column on which stood a series of miniature buildings and two barely adorned gateways. The temples, and the gates to heaven and hell, I knew without a doubt.

In desperation, I put as much energy as I could into the need to get in front of her, to stop her. There was a sputter of movement, but before I even knew whether I'd succeeded, two bolts of lightning hit my middle and sent me flying backward—straight into the arms of the obelisk.

Malin laughed. "And so, dear Risa," she said, as she pressed a hand against the stark white stone of the column. "You have the pleasure of watching this place die, and a moment to reflect on your failure before the creature that holds you tears you into infinite pieces."

"Go fuck yourself, Malin." In a last, desperate effort to be free, I thrust Amaya into the middle of the obelisk creature. He exploded. The force of it ripped Amaya from my grip and flung me forward. I hit the ground hard and pain bloomed, but I ignored it and rolled forward and up, and ran, with every ounce of strength I had left, straight at Malin.

She pressed her other hand against the column and pushed it. It began to rock, gently at first, then with greater speed.

"No!" She wasn't going to win. No way in hell was I going to let her win.

I launched myself into the air and desperately arrowed forward. Not at Malin, but at the miniature itself. I grabbed it from its precarious perch, twisted around in the air, and flung it to the side.

Amaya, shield and protect, no matter what happens!

I couldn't see whether she obeyed. I hoped she did. Hoped I hadn't completed what Malin had started. I hit the ground, heard the groan as the column reached full tipping point, and looked up to see it hurtling toward me.

I imagined myself out of the way, but there was no sense of movement and nothing but the column filling my vision. I rolled. It was all I could do.

The column crashed to the ground inches from where I lay, and the impact shuddered through every part of my being. Malin screamed, and once again I looked up. This time, it was she who was coming at me, a bloody sword held high above her head and vengeance oozing from every pore.

I had nothing left.

Nothing but one desperate hope.

Priests of Aedh, if you're out there, if you're watching and listening, you need to get your asses in here and give me a little help.

The bloody sword came at me. I flung my hands up,

imagined a shield, and prayed like hell. Metal hit metal and again the sound rang out like a clarion bell.

She raised the sword and hit the shield again. This time, it cracked. As she raised her sword for a final blow, I twisted and kicked, with all my might, at Malin's gossamer legs. I didn't have much strength left, but it was enough to unbalance her. What would have been the death blow skittered off the shield and hit the darkness just to my right.

I scrambled up, clenched my fists, and hit her full in the face. It might not have been a strong blow, let alone a killing one, but damn, it felt good.

She raised a hand as she staggered away, and suddenly there were vines twining up my legs and pinning my arms to my body.

"Now," she said, as she stalked toward me, her face twisted and ugly with malice. "We end this—"

Enough. The voice was male, and it came from everywhere and yet nowhere. It echoed through the shadows and reverberated through my mind. It held no threat, yet I sensed it could kill without a moment's hesitation or thought.

And it was a voice I had heard before. It was the remnant I'd spoken to the last time I'd been here in the temple.

"You have no power over me," Malin snarled. "Begone—"

Her eyes went wide and she froze. The vines that bound me withered away, but without their support I ended up on my ass.

You have caused enough damage to this place, Malin. For that alone, we could end you. His tone was calm, collected, but filled with a sense of regret. *We had hoped, until the very end, that you would come to your senses, that the last of the Aedh priests could not possibly want the destruction of all that we hold sacred.*

Malin made a muffled retort. Energy radiated off her, but whatever she was trying to do, it had little effect.

But in attempting to destroy the archive of both the temple and the portals, you have shown a malignancy that cannot be tolerated. There was a soft sound, like a sigh of wind. *It is with great regret that we are therefore forced to end you.*

And just like that, she was gone.

I blinked. "So she's dead?"

No, because with death comes eventual rebirth. She is scattered, never to re-form, never to know the kiss of the stars or the bliss of being in the presence of the fates.

Wow. Although it wasn't like the bitch didn't deserve it. "And the others?"

Even now the reapers finish the last of them. He paused. *Your reaper heads this way, but he has no need to fear. We owe you and him a great debt.*

"I was just trying to save my world."

Yet the fate of your world still hangs in the balance.

"Yeah, I know." I sighed and rose. "Is it safe to recall my sword?"

Yes.

I held out my hand and Amaya thudded back into it. I sheathed her, then said, "What happens now?"

And now we will ask something else of you.

I blinked again. "What?"

That you take a message to she who bears the Aedh's child.

I frowned. He could only be talking about one Aedh—Lucian, whom I'd once thought of as a friend, and who turned out to be one of the major players in the whole key-theft saga. He was also the man who'd kidnapped and impregnated my best friend—and had tried to do the same to me. Thankfully, I was already carrying Azriel's child by that time. "What has Ilianna to do with any of this?"

The child she carries is the future of this place. Her daughter must undergo priest training. The fate of those she holds dear will depend on it. And when she dies, she will come here and guard this place.

"One person cannot possibly—"

She will not be alone. We will train the reapers as well.

You will? a familiar voice said, as the warmth of his particles wrapped around mine and gave me strength.

Yes. For too long we have watched while you fought. It is time we helped.

It would be greatly appreciated, Azriel said, his voice formal.

We cannot, however, intervene in the search for the remaining key. That task still falls to you.

"What if hell *doesn't* hold the sorceress? What if she appears in the temple grounds again, or attempts to open the final gate?" I asked.

If we sense her, we will stop her. But if she uses Aedh magic to conceal herself, as she did previously, we may not know of her until it is too late.

"And you can't undo what she's done and close the two gates that are already opened?"

No. For that, we would need the blood of their creator.

I closed my eyes and cursed. Maybe it *hadn't* been such a great idea to kill my fucking father.

What he tried to do to Mirri he would have done to all of those you cared for, Azriel said. *To protect them, you had no choice but to kill him.*

Yeah, but now we're stuck with no way to close the gates and one gate standing between us and hell.

One portal is enough, the voice said. *And more can be built once we again have fully trained priests in the temples.*

It was a hope. Not much of a hope given all the shit that was still out there, ready to fling itself our way, but at least it was something.

Thank you, the voice intoned again.

And with that, he left.

I blew out a mental breath, then turned and wrapped myself around Azriel. *And now, James, you may take me home.*

I would love to, he said. *But that, unfortunately, is not something I can do. You must return to your flesh by yourself. I cannot help you with that.*

Then I'll see you at Riley's.

You will. The energy of his being briefly ran through mine, a sensation that was the reaper equivalent of a hug, and one that left me feeling both safe and loved. Then he left.

I closed my eyes and did the same.

Chapter 3

The minute I opened my eyes, the pain hit. I gasped, bent over double, and wrapped my arms around my body. Every muscle I possessed seemed to be on fire. God, it even hurt to breathe ...

Arms scooped me up and held me close to a chest that was warm and muscular and smelled of blood and sweat.

Azriel.

As I wrapped my arms around his neck, his heat and strength infused me. Although it didn't chase away all the hurt, it went damnably close.

"Fucking hell," Riley said, her voice a mix of concern and anger. "You both look like *shit*. What happened?"

"We don't just look like it," I muttered without opening my eyes. Doing so would have been too much of an effort. "We feel like it, too."

"Speak for yourself," Azriel said, amusement touching his rich tones.

"What do you need?" Quinn said, ever the practical one. "And is there any immediate danger to either of you, or to us?"

"No," Azriel said. "But Risa is in need of a shower, clothes, and food."

"Risa knows where the shower is, and I'll grab some clothes. Quinn can cook something up for Risa and me to eat," Riley said. "But when all that is done, I want a full and concise summary of what the fuck just happened."

"Agreed," Azriel said.

His energy burned around me briefly, and I opened my eyes to discover we were in Riley's huge bathroom.

"Christ," I muttered, wobbling a little as he placed me back on my feet. "Despite your energy boost, I'm as weak as a damn kitten."

"That is natural after everything we just went through."

He was still gripping my arm, which was just as well. My legs were jelly and I had a bad feeling I'd topple if he let go.

"Then how come you're standing there, as rocklike as ever?"

He half smiled. "Because whatever else you can and will be, you are still flesh. And flesh does not recover as quickly as energy."

"I thought that would have changed when you shared your life force."

"It did, in that you will now recover faster and I will recover a little slower, but it has not altered the basic fact that you are still flesh rather than Mijai."

I grunted. "So is it really over? Malin and the Raziq really *are* no more?"

His gaze met mine, and his blue eyes—one as dark as the storm-held seas, the other sapphire bright—showed an odd mix of sadness and satisfaction. "Yes. As the remnant said, they are little more than particles adrift in the endless night of space."

I raised a hand and thumbed away the bead of blood tracking down the side of his face. "And you regret that?"

"I regret that it came to that, yes. Killing is not something any Mijai rejoices in, despite the fact that it is the reason we exist." He hesitated and grimaced. "Although I cannot deny there is a degree of pleasure in the knowledge she and her kin can never harm you—or anyone else—ever again."

"And thank the fates for that." I swept a hand through my sweat-matted hair. "Now if we could only get them to deal with the bitch who stole the keys and *then* Hunter, I'd be one happy woman."

"The fates have never been *that* generous, as you yourself have often noted."

"Yeah, but I keep hoping for a miracle."

"I believe we just got one." He paused, and his gaze swept me almost critically. "But before we worry about the keys or Hunter, you need to shower."

I raised an eyebrow. "Are you saying I stink, reaper?"

"Certainly not." It was solemnly said, but the twinkle in his eyes and the smile that teased the corners of his lips somewhat spoiled the effect. "Although I cannot deny the air around you is somewhat odorous at the current time."

I lightly whacked his arm. "You don't exactly smell like a rose yourself, reaper."

The lurking amusement grew stronger. "Why would I, when a rose is a plant and I am energy?"

I snorted softly, then stood on my tiptoes and dropped a quick kiss on his lips. It was tempting to do more, but that could come a little later—when we were both smelling better. "You, reaper, are an idiot."

"*That* is a claim that could be laid at the feet of both of you," Riley commented, as she came into the room with an armful of clothes and towels. "You have three people who are not only well trained and fight ready, but willing to help you in your quest, and you keep damn well refusing their help."

"For good reason—"

"Good reason, my *ass*." She dumped the pile of clothes on the ornate chair sitting in the corner of the bathroom, then thrust a hand on her hip and added, her voice full of censure, "It has to stop, Ris. I promised your mom I'd look after you if anything ever happened to her, and I intend to keep that promise, one way or another."

I held up my hands. "I know, and I'm sorry I'm making things difficult for you. But I have my reasons—"

"Hunter, I'm gathering," she cut in grimly.

My stomach dropped. How the hell did she find out about Hunter? I doubted Rhoan would have said anything, and she couldn't have plucked it from his thoughts. He might be her twin, but he was also a telepathic dead zone. It's one of the things that made him such a good guardian—vampires could neither read his mind nor influence his actions in any way.

So who would have spilled the beans? Not Quinn, surely. He undoubtedly knew far more about what was going on thanks to his position in the vampire high council, even if he hadn't yet said all that much to me. But would he have said anything to Riley? I very much doubted it, given that he also had to know just what Hunter was capable of.

"What makes you think—"

"Don't play possum with me, Ris. Not now."

I didn't reply. There was obviously no point in attempting to lie about Hunter's involvement in my life, but, by the same token, I wasn't about to say or do anything to confirm it. Not until I knew exactly how much she *did* know.

"You can't keep secrets from a strong telepath for very long," she continued. "So get your ass into the shower, then come out and tell me everything."

"Yes, ma'am."

It was meekly said, and she smiled grimly. "I know *that* tone, but enough is enough, Ris. I've been patient, I've stood back, but you obviously can't—"

"What I can and can't do," I interrupted quietly, "is no

business of yours. I love you both to death—you know that—but this situation is mine and Azriel's to handle, not yours."

Her gaze met mine, her expression giving little away. "Perhaps," she said eventually. "And perhaps not. Breakfast will be in ten minutes."

With that she turned and walked out of the bathroom, closing the door behind her.

"She is an extraordinary woman," Azriel commented, then added silently, *But she cannot get involved in our dealings with Hunter. As powerful as she is, she would be destroyed.*

Which is why I don't want either of them involved. Although we might yet need Quinn's advice—especially when it came to dealing with Hunter. *Can either of them hear us when we speak like this?*

No. This is not telepathy as such, but more a melding of spirit and mind that allows communication. He hesitated. *Have you never wondered just why the fates chose me over all the other Mijai?*

I raised an eyebrow, amusement lurking on my lips. *Because you were the only one with enough patience to put up with my stupid tendency to ignore what is obvious to everyone else?*

His smile creased the corners of his eyes and made my heart do a happy little dance. *Aside from that.*

Not really. I shrugged. *I just thought it was the luck of the draw.*

There is no such thing as luck when it comes to the fates. I was chosen because you were my Caomh.

Which meant life-mate—and a whole lot more—in reaper terms. *And you knew that from the very beginning? Fuck, Azriel, why didn't you say—*

What could I have said to convince you, given your determination to keep me at arm's length? Besides, the fates order, not explain, and while I wondered why they were able to link me to your chi so easily, I did not suspect the reason. Not initially.

But once you knew what was going on—

I still could not say anything. We are, as you noted many times, from two very different worlds. And the fates don't always believe in happy endings.

After all the shit they've put us through, they'd better give us one, I growled, *because, believe me, if they don't, there will be trouble.*

I suspect even the fates would be wary of your kind of trouble.

I grinned, but it faded quickly as my thoughts returned to the problem at hand. *So why can't Quinn hear us? He's part Aedh, after all.*

And although reading the minds of those in the immediate vicinity was one Aedh talent I *didn't* get, Quinn was an extremely strong telepath. For the first time I wondered just how much of that was due to his Aedh heritage.

He can and does read your surface thoughts, but our connection is at soul level, and not something he can access, Azriel said.

Then I'd better watch my thoughts. The last thing I want is to endanger either of them. I pulled my sweater off and dumped it on the floor. *Although it has to be said, the two of them together are a force to be reckoned with.*

Against Hunter, who has the force of a god behind her, they are still nothing.

I doubt Quinn would be so easy to beat. Hell, if Hunter had any *inkling she could defeat him, she would have done so by now, surely.*

She has not done so because she is not ready. And while he may be one of the few here on Earth capable of defeating her, he is now vulnerable because he has a family. Hunter is not above using such a weakness, as you well know.

I did know. The bitch wasn't above using anyone and anything she could to get what she wanted. She'd certainly used my grief and my bitter need to avenge my mother's death to hook me into working for her. And when common sense finally *did* hit me, she'd reverted to threatening my friends and family. It was the reason Jak—a former lover, and a reporter who'd been helping us in our search—was now dead. She'd had him gutted as a warning of what might happen to others if I didn't start toeing her line.

Even if I can convince Riley and Quinn to play it safe, I know for sure Tao and Ilianna won't go anywhere. I kicked off my shoes, then peeled off my jeans. *Hunter still has their lives to hold over me, no matter what I do.*

I could force them to leave.

It was so casually said that I blinked, not entirely sure I'd heard him right. *What do you mean?*

He half smiled. *What I said. I am reaper, remember, and able to touch the minds of humanity.*

Even someone as strong as Riley?

Yes. He hesitated. *Although not Quinn. He is a former priest and, as such, immune to my influence.*

It was tempting. *Very* tempting. If we could force everyone but Quinn out of the way, it would minimize the risk and make dealing with Hunter so much easier.

Because as much as I was trying to avoid a confrontation with Hunter, I knew it was coming.

But as easy as it might be to take that route, it was also an action that should be used only as a last resort. Taking away free will was never a good thing. Lucian had basically done that when he'd used magic to ensure that I was unable to resist him sexually. My intentions might be a whole lot more honorable than his, but it didn't alter the fact that by taking away their freedom to choose, I would be forever altering my relationship with all of them. It might even destroy it.

And I'd already lost far too much.

You might have no other choice. Azriel's mental tones were grave. *I fear she will not accede to your desire to fight Hunter alone without some sort of intervention.*

And I feared he was right. I sighed. "I better go shower before Riley gets antsy."

"Do you wish company, or would you prefer to be alone?"

"That is the stupidest question I have ever heard." I glanced down his bloodstained torso. "And a good start to proceedings would be removing those jeans."

"Given the jeans are little more than an illusion of energy, that is no problem." Even as he spoke, the jeans disappeared and he was standing there in all his muscular glory.

I had no idea whether Azriel's energy form was considered handsome by other reapers, but when he wore "human" form, he certainly was. His face had a chiseled, almost classical look, but its beauty was tempered by a hard edge that spoke of a man who'd survived many battles. His well-defined body held a similar hardness, though he now bore scars from his more recent battles. One of them—a jagged tear that ran from the left edge of his belly button and up under his arm, slashed through the middle of the stylized black tattoo that was his Dušan, which all but dominated the left side of his torso.

"Better," I murmured, then caught his hand and tugged him toward the vast shower.

The water came on the minute we stepped into it, and at just the right temperature. The needle-sharp jets that hit my skin both soothed and exhilarated. I closed my eyes, enjoying the sensation for several heartbeats before I turned around and stepped into Azriel's waiting arms.

His lips met mine; warm, familiar, and oh so wonderful. We kissed, touched, explored, until there wasn't an inch of me that didn't burn with need.

Then he turned me so that my back was against the hard heat of his body and his erection nudged my butt. He kissed my neck, my shoulders, then reached for the soap and began washing me. The sweet scent of orange touched the air as he gently—lovingly—soaped every inch of me, and oh, it felt *good*.

But being caught between the heat of his body, the drum of the water, and the caress of his hands was nothing short of torturous. When I could stand it no more, I grabbed the soap from him and turned around. The water seemed to reverently caress every muscle, every scar, as it rolled down his beautiful body, and I followed its lead, soaping every marvelous inch, until he was quivering as badly as I was.

He reclaimed the soap and put it back in the holder, then twined his hands in mine, raising them above my head as he pressed me back against the wall. The heat of him flowed around me, through me, a sharp and delicious contrast to the coolness of the tiles pressed against my spine.

His gaze met mine. The blue depths gleamed with desire, and something else. Something that was raw and very human. I was his Caomh, and as vital to him as life itself, but the intensity of emotion so evident in his gaze had my breath catching in my throat and my heart dancing.

"I cannot wait," he said softly, as he nudged my legs wider with one knee, "for the time when there is just you, and me, and the family we will create together."

"Neither can—"

The rest of my words were lost to a moan of pleasure as he slid into me. He began to move, slowly at first, then with more urgency, and god, it was glorious. Energy flickered across our skin, gentle sparks that grew ever stronger as the music of his being began to play through me, and mine through him. It was a dance, a caress, a tease. It was movement, heat, and desire. It was an electric firestorm that grew and grew, until we were both more energy than flesh, and it both fueled the urgency and heightened desire. It was a maelstrom of sensations that assaulted every part of me, until pleasure was so fierce it was almost agony and I couldn't think, could hardly even breathe.

Then my orgasm hit and I gasped, grabbing his shoulders, clambering up his body to wrap my legs around his waist and push him deeper still. Rapture exploded between us and shuddered through my soul. He cried out, his body stiffening against mine as he came.

For several minutes neither of us moved. He leaned his forehead against mine, his breathing harsh against my lips as the shower continued to rain hot water down on us, though its touch was cool compared to the heat still burning between us.

"That," he said, after several minutes, "was very invigorating."

"It certainly was." I felt a whole lot better—and a whole lot stronger—than I had only minutes ago, and *that* wasn't merely a result of great sex. I wasn't only his Caomh, but his "recharge" partner. Reapers didn't keep themselves alive by eating or sleeping or any of the other things humanity did. Instead, they mingled energies—which was the reaper version of sex—with those who possessed a harmonious frequency. Up until very recently that recharge had gone one way—his, although he'd always been able to heal me—but this time, it had been different. I was now a reaper in waiting and, in reality—thanks to his sharing part of what he was to save my life—more energy than flesh these days.

"Your aunt grows restless," he murmured. "We should move."

"My aunt knew exactly what was going to happen in this shower and would be shocked if we rushed." I dropped a quick kiss on his lips, then unwrapped my legs from his waist and stood. "But given her mood, she's just as likely to march in here and tell us to get a move on, so I think we'd better dress."

We did so—although it didn't take Azriel long. All he had to do was imagine his jeans back on. My borrowed clothes smelled faintly of vanilla and musk, which meant the jeans and the beautiful lilac sweater were once again Darci's. She was Riley and Liander's middle daughter, and the only non-twin in their brood of five. I'd grown up with them all, and no more wanted to endanger them than I did their parents. And I sure as hell *wasn't* above using them as leverage in the upcoming battle with my aunt.

Riley might be fierce in her desire to protect me, but when it came down to it, I was neither pack nor blood. She'd fought long and hard to get her brood; given the choice between me and them, she would naturally always choose them.

And that gave me an angle of attack.

I dumped my towel down the laundry chute, my clothes in the bin, then—after a deep, steadying breath that did nothing to ease my nerves or shore up my courage—headed out.

"So," Riley said, once we'd demolished the toasted egg and bacon sandwiches Quinn had made for the two of us. "Explain."

I hesitated. "Before I do, there's one thing you should be aware of. Hunter has Cazadors following me about astrally. She'll now know—"

"Nothing," Quinn interrupted. "At least nothing when it comes to what is said in this house. I'm well aware of Hunter's predilection to use the Cazadors as her own private army and have taken steps to ensure they have no access to any of my houses or workplaces—physically or astrally."

Meaning, no doubt, magic had been employed. There was little else that could stop astral travelers. It surprised me, but I'm not sure why. After all, he'd been around almost as long as Hunter, and while I'd never seen or heard anything that suggested he could perform spells, there was also no evidence saying he couldn't—especially given that he not only was part Aedh, but had undergone priest training. But even if he couldn't perform magic himself, I was betting he knew some very powerful individuals who could.

Either way, it was good to know that Hunter would have no idea what was said here. It gave us time, if nothing else.

So I filled them in on the loss of the second key, the opening of the second gate, the death of my father, and the intervention of the remnants, as well as their subsequent destruction of the Raziq.

"I'm surprised the remnants intervened," Quinn commented, once I'd finished. "It is very rare."

"Not that rare," Riley commented. "Your father contacted you once, remember."

I raised my eyebrows. "Your father is a remnant?"

Quinn nodded. "He is one of six who remained to protect the temples from outside forces."

"Outside," I said. "Not inside. Not the Raziq."

"No." Quinn's brief smile held a grim edge. "Their reluctance to act against the Raziq is the reason they are remnants in the first place. Hence my surprise at their actions now."

"They were left with little choice," Azriel commented. "As it was, Malin very nearly destroyed both the temples and the gates."

"So both Malin and the Raziq really *are* dead?" Riley asked. "No chance of resurrection?"

"No chance," Azriel replied. "They are little more than scattered particles in distant skies."

"The priests may be slow in acting," Quinn noted, voice dry, "but they are very thorough when they do."

"Well, good," Riley said. There was something in her tone that had me picturing her mentally rolling up her sleeves. I tensed, not sure I was entirely ready for the fight ahead. She added, "Now, about Hunter—"

"No." I said it quietly but firmly.

Riley raised an eyebrow. "What do you mean, no?"

"Just that. I don't want you involved. Not in any damn way. Hunter is my problem, not yours."

"You can*not*—"

"What I can*not* do," I cut in again, "is allow you, Quinn, and Rhoan to step into the middle of a situation that will endanger not only your lives, but those of your children. I won't risk your future—or theirs—as I risked my mother's. I couldn't live with any more guilt like that. I won't."

She reached across the table and caught my hand. Her fingers were warm against mine, but her palms were calloused. It was a reminder that whatever else she was, she was first and foremost a fighter. She'd been through the mill and survived, but that knowledge served only to strengthen my resolve.

"Your mother's death was not your fault, Ris—"

I pulled my hand from hers. "But it was, even if indirectly. She was targeted to create a void in my life. Your death—or Quinn's, or Rhoan's—would create the same sort of void, and Hunter is more than aware of that fact."

"Hunter may threaten such an action," Quinn said quietly. "But she would not take such a step; not until she is truly secure in her position and her power. She is close to that, but there are still those who oppose her."

My gaze met his. "Harry Stanford?"

"He is her main adversary, yes."

"And Stanford himself?"

"Cannot and will not defeat her alone." His gaze held mine for several seconds, as if to add weight to his words. "Do not get involved in vampire politics, Risa. It will only end badly."

It probably would, but it wasn't like I had much of a

choice. Like it or not, I was already involved. "Meaning you know what she is?"

"Yes, but few others do."

"Well, I'm obviously one of the ones who missed that particular bulletin," Riley cut in. "Here I was thinking she was just queen bee of the Directorate and one of the head honchos of the vampire council. Obviously, there's a whole lot more to her story than that."

"She's a maenad—a worshipper of the Greek god Dionysus, and imbued with his magic and power," Quinn said, keeping his gaze on mine. "And it is part of the reason I have never challenged her."

"The other reason being you now have too much to lose."

A smile ghosted his lips, but it failed to lift the concern in his dark eyes. "Yes."

"Then you understand my reasons."

"Understanding them does not mean I agree with them."

"No." I took another of those noncalming deep breaths. "I appreciate your concern and your desire to help. I really do. But this is my fight—"

"No one in this family fights alone, Risa." Riley's voice was as steely as her gaze. *"No one."*

"But this time, we have no choice. I'm sorry, Aunt Riley, but as amazing as you are, as skilled as you are, you are, in the end, only mortal. Unfortunately, Hunter is not." I hesitated. "And neither am I."

She raised an eyebrow, her expression unconvinced. "Last I heard, you were only *half* Aedh. That makes you as mortal as everyone else in this pack."

"Perhaps when this quest first began that was true," Azriel said quietly. "But no longer."

Riley's gaze flicked to him. "And how, exactly, did you manage that little—" She hesitated. "It has something to do with you pulling her back to life, hasn't it?"

"Yes. I imbued her with my life force."

"That does not make her immortal," Quinn said. "She can still die, just as you can."

"Yes, but because we can draw on each other's energy, we have a greater chance of survival." He paused, his expression giving no hint of the fierceness I could suddenly feel within him. "Trust me when I say that Hunter—or anyone else in either this world *or* the next—will not take her away from me."

"Sentiments I totally understand," Quinn said. "But the fact still remains—the sharing does not make her immortal."

"No one is truly immortal," Azriel agreed. "Even the fates can be destroyed given the right knowledge. But she will become Mijai on death, and we are far harder to destroy."

Harder, but not impossible, I thought grimly. The reason he became a Mijai in the first place was because he'd sought revenge for the murder of a reaper friend. But I didn't say anything—there was no point in giving my aunt any further ammunition. And although Quinn was undoubtedly aware of both the strengths and the weaknesses of the reapers, I had to wonder how much of that knowledge he'd passed on to Riley. He wanted to keep her as safe as we did, after all.

"All of which sounds very convincing," Riley commented, "but it doesn't alter the fact—"

"Riley," I said softly. "You know how much I love you, so please don't take this the wrong way—"

She raised her eyebrows, a faint smile touching her lips despite the seriousness in both her expression and her eyes. "But I'm not your mother, so kindly butt out. Or words to that effect, right? You do know how impossible that is for me, don't you?"

"Yes, and yes," I said. "The thing is, you have a family now—a family you've fought long and hard to have—"

"Which is why I won't—"

"But I'm *not* one of them," I continued over her voice. "And if it comes to a battle with Hunter, then the task is mine and Azriel's. Not yours. Not Quinn's. Not Rhoan's. You all have too much to lose if you go up against her."

"And you haven't?" She snorted. "You're pregnant, are you not?"

I blinked, but I guess it shouldn't have come as a surprise that she knew, given that she'd spent so much time by my bedside after Azriel had pulled me back from death. She might not be able to hear the deeper lines of communication between Azriel and me, but if Quinn could read my surface thoughts, then she undoubtedly could. Azriel—and the child we'd created— would have been uppermost on my mind even when I'd been unconscious.

"Yes, I am," I said. "And that is why I cannot understand your willingness to risk the lives of your own children for someone who is not, in the end, of your bloodline."

Silence filled the room. A silence heavy with emotion—surprise and anger being the strongest, but there was a torrent of other emotions swirling underneath, each one moving too quickly to define.

Eventually, she said, "Hunter would not—"

"Hunter would, and will." My gaze flicked to Quinn. "You know that, don't you?"

"Yes," he agreed. "But, as I've already said, she would not do so until she was completely sure of her position and her ability to beat me. She is neither of those things right now."

"And hopefully, never will be." I felt like crossing my fingers and praying to the fates even as I said it—except that the fates were just as likely to do the opposite of what I wanted. They were contrary like that—at least when it came to my desires. "But the fact remains, Hunter is using the Jenson pack to control my actions. I need you out of the equation, not stepping further into it."

"You want me to *run*?" Disbelief edged Riley's tone. "I have never—"

"And Hunter is as aware of that as I am. And as long as she has the threat of your deaths, she has me on a leash." I hesitated, then added softly, "If you do not go willingly, then you *will* do so unwillingly."

She stared at me for several seconds, then leaned back in her chair. "And that is a threat you would not make if you could not back it up." She sighed in frustration and thrust a hand through her red hair. "Damn it, Ris, I'm not happy about this—"

"And you think I am?" I cut in. "Trust me, I'd like nothing better than to have you and Rhoan and Quinn back us up if we're forced to confront Hunter. But it's better this way—if Hunter can't find you, then she can't use you against me."

"And how long are we expected to disappear? We all have lives; we can't put everything on hold indefinitely."

"It would be no longer than a week," Azriel said.

I glanced at him sharply. "What?"

He shrugged. "So the fates said."

I wondered what else the fates had said that he wasn't telling me. Heaps, I suspected. It seemed the more some things changed, the more some stayed the same.

Riley studied the two of us for what seemed like an eternity—though I very much suspected she was conversing with Quinn. Finally, she grunted. "A week we could do."

It felt as if a huge weight had been lifted from my shoulders. Against all the odds—against pack instinct and her natural desire to fight and protect—she was going to leave.

But then, she *was* a mom, and as I'd already said, I

wasn't blood related. As much as she might want to protect me, her own family had to come first.

"Thank you—"

"Don't thank me yet," she interrupted. "Not until you've heard my conditions."

My heart sank again. "And what might they be?"

"One, that you keep in contact—and by that I mean every damn day. Given Hunter could very easily track us by phone, we won't be taking them with us, but you find a way. You could send a message via a damn carrier pigeon, for all I care. I just want to know you're alive and well; otherwise, I *will* come running."

"That is easily achievable," Azriel said. "Even if inconvenient."

Riley snorted and glared at him. "Don't give me that inconvenient crap, reaper—especially when you can pop in and out of existence at will. It'd take less than a few seconds of your life to update us, and we both know it."

"And the second condition?" I replied, cutting off any reply Azriel might have made.

"That you do not go up against Hunter without contacting me first," Quinn said.

"Didn't we just finish arguing—"

"We did, and I must—somewhat reluctantly—agree that for the time being, we *are* better out of the picture. But you cannot go up against Hunter without help—or, at the very least, advice."

My smile was grim. "Advice, I'd appreciate. Help, not so much."

"We can argue about that closer to the time," Riley commented. "But for now, you be careful."

"Oh, I will." I smiled. "After all, I do have a couple of reasons to live."

"And I have always had a desire to be a grandmother," Riley said. "So make damn sure you're around to make me one."

Tears stung my eyes. "I will."

She pushed upright. "Then we had better get moving."

I rose, moved around the table, and hugged her. "Thank you."

She grunted and wrapped her arms around me fiercely but briefly. "Just keep safe, and keep in contact."

"I will."

"Then go, so I can call the tribe and get everyone moving." She hesitated, frowning. "Rhoan won't go. You know that, don't you?"

I did, but I had to at least try. "I'll talk to him."

She half smiled. "Good luck with that."

"Thanks. And be safe—all of you."

With that, I stepped back and placed my hand in Azriel's. A heartbeat later we were standing in the middle of a rather luxurious bedroom. It wasn't one I recognized.

I frowned and looked around. "Where are we?" But recognition stirred even as I asked the question. He'd brought me to my favorite hotel.

"We are at the Langham," he confirmed. "You need to rest, and you enjoy this place, do you not?"

"Yes, but you just can't pop in and take over a room like this. They're a business. Hell, they might have already rented the room out to someone—"

"I will go down to reception and ensure that cannot happen," he said. "In the meantime, you should sleep. You cannot continue to go on as you are."

"But the sorceress—"

"May yet be locked in hell, for all that we know." He placed his hands on my shoulders and gently but firmly pushed me toward the bed. "If you care nothing for your own health, then at least think about the health of our child. Please, get some rest."

"That's not playing fair, reaper," I muttered, as my butt hit the bed. "Besides, we did that whole energize-through-sex thing not too long ago. If you can go on without any other rest and sustenance, I should be able to."

"When you are full energy, yes, you will be able to." There was little inflection in his voice, but more than a little impatience in his thoughts. "But you are not that yet. Rest."

Tiredness washed through me at his words, and I had to wonder if perhaps he was subtly forcing me to obey.

"No," he said, the impatience evident in his voice this time. "I cannot. It was one of the more unfortunate effects of sharing my life force."

I raised an eyebrow. "I'd hardly call it unfortunate."

"It is when you are being unreasonably stubborn."

I touched his arm lightly, my fingers cool against his more heated skin. "Azriel, I'm not being stubborn. It's just that we've been three steps behind the sorceress up until now. We have a chance—and possibly only a *brief* chance—to get ahead of her and find the key, and we need to grab it."

"A few hours will not make a great deal of difference to our chances of finding the key," he said grimly. "But it might well make a vast difference to our chances of surviving whatever fights the fates have in store for us."

"Fair enough," I muttered. "But if you're going to nag me like this for the rest of eternity, I won't be a happy woman."

"If we survive the next few days, then I promise, I will do all in my power to ensure your happiness."

He was half smiling as he said it, but there was a seriousness—a darkness—in his eyes that had my stomach churning. "What aren't you telling me?"

"Nothing—"

"Damn it, Azriel, you agreed to stop that. You said you'd be honest—"

"And I am." He took a deep breath and released it slowly. "We are both in a precarious situation. The fates have given no certainty of life for either of us, but that has been our situation since this quest first began."

"But the fates have said something since this quest began, haven't they? I can feel it, Azriel. It hangs like a weight in your eyes and your soul."

"They have done nothing more than emphasize the precariousness of the situation, but that is something we have long been aware of." He shrugged. "Now, please, rest."

He was lying. I knew it; he knew it. The fates *had* said something else, something he feared to tell me. I swore softly but knew my reaper well enough by now to know he was never going to tell me what it was.

I tugged off my clothes and climbed into bed. As I pulled the blankets over my shoulders, I met his gaze, a smile teasing my lips. "Seeing you're forcing me into bed, the least you could do is give me a kiss good night."

He raised an eyebrow. "Is this a required custom here on Earth?"

"Totally," I said. "And if you don't kiss me good night, I'll only get moodier."

"Heaven forbid *that* happen," he murmured, then bent down, his lips brushing mine briefly, before the kiss deepened, becoming a long, slow exploration that had desire curling through me again and heat sparking the air between us.

"That," he murmured eventually, "is a very dangerous custom. And if you did not need sleep so badly, I might be tempted to join you under those sheets."

"You still can." I traced a line down his chest with a fingertip and lightly played with the button of his jeans. "Twenty or so minutes isn't going to matter one way or another to my strength."

"Twenty minutes hardly does justice to the fire that plays between us," he said, and pulled away from my teasing touch. "Sleep, Risa. It is for the best, trust me."

"You, reaper, obviously have a core of steel somewhere inside that rather enticing exterior of yours."

"Believe me, I have not." He caught my hand and kissed it. "I merely wish us both to survive the next couple of days."

With that, he released my hand and disappeared. I sighed, then snuggled deeper into the blankets. And, despite the desire that still spun through my body, fell to sleep almost instantly.

A few hours later—feeling refreshed but still somewhat unsatisfied sexually—I leaned back in the office chair and rubbed my forehead. We were now back in the office above the café I owned with Tao and Ilianna, and the sounds of a world going about its business as usual drifted upward—sounds like the murmur of conversation, the clink of cutlery being polished, or the happy whistle of our sous chef as he prepared for the next influx of customers. Normal, everyday sounds in a life that had become far from normal.

At least for me.

But they were also sounds that would no longer exist if we didn't find the remaining key damn soon. Unfortunately, the search was going nowhere fast. My father might have said that the key could be found in a palace whose coat of arms lay the wrong way around, but there were no actual palaces in the state of Victoria, and Google had thrown up hundreds—if not thousands—of places that used "palace" in their names. It was going to take forever to check and eliminate every one, even with Azriel's ability to zip from one place to another in seconds flat.

"Perhaps it is time to call on Stane's skills again," Azriel commented. He was sitting on the sofa at the other end of the room, outwardly relaxed but not so inwardly.

His frustration swirled through me, as sharp as anything I was feeling. "Cannot a computer work far faster than either of us?"

Stane was Tao's cousin, and a black marketeer who just happened to be able to hack into any computer system ever created. It was an ability I'd made full use of when it came to Hunter's cases as well as the search for the keys.

"Yes, but while a computer can check location, it can't visually visit every place and check whether it bears a coat of arms that lies the wrong way around."

"But could he not write a program that would at least list those buildings that bear a coat of arms? Surely not every building would do so. It would, at least, shorten the list."

I frowned. "I guess—"

The phone rang, cutting off the rest of my words. I glanced at the caller ID and groaned. It was Hunter. I guess I should have known the bitch would catch up with me sooner rather than later.

"You do not have to answer it," Azriel commented. "Although doing so might cause the very problem we are trying to avoid with her."

"I know. Trust me, I know." I reached for my Coke, taking a sip to ease the sudden dryness in my throat, then reluctantly hit the vid-phone's Answer button.

A brief, psychedelic pattern ran across the screen; then Hunter's countenance—which seemed oddly sharper—glared back at me. Her shadowed green eyes were filled with the promise of death, and a tremor that was part fear, part foreboding, ran through me.

"Good morning, Risa Jones." Her voice was soft— pleasant, even. But there was something in the way she said my name that increased my fear. Or maybe it was the fact that she'd used my *full* name, something she hadn't done in a very long time. "I appear to be missing a Cazador. You wouldn't happen to know anything about that, would you?"

"And why would I know anything about the disappearance of a Cazador?" I replied, feigning a calm I certainly didn't feel and damn thankful she was at the other end of the vid-phone rather than standing in front of me. Hunter always seemed to catch my thoughts at the worst possible moment, despite the fact that I had superstrong nano-microcells inserted into my body. With them in place, no one should have been able to get inside my head—but she had a habit of doing things she shouldn't be able to.

"Because this particular Cazador was one of the three who was astrally following you."

I knew that. Just as I knew his name—Nick Krogan.

Just as I knew he wasn't missing, but rather dead.

"Not Markel, I hope."

Markel was the only one of the three I'd had any sort of contact with—outside of killing Krogan, that was. He also happened to be a supporter of the "get rid of Hunter" portion of the high council. Whether Hunter was aware of this was anyone's guess, but given that he was still alive, I'd have to guess she wasn't. Another of Hunter's habits was getting rid of the opposition. Hell, she had a habit of getting rid of people just to teach someone a lesson.

Like Jak.

Tears stung my eyes, but I blinked them away and hoped like hell she hadn't noticed.

"No, not Markel." She paused. "But it is interesting you know his name."

Oops. Trouble headed Markel's way if I wasn't very careful. "Hardly," I replied, my voice coming out surprisingly even given the butterflies going nuts in my stomach. But then, I'd seen what this woman could do. I wouldn't wish that sort of death on anyone—not even my worst enemy—which Markel most certainly was *not*. In fact, he was something of an ally, even if he—like just about everyone else who'd come into my life over the last few months—wanted something from me. "He was on duty when I astral traveled to talk to that ghost. As you undoubtedly know."

"Indeed." She contemplated me for several seconds, and my heart began to beat so fast it felt like it was going to tear out of my chest. Because I knew what was coming.

Feared it.

Or rather, feared her reaction to my answer.

That's presuming you tell her the truth, Azriel said. *I would advise against doing so.*

Not telling her the truth could be a whole lot more dangerous. I took another sip of Coke. It wasn't doing a whole lot to ease the butterflies in my stomach, but then, I doubted if even several bottles of the strongest alcohol ever made would do that. Hunter had that sort of effect on me—which I guess is why I tended to bite back at the bitch more than was wise. An illusion of bravado was better than none.

Perhaps, but it gives us time, Azriel replied. *Right now, that's what we need, more than anything.*

No, what we needed right now was for the whole fucking lot to get lost and just leave us alone. But that wasn't likely to happen. Not when the fates seemed to be using me as their own personal punching bag.

I returned my attention to Hunter and—trying to delay the inevitable—said, "Have you asked Markel about the missing Cazador? I mean, surely he'd know, given he had to change shifts with them."

"That's what is strange," she drawled. Not believing me, not for an instant. "Markel claims when he came on duty, Krogan had already gone."

Meaning Markel had removed Krogan's body from

wherever it was they set themselves up to astral travel and, in the process, saved me from a whole lot of Hunter-type grief. Because while the life of a Cazador was usually a short and violent one—exceptions like my uncle Quinn and Markel himself aside—Hunter would have taken one look at Krogan's body and known who and what had placed the killing blow.

While you couldn't *technically* die on the astral plane, what happened to you on the plane *could* become reality here if the illusion was powerful enough. When I'd stabbed Amaya through Krogan's heart, it was a combination of his belief *and* her power that had killed him, both on the field and here on Earth.

That I'd done it out of necessity—to save Uncle Rhoan—wouldn't have mattered to Hunter, especially given the fact I'd done it to save Rhoan from *her*. And I had no doubt she would go after him *because* of it.

I raised my eyebrows, somehow managing nonchalance as I said, "And you don't believe him?"

"Oh, I believe he was gone. I'm just not entirely sure Markel had nothing to do with it."

Because he more than likely did. If the third Cazador following me had discovered the body, she would have reported it. I shrugged. "Well, I'm not sure how I'm supposed to help you given I have as little to do with them as possible. But hey, if you think it's too dangerous for them to be following me around, feel free to remove them from the task."

She smiled. It was not a nice smile. "Oh, they're staying, whatever the danger. I want those keys, and you *will* give them to me, won't you?"

Keys, not key. She had no idea the second gate was already open. Relief swept through me, its force strong enough to leave me shaking. Coke splashed over my hand, and I put the can down, hoping like hell she hadn't noticed.

I had about as much chance of *that* happening as I did the full moon failing to rise tonight.

"Why, Risa, anyone would think you were nervous." Her expression was that of a cat who'd just eaten the cream. "You weren't planning on double-crossing me, were you? Because you know the consequences of such an action, don't you?"

I had to clench my fingers against the sudden urge to grab the vid-phone from the desk and heave it across the room. As much as seeing her smug face smashing against the wall might give me a moment of pleasure, it wouldn't really achieve anything more than a smashed phone.

"Yes," I bit back, voice tight.

"Good," she all but purred. "So tell me, how goes the hunt for the sorceress?"

"It doesn't."

She arched one dark eyebrow. "And why not?"

Because the bitch had been dragged into the pits of hell, and hopefully, that was *exactly* where she'd remain. Not that I could tell Hunter that, because I wanted to keep the truth about the second key from *her* for as long as possible.

"Because we're having trouble finding Lauren Macintyre, the sorceress behind the theft. It appears she's not only a face shifter, but a hermaphrodite capable of full-body transformation."

Hunter raised her eyebrows. "That is an ability I've only ever seen once in the thousands of years I've been alive. Are you sure she's not just using magic to transform herself?"

"We're sure." After all, Lauren had even used *my* face at one point . . . The thought stalled, and I swore. If she *had* somehow managed to break free from hell, what was stopping her from taking on my appearance and questioning—or even killing—someone I loved? If she could do it once, she could do it again. I scrubbed a hand across my eyes. This whole fucking thing was getting more and more complicated. The sooner we found Lauren, the better—for both the quest and everyone I'd dragged into it. "I don't suppose you know of any way to track someone like that down?"

"As a face shifter yourself, surely you should sense when you are in the vicinity of another?"

I grimaced. "If she were a werewolf and vampire or another kind of shifter, I'd sense that. But face shifting requires a different type of internal magic, and it's not one that can be picked up by normal sensory means."

"That is unfortunate."

"Yeah," I agreed. "We're trying to track down a couple of aliases we think she might be using, but it's taking time."

"Time you haven't got," she drawled. "I really do need the remaining keys in my possession by the end of the week."

The fear churning my gut rose in my throat, and it was all I could do not to puke all over my damn desk. "It's impossible to give you that sort of guarantee. I have no power over the speed of computers, for starters—"

"Then use other methods, my dear," she continued evenly. I might not have spoken for all the impact my words seemed to have made. "You seem to be very chummy with the Brindle witches at the moment, so why not ask one of them to do a scrying for you? Or perhaps use some item of the sorceress to uncover a location?"

"Great idea, except we've tried the first and can't do the second until we actually have something of the sorceress's."

That we actually *did* have something was a point I wasn't about to mention. We'd already tried to use it to find the sorceress, and we'd come damn close to snaring her, too. But events since then had left us with little time to make a second attempt.

Besides, if the sorceress *was* still in hell, how would that affect any attempt at scrying? Or even the use of psychometry? Would it actually work? Or would it be dangerous for the practitioner to even *try* to locate our sorceress? Hell wasn't a place you messed with, in any way, shape, or form. Unless, of course, you were a dark practitioner—and our sorceress had certainly shown very little fear or concern about playing in the underworld's gardens.

"I do not care about your problems," Hunter said. "I merely care about the end results."

I closed my eyes and resisted the urge to scream. We had a week. The fates had also warned that this would all end in a week. Did Hunter have a direct line to those in charge? She drew her power from an old god, after all, so it wasn't beyond the realm of possibility.

You have nothing to lose by agreeing to her demands, Azriel noted. *And time—as well as the space to move—to gain.*

But only if she doesn't throw another wrench in the works. I opened my eyes and stared at Hunter for several seconds. I don't think I'd ever hated anyone as much as I hated her right then, and it was galling to think that I hadn't seen what she was—or what she was capable of—from the very first moment our paths had crossed and I'd agreed to work for her. And sure, she hadn't exactly made it easy for me to refuse, but the truth was, it was my desperate need to avenge my mother's death that had gotten me into this pickle, nothing else.

"Why," I asked eventually, keeping my voice as even as I could, "is it necessary for you to have the keys within a week? It's not like hell's going anywhere." Although it *would* bleed all over Earth—create a new playground for all hell's nightmares—if we didn't stop the sorceress from opening the final gate.

"Because I find it necessary to bring forward my own

plans," she answered blithely. "There are certain . . . shall we say, elements . . . within the council that are gathering momentum. I find myself in need of a little something extra to contain the groundswell before it gains too much force."

Meaning, in other words, that Harry Stanford, Markel, and everyone else involved with the "get rid of Hunter" movement had better start watching their backs *very* carefully.

"I really don't think it's wise to be using hell as some sort of—"

"And I really don't care what you think," Hunter snapped, green eyes glittering with both anger and darkness. And perhaps, if I looked closely enough, madness. "You will do as I desire or pay the price."

"Fine," I growled, clenching my fists under the desk in an effort not to smash one through her image on the vidphone's screen. "You'll have both keys by the end of the week."

"Good," she murmured. "Although there is one additional point I forgot to mention."

Of course there was, I thought darkly. There was always one more damn point. "And what might that be?"

"The second key. I want it in my hands by eight o'clock tomorrow morning, or people will start dying."

Chapter 4

My breath caught somewhere in my throat, and for several seconds I couldn't do anything more than simply stare at her. Horror, disbelief, anger—it all curled through me, and when combined with my already churning stomach, there was no containing it. I lurched out of my chair but didn't make it any farther than the nearest trash can, where I was thoroughly and totally ill.

Azriel was beside me in an instant, holding back my hair as I lost every single bit of food I'd eaten only hours before, and then some.

"Water," I croaked eventually, as I wiped a hand across my mouth. "Please."

Azriel immediately disappeared but was back within seconds, a cup of cool water in his hand. I took it, rinsed my mouth out, then spat into the bin.

"Why, Risa dearest," Hunter drawled, amusement heavy in her tone, "don't tell me you're coming down with something. That would be unfortunate timing indeed."

Fury hit me; fury that was so deep, so fierce, it just about short-circuited my brain. I reached out, catching Azriel's fingers, feeling the tremble in them, a physical echo of the emotions surging from his mind to mine.

You have no idea, he growled, *how tempting it is right now to go find that woman and cut her into very tiny little pieces.*

Which I'm guessing is exactly what she wants, I replied. *She's trying to goad you into an action we'd both regret.*

I am well enough aware of that; it's the reason I still stand here.

Her time will come, Azriel. It has to.

I hope so. But he didn't look convinced and again I was left with the feeling that the fates had told him far more than he was letting on.

If they let her live, there *would* be hell to pay.

"It would seem," I said, squeezing Azriel's hand a final time before releasing him and moving back to the desk, "that I ate something that disagreed with me."

A more logical explanation would have been the fact that I was pregnant, but I wasn't about to hand Hunter that sort of information. Whether the Cazadors had it was another matter entirely.

"I'm so glad it wasn't something I said."

"Hardly," I murmured. "I mean, it isn't like we haven't heard that particular tune before."

"So true." Her voice was philosophical, but the darkness and madness in her eyes were oddly sharper. "Which means, of course, that you are well aware I will carry through with my threat."

"I'm aware."

"Good," she said, voice suddenly brisk. "I shall expect to see you within the next twenty-four hours, then."

"You will." I hit the End button, then swore like there was no tomorrow. It didn't help the situation one little bit, but it at least made me feel a little better.

Azriel merely raised his eyebrows and waited until I'd finished. "I had no idea there were *that* many swearwords in this world."

I half smiled, as he no doubt intended. "There's probably not. I just got creative with some non-swearwords." My smile faded. "What the fuck are we going to do, Azriel? I very much doubt that we can find the key in twenty-four hours—and even if we did, there's no way in hell I'd give it to her."

"No." He rose and walked over, dragging me upright, then wrapping me in a hug that was fierce and warm. One that made me feel safe, looked after. Of course, it was a lie—or the safe part of it was. At least until we sorted out this whole key mess. Then there was Hunter . . .

"Let's worry about her when we have to," he said, being his usual practical self. "It is pointless doing so before the need arises."

"Totally true, but, unfortunately, I'm not built that way."

"No, and I am extremely grateful for the way you *are* built."

I snorted softly and lightly punched his arm. "You, reaper, are incorrigible."

"Is that not an acceptable thing to say in this world?"

I pulled away. Though his voice was solemn, his blue eyes twinkled with mischief. "It's totally acceptable. So, shall we head to Stane's?"

"His system is far more able to search quickly than the computer you have here."

Which was a given, simply because Stane's computer was megapowerful *and* worth megabucks, where as my poor little thing barely had the power to cope with the tax and wage tasks of the restaurant. I really would have to buy a new one when all this was over and things got back to normal.

"Or as normal as they can be given you carry my child," Azriel murmured. "You have no idea how desperately I desire to see you round and fat."

"Round I can cope with. Fat, not so much." I grinned, dropped a kiss on his lips, then said, "To Stane's, please, driver."

He wrapped his arms tighter around me; then his energy surged around us and in no time flat we were standing inside the foyer of Stane's West Street shop. It housed not only his electronics business, but his living quarters and black market business as well. The camera above the door buzzed into action the minute we appeared, swinging around to track our movements. Not that we could go far—the shimmer of light surrounding the small entrance was warning enough that his containment shield was active. Azriel could—and had, in the past—deliver us upstairs, where Stane's computer "bridge" and living quarters were, but the last time we'd done that, our sudden appearance had just about given Stane a heart attack.

"Hey, Stane, it's Risa and Azriel." I smiled up at the camera. "Turn off the shield so we can come up."

"Hey," he replied, his warm tones sounding slightly tinny through the small speaker near the camera. "Welcome back. I was beginning to think you'd abandoned me."

"What, you've grown so used to me bugging you daily with urgent tasks that you feel lost without me?"

The shimmering field surrounding us died, allowing us to walk toward the stairs at the rear of the shop. Of course, this meant we had to go right through the middle of all the shelves holding the tons of dusty junk that were little more than a cover for his real business—black marketeering. And no one, not even Stane's mom the last time she'd been down here, had dared to clean this room for fear of suffocating in the resulting dust storm.

"Well, not so much you," he said, voice amused. "It's more the champagne you supply with each task."

I grinned. "You, Stane, are becoming a lush."

"And damn proud of it," he agreed. "Come on up, folks. I just made coffee."

"Excellent."

I bounded up the steps. He met me at the top, a grin on

his face and a coffee in his hand. "Here you go," he said, honey-colored eyes amused as he offered me the cup. "It's even the good stuff."

"You have good stuff?" I said, feigning shock. "Since when?"

"Since I made a most excellent sale of the latest in limpet lasers."

Limpet lasers were small but powerful lasers that clung to the palm of your hand, and could be fired through various finger movements. "They aren't exactly a new development."

He stepped to one side, then swept an arm forward, ushering me on. "These were, trust me."

I stepped past him, not bothering to ask what made them special. Just as I didn't ask where he got them. Sometimes it was better *not* to know.

Unlike the lower portion of his building, this floor was pristine and dust-free. It had to be, because dust damaged computer systems, expensive electronics, and possibly whatever other black market items he happened to have, all of which were kept on this floor. Stane himself, however, could only be described as a mess, with unkempt brown hair, an ill-fitting blue sweater with holes in the elbows, and wrinkled jeans. But at least he was neither dusty nor dirty.

I glanced around the open living and kitchen area, hoping to see Tao. He wasn't here, and his scent was little more than a hint in the air, suggesting he hadn't been here for at least twenty-four hours. I frowned. "I thought Tao was staying with you."

"He is," Stane said, expression suddenly grim. "Or rather, he was."

I swore softly. "When did he disappear?"

"Early yesterday morning."

He hadn't been sighted at the café in the last twenty-four hours, either—something I knew because I'd checked when I was there. I swore again and thrust a hand through my hair. "You tried tracing him?"

"Of course I have." His voice was filled with anger, but I knew it wasn't actually aimed at me. Rather, it was a result of frustration and worry. "There's nothing. His phone is sitting in the spare bedroom, as is his wallet. And he hasn't contacted any of his other friends."

Meaning, more than likely, the fire elemental he'd consumed to save Ilianna had taken control of his body again. "How was he the last time you saw him?"

"Strung out. Fiery." Stane shook his head. "I've seen him play with fire before. I mean, he's pyrokinetic, so that's not unusual in and of itself. But this time . . . it was bleeding from his skin, Risa. There was no *way* it was controlled."

"Fuck," I muttered.

"Yeah," Stane said. "I tried to get him into an icy shower—I figured it couldn't hurt—but he practically threw me across the room, then ran down the stairs. By the time I got up and went after him, he'd disappeared."

And no doubt headed once more for the sacred site in Macedon, the place where the fire elemental within Tao had been created.

With the clock counting down on Hunter's deadline, you haven't the time to chase after him, Azriel warned softly. *If the fire elemental is in control, then there might be no bringing him back this time. Nor will I allow you to endanger yourself again by touching him while the elemental holds sway. It might just kill you this time.*

Which technically wasn't a problem given that I'd just become a dark angel. But that wasn't something I actually wanted; I wanted to live a full and happy life here on Earth first. Wanted to bring my child into this world, not the other.

But Azriel was right. I really couldn't afford to lose any time, even if it was a matter of minutes.

Let's just hope he comes back from this, I said. *He has before.*

By this time, the elemental will have reached Macedon's sacred site. And given the fire that created it still burns within that place, its very closeness to it may provide the creature with enough strength to completely block Tao out.

I know. Believe me, I know.

He smiled grimly, adding, *Then you should also remember that I can't get into that site, so it's not as if I can even check whether he is there or not.*

"Damn it!" I plonked down on a chair and watched as Stane resumed his usual position on his captain's chair in front of his computer bridge.

"Yeah," Stane said. "Can you get into that site and check that he's there?"

"Maybe." I hadn't actually tried since I'd become a dark angel in waiting. But given that the place had banned reapers and Aedh from entry, it might just ban me now that I had both their energies running through me. "Only problem is I haven't got the time to find out right now. I have a deadline and people will die if I don't meet it."

"Tao might die if you don't," Stane replied, grim faced.

"Don't you think I fucking *know* that?" I took a deep breath and tried to calm the anger and fear running through me. "I'm sorry. I shouldn't have responded like that. But the thing is, Hunter's given me a twenty-four-hour deadline, and if I don't come through with the key, she's going to start killing people. People like Ilianna and Tao and you."

He blinked. "Why would the psycho want me dead?"

"For the same reason she wants the keys to hell—for

control. In your case, control of me. Or rather, my actions."

I took a sip of the coffee, noting somewhat absently that it was indeed the good stuff. "I have a choice, Stane. Save Tao and risk everyone else, or simply try to save everyone the best way I can."

"Hell of a choice," he muttered.

"Yeah, tell me about it." I paused. "I don't suppose you want to evacuate the immediate area and go hide somewhere, do you?"

"I'm thinking you can probably guess the answer to that." He patted the desks holding his range of light screens and keyboards with affection. "I'm not leaving my baby, and I can't exactly pack her up with me. Besides, someone has to be here in case Tao does turn up."

"What, no mention of a particular upcoming sale of the generous-to-your-bank-account but definitely black market type?"

He grinned. "Well, there might be a couple of sales in the works over the next couple of days that I can't afford to walk away from, now that you mention it."

I snorted. Of course there were. "It could be dangerous. I've already lost Jak to the bitch. I don't want to lose anyone else."

"Then I'll install a secondary energy shield around all internal walls. Trust me, no one—not even a vampire hell-bent on destruction—will get past it."

I hoped he was right. I didn't want to lose Stane any more than I wanted to lose anyone else.

"So," he said, grabbing his coffee, then swinging around to face me. "Do you want to tell me why you're here, or do you wish to see my results first?"

I blinked. "On what?" To be honest, we'd asked Stane to do so many searches over the last few weeks that I'd totally lost track of them all.

"You know those index cards you swiped from the dead jeweler's place?"

I nodded. We'd gone to the jeweler's after discovering his maker's mark on the antique silver cuff link we'd found in Lauren Macintyre's Gold Coast home, hoping he'd be able to tell us whom he'd made it for. As per usual when it came to our sorceress, we'd been a couple of steps too far behind. Not only had she fled her Gold Coast home before we'd arrived there, but she'd also made a visit to the jeweler and slashed his throat from ear to ear. Which meant the index cards, with their list of client names, had become our only chance of possibly tracking down another of Lauren's alternate identities — an almost impossible task given that she could take on both male *and* female personas.

"Well," Stane continued, a pleased grin stretching his lips, "I found a connection between the jeweler, the names on the cards, and your mad sorceress."

I smiled at his enthusiasm. He really *was* going to be lost when all this crap was over with and life got back to normal. "The connection being?"

"Harry Bulter."

I blinked. For some reason, that name rang a bell. Then the connection hit and I sat up a little straighter. "Harry Bulter — as in, one of the names mentioned in John Nadler's will?"

John Nadler had been the man behind the consortium that had bought up most of the land all around Stane's shop. Not that Nadler — or rather, Lauren, because the real Nadler had been long dead by the time the buyout had happened — had wanted the land per se; he'd just wanted to control what lay underneath it — a major ley-line intersection. Such intersections were places of great power and could be used to manipulate time, reality, or fate. But they could also be used to create a rift between this world and the next, enabling those with enough power here on Earth to step onto the gray fields. And that's exactly what Lauren had succeeded in doing, too, but only with the help of Lucian, a rebel Raziq with destruction plans of his own.

And to think I'd not only bedded that bastard, but trusted him, too. My instincts had been way, *way* off as far as he was concerned.

At least he was dead. At least he couldn't do any more harm to anyone I cared about. Couldn't rape or impregnate anyone else, as he had Ilianna, and more than likely the sorceress.

If she *was* pregnant, I thought suddenly, how would that affect her ability to take other forms? While face shifting shouldn't hurt any child she carried, I had no idea whether attempting a full-body transformation would. I imagined it would be rather hard to disguise a rounded belly, as she wouldn't be able to manipulate the flesh of the child within her. Even if it was little more than a few weeks old, it would have a soul and a power all its own. She could change *her* flesh, but not her child's. Nor, I imagined, could she change the physical space that child used.

Maybe we'd better start looking for men who looked pregnant—although given the number of middle-aged men who seemed to have beer bellies these days, *that* might not be such an easy task.

"So Harry Bulter was one of the names on the index cards?" Azriel asked.

"No, of course not. That would be too easy."

"Yeah, I guess it would," I agreed, amused. "So how did you find him?"

"By following the connections." Stane shook his head, something close to admiration in his expression. "I can tell you one thing—the bitch may be as mad as a hatter, but she certainly knows how to cover her tracks."

A skill no doubt garnered from her association with Lucian, who'd been banished to Earth's plane for centuries, and who'd had the time to learn not only the art of deception, but also, we suspected, that of dark magic.

"So how did you find her in the end?"

"By tracing back not only every single name, but all the traceable connections each name had."

He spun around and flicked a finger across one of the light screens. An image appeared on the next screen—a tall, gray-haired gentleman with stern features and a somewhat forbidding nose. "This is Harrison Jantz, a stockbroker who has purchased several items from our dead jeweler. His address on file was Elizabeth Street in Sydney, right opposite Hyde Park."

"Expensive," I murmured. "He's obviously a very *good* stockbroker."

"*Was* a very good stockbroker," Stane commented. "He was reported missing yesterday, after not showing up for work several days in a row."

"Coincidence, or the sorceress simply killing off another of her identities?" Of course, it hardly mattered, given that she sure as hell seemed to have enough of them—but it was damn frustrating to once again be a step behind her. Though *how* she managed to keep track of them, let alone keep them all alive as viable identities, I had no idea.

If she is responsible for this man's disappearance, Azriel commented, *then she is well and truly out of hell.*

A point I hadn't even *thought* about. *You'd think just once the fates would give us a break,* I all but grouched. *Just once. Is that too much to ask?*

Apparently, he said, with a mental shrug. *You'll get used to it.*

I bet I won't. And they had better get used to me complaining. Azriel might be all stoic and accepting, but I wasn't about to be. Not if this was the pattern they'd set for the rest of our lives together.

If they'd planned a "rest of our lives" for us, that was. I very much suspected that was still up in the air, especially given Azriel's nonanswer earlier.

"I can't tell you whether it was the real Jantz that was reported missing or the fake," Stane said. "They did a search of his apartment, but there was no evidence of any sort of foul play. Nor has his body been found—and remember, Nadler's corpse was found pretty quickly after our mad sorceress decided to shed the identity."

"Is it common for Jantz to disappear like this?"

"No. According to the people who filed the missing persons report, it was extremely unprecedented for him to go away without at least informing one of them. I think we'd be wise to presume death."

Totally wise. "So how did uncovering Jantz lead you to Bulter?"

"Ha. That's where it gets interesting," Stane said. "The apartment Jantz lived in is owned by a private consortium. As is usual with those sorts of companies, there are a couple executives who are responsible for securing targeted business, real estate, or whatever else the consortium might wish to purchase, and who play a central role in negotiations relating to all elements of the deal. It's the consortium's name on all legal documents rather than each investor."

I nodded. "This is sounding very similar to the consortium Nadler set up."

"That's because it basically is. We couldn't find anything about *that* consortium because the paper trail led to a company that was listed offshore, and it's damn near impossible to trace the details of who might be involved with offshore businesses."

"But you've had a breakthrough," I said, smiling.

"But I've had a breakthrough," he echoed. "A mob called the International Consortium of Investigative Journalists has spent years sifting through millions of leaked documents and recently released an updated report on those involved with offshore accounts, trusts, etcetera. And one of the names in that report just happened to be Harry Bulter. And this," he added, swinging around to grab a piece of paper from his desk, "is his address in Sydney."

I glanced at the address and frowned. "He lives in the same building as Jantz?"

"No only the same building, but the same *apartment*. But, according to those who filed the missing persons report, Jantz lived alone and rarely had visitors."

"Meaning Jantz was either in cahoots with Lauren, or she was simply using his name and face when it suited her." I hesitated, my frown deepening. "Did Jantz have any special delivery instructions on his index card?"

"None—though some of the others have 'pickup only' noted on them, so that would suggest Jantz's items were posted."

"Then we definitely had better go investigate the apartment." Jantz might be missing and presumed dead, but there could be a faint hope that he—or even Lauren, if he was involved with her in some way—had left something behind that would clue us in as to where Lauren might be.

It is a very faint hope, Azriel commented. *Our sorceress has shown no inclination so far to leave things to chance.*

Granted, but it's not like we've got many other choices right now. And until we'd cut down the huge number of possibilities when it came to the placement of the final key, there wasn't much we could do there, either. No matter how much Hunter might threaten or wish otherwise.

"So," Stane said, "my news has been dealt with. What's the next delicious puzzle you want me to solve?"

"I'm afraid it's a rather tedious one."

"Which is precisely what computers are designed for. Give."

I hesitated, my gaze sweeping the room. "You *have* checked for bugs recently, haven't you?"

He snorted. "Daily, my dear. And I have several of the latest noise screens up and running, just in case the Directorate or some other government department decides to get long-distance nosy about my activities."

"Good." Because I wouldn't put it past Hunter to have this place wired for sound. Of course, I guess she really didn't *need* to, given that she still had at least two Cazadors following me about astrally, and at least one of those was still reporting back truthfully. I supposed I just had to hope it was Markel on duty right now, not the other one. I took a deep breath in an effort to calm the tension running through me, then added, "According to the bastard who was my father, the third key lies in the southeast, on a palace whose coat of arms lies the wrong way around."

Stane blinked. "Well, that's not exactly an expansive clue, is it?"

"No. I've done a search and come up with thousands of possibilities. I need you to pin it down—and, if possible, within the next six hours."

He clasped his hands, then stretched them out in front of his body, cracked his knuckles. "Well, we'd better get down to it, then, hadn't we? You waiting around, or checking out Jantz's address?"

"The latter."

"Then come back in six hours if I haven't contacted you sooner."

"Will do." I gulped down the remainder of my coffee, put the cup in the sink—which was already half-filled with unwashed dishes—then walked back over and dropped a kiss on Stane's cheek. "Thank you."

His grin was decidedly impudent. "You *do* know that another crate of bubbles would be far more appreciated than a kiss—as lovely as a kiss is, obviously."

"Consider it done." I got out my phone and ordered him two. Who knew when I'd get the chance otherwise.

"Thank you, my dear. My liver appreciates it."

"So does your wallet, no doubt," I said, voice dry, "especially considering you're undoubtedly making a nice profit on them."

"On some of them, definitely. But me and the liver have acquired quite a taste for bubbles."

I stepped toward Azriel, then hesitated and glanced back at Stane. "Get the rest of those screens up. Now."

His smile faded. "On it, boss. You take care yourself."

"We will."

With that, Azriel wrapped his arms around my waist, tugged me closer, then whisked us out of there. We reappeared in the middle of a park. A pretty park, but still a park rather than the expected apartment. I blinked and looked around, then caught sight of the golden turret atop the Sydney Tower and realized what had happened. Azriel couldn't actually take us to anyplace neither of us had been. We were here rather than Jantz's apartment simply because I'd been through Hyde Park, and this was the closest we could get to the Elizabeth Street building.

"I *can* use static images as reference points," he commented, "as long as they're detailed enough."

"Which is something we'll undoubtedly have to do later." I stepped away, then caught his hand and led the way. "A building in this part of town is going to have high-level security. You might have to influence the guard to get us in."

"That will not be a problem."

It never was. We walked down to the streetlights—dashing through Sydney traffic was never a good idea; not if you valued your life, that was, and I hardly wanted to survive the Raziq only to get sideswiped by a mad Sydney motorist—then back to the building. The entrance was discreet and the foyer plush—a palette of golds mingling with dark woods and clever lighting. A guard—also clad in muted gold—looked up from his desk and gave us a smile.

"And how may I help you folks today?" His voice was as smooth and welcoming as his smile, despite the fact that we certainly didn't look like the type of folks who would know anyone wealthy enough to own a place like this, let alone be able to afford it ourselves. Which, of course, was rather deceptive, given that I *could*. Hell, I could buy the whole damn building had I wanted to. Mom certainly hadn't left me poor, in any way, shape, or form.

"We have a meeting with Harrison Jantz in"—I hesitated, making a show of looking at my watch—"precisely five minutes."

The guard frowned. "I'm afraid that's impossible, because Mr. Jantz—"

"Mr. Jantz said it was urgent," Azriel cut in, and waved a hand, doing his thought-altering bit.

The guard's expression didn't change. "Of course, but I'll have to speak with Mr. Jantz first."

"Fine," I said, but raised my eyebrows at Azriel. *How is that going to get us in when Jantz isn't there?*

He might not be, but our guard will nevertheless hear the expected response, and we will be cleared to go upstairs.

You're a man of never-ending talents.

And I haven't even begun to unveil the full depths of some talents yet. His mental tones were bland, but there was a hint of amusement running through the background of his thoughts, and a decidedly cheeky smile creasing the corners of his blue eyes. *But it will be my great pleasure to reveal one particular talent over our years together, if the fates so allow.*

I grinned. *And I, dear reaper, cannot wait.* Especially if that so-called talent was what I suspected it was. And really? If what we'd shared was but a taste of what he could do to me, then I was going to be happier—and far more contented—than a pig in shit.

I cannot see why you would equate a pig to your own future happiness. That makes no sense. His reply was distracted. The guard had made the call and was currently have a conversation with the nonexistent Jantz.

You've obviously never witnessed the joy of a pig rolling in mud and shit.

Nor do I want to.

How about if I roll around in mud?

That I would definitely watch. He glanced at the guard, who froze instantly, the phone still held to his ear, then added softly, "But then, my idea of heaven is being with you, no matter what you do or where you are."

I smiled, twined one hand through his, then rose on tiptoes and kissed him, long and tender. Eventually, I added, "Who knew you were such a romantic, reaper."

He raised a hand and brushed my cheek gently. "Who knew I would have so much to live for. Certainly not me. Not before I met you."

"And who knew everything I was looking for would come wrapped up in such a stoic, stubborn, frustrating, and absolutely wonderful being who isn't even of this world."

He laughed, the sound warm and rich. "There's a compliment in there somewhere, I'm sure."

"Maybe. Maybe not," I replied, amused.

He smiled, then glanced at the guard and released him. The guard placed the phone receiver down, then said, "Mr. Jantz has cleared your entry into the building."

"Excellent," Azriel said. "Thank you very much."

"No problems." The guard put a couple of security cards on the table, followed by a sign-in book. "ID?"

I showed him my driver's license, then signed for both of us. He added, "These will get you into the elevator area, and through security screens on the seventh floor."

"And Mr. Jantz is apartment A?" Azriel said.

"He certainly is." The guard smiled again. "Just return the passes as you're exiting."

"Thank you," Azriel repeated, then tugged me forward, leading the way to the lift area.

I swiped the card through the slot, then pressed the button for the seventh floor. As the doors closed and the lift began to move smoothly upward, I said, "Given Lauren has a habit of setting traps or blowing shit up, it might be wise if we presume the worst and reconnoiter in energy form before we physically enter Jantz's apartment."

"There is also the apartment's security system to deal with. It is activated, so even if there are no sorcery surprises, we would need to disconnect that."

I glanced at him. "How did the police get in if the place was alarmed?"

"Building security has an override. I retrieved it from the guard's thoughts." He glanced at the floor indicator. "You had better become Aedh. We're almost there."

I wrapped my fingers around my phone, then took a deep, steadying breath and reached for that part of me that was Aedh. Energy surged in response, sweeping through me like a heated tide, numbing pain and dulling sensation as it invaded every muscle, every cell, breaking them down and tearing them apart, until my flesh no longer existed and I became one with the air. Until I held no substance, no form, and could not be seen or heard or felt by anyone or anything who wasn't reaper or Aedh.

The lift came to a halt and the doors opened. Azriel led the way, his reaper form bright and golden in the warm light of the corridor. We swept under the glass security doors, then headed toward the apartments. There were only two on this floor, and Jantz's was the one on the Hyde Park side of the building. I slithered in through the small gap between the door and the floor, then paused and looked around. The apartment was absolutely beautiful. It was minimalist in design and one vast open space, the kitchen, dining, and living areas flowing into one another seamlessly. The wall facing the park was all glass doors that could fold back completely, allowing entry onto the gently curving balcony from wherever you were in the main room. Chairs, tables, and mats were the same white as the walls, and the floor was white marble. The only color in the place was the dark wood of the kitchen cabinets and the long entertainment unit that lined one internal wall. There was nothing out of place, and nothing, as far as I could see or sense, that spoke of our sorceress or any of her nasty spells or creatures.

Not yet, anyway.

I moved into the bedroom. There was more color here—splashes of red among the bed furnishings and deeper gold in the en suite. Still no magic, and no obvious bombs.

If she has set such a trap, Azriel commented, *she would hardly make it obvious.*

True. I drifted back into the main room and headed left, past the entrance door and into the three rear rooms. One was a laundry, one was a bathroom, and the final one a spare bedroom. I still couldn't feel any magic, and there certainly wasn't hell spawn of any kind waiting for us. I went back to the main living area and stopped. *You know, this doesn't feel right. At every other place she has had something prepared for us, so why not here?*

It could just be that, in these forms, we are unable to sense whatever it is she has waiting.

Maybe. I spun around and headed for the security pad near the front door. *What's the override code?*

Seven-four-nine-one.

I called to the Aedh again but siphoned the power into my arm, down into my fingertips, imagining them alone gaining flesh rather than the rest of me. The energy surged and, in an instant, fingers appeared, seemingly floating in midair. I typed in the override code and watched the light stop flashing and turn green.

We should be all right, I said, half turning around.

And in that very instant, the apartment exploded into a million different pieces.

Chapter 5

Heat hit me, a wave so fierce and strong that I was little more than dust before it, tumbling and twisting and burning as it blew me through the apartment, then out the window. Concrete and metal, glass and wood, and god knows what else surrounded me as I was flung from the building, the force of the blast throwing me over the street and into the park.

I hit the ground hard enough to bounce even in energy form, and tumbled several feet farther before I came to a halt. I lay where I fell for several seconds, winded and shocked. Every part of me burned with the force and the heat of the blast, and yet, incredibly, I was alive and *not* hurt. Being in energy form had undoubtedly saved my life.

Azriel? My mental tones were little more than a croak.

Here. His energy briefly ran across the edges of me, as if he were reaching out with one hand and clasping mine. *I think that is what you would call a lucky break.*

Yeah. But it also means Lauren was here after *the police had investigated Jantz's apartment—otherwise, it would have taken them out rather than almost getting us.* And that meant it might be worth pulling up the security tapes to see who had entered Jantz's apartment *after* he'd been reported missing. Unless, of course, Lauren had used magic to get in and out of the apartment. If she'd known Jantz well enough to either use his name and identity or employ him to pick up her parcels, then she would have been familiar with his place. Magicking in and out in that case certainly wouldn't have proved a problem.

I shifted my still-tingling particles enough to see the building. On the seventh floor, where Jantz's apartment had been, there was now a huge, gaping hole. The apartments above and below had sustained some damage, but not as much as I'd expected from the force of the explosion. Or maybe it just seemed huge because we'd been energy ourselves. Smoke and dust billowed through the shattered remains of the glass doors, though from where I was, I couldn't see flames. Sirens were going off everywhere, and people were evacuating both Jantz's building and the buildings on either side, running down the pavement, away from the destruction.

If that is the case, there might not be anything in that apartment to find. Maybe it was Jantz himself who was the danger.

Possibly. But we should—

—check what is left of that apartment, just in case any fires within destroy what the blast did not, he finished, resignation heavy in his mental tones. *Are you sure you're feeling up to it? It has not been an easy few days and your energy levels are yet to recover, despite both our revive session and the sleep you've had.*

Revive session—what a nondescript way of putting great sex.

Amusement ran through his thoughts. *Economy of words is always best when even the most descriptive of sentences could never do justice to what we share.*

And if there's one thing that's been a constant since you arrived on the scene, it's your economy with words. I forced myself upward. Pain slivered through my particles, but it was distant, dull. No major damage, I gathered, though I suspected I might have one hell of a headache when I finally regained human form.

We went back to the apartment, slipping quickly through the smoke and into the ruins of the once beautiful main living area. Everything that had survived was little more than broken, scorched bits. Even the marble floors were blackened and cracked. There wasn't much hope of finding anything here.

I drifted into the bedroom. Though this room had sustained less damage than the living room, a fire was beginning to burn here, and it was catching fast. I did a quick look around but didn't see anything more than the last time. I retreated and moved to the rear of the apartment.

There's less damage here, Azriel commented. *It does look as if the bomb had been positioned to take out whoever disarmed the security system.*

And that *suggests maybe Jantz disappeared of his own accord and this bomb was a security measure on Lauren's part, just in case he came back.*

Possibly.

I still think there has to be something here. Something we've missed.

If there was something to be found in the living area, then there is little chance of recovering it.

I know. Just as I knew the only way I might be able to feel something was to regain human form. I swung around, studying the floors and walls. There were no gaping holes and, aside from a few cracks, nothing to indicate that any of the walls in this area was in immediate danger of collapse. The smoke and the fire were both a threat, but if I was quick, it should be okay.

Let me re-form first, Azriel said, and immediately did so. I watched, body tense—or as tense as energy particles could be—waiting for something to happen. For the broken building to react in some way or for some spell or demon to materialize.

Nothing did.

He glanced at me and nodded. I called to the Aedh, felt her sweep through me, and in very little time I was standing beside Azriel. A heartbeat after that, the air—thick with dust and smoke and heat—caught in my throat and sent me into a coughing fit. But as I half bent over, trying to get clean air into my lungs, I felt it—a sliver of dark energy. One I'd felt before, and which belonged to our sorceress.

"This is insane," Azriel growled. "You shouldn't—"

"There *is* something here," I cut in hoarsely. "Some sort of magic."

He frowned. "I cannot feel anything beyond your discomfort."

"That doesn't make it any less here." I stood upright, but the minute I did, the sensation went away. All I could feel was the thick dust; all I could hear was the crackle of fire, the groan of broken walls, and the wail of sirens drawing close. I frowned, bent over again, and the sensation reappeared. "This way."

I followed the tenuous trail out of the bedroom, stepping over chunks of marble and concrete, trying not to breathe in too much of the dust and smoke. My throat burned, and I needed water badly, but there was no way I'd leave this place until I found whatever that slight tease of magic was.

The trail led into the small laundry, of all places. I paused, looking around, trying to pinpoint the sliver of darkness. After a moment, I moved to the cupboard near the washer/dryer. When I opened the door, a laundry hamper slid out, half-filled with shirts, undies, and socks. Somewhat reluctantly, wishing I had some gloves so I didn't have to touch used undies with bare hands, I fished around. My fingertips soon brushed something solid near the bottom. I caught it and pulled it out.

"As dark magic goes, that pair of trousers looks particularly unthreatening," Azriel commented.

"Don't they just." They also felt rather heavy. I explored each of the pockets and, from the last one, pulled out a phone. Its surface crawled with the dark sensation of magic. I handed it to Azriel, then tossed the pants back into the hamper. "Can you feel it?"

He nodded and turned the vid-phone over, studying it. "I do not believe it is spelled, as such. It simply feels as if magic has leached into its surface."

"*Can* magic leach into surfaces?" I barely managed to get the words out when I started coughing again. The smoke was getting thicker, the heat stronger, and the emergency response vehicles had stopped on the street outside. We had to get out of here.

He shrugged. "I am not familiar enough with magic to answer that question, but the Brindle witches might be able to."

They probably could, but I'd already jeopardized their safety enough. I wasn't about to take this phone to them and risk either setting off a spell we couldn't detect or bringing the wrath of the sorceress down on them.

"Then what do you wish to do?" Azriel said. "As you noted, we must get out of here."

"Let's go to the Directorate," I said. "Maybe Uncle Rhoan—or at least someone in the Directorate—will be able to break whatever security is on the phone and trace who it belongs to."

He raised his eyebrows even as he reached for me. "And if there *is* a spell?"

"They have more than enough witches and plenty of spell-nullifying rooms to cope with it." I shoved my hand into my pocket and wrapped my fingers around my phone again.

"Good plan," he said, and zipped us out of there.

"I do have them occasionally," I said, as we reappeared in front of the inconspicuous green-glass building that housed the Directorate.

"Apparently so." His voice was dry.

I ignored the comment and, after tugging my clothes into some semblance of order, fished my phone out of my pocket and walked toward the Directorate's main entrance.

"Call Rhoan," I said, and a heartbeat later, his image appeared on the vid-screen.

"I was wondering when you'd get around to me," he said, a smile touching his lips but little in the way of amusement in his eyes.

"I need to talk to you ASAP."

"Don't bother, because I have no intention—"

"It's not about that," I cut in, not wanting him to say too much in case it wasn't Markel astrally following us about. The Cazadors generally weren't able to track our movements through the gray fields, but they would have heard me mentioning going to the Directorate and might already be here. Traveling on the astral field was as simple and as easy as traveling via reaper. "Well, not entirely. I need your help."

"Where are you?"

"Just about to enter the Directorate foyer."

"I'll be down in a minute."

The screen went dead. I shoved my phone away and stepped through the Directorate's main entrance. Pale blue light swept my length as I did so, the only visible indication of the vast array of scanners installed in this place. They all had one purpose—to protect those within. Not even a gnat could get into the Directorate without security being aware of it, let alone anyone armed with some form of weapon—be it metal, plastic, or laser. Of course, there wasn't a sensor in the world capable of detecting the presence of our swords.

Naturally, Amaya commented, her mental tones haughty. *Superior we are.*

A point with which I couldn't disagree. Even so, I couldn't help saying, *At least the weapons of this world don't scream at inopportune moments.*

Problems theirs, she said. *No point in* not *screaming. It scares more than steel.*

I guessed *that* was another point I couldn't argue with. I walked over to the comfy chairs situated to one side of the foyer and sat, legs crossed, to wait for Uncle Rhoan.

Security frowned at us. "Can I help you, miss?"

"It's all right, Mac," Rhoan said, as he came around the corner. In the foyer's light, his red hair gleamed like fire. "These two are here at my request."

I rose and walked toward him. His sharp gray gaze briefly swept me. "You really need to get some rest in the next twenty-four hours. You look like shit."

"Well, thanks." I kissed his cheeks. "It's good to see you, too."

He half smiled, but it didn't lift the seriousness in his eyes. "I mean it. You can't keep running on empty, Ris. It won't do anyone any good." His gaze moved beyond me, and he made a slight nod of acknowledgment. "Nice to see you, reaper."

See? I am not the only one who notices these things, Azriel said, even as he said out loud, "And you."

Rhoan's gaze returned to mine. "What's the problem?"

"I prefer it if we were somewhere secure. Too many possible listeners hanging about out in the open."

"The Directorate's foyer has more antilistening devices than most secure offices could even dream of." But his gaze flickered briefly beyond me, and I knew then he'd caught my meaning. "But if it would make you feel better, come along."

He swung around and led us to the lifts. No one spoke as we headed down into the true heart of the Directorate. The ten levels aboveground might be the public face of the Directorate, but it was here, in the five stories underground, where the guardians were housed and trained, and where the liaisons—the people who filed the guardians' reports, who catered to their everyday needs, and who gave them their assignments—operated.

The lift came to a halt and the doors slid open. The thick smell of vampire swept in, but underneath it ran the sweeter scent of shifters. Once upon a time, this section of the Directorate had operated mainly at night, simply because most guardians had been vampires. But over the last fifteen years or so, more shifters and psychics had been employed to cover daytime operations.

Rhoan led us through a maze of halls, then finally stopped and slapped his palm against a scanner. The door slid open. He stepped to one side and waved me in. The room was small and sparsely furnished, with little more than a coffee machine and a table that had half a dozen chairs scattered around it. It was also a room protected by magic. It caressed my skin, a touch that was warm and yet filled with power. It wasn't as strong or as ancient as the force that protected the Brindle, but it wasn't something anyone sane would want to mess around with.

"Okay," Rhoan said, heading for the coffee machine. "What's the problem?"

"Our sorceress just blew up a rather expensive Sydney apartment—"

"Which undoubtedly explains the torn state of your clothing and the smell of smoke," he cut in. "I gather the bomb was meant for whoever owns the apartment, rather than you?"

"We think so," I said. "It didn't detonate until we deactivated the security system."

Rhoan punched several buttons on the coffee machine, then said, "How did you survive the blast?"

"We were in energy form, so it simply blew us out rather than up. We were lucky."

"Apparently so." He didn't make the obvious comment—that one day we wouldn't be—though I could almost see the thought cross his mind. "Why did she destroy the apartment? Who owned it?"

I pulled a chair closer to the table, then sat down and told him about Harrison Jantz. "We're not sure why Jantz has disappeared, but if our sorceress set the bomb to take him out rather than destroy any evidence she might have left there, then we need to find Jantz ourselves, and fast."

"Which is why you're here?" He carried two mugs of coffee over and handed me one.

"Yes, but also because of this." I glanced at Azriel. He placed the phone we'd discovered at the apartment on the table. "The same sort of magic Lauren uses clings to its surface, so we doubt it's Jantz's. We were wondering if the witches here could defuse whatever spell might be on this thing, then trace the owner."

"It's more than likely a burn phone. I mean, surely your sorceress wouldn't be daft enough to leave something like this behind at the scene of her crime."

"It was in a pair of men's pants. Maybe she forgot it was in them when they were tossed into the laundry basket."

He frowned. "Why would your sorceress be leaving men's pants in Jantz's apartment?"

"Because she's a multishifter who can take on both male and female forms." I hesitated. "She has, in the past, taken my form, so be really careful if you get an unexpected call from me requesting a meeting somewhere private."

"All the calls I get from you are unexpected." His voice was dry. "But I do see your point. No clandestine meetings with you from now on, then."

"I'm serious, Uncle Rhoan. I have no idea how much this bitch knows about me, but I don't want to risk your life any more than I already have."

"Ris," he said gently, "I'm a guardian. Danger is an inherent part of my job."

"I know, and that's not what I meant."

He smiled. "I appreciate the concern, but I will not—"

"I know, but you don't understand. Lauren is the *least* of your problems when it comes to danger. Hunter is not only head of the organization you work for, but undoubtedly knows which buttons she needs to push to get to you. She's already killed Jak, and she's threatened me with not only your safety, but *everyone* else I care about. She *will* carry through with those threats. And nothing, not this place, not being a guardian, will protect you from her. She's not human. She's—"

"No one you should be going up against," a deep voice said.

I jumped, splashing coffee across my hand as I swung around. The man who'd entered was bald, average sized, with weatherworn features and sharp green eyes. He neither looked nor felt dangerous, and yet he was possibly the most dangerous person inside the Directorate aside from Hunter herself.

This was Jack Parnell, senior vice president of the Directorate, and the man in charge of the entire guardian division.

He also happened to be Madeline Hunter's half brother.

"It's not like I want to go up against her." I put my coffee down and rubbed my hand on the leg of my jeans to dry it. "In fact, it's the one thing I'm trying to avoid. But she's—"

"I know what she is," Jack cut in. He walked across to the coffee machine and pressed a button. "I'm also aware of what she might desire."

"I think 'might desire' is putting it a little too mildly, don't you?"

He flashed me a smile, but it held little in the way of warmth.

"Perhaps. But I have been aware of my sister's ambitions for quite a while and, as much as I am able, have been attempting to keep some control over them."

"Control?" I retorted. "How is allowing her to kill Jak keeping some control over the situation?"

"Ris," Rhoan murmured. "Calm down—"

Something within me snapped. "Damn it, *no*! I won't. I *can't*. I've been pulled from pillar to post by the wants and desires of just about every other damn person on this planet—and some beyond it—and I'm getting a little tired of it. This isn't about me calming down. This is about me trying to save not only your butt, but the butts of everyone else on this planet if either of the psycho bitches who have designs on the last key actually gets her mitts on it."

I stopped and took a deep breath. Uncle Rhoan's expression swung between surprise and amusement. I couldn't say what Jack was feeling, because—like most vampires—he could control his emotions to the extreme when he wanted to.

And, right now, he apparently wanted to.

I met his bright gaze. "I know she's your sister, but surely to god even you can see that her gaining control of both the high vampire council *and* the key would *not* be a very good thing."

"I didn't mention the keys when I talked to him about Jak," Rhoan murmured.

"No, he didn't." Jack gave Rhoan a somewhat severe look. "But he didn't need to. I have, as I said, been aware of the situation for some time. And I'm sorry about Jak. That was . . . unfortunate."

He'd been aware . . . and yet hadn't done a damn

thing. And because of that, Jak had died. I slapped a hand on the table and thrust to my feet. "And will Rhoan's death be unfortunate?" I exploded again, waving a hand at him. "Will Aunt Riley's? Where are you going to draw the line?"

"Ris, enough," Rhoan warned softly. "Let the man explain."

I opened my mouth to argue, then met Rhoan's gaze and closed it again, suddenly aware of the fury building near the coffee machine. Jack might be able to control his emotions, but right now they were extremely close to erupting.

I sat down, wrapped my fingers around my coffee cup, and waited. After a moment, Jack walked across to the table, pulled out a chair, and sat down. Every move was measured, considered. He sipped his coffee, saying nothing, and while that sense of fury didn't ebb, the sensation of imminent danger eventually did.

"My sister," he said, after a few minutes, "deserves the chance to step away—"

My gaze flashed to his. *"What?"*

"Ris," Rhoan warned again.

I glared at him but shut up.

"She started the Directorate," Jack said. "And she has spent centuries protecting this world *and* its people. I cannot and will not go up against her without giving that history the respect it is due."

"Whatever good she's done here and elsewhere in the past doesn't give her a pass for unleashing known killers on innocent people," I said. "That's the premise the whole Directorate was built on, wasn't it? Protecting humanity from supernatural predators?"

"I'm *well* aware of what the Directorate stands for." Jack's voice was mild, but there was a note in it that chilled. "My sister may have founded the Directorate, but *I* helped build it to what it is today. *Never* forget that."

I wouldn't, but I had to wonder if Hunter had. Had to wonder if, in the end, it came down to a choice, whether Jack would side with his sister or the organization he'd helped build.

His comments earlier suggested the latter, and I certainly hoped that was the case. I very much suspected Jack was, in his own way, as dangerous as Hunter. The two of them together might be nigh on unbeatable.

"Besides," he continued, "there was no confirmation that the vampire who killed Jak was sent there by my sister. Rhoan interviewed him when he was first captured, but a formal interview never occurred and the suspect died while being transported here. I will not move on her, officially or otherwise, without definitive proof of wrongdoing."

"Oh, how convenient," I muttered, though I had to admit, the news *did* surprise me. I really *had* thought Hunter would use that vampire to lure Rhoan into doing something rash—like confronting her. Instead, he'd confronted me and had probably saved his life by doing so. Of course, once her plan was so obviously foiled, Hunter had simply erased the evidence by erasing the vampire.

I contemplated Jack for a moment, then slowly said, "I guess it's fortunate that I taped his confession, then, isn't it?"

"You did?" Rhoan said, expression annoyed. "And why didn't you hand it over when I confronted you about Jak's death?"

I raised an eyebrow. "Would you, given the situation? The woman who runs this place is your boss, and she has god knows how many people under her thumb. Even if you didn't do as she wanted—confront her—I'm betting the taped confession would soon have disappeared."

"I want you to hand over that confession to *me*," Jack said. "That is evidence, and you should not—"

"I'll send you a copy," I cut in. "But I'm keeping the original as a security measure."

Jack smiled, and there was something almost sad about it. "Do you think, for a second, that one vampire's confession will be enough to curb my sister's activities? If you do, then you have no real understanding of her."

"I understand her *plenty*." I met his gaze, judging him as he undoubtedly was judging me. Seeing not only the remaining embers of fury in his eyes, but the growing fires of resignation. He knew a war was coming; he knew the time had come to make a stand. "But she hasn't got the key yet, and she hasn't taken over the council yet, and the existence of that tape might well force her to at least place her plans on a temporary hold. And *that* might just give us the time we need to find the key and stop darkness being unleashed on the world."

Whether that darkness was hell itself or Hunter didn't really matter.

Jack drank some coffee as he contemplated me. Eventually he said, "She will know where the confession came from. That might well place you in a difficult situation."

"It *couldn't* be any more difficult." My voice was grim. "She's given me twenty-four hours—of which there are now just under twenty-two hours left—to find and hand over the next key; otherwise, she'll start picking off people close to me."

Jack closed his eyes. Rhoan swore and said, "Which is the reason you told Riley and Quinn to get the hell out of town."

"And why I need you out." I held out a hand to halt his almost instinctive refusal. "I know, I know. But you could at least get Liander somewhere safe. She may value you too much to actually kill you—no matter what she's threatened otherwise—but Liander is another matter entirely."

That hit home. Liander was, after all, his soul mate,

and very few wolves could survive such a death. Riley *had*, but then, she'd also had Quinn. "Done," he said, and jumped up. He moved across to the other side of the room and made the call.

I met Jack's gaze again. "You said you were keeping some control over the situation—is there any way at all you can protect Rhoan?"

"I will talk to her," he said heavily. "And make it known that all Directorate personnel are off-limits. That by touching one, she sets the guardian division on a collision course with her."

How much protection that would provide was anyone's guess, but given that Hunter appeared to value her brother's opinion—or rather, she did if comments she'd made in the past were anything to go by—it was better than nothing.

"And the keys? Or her takeover attempt of the high council?"

He half shrugged. "I have never gotten involved in high council politics, and have no intention of doing so now. I do not care, one way or another, whether it is ruled by a committee or a force of one."

"Others don't quite see it that way."

"I'm well aware of that." His expression was grim. "I have been on this earth for a very long time, young Risa, and I have *not* survived by keeping my head in the sand and being unaware."

Duly chastened, but still not backing away, I said, "Will your sister listen to you? She's . . . well, she's gone a little off the deep end since the death of her lover."

Though I personally suspected she'd well and truly jumped into the crazy pool *before* that death. Her lover's murder had just made it more obvious.

"I have not seen her much since then, so you could well be right." Jack drained his coffee, then tossed the cup in the bin and rose. "I'll arrange a meeting with her immediately. In the meantime, do nothing to antagonize her."

"I have no intention of contacting her until the twenty-four-hour deadline is near." Whether she'd contact me—antagonize *me*—was another matter entirely.

If you don't bite back at her, it should not provide a problem, Azriel commented.

Easier said than done, I'm afraid.

Not if you recall the faces of those she might destroy out of sheer spite.

I glanced at him. He raised an eyebrow, as if daring me to contradict the statement. But I couldn't, because it was true. I simply *had* to control my temper. No ifs, buts, or maybes.

"Good," Jack said. "But be careful, Risa. Those who oppose my sister are no angels, either."

"Something *I'm* well aware of." But if push came to shove, I'd use them—and anyone else, for that matter— to protect my friends and to stop the crazies from ruining the world.

Jack walked from the room. I released a long, slow breath, then downed my coffee in several quick gulps. *That* had turned out a whole lot better than I'd hoped— but it could have very easily gone the other way, and I knew it.

"Liander is, as we speak, jumping in his car and heading to parts unknown," Rhoan said, as he returned to the table. "He won't contact me for the next forty-eight hours."

"What about his phone and the GPS in his car? They can both be used to trace him—"

"He'll disable both. He has not been the soul mate of a guardian for so long without picking up a trick or two."

"Forty-eight hours is long enough," Azriel commented. "One way or another, things will be sorted by then."

I shot him another glance. *I thought you said we had a week?*

No, I said we had no more than a week. His expression gave little away, but I could feel the turmoil in him, the uncertainty, and that scared the *hell* out of me. *That timetable has since been revised.*

Meaning our actions have revised it? But what actions? Finding Jantz, blowing up his apartment, or talking to Rhoan and Jack?

It doesn't matter, Azriel said. *The timetable is what it is now. And, at the very least, it gives us a shorter period to survive.*

And you'd better survive, reaper, I said, mental tones fierce. *Or I will not be happy.*

You can be assured that I would be decidedly unimpressed with anything short of survival myself.

"I get the feeling," Rhoan commented, "that there's a completely different conversation happening right now."

I glanced at him and smiled. "Yeah, sorry." I slid the phone we'd found at Jantz's across to him. "Can you let me know the minute you find any information about who owns this?"

"Can do," he said. "And I'll watch my back. I'll even ensure I have people I trust around me at all times. Will that assuage your concerns?"

"Some," I admitted.

"Good." He studied me for a minute, and something in his eyes hardened. The guardian, rising once more to the surface. "Then you need to assuage mine. You will *not* tackle Hunter without outside help, will you?"

I licked my lips. "Look, I know you mean—"

"This *isn't* a request," he cut in, voice flat. "And there *is* no refusing. There is only yes, or there's me walking out of this room right now and confronting her myself."

I stared at him. "That's blackmail."

"Too right it is, and I don't care. I want your word,

Risa, that the minute you even *contemplate* contacting the forces that oppose Hunter, you'll also contact me. I know that you've already made this promise to Riley and Quinn, and you will damn well extend it to me—and keep it. Otherwise, I'll do as I threatened."

He would, too. To keep me safe, he'd risk his own damn life. "You're fucking crazy, Uncle Rhoan," I muttered, then flung myself into his arms. "And god, I love you for it."

His arms went around me and held me tight. After a moment, he kissed the top of my head and said, "I can take that as a yes?"

"You can." I stepped away, then thrust a hand across my eyes, wiping away a defiant tear. My phone rang, and the tone told me it was Ilianna. My stomach flip-flopped, though I wasn't sure whether it was fear or just pregnancy reasserting itself.

I dragged the vid-phone out of my pocket, hit the Answer button, and said, "Is there a problem?"

"Other than you and then Azriel making quick exits and not getting back to me to let me know you're both okay?" she said, voice mild but holding a hint of censure.

"Yeah, besides that," I said, voice contrite. "And I'm sorry—"

"I know," she cut in. "I'm just feeling tired and stressed, and bitchy because of it. Anyway, you need to get your butts over here. We have to talk."

"How urgent is this?"

"Very, if you want to protect the people you care about."

"Then I'll be right over."

"See you soon." She hung up.

I put the phone away, then gave Rhoan a smile. "Gotta go. Talk to you soon."

"I damn well hope so."

I half stepped toward Azriel, then stopped and turned

to face Rhoan again. Clairvoyance wasn't one of my stronger psychic skills, but when it hit, it wasn't often wise to ignore it.

And right now, it was hitting hard.

I hesitated, then said, "I don't suppose I could borrow that ring Liander gave you for your anniversary last year, can I?"

He glanced down at the small, unobtrusive ring on his left hand. "Why?"

My hesitation was longer this time. "Because, as of this minute, I have a horrible feeling I might need it to find you sometime in the future. And while I hope to *god* I'm wrong, given everything that has happened over the last few days, I just don't want to take any sort of chance."

"If something went wrong, and I went missing, Riley would find me." He eyed me for a minute, his expression thoughtful. "You know that."

"I know, but the twin connection *can* be disrupted by magic *or* drugs—and you know *that*."

"True." He studied me for a moment longer, then tugged the ring off his finger and dropped it into my hand. "Just don't lose it. Liander will kill me—and you."

"I won't." I shoved it onto my left thumb—the only place it was secure given that his fingers were thicker than mine. Plus, it was safer than merely putting it in my pocket. "But if either our sorceress or Hunter decided to snatch you—and there *was* no way we could find or rescue you—then Riley would likely kill *me*."

Amusement filled his tone, though it failed to break the concerned glitter in his eyes. "But only after she'd rescued me—and you wouldn't be the only one on the receiving end of the lecture."

I half smiled. Riley's lectures had become somewhat infamous over the years, but they were born from both fear and relief, and we all knew that. They usually ended with a fierce hug and a plea not to scare her like that again, anyway, so it was all good.

I stepped forward, dropped a kiss on his cheek, then said, "Just be careful. This is one case where I'm more than happy to have instinct proven wrong."

"As am I. Go. I'll get the phone information to you the minute I can."

We went. A heartbeat later we were once more standing within the halls of the Brindle. The magic reacted immediately, crawling across my skin like electric gnats, its feel sharp. Probing. Kiandra might have recently woven some exceptions into the barrier that protected this place to allow for our comings and goings, but the Brindle wasn't about to let us enter unchallenged any more than it would evil. And while I wasn't evil, I was no longer flesh and blood, and the magic was always going to react to that, regardless.

"You were never *just* flesh and blood." Azriel caught my hand and tugged me forward. Up ahead, near the door that led into the Brindle's shadowed inner sanctuary, a tunic-clad witch waited. "Your heritage is Aedh just as much as werewolf, and it is *that* bloodline which has always allowed you to sense the magic in this place."

"Just this place?" I queried, remembering my reaction to the sacred site where Tao had consumed the fire spirit to save Ilianna's life.

Azriel glanced at me. "Neither Aedh nor reaper can enter that place. That the magic lets you pass rather than forbid your entry is something I cannot explain."

"Risa, Azriel," the brown-haired witch said softly, as we approached. "Please follow me."

She turned and led us through the door, then down a flight of stairs to a hall that was lined with darkly stained timber and filled with shadows. Sconces flickered on as we approached, then went dark once we'd passed, fueled by magic rather than electricity.

We turned right at the end of this hall and went down a second set of stairs and into another hallway. Our guide stopped about halfway down and knocked on a plain wooden door. Then, without waiting for an answer, she opened it and ushered us in. I realized almost immediately where we were—Zaira's office. It was a small and sweet-smelling room, with little more than a very large old wooden desk, a leather chair that had seen better days, and shelves that lined all available wall space. Books were everywhere—crowding not only the shelves but much of the floor space, a riot of leather-bound color that lent warmth to the otherwise barren room. The smell within the room was divine, and I took a deep, appreciative breath. There was nothing quite like the scent of old books, even when it was almost overwhelmed by the richer scents of lavender and rose.

Ilianna and Kiandra were both sitting near the old desk, and they looked up as we entered. Ilianna's gaze skimmed us; then she smiled. "Not only alive, but apparently in one piece. It's a miracle."

"You have no idea just *how* much of a miracle it is." I wrapped my arms around her and gave her a brief but fierce hug. "I really *am* sorry I didn't let you know earlier."

"Forgiven," Ilianna said. "I guess you have been kinda busy, what with trying to save the world and all."

"Yeah." My gaze went to Kiandra's. "The Raziq are no longer a problem. There was something of an intervention by both the fates and the Aedh who still haunt that place."

She nodded, her expression pleased, though I had a suspicion it wasn't exactly news to her. "And the sorceress?"

"Went to hell—literally. I'm not sure she stayed there, though."

"Which is the *precise* reason we made these." Ilianna

held up what looked like a half dozen multicolored ribbons twined together, then looped through several creamy white stones to form a bracelet.

I frowned. "And what might they be, besides pretty?"

She grinned. "Do you remember asking me to create something along the lines of the wards your father gave you, but for personal use?"

I nodded. I'd figured at the time it might be the only way to protect everyone I cared about from the Raziq. It was a shame said stones couldn't also ward off the crazy that was Hunter.

"Well, when you made the mad dash home and Azriel came back with the wards, Kiandra said that personal wards against the Raziq was no longer the problem, and that wards against magic would be far more beneficial. Hence, pretty bracelets."

My gaze met Kiandra's. She smiled. "And I was right, was I not?"

"You certainly were. And thank you."

She nodded and rose. "Before I leave, is there anything else you wish help with?"

I hesitated, then said, "You wouldn't be able to recommend someone with psychometry skills, would you? I need to trace the owner of a cuff link I found."

"And the owner is the sorceress?"

"We think so."

"Then you will need a practitioner who has some ability to protect both herself and you against the dark magic should there be a spell of some kind infused within the object."

I frowned. "If there was a spell, wouldn't I have set it off by now? I've had it for a while."

"Not necessarily. If the object were mine, I'd set the spell to trigger only when someone attempted to use it against me in some way." She pursed her lips for a moment, her expression thoughtful. "Unfortunately, we have none capable of psychometry here at the Brindle at the moment, but I do know of someone outside these walls who may be able to help. I shall contact her and see if she is willing to see you."

"That would be fantastic. And again, thank you."

"It is in all our interest to aid you in whatever way we can." She paused, her gaze suddenly unfocusing. Power shivered through the air, its touch as sharp and as electric as the power that protected this place.

"You must trust your instincts, Risa," she said, voice soft. "No matter how incredible it might seem at the time. And remember, safety lies in four."

Safety lies in four? What the hell was *that* supposed to mean?

Kiandra blinked, and life came back into her eyes. She smiled, but there was concern in her expression. "I told you once before there was someone in your life who was not what they seemed. That impression has grown stronger. Watch your back." She paused, her gaze flickering to Azriel. "And you, reaper, had better watch yours."

Azriel bowed slightly. "I thank you for the warning."

Kiandra half smiled. "I shall leave Ilianna to explain the intricacies of the bracelets. I will be in contact if I find someone willing to help you with the cuff link."

With that, she left. I looked at Ilianna. "I don't suppose you can explain that somewhat cryptic message?"

"The 'safety lies in four' bit, you mean? Not a chance. Kiandra's visions are often less than informative, unfortunately."

Great. Though it wasn't like I could bitch given all the help she was giving me otherwise. "So, these bracelets." I carefully hooked a finger around one of them and plucked it from Ilianna's hand. Energy tingled across my fingertips, and the Dušan reacted immediately, spinning around to glare at it.

Ilianna blinked. "That thing just moved again."

"Yeah, it does fairly regularly these days."

"Huh. I would love to know how."

"So would I," Azriel commented. "The Dušan are not supposed to be active on this plane of existence."

Ilianna raised an eyebrow, amusement creasing the corners of her green eyes. "So it's like its owner, and keeps doing the unexpected?"

"Definitely," Azriel commented, voice dry. "But it does make for a more interesting existence."

"Undoubtedly." Ilianna's amusement grew stronger. "But to get back to the point, these will protect their wearers from most incantations and spells. Given you're somewhat more sensitive to magic than most nonpractitioners, I imagine you will probably still feel any attack on you, but it will not be enough to influence you—or anyone else who wears them—in any way. It will not protect you from the darker forces, however."

"Darker forces meaning demon attack and the like, rather than actual spells and incantations?"

She hesitated. "I'm not sure it will protect you against a spell with the full backing of blood magic behind it, but it should withstand most other magic."

Which was a damn sight better than nothing.

"We've only managed to make three of these things," she continued. "For safety's sake, Mirri and I are going to stay here at the Brindle, so you might want to give one to Tao and the other to Stane."

"Not Tao," I said immediately. "Aside from the fact that if we can't find him, it's doubtful the sorcerer or even Hunter could, he at least has the elemental for protection. That thing seems to have a sixth sense when it comes to attack."

Or even being touched. I shivered, and pain ghosted through my hand as I remembered my attempt to stop the elemental reaching Macedon. If Azriel hadn't been able to heal me, I would have been left with a useless limb.

"You're right." Her expression was thoughtful. "And it's probably the only real protection he needs, when I think about it."

I frowned. "How so?"

"It's obvious the fire that gave birth to the elementals still burns within the Macedon sacred site, and as long as it does, the elemental cannot be controlled by other forces of magic."

"But it can be destroyed by them—can't it?"

"Yes, but it would take a lot of energy and strength. The elementals are a force of *being* as much as magic."

"Our dark sorceress has the strength, though."

"Yes, but it would drain her. With you so close on her tail, I don't think she'd risk it."

Neither did I. Then what she'd said earlier actually hit me. "Ilianna, if destroying the fire will destroy the elemental, why don't we just do that to free Tao?"

"Because it won't free Tao. It'll kill him." She grimaced. "Trust me, I *did* think of that solution, but I'm afraid when Tao consumed the elemental, he forever changed his body chemistry. They are too intertwined now to separate. Kill one, and you kill the other."

"So our only hope is praying that Tao wins the battle for control?"

"Or that, at the very least, they come to some sort of truce."

I snorted. "It's hard to imagine what sort of truce would work for two very different beings."

"Yes." There was sadness in her expression. She crossed her arms and said, "Who do you plan to give the spare bracelet to?"

"Uncle Rhoan. He adamantly refuses to retreat to safe ground, so this bracelet will at least afford him some protection." I handed the bracelet to Azriel. "Could you please take it to him?"

"As long as you remain here, under the Brindle's protection, while I am gone."

"I will."

He immediately disappeared. I took the remaining two, slipping one over my right wrist and shoving the other into a pocket to give it to Stane later. The Dušan reacted immediately to the presence of the bracelet on my wrist, slithering up my arm, across my shoulders, then down my right arm. It was a weird sensation, not unlike my skin crawling, but interspersed with needle-sharp pinpricks that were a result of the Dušan's claws cutting into my skin—though she didn't draw blood. As the Dušan reached the ribbon-and-stone bracelet, her tail lifted from my skin, curled around the bracelet, then returned to my flesh. The bracelet went with it, prickling and itching as it leached into my skin. After a few seconds, it was little more than a multicolored tattoo that encircled my right wrist. The Dušan then retreated to my left arm and entwined around the leafy charm Ilianna had given me earlier to protect—or at least mute—the force of any ordinary spell or *geas* used against me. Though Lucian—who'd placed one such *geas* on me—was no longer a problem, the sorceress was still out there, and who knew what kind of compulsion she might try if given half the chance.

I held out my wrist. "Is the magic still active?"

Ilianna ran a hand around my wrist, her expression thoughtful. Contemplative. "Definitely. I wonder if I can figure out how the Dušan does this. If I *could*, it could herald in a whole new era in spell protection."

"And make you rich," I said, with a grin.

She glanced up, expression cross. "I'm already rich. This is about—"

"Ilianna," I said gently, "I was joking."

She took a deep breath and slowly released it. "Sorry. As I said, the pregnancy is making me bitchy. Of course, it could also be the meeting we've planned with Carwyn tonight."

Carwyn was the stallion whose herd Ilianna's parents—who were unaware Ilianna was gay and already in a committed relationship with Mirri—were pushing her to join. Ilianna had been fighting against their wishes for a while now, but the truth was, mares rarely remained without a herd. They usually went from their father's herd to their stallion's, and quite often the match was chosen for political or monetary advantages rather than love.

"I hope he's coming here—"

"He is," she cut in. "I'm hoping the Brindle will make him see that I belong here, not with him."

I frowned. "But you don't belong here. You said that yourself, more times than I care to remember."

"I know. It's just—" She paused and rubbed her arms. "Ever since I came back here, it's felt oddly right. It's almost as if I've come home."

A vague and definitely selfish sense of alarm ran through me. Things were changing—we were *all* changing—and no matter how much I might wish otherwise, there was no going back. Not to the way we were before my father, the Raziq, and Lucian stepped into my life, anyway. And while that might not necessarily be a bad thing, it nevertheless made me sad.

But all I said was, "Your mother was under the impression you could never return to the Brindle until Kiandra was gone."

"She's right—I couldn't. At least, not until recently. Not until all this key business started. It made me realize however much I might have disagreed with what was done so long ago to maintain the safety of this place, there *was* a need for it."

"And what was done?" I said softly.

Her gaze met mine. "Sacrifices. Blood sacrifices."

I frowned. "But witches are against blood magic."

"Yes, we are. It is the reason I swore never to return to the place while Kiandra was present. She was the instigator. She raised the magic and forever tainted the soul of this place. Or so I thought." She took a deep breath and released it slowly, then gave me a quick, sharp smile. "Anyway, I'm hoping Carwyn will see this place, see my place in it, and make the only logical decision."

"That being to walk away and not attempt to add you and Mirri to his herd?"

"No, because that would hurt both our families." She shrugged. "The logical solution is to make it a joining in name only. That way, he gets the alliance he wants, and I get the protection of his brand."

"And Mirri? What does she get out of the deal?"

"She, like me, gets the protection of his herd while still retaining her freedom. Plus, if she wants, she gets babies." She half smiled. "She's bisexual, remember, and me being pregnant has made her somewhat broody."

"Then I hope Carwyn sees sense."

"So do I," she murmured. "So do I."

Azriel returned. "Rhoan is not happy about wearing something so feminine," he said, "but has agreed to do so until told otherwise. He did comment that it was more Liander's style than his."

I smiled. Liander would probably have painted his fingernails all the different colors of the ribbon, just for the fun of it. I gave Ilianna another hug, wished her luck, then stepped into Azriel's arms and said, "Let's head back to Stane's and see if he's had any luck with pinning the key location down."

"It is unlikely," he said, as we reappeared once again within the security shields protecting Stane's place. "Not enough time has passed since we assigned him the task."

"I know, but what else can we do?" I glanced at the camera. "Stane, it's us again."

"Come on up."

The screen briefly shimmered, then died. I headed for the stairs and lightly ran up them. Stane was stationed at his bridge but glanced around as we entered the main living room. "As Azriel has already noted, even my computers can't come up with answers that fast."

I plopped down on one of the chairs and handed him the ribbon bracelet. "Put that on and don't take it off."

He raised his eyebrows, even as he did as I ordered. "What is it?"

"An early warning system against any sort of spell headed your way."

He studied the twined ribbons, expression bemused. "Does it also protect against it?"

"Against all but the really dark stuff."

"Then it is now a permanent feature on my wrist."

I smiled and got back to the business at hand. "So you have nothing for us yet?"

"On the contrary, I currently have a list of over a thousand places," he said. "Right now, I'm programming in variables using historical records and photographs in an effort to cut down the numbers."

I blinked. "Why are you using old records and photographs?"

"Because it's rare for modern buildings to have a coat of arms designed onto them, let alone one that's been placed upside down or the wrong way around. And given it's not unusual for a building to be renamed when a new business takes it over, I'm also doing a search through business registration records."

"Good point. But I can't justify sitting here doing nothing while the computers work. I need to be doing something." Needed to be *seen* to be doing something. I very much suspected Hunter would not be pleased to hear that I was sitting around twiddling my thumbs, waiting for answers to appear on-screen.

Stane blew out a somewhat frustrated-sounding breath. "I guess there's always a chance you could stumble on the right one." He leaned over and flicked a list across to another screen. A second later, my phone beeped. "That's the entire list of possibilities. I'll continue sorting through them, so let me know if you do find the correct building."

"I will." I jumped to my feet, dragged out my phone, then brought up the list. The first town listed was Bairnsdale, which was one of the largest towns in the East Gippsland region. I'd only ever been there once, and that was when Ilianna and I had decided to spend a week or so exploring the Gippsland Lakes district. I glanced at Azriel. "Can you take us there?"

He nodded. "Your memory of the place is hazy, but there's enough information for me to get us there."

"Good." I glanced at Stane. "Talk to you soon."

He nodded. Azriel whisked us out of there, and in very little time, we were standing in the shadows of Bairnsdale's beautiful old rotunda. It was situated in the gardens that were maintained on the wide median strip that divided the two sections of Main Street. I glanced around, vaguely recognizing several of the shops, then brought up maps on my phone and plugged in the addresses of the possible key locations. More than an hour later, we'd checked out all of them, and there was nary a key in sight.

We repeated the process at the next two—much smaller—towns, with exactly the same results.

"This is next to useless." I collapsed back onto a park seat somewhat dispiritedly.

"Yes," Azriel said. "But you were well aware that was a possibility before we started."

"Yeah, but I guess I was just hoping we might catch a

break." I scrubbed a hand across my eyes. "I suppose the only thing we can do is head back to the office and hope like hell Stane comes through with a smaller list of possibilities sooner rather than later."

Although, if I was being honest, all I really wanted to do was head back to the hotel and catch some sleep. Nothing major—a week or two would do. But with Hunter's deadline looming over our heads, I doubted I'd be able to sleep even if we could spare the time. At least if I was at the office, I could search the Net and make like I was looking even if Stane had more hope of getting a result than I ever did. At least on a computer, anyway.

Azriel didn't say anything, but a second later, his energy surged around us, and I found myself sitting in the chair in the café's office rather than on a park bench.

I raised an eyebrow, a grin teasing my lips. "So you really *don't* need to touch me to transfer us both."

"Of course not. As I've said previously, I merely prefer it."

"You, reaper, are a lecher in the making."

He raised an eyebrow. "If by that you mean I have a strong, sexually based desire to hold you in my arms, then yes. And I see nothing wrong with it."

"Neither do I," I replied mildly. "Except for the fact that until recently, you seemed quite determined to keep me at arm's length."

"Which was self-protection, as you well know." He hesitated and tilted his head sideways slightly, as if listening to something. "It might interest you to know that Tao is downstairs."

I stared at him for a minute, not quite believing I'd heard him right, then thrust up from the chair and bolted downstairs for the kitchen. I slammed through the kitchen's double doors, saw Tao, and all but threw myself into his arms.

"You're okay," I murmured, as I hugged him fiercely.

The heat radiating off him was as intense as a flame and had pinpricks of sweat breaking out across my body in an instant. I didn't care. He was here, he was whole, and that was all that mattered for now. "I'm so glad you're okay."

"So am I," he replied, voice cracking with emotion and weariness. His arms briefly tightened around my waist; then he pulled back.

I released him somewhat reluctantly. His face was thin, his cheeks hollowed, and his body—which had always been wolf lean—was now whip thin. It was almost as if the elemental had melted every single ounce of fat from his body, leaving only muscle, bone, and skin. "What happened? How did you get here?"

He hesitated, glancing around at the kitchen, then said, "Why don't we take this outside?"

I waved him ahead of me, and we headed for the rear of the kitchen and the door out into the lane. The air was cool, thick with the smell of the nearby rubbish and an oncoming storm.

He swung around and crossed his arms, tension evident in the set of his shoulders. "Did I hurt Stane?"

My eyebrows rose. "Of course not," I said, surprised. "Why would you—"

I hesitated, remembering what Stane had said about being thrown across the room, and Tao smiled grimly. "So I *did* attack him?"

"Not really. And you certainly didn't hurt him."

He swore and thrust a shaky hand through his hair. "But I so easily *could* have. I have no memory of leaving Stane's, Risa. No memory of anything until I woke up in the middle of that damn forest where the thing inside me was created."

"At least you *did* wake up. It hasn't won the battle yet, Tao."

I took a step toward him, but stopped when he retreated. He must have caught the instinctive flash of surprise and hurt that ran through me, because he grimaced and said, "Sorry, it's just—" He stopped. "I don't want to hurt you. I don't want to hurt anyone."

"Then why come here?" Azriel asked softly from behind me. "If you are worried about control, is not the kitchen the worst place you could be right now?"

It was a question that had echoed through me, as well, but one I'd been afraid to give voice to.

Tao didn't immediately reply. He simply stared almost blindly at the two of us, then made an abrupt, chopping motion with his hand. "No, it's not. It's a compromise. A kitchen has enough heat to keep the elemental satisfied while still allowing me some degree of control."

"The last time you were in the kitchen, the heat made you *lose* control," I said, trying to keep my voice even. "I really think—"

"Then don't think," he snapped. "You know *nothing* about the thing inside of me, Risa. None of us have any idea what will or won't work when it comes to control—or even if control is possible."

"Which is why—"

"No," he said, his eyes bleeding heat, with sparks of flame shooting from his fingertips. "It needs heat and I want to survive. I don't want to hurt anyone, but I also do *not* want to spend the rest of my life playing solitaire in some godforsaken forest. There has to be some compromise everyone can live with."

"I agree." I somehow managed to keep my voice calm, despite the turmoil and fear surging through me. It wasn't the Tao I knew and loved speaking right now. It was a desperate stranger—a fiery combination of elemental and wolf, both of whom were struggling to meld and survive. "There *has* to be a compromise. But until we find it, you can't be here. You can't jeopardize the safety of both our employees and our customers."

He began to pace, his strides long, angry. "The only way I'm going to maintain any sense of normality is to keep doing what I've always done. And that means working. I have to do it, Risa. I can't *not* do it."

"And until you gain control of the elemental, I can't let you in the kitchen."

He stopped and stared at me. It wasn't a pleasant stare. It was angry, alien, and filled with fire. It bled from him, filling the air with the threat of an inferno. I clenched my fists and resisted the urge to back away from him. Tao *wouldn't* hurt me; I'd believed that from the very beginning and I still believed it, despite growing evidence to the contrary.

You may believe it all you want, Azriel commented. *But that does not make it a truth you should entrust your life to.*

Shield will, Amaya commented. *Flames not touch.*

That, Azriel said, mental tones little more than a growl, *is not the point.*

Point, Amaya growled. *I protect.*

I couldn't help smiling. My sword had never been afraid to throw a little attitude around, but it surprised me that she so readily flung it at Azriel. I said, *He hasn't lost control yet.*

Even if he was very obviously close.

The only safe place for him to be is the sacred site the elemental keeps going back to, Azriel said. *I'll take him there by force if I have to.*

You can't get him into the site itself. Besides, he'll only keep coming back. We have to get him there willingly, or there will be little point. To Tao, I said, "Look at what you're doing, Tao. Look at your skin, and try to convince me you're in control at this moment."

He stared at me for several minutes longer, then slowly, like a dreamer coming out of a dream, raised his hands and stared at them. After a few minutes, the flames that flickered and danced across his fingertips began to die, and the inferno threatening the air eased. He closed his eyes and swore softly.

"I'm sorry. I just thought—"

I closed the gap between us and touched his arm. His eyes opened, the brown depths filled with desperation and the ever-lurking threat of flame. "I understand what you're trying to do, but you can't do it here. It's simply too dangerous."

"Everywhere is too dangerous," he said bitterly. "Maybe it would be better for everyone if I simply killed myself."

"No!" It came out panicked. My grip on his arm tightened, and I shook him, violently. "Don't you dare give up on me. You can win this battle, Tao. I believe that with all my heart."

"Then you would be the only one." His gaze moved past me. "Even the reaper believes otherwise."

"You fate is in your own hands," Azriel commented. "Live or die, the choice is yours."

Tao snorted. "Live or die as *what* is the question, though, isn't it?"

Azriel shrugged, something I felt rather than saw. "The fates have no answer in that regard. The decision, as ever, comes down to your own actions."

The fates have a great way of passing the buck, I commented, somewhat sourly.

It is hardly "passing the buck," as you say, to let a person's fate ultimately reside in his own hands. There was a hint of censure in his voice. *They can and do plan a common course for all, but it is neither practical nor logical to expect all of creation to follow such guidelines rigidly. Especially when humankind have a habit of doing the unexpected.*

A trait that doesn't belong to only humans, I reminded him. *Or was it in the fates' grander scheme of things for you to ignore every reaper rule in existence to hunt down your friend's killer?*

Perhaps not, but once I became a Mijai, I have no doubt this is what they intended.

I'm betting they didn't intend you and I to get together.

On that aspect, they are playing their cards very close to their chest. They have never said much about you and I, and they still don't.

"My own actions," Tao echoed, and laughed. It was a short, sharp sound of bitterness. "Except it isn't *just* my actions involved, is it?"

"The elemental has no more desire to die than you," Azriel commented. "It lives because the flame that gave it birth still burns in that sacred place. Perhaps it merely wishes to return in order to protect it."

"Meaning if I destroy the flame—"

"It will kill you both." My grip tightened on his arm again, forcing him to look at me. "Don't you dare even *consider* that."

"Risa," he said, voice soft. Desperate. "You expect too much of me."

"I expect *nothing* of you that I haven't expected of myself," I said, voice fierce. "Do you think these past few weeks have been easy for me? I've been to hell and back—literally—I've welcomed death, and I've been forced back to life. And I can tell you from experience that even though death may seem the better option, it *isn't*. Life is worth the fight, however much it might seem otherwise at the time."

"I don't know—"

"Tao," I said. "Go back to the sacred site and talk with the elemental. It is within you, remember. Instead of trying to control it—or it you—maybe what you need to do is come to a resolution that suits you both."

Tao snorted. "It's hard to talk to something when it has no understanding of the human language."

"Except that it has, through you," Azriel commented. "It is no longer just an elemental, as you are no longer just a wolf. You may be two separate souls, but you now inhabit one body and share thoughts and memories. If you wish to communicate, you can."

Tao stared past me, and though the desperate light never really left his eyes, some of the tension did. He might still be afraid, but maybe—just maybe—we'd given him a reason to hope.

"You really think that's possible?"

"I don't think," Azriel said. "I know."

Tao straightened just a little. The determined light in his eyes became stronger. "Then I should at least stop my whining and give it a try." He gave me a somewhat wan smile. "Because if I give up and take the easy way out, I have no doubt that, being a Mijai in waiting and all, you'll find a way to make my afterlife hell."

"Too damn right." I threw my arms around him and hugged him tight for several seconds. When I finally stepped away, I added, "Do you want me to send a boat-load of supplies up to the sacred site?"

He scrubbed a hand across his jaw, the sound not unlike sandpaper across a wall. "Might be wise. There's a ton of rabbits up there, but I have a feeling it might not be a good idea to hunt and kill anything within the walls of that place."

"Well, it *was* a witch sacred site." Besides, spilling blood tended to raise darker magic, and given that wild magic was alive and well within the boundaries of the place, who knew what might happen.

"Yeah, that's what I was thinking." He touched a hand to my face, his fingers warm against my skin but no longer dangerously so. "I'll see you soon."

It was more a question than a statement, and I smiled. "You will."

He glanced past me, nodded at Azriel, then turned

and walked away. I crossed my arms and watched him leave.

And wondered whether I'd ever see him again.

"That," Azriel said, "depends entirely on what now happens between him and the elemental."

"And whether we actually survive."

"That, too." He stepped up behind me and rubbed my arms lightly. "You should go inside. You're cold."

"Yes, I am." But I didn't move. Not until the very last traces of Tao's scent had left the air, and all that was left was the gathering sense of the storm and the aroma of rotting rubbish.

On my way through the kitchen, I grabbed some bread and a couple of thick slices of beef, munching on them as I made my way through the café. The news was being shown on one of the TVs, and the picture of a tall, thin man with dark auburn hair and muddy, empty eyes flashed onto the screen. I frowned, trying to remember where I'd seen him before.

"He was one of the three vampires who was with Hunter at that blood-whore establishment," Azriel said. "It was he who commanded you to stay in that room with the ghosts until the Rakshasa appeared."

The vampire with the silky-smooth voice, I thought with a frown. The councillor whose energy had felt dark and coiled. But why had he suddenly made a news report? I was under the impression those on the high vampire council preferred to fly under the radar. I stepped closer to listen to the report.

The body of high councillor Angus Donvale was found in his home today, the newsreader said. *Police indicated that while there was no sign of either a break-in or a struggle, Donvale's body had been mutilated almost beyond recognition.*

The news went on, and it got worse. Two more murders, both prominent businessmen, both vampires. Both attacked with a ferocity that went beyond mere murder. The newsreader noted that the Directorate had been called in but at the moment had no comment. Nor were they discounting a possible link between all three murders.

I had to wonder whether they would ever actually find that link, or if this case would simply become yet another in a long list of unsolved crimes.

Because I had no doubt who was behind these murders. Had no doubt why.

My stomach began to churn, and my sandwich suddenly lost its taste. My gaze met Azriel's. His expression was grim.

"It would seem," he said, saying what I feared, too, "that Hunter has begun to exterminate all those who would oppose her."

Chapter 6

I dumped the uneaten portion of my sandwich in a nearby bin, then tucked the plate behind the counter, out of the way. "Angus Donvale didn't seem to be in opposition to Hunter the day we met him. Quite the opposite, in fact."

"The fact that he apparently supported Hunter in her dealings with you does not mean he supported her overall," Azriel noted. "The majority of vampires, from what I have witnessed during my time here on Earth, always seem to put their own interests first and foremost."

I snorted softly. "If they were putting their own interests first, they sure as hell wouldn't be going up against Hunter in *any* way."

"Unless, of course, they thought the end reward was greater than the risk."

"Which I guess they did. And because of that, they're dead." As dead as we would be, if we weren't very careful.

"Except for the technicality that you can't actually die this time around," Azriel noted, pressing his fingers against my spine and gently guiding me toward the stairs. "You become a Mijai on your death, and that does have certain benefits in this particular case."

I raised my eyebrows as I began to climb the stairs. "How is becoming a dark angel a benefit in this case?"

A smile lurked in the mismatched blue of his eyes,

despite the seriousness of his expression. "It means you could come back and kill her. I'm sure Amaya would be willing enough to help out."

Be good to consume, Amaya agreed. *Provide plenty of dark energy, that one.*

I snorted, though the sad truth was, Amaya probably *could* survive months—even years—without consuming the energy of anyone else. Hunter was a feast of all sorts of evil.

"I thought the powers that be frowned on that sort of behavior," I said, as I reached the landing and headed for the office and my desk.

"They do," he said. "But in this case, I think it would be worth it."

"You could be right," I agreed. "The whole trouble is, I'd have to be dead first, and I'm seriously wanting to avoid that right now."

"A goal we are, for once, in complete accord about." He stopped long enough beside me to brush a kiss across my lips, then moved on to his usual post near the window.

I booted up the computer, then Googled the latest news reports, but they didn't really reveal much more than the names of the other two murdered men.

I scrubbed a hand across my eyes and leaned back in the chair. "These murders have to be the reason why she's given us twenty-four hours to find the second key. She's decided to move up her domination schedule."

"It would appear so." Though he stood several feet away from me, the warmth of his presence chased away the chills. "The question is, why?"

"Who fucking knows!" I waved a hand in irritation. "It's not as if the mad bitch actually needs a reason."

"True, but it is nevertheless unusual, especially given her brother had no inkling that this was her plan."

I spun around to face him. "You read Jack's mind?"

He raised his eyebrows. "Why do you always seem so surprised, given you are well aware that I can touch the thoughts of any I choose?"

"It's just that Jack is one of the strongest telepaths around, aside from Aunt Riley and Uncle Quinn."

"Even the strongest telepath cannot prevent a reaper's access."

The thought made me frown. "Maybe that's why she's been contacting me via the phone these last few days—she wanted to keep you out of her thoughts and her plans a secret."

"That is entirely possible." He shrugged. "It is, however, not a concern right now. Nor is the murder of those three men. The key has to be our priority."

"Except that we haven't got a fucking clue about *that* right now, either." I swung around again, and for the first time noticed the small white envelope sitting in the middle of the desk. I stared at it for several seconds, that sick feeling in my stomach growing.

Because I'd seen such envelopes on several occasions now, and recognized the handwriting. It was from Markel.

I took a deep, somewhat quivery breath, then slowly picked it up it. After sliding my nail under the edge of the flap to open it, I pulled out the crisp white paper. The message was short and to the point:

> *Meet me where we first met. It is a matter of urgency.*

I stared at it for several minutes longer, then screwed it up into a tight ball and tossed it into the bin. "What the fuck am I going to do now?"

"You have two choices—either you go, or you don't," Azriel said.

I swung around to face him again. "You have no thoughts on the matter?"

He half smiled. "Oh, I have plenty of thoughts. Whether you will take any notice of them is an entirely different question."

"Azriel, I wouldn't ask for your opinion if I didn't want it."

"Which is no indication that you will actually *act* on such advice." There was amusement in his voice, but it faded quickly. His mental tones were somber as he added, *I believe that both your uncle's and Jack's advice was sound. It is not wise to get involved with those who would use you to oppose Hunter.*

But in many respects, I am *already involved. I'm on a collision course with Hunter—you know that; she knows that. And I've got a bad feeling that you and I may not be enough to cope with the bitch. She's had a long time to plan her accession, Azriel, and time enough to learn how to cope with a reaper.*

Which is why I suggest you do go talk to Markel.

Surprise rippled through me. *Now, that was an answer I wasn't expecting.*

And yet it is the only sensible option right now. Markel will surely be aware of her movements, and that, at the very least, might give us some clue as to what she plans next. He paused, his blue eyes narrowing slightly. *Just talk. Nothing more. No promises or agreement.*

Don't worry, I said grimly. *I've learned my lesson about jumping into agreements before thinking about the long-term consequences.*

Then perhaps your agreement with Hunter did have some benefit. A touch of amusement swam down the mental lines. *Where would you prefer to astral travel from?*

Where I'd prefer was my bedroom, but that had been blown to smithereens, perhaps never to be resurrected. I waved a hand to the sofa. "I can get comfortable enough there."

"Then do so. I will guard."

I moved across to the sofa and lay down, getting as comfortable as was possible stretched out on a two-seat sofa. Once I was settled, I closed my eyes and concentrated on my breathing, slowing it down, drawing it deep. As my pulse rate dropped, a sense of peace enveloped me and all the tension that rode my body began to slip away. Then, as I'd been taught, I pictured a rope hanging above my head and reached up with imaginary hands to grasp it. It felt thick and real against those fingers, and steel strong as I pulled myself upward along it. Dizziness briefly swept over me, seeming to come from the center of my chest. I ignored it and kept pulling myself up that rope. A pressure began to grow inside me, getting ever stronger, until my whole body began to vibrate under its force. Then, suddenly, I was free and floating above my prone form.

I didn't hang about, simply imagined myself standing in front of the gigantic shed that was the Central Pier function center in Melbourne's Docklands district—the place where I'd not only first met Markel, but interviewed the ghost of Frank Logan. In an instant I was there.

And so was Markel. He was tall, with regal features and a body that was as lean as a whip. He bowed rather formally when my gaze met his, and while his expression gave little away, his brown eyes showed a touch of relief.

But it was the man who stood beside him who caught my attention. It was Harry Stanford, Hunter's archrival and the man who planned to use me to destroy her. He was also tall, with dark hair and skin, and incandescent green eyes that glowed with an unearthly fire here on the astral plane. He'd once been a Cazador, and *that*, in my estimation, made him the more dangerous of the two, if only because so few of them actually came out sane and whole on the other side. At least according to Uncle Quinn, anyway, and he should know given he was one of those few.

I'd like to say it's a pleasure to see you both here, I said, unable to hide the edge in my mental tones, *but that would be a lie.*

Believe me, Markel said, his voice cool, without inflection but oddly pleasant, *this is not something I desire, either. Hunter suspects my part in Krogan's death and watches my every move.*

Guilt swirled through me at the mention of his name, and it was a heaviness I doubted I'd ever be free of. I might have killed him to protect those I loved, but that didn't make his death any easier to bear. And it certainly didn't make it right.

Given you didn't actually kill him, I replied, *you hardly need to fear her wrath.*

No, but I did get rid of his body. I also failed to report your actions to her. Either of those two events would normally bring down her wrath. Together, they mean death.

I frowned. *Surely Hunter is not so sure of her position that she would start killing off Cazadors?*

Have you not seen the news reports? Stanford's deep voice held an edge that spoke of frustration and anger. He was a man standing on the precipice of doom, and he was all too aware of it. *Hunter begins her battle for supremacy, only she does it via stealth and murder rather than openly.*

Besides, Markel added, *why would you think Cazadors are any safer than high councillors?*

I don't. Hell, I didn't even consider *myself* safe. Hunter was just as likely to turn around and kill me the moment she got anywhere near the key—especially if she'd figured out a way to nullify Azriel's presence. *But if you've called me here in the hope that Hunter's recent action would force me to your side, then you're out of luck. The only side I'm on right now is my own.*

Your side, Stanford said, the edge stronger this time,

is a losing one. You cannot defeat her alone, Risa. It will be the end of not only yourself, but all you hold dear.

But I'm not alone. Even as I said that, my stomach tightened and the bitter taste of bile rose in my throat. It was fear of what was coming, and fear that he was right. That in the end, I *would* be alone. That for me, there was no other choice. Not when it came to Hunter. Even so, I couldn't help adding, *I have Azriel, and I have my sword. Neither should be taken lightly.*

Though I wasn't entirely sure whom I was trying to convince—them or me.

No, they shouldn't, Markel agreed, his mental tones still very controlled. Maybe he didn't have as much to lose as Stanford. Or maybe he'd simply accepted that death was a likely outcome no matter what path he took. *But Hunter is a maenad and has the force of a god behind her. It gives her power beyond anything on this earth.*

Azriel isn't of this earth, I reminded them. But the bitter taste of bile was growing. I half wondered whether it was possible to throw up on the astral plane—and what would happen if I did. Because as much as I wanted to ignore what they were saying, as much as I knew they were only trying to get me to aid them, I also knew their words held an undeniable weight of truth.

Reapers can die. Demon swords can be nullified, Stanford said. *It is only a matter of know-how.*

Nullify them, Amaya said. *Chance give.*

No, I said to her, amused despite the growing sense of dread. *They're friends—of sorts. You don't nullify friends.*

She muttered something I didn't quite catch, although it wasn't hard to guess it was something along the lines of her being willing to make an exception.

I studied Stanford for a moment, seeing the tension in the small lines near his eyes, feeling it in the unpleasant vibration that ran through the ether around us. *If Hunter is all-powerful, how do you plan to uphold your end of the deal and give me the means to negate her connection to her god?*

I am not the oldest vampire currently living, but I am old enough to remember a time when the gods—and maenads—were more prevalent than they are today, Stanford said. *And I am not the only one. More important, those others also remember how to counter them.*

Then I'm surprised Hunter hasn't tracked them all down and killed them. If Stanford knew of their existence, Hunter surely did as well.

She can't, because they already are *dead,* Stanford said. *But, as you are no doubt aware, not all souls move on. Some stay because they have no choice, but others remain because they know their task on this earth has not yet finished.*

I raised an eyebrow. *Meaning your source is a ghost who's hanging about waiting for the chance to off Hunter?*

Basically put, but yes. Amusement briefly lit his eerie eyes, but it just as swiftly disappeared. *It gives us—and you—a small but important advantage.*

It gives me *nothing,* I shot back. *Because I'm not going to help you kill Hunter. Not unless I have absolutely no other choice.*

It will come to that point, Markel said softly. *You are walking a knife-edge with her now. In the end, she will leave you no other option but to act.*

Perhaps, I said, still desperately trying to ignore both the bitter taste of bile and the knowledge that he was right. *But, for now, there's wiggle room.*

Those you care about cannot remain hidden and safe forever. They all have lives, and people who depend on them, Stanford growled. *It is always better to be on the offensive rather than the defensive.*

Better for whom? I said. *Not for me. Not at this particular moment in time.*

You now have less than twenty hours to find that key,

Markel said. *What do you think will happen when you don't hand it over?*

That is something I'm actively avoiding thinking about.

Then you are a fool. Stanford thrust a hand through his hair, an action that was violent, frustrated, and had the ether around us spinning away in agitation.

Markel stepped forward and caught my hands in his. His fingers were cool in this place, ghostly, and yet a sense of strength and calm seemed to flow from his touch. It eased the sick sensation of fear but didn't do a whole lot against the certainty that the confrontation that scared the hell out of me—the very one *they* wanted—was steamrolling toward me, and there was absolutely nothing I could do to stop it.

I understand your desire to avoid any sort of battle with Hunter, Markel said. *Once, I would have done the same. But it cost me all that I held dear, and it will cost you as well if you are not prepared.*

My gaze searched his. I saw no lies in the brown depths, only a sorrow deeper than anything I could imagine. I may have lost both my mother and a former lover, but he'd lost a whole lot more than that. Curiosity stirred, but this was neither the time nor the place.

But he was right. Besides, it cost nothing to be prepared. Cost nothing for *them* to be prepared.

Okay, I said, gently pulling my hands from his. *Whatever it is you need to do to nullify Hunter, do it. I'm not guaranteeing I'll help. Not yet. But if I feel her web closing in any tighter, I'll need you to be ready.*

Markel smiled, though it was still tinged with that haunting sadness. *As the saying goes, it is always better to step into a battle fully armed than not.*

I snorted softly. *And sometimes it is better still* not *to step into battle at all.*

With that I can only agree, Markel said. *But I fear fate will give us little other choice.*

From what I've seen, she rarely does. I studied the two of them for a moment, then added, *Is that it?*

For now, yes, Stanford said. *But be wary of Hunter. She may have given you twenty-four hours to find the key, but there is no guarantee she will actually allow you to take the entirety of that time.*

She can't have what I haven't got, and she can't kill me until I've got it. And if I repeated that often enough, I might just believe it.

I gave them a nod good-bye, then imagined myself back in my body and got the hell out of there. I didn't immediately move, however. I just lay on the sofa for several minutes, drawing in air and trying to ease the queasiness still threatening to jump up my throat.

"Here," Azriel said softly. "Drink this."

I opened one eye and discovered a can of Coke hovering a few inches from my nose. For normal people, Coke would probably be the very worst thing they could drink to ease a less-than-stable stomach, but I'd grown up on the stuff, and it pretty much ran through my veins.

"Thanks." I plucked the can from his grasp, then sat up. After consuming several mouthfuls of the brown fizz, I silently filled him in, then added, *He's going to contact a ghost who apparently knows how to stop a maenad. Just in case we need to.*

As I believe you said, it never hurts to be prepared. He squatted next to the sofa and brushed some hair away from my cheek. His caress was warm against my skin, and all I wanted was to be taken into his arms and have his heat and strength and love wrapped around me. But that wasn't a desire I could indulge in right now.

"Perhaps later," he said, voice wistful. "When we do have the time."

"When we *do* have the time," I echoed, with mock fierceness, "I expect you to do a whole lot more than just hold me."

"*That* you can be assured of." He leaned forward and kissed me. It was a promise, a hope, and one I could only pray the fates would let us fulfill.

My phone rang, and the tone told me it was Stane. I tugged it out of my pocket and hit the Answer button. "Hey," I said. "Does the fact you're calling mean you've pinned down a possible location for the key?"

"Not as yet, unfortunately," he said. "Who knew there were so many places in Victoria that were using—or had used—the word 'palace' in them?"

"Meaning there's not even a short list yet?"

"There's a short list of a hundred. I'm still whittling them down." He shrugged, his expression bemused. "I can and do provide computing miracles, but some of them take longer than others."

I half smiled. "I know, and I really *do* appreciate the effort."

"So you should," he said, grinning. "Although it's not like I'm actually doing anything harder than programming. Speaking of which, another of your requested searches has come up trumps."

I raised an eyebrow. "Which one this time?"

"It was the one looking for any other property connections between Lauren Macintyre, Genevieve Sands, and John Nadler."

"I vaguely remember that one." It had come about after a search on Pénombre Manufacturing—the company that supposedly owned the old warehouse in Maribyrnong in which we'd found a sorceress's lair—hadn't revealed any actual connection to either Macintyre or Sands. It had, however, revealed a different connection between the two women, in that twenty-eight years ago, Sands invested in a property that Macintyre subsequently purchased. Then, five years ago, Sands had sold the property, and it had ended up in the hands of one John Nadler—another of the identities Lauren had taken. As Tao had noted at the time, around and around the circle went.

"Well, it revealed a number of properties across both Victoria and New South Wales that at least two of Lauren's aliases have owned over the years." He hesitated, grimacing. "Unfortunately, it also revealed a connection between several of *them* and another name I think you might be familiar with."

Kiandra's warning—that someone in my life was not what they seemed—rose like a ghost to taunt me. I'd hoped against hope that she'd read things wrong, that there was no wolf in sheep's clothing hiding in the closet of anyone I knew. I guess I should have known better.

Resignedly—wearily—I said, "Familiar how?"

"As in, it's one Michael Judd."

It took a moment for the name to register, simply because Michael Judd was not a name I'd ever used for him. He'd always been simply Mike—the accountant who looked after all the tax stuff for both me and the café, as well as my mom's former lover.

But he *couldn't* be the traitor. It *had* to be a coincidence. He'd loved my mom, damn it, and he'd been with her for as long as I could remember—for as long as I'd been alive.

And yet . . . I remembered the uneasy feeling I'd gotten when I'd read his note inviting me to dinner. Remembered the steely calculation so evident beneath the outrage when I'd gently suggested that maybe he was seeking to fill the void of my mother's loss with a deeper—though not sexual—relationship with me.

Damn it, no! It *couldn't* be Mike. Mom had been a psychic of formidable power and there was no way in hell she would have been fooled for long if Mike was not what he'd claimed.

Do not forget we are dealing with a powerful sorceress,

Azriel noted softly. *Even your mother could have been fooled by one such as Lauren.*

Mike isn't Lauren. Surely to god we hadn't been *that* fooled.

I'm not saying he is, but if there is a connection between them, then the possibility of it being a coincidence really is only slender.

Because chance hadn't played a very major part in this whole mess so far. I briefly closed my eyes, then said to Stane, "What sort of connection are we talking about?"

"Legal only, at this stage," he replied. "At least from what I can see. He acted as a financial adviser to Genevieve Sands—"

"The real Genevieve or the fake one?" I cut in.

"It's beyond even the scope of my computers to answer that one," Stane said, voice dry. "Though it was over fifteen years ago, so the possibility is there that he advised the real one."

"It may be beyond the scope of your computers, but maybe *not* beyond that of the coroner," I said. "When they autopsied the bits of Sands they found after the bomb blast, was there any indication just how long she might have been frozen?"

"Hang on a sec." He spun away from the vid-phone's camera and for several seconds there was silence. Then he reappeared. "The report said she'd possibly been frozen for somewhere between five and eight years."

"So it's entirely possible Mike was dealing with the real Genevieve."

"Entirely possible," Stane agreed. "But don't forget to factor in his other connections—namely one Jim O'Reilly and an M. R. Greenfield."

"As in, Michael Greenfield, the registered owner of Pénombre?"

"The very same one."

And around and around the threads went. Fuck it, when were we going to get a break from the shit being flung at us?

Stane hesitated, then added, "Do you want me to do a background check on your Mike?"

If Mike was involved, then doing a check on him might well be akin to closing the barn door *after* the horse had bolted. Still, it wasn't like we had any choice. "I guess it can't hurt. In the meantime, I might ring him."

"Do you think that wise?" Stane frowned. "It might achieve nothing more than alerting him that you're on to him."

"That's a chance we'll have to take, because we're running out of time."

Stane grunted. "I'll make the background search a priority. Meanwhile, be careful. I'd hate to have to find another source of the best bubbly in town."

I snorted. "You could, as has been suggested before, buy it yourself."

His expression became one of shock, though amusement gleamed brightly in his eyes. "Wash your mouth out with soap, woman! I never buy anything." He paused. "Except the perishables. When it comes to meat and chicken, I do prefer to know and trust the source."

Suggesting that many of his sources weren't trustworthy. But then, it *was* the black market we were talking about. "Contact me the minute you get anything vital. No matter what the time."

"Will do."

He hung up and I raised my gaze to Azriel's. "Do you think he's right—is it too much of a risk to ring Mike?"

He shrugged. "Perhaps, perhaps not. You do have a legitimate reason to ring—a past connection with a building we are investigating. If he is *not* involved with our sorceress, then there is no problem."

"But if he *is*, he might well run." I paused and swung my legs off the sofa. "Maybe you need to be there. That way, if he *does* bolt, you can track him."

He raised his eyebrows. "That is a good idea, although surely if he *is* connected to Lauren, it would be one they would be aware of and prepared for."

"If there is any sort of shielding or protection against your presence, it would be within the offices." I thrust to my feet, unable to stand still. "But you don't really have to be present in his room. You could hang about the outside of the building and see if he reacts in any way—like suddenly deciding to leave."

"And if he does?"

"Then you come and get me, and we'll question the bastard together." My gaze met his, my expression grim. "If he *is* involved, then it's more than likely he's been there from the beginning."

Which meant his relationship with Mom might have been nothing more than a sham. That he'd been using her just as much as Lucian had used me. And as much as I didn't want to believe that, I couldn't escape the possibility of it, either.

"It would seem the threads of the Aedh's deceptions go far deeper than we had imagined." Azriel's voice was grim.

"Don't they just." I leaned forward and kissed him. "Be careful out there."

He smiled but didn't say anything, simply disappeared. I took a deep, somewhat quivery breath, then called Mike and walked over to the window as I listened to the vid-phone ringing. There was a brief pause in the dial tone; then Mike appeared on the screen. I didn't actually know how old he was—he looked to be in his early forties, but I knew, from various things Mom had said, he was a lot older than that. His hair was black and short, the dark curls clinging close to his head like a helmet.

His eyes—a clear, striking gray—seemed to hold aeons of knowledge behind them, and for the first time since I'd known him, I wondered if they actually *did*. Dark sorcerers had the power to extend life through blood magic, and *this* dark sorcerer had been involved with an Aedh who knew the magic of an entirely different world.

"Risa." His voice was deep and as aristocratic as his features. "This is a lovely surprise. I do hope there's nothing wrong."

I hoped there wasn't, either. "I just wanted to ask you a question about a property."

"One you wish to buy?"

"No." I hesitated, not sure of the best way to broach the subject. He'd been in my life—or, at least, my mother's life—for as long as I could remember, and while I didn't want to upset him if he *was* innocent, I also needed answers.

He frowned. "I'm an accountant and investment adviser, not a real estate agent, but I shall nevertheless do my best to answer it."

"But you have assisted clients over the years to purchase properties, haven't you? I mean as investments."

"Well, yes." He paused, frowning. "Why do you ask?"

"Because," I said, thinking fast, "a friend is interested in purchasing a couple of rental houses, but an in-depth search on them revealed a few paperwork oddities. He saw your name on one of them and asked me to ask you about them."

"If there were paperwork oddities, my dear," he said, frown increasing, "I'm sure they would have been picked up by the appropriate authorities at the time."

"Well, apparently they weren't."

"How odd." Despite the frown, there was little in the way of confusion in the steely depths of his eyes. Nor was there any sign of wariness, guilt, or any other sort of emotion. And it was that very lack that made me uneasier than any actual emotion could have.

But was I reading things into his expressions—or lack thereof—and looking for a reason to believe his guilt because of what Kiandra had said? Maybe. I mean, a few tenuous links did not a villain make—but they couldn't exactly be ignored, either.

He added, "What properties are we talking about?"

I hesitated, then said, "One was a little terrace in Argyle Place in Carlton, and the other was an apartment in Greeves Street, St. Kilda."

"Good rental locations, both of them." His expression was thoughtful. "But neither property immediately rings any bells. How long ago were these discrepancies?"

"He didn't actually say." I shrugged. "But a while ago, I think. He's basically just dotting his i's and crossing his t's before he lays his money on the line."

"And he hasn't a solicitor? Surely that's what *they're* supposed to do?"

"Well, yeah, but he's one of those thorough types who likes to double-check everything himself. Look, I'm sorry to have bothered you, but I said I'd ask—"

"My dear Risa," he said, voice grave, "you're not bothering me. I told you once before, if you ever need anything, I'm here. I do not intend to go back on that, even for a request as odd as this."

"Well, if you could just check your files and see what information you might have on either of those properties, that would be fabulous," I said. "But don't go to too much trouble if the information is difficult to get to. It's not that important."

"I have to keep all records for seven years for tax purposes," Mike said, with a half shrug. "So if the information is within the files I hold here, then you may have it."

There was nothing in his manner that spoke of suspicion. Nothing that spoke of guilt. It made me feel bad for suspecting him, but, at the same time, I couldn't escape the notion that there *was* something going on. "Thanks again, Mike."

"Anytime." He hesitated. "You do remember we're having dinner tonight, don't you?"

I blinked. We'd agreed to meet for dinner, but I couldn't actually remember anyone suggesting *tonight.* Sure, time was something I hadn't had a great grip on lately, what with everything else that was going on, but my memory wasn't that *bad.* Not yet, anyway.

"You've forgotten," he added, when I didn't immediately answer. "If you can't make it, I understand—"

"No, it's okay," I said, though it wasn't. The very last thing I needed to be doing right now was wasting time going to dinner with my mom's ex. At the same time, could I afford *not* to go? Especially if he was somehow involved with Lauren?

"If I can find the files," Mike added, "I'll bring them along. I can't, of course, allow you to take them away, but I can bend client confidentiality rules enough to let you look through them."

"That would be fabulous." I hesitated again. "When and where shall we meet?"

"There's a new restaurant that just opened on Smith Street that Beatrice recommends I try—Winter's, I believe it's called. I can get her to book us a table for seven, if you'd like."

Beatrice was Mike's secretary and had been with him from the very beginning. If Mike was holding any secrets, then surely she would be aware of them—and that meant maybe she was someone Azriel should use his skills on.

"That would be great. Thanks, Mike."

"See you at seven," he said, and hung up.

I blew out a breath and wondered if I'd done the right thing. Time really *was* tight—did I really need to be wasting it on the slight chance that Mike might just lead us to the sorceress?

But what other choice was there?

Every single time we'd found a clue that led us to one of the keys, the sorceress had gotten there before us, stealing the thing from under our noses. I couldn't let her get this last one—not when all that stood between us and hell was that one remaining gate. And it was all well and good for the remnants to suggest that new ones could be built, but how long would that take?

We needed the key and we needed to place it somewhere safe—not just safe from the likes of Hunter and the sorceress, but safe from anyone else who might fancy themselves as the king or queen of hell, now or in the future.

But maybe before we did *any* of that, it would be better to track down and take out the sorceress. At least then there would be one less nutter for us to worry about.

I swung away from the window and ordered some food from the kitchen downstairs, then began to pace. There wasn't a whole lot else I could do, not until Azriel got back or Stane came up with a list of possible locations for us to check out.

I'd finished a second can of Coke and was just scooping up a last bit of chocolate cake by the time energy and heat stirred the air, signifying Azriel's return. I dumped the plate on the desk and swung around to face him, my gaze sweeping him to make sure he was okay.

"I am whole and unhurt," he said immediately, amusement in his voice and his expression warm. "But I do thank you for the concern, even if it was not really required in this instance."

"Hey, when you're dealing with a dark sorceress, even the most innocent of quests could turn deadly." I tugged him closer and dropped a kiss on his lips. "Did anything untoward happen?"

"Unfortunately, no." He wrapped his arms loosely around my waist. "He didn't call anyone, nor did he appear overly anxious after your call. He certainly didn't leave."

"Damn."

"Yes. I did try to read the secretary's thoughts, but she is another of those rare people I cannot access."

"We seem to be striking more than our fair share of those types of people in this quest," I grouched.

"Yes, but remember, the Aedh had been on this earth for a very long time before you came along. He had the time to gather those necessary to his cause, and—given his knowledge of who and what would be involved in any search for the key *before* he was sent back in time—that would include people a Mijai could not read."

I smiled up at him. "You do know Lucian's dead, right?"

He frowned, his confusion evident. "I cannot see the point of that question."

Of course he couldn't, because reapers supposedly didn't do emotion, particularly jealousy. "Well, being dead, he's no longer a rival or a threat. Surely that means you can actually say his name now."

Amusement briefly flirted with his lips. "Actually, I don't believe I can. Or, at least, I have no desire to grace the air with his foul presence, even if it is something as simple as giving him the courtesy of a name."

Since I couldn't really argue with *that* sentiment, I said, "Do you think I should still meet with Mike for dinner tonight, as planned? I mean, if he's shown no concern over my questions, maybe his links with Sands and the others *are* innocent."

"They possibly are, but we cannot afford to ignore any link right now, no matter how tenuous." He shrugged. "Unless you wish to arrange for someone to watch him twenty-four hours a day, there is little else we can do but meet him tonight and see if his files lead anywhere else."

"They won't if he's involved." Or they'd take us off on some wild-goose chase.

"Either way, unless Stane comes through with a short list of key locations, we must pursue every possible lead we can. Especially given we have no idea which lead could take us to our dark sorceress—and as you noted, it would be far better to deal with her before we found the key than after."

"Finding her is the whole problem," I muttered. "It's a shame hell did not seem to impede her in any way."

"She is a *dark* sorceress," Azriel noted, with a trace of amusement. "It gives her a far greater understanding of that place than even we reapers have."

I guessed it did—but it still didn't stop me from wishing that hell had provided at least *some* impediment. Even a few weeks could have made the difference for us. I sighed and stepped away. "So what next?"

Just as Azriel opened his mouth to reply, my phone rang sharply.

"Answering that, obviously."

I smiled and hit the Answer button. Kiandra's image came up on the vid-screen. "Risa," she said, by way of hello. "I've spoken to a witch capable of psychometry, and she is willing to attempt a trace of the cuff link's owner."

"That's brilliant! Thank you."

Kiandra nodded. "Her name is Maggie Stiller, and she runs Found Treasures, a small lost-and-found business in the city. You can visit her anytime you desire during normal business hours."

"I have to say, that's a *perfect* occupation for someone with a finding skill."

"Yes," Kiandra said, with a smile. "She does make a very decent living out of it, too. However, there is no guarantee she will be able to help you with the cuff link's owner. Given we are dealing with a dark sorceress, she more than likely would be aware of such an eventuality and have measures in place to take care of it."

I frowned. "And is Maggie aware of this?"

"Yes. I would not ask this task of anyone without providing full disclosure of who and what might be involved."

Fair enough. "I'll head down there now. We seem to be at something of a standstill at the moment."

"That," Kiandra said, her expression grim, "will not last."

A chill ran through me. I knew well enough that sooner or later we'd be up to our necks in deadlines *and* trouble, but hearing Kiandra say it—or rather, hearing the heaviness and perhaps even the touch of fear in her voice—was as scary as all hell breaking loose.

"The next nineteen hours will make or break your cause, and our world," she continued softly. "Be wary, both of you, or all will be lost."

I nodded. I couldn't do anything else right at that moment—fear and panic and an almost overwhelming sense of doom had my throat locked so tight, words just couldn't get through.

"And while I think about it," she added, "Rozelle mentioned that you'd found a second barrier in the basement of that warehouse that she didn't have the skill to counter."

Rozelle was one the Brindle's trainee witches, and the woman who'd helped weave an exception into the magic protecting that warehouse so that Azriel could enter it without harm. "We did, but it's undoubtedly dangerous—"

"Which only means," she cut in, "that it is also undoubtedly vital. No sorceress would waste energy creating such a strong barrier if there was nothing worthy of protection within. I have assigned a team to it."

"Did Rozelle also tell you that our sorceress is a multishifter who can take on any form she desires? She could approach them as me, or even you, and they'd never know until it was too late."

Kiandra smiled, and it was a dangerous thing to behold. "Trust me, she would not want to try. She is not the only one with a trick or two up her sleeve."

And *that*, I thought with a shiver, was the reason why Kiandra was the head of the Brindle.

"I just don't want anyone else in the line of fire because of me—"

"It is not because of you, but rather this quest. You fail, and it will not go well for the rest of us."

I swallowed heavily. Nothing like having your fears so boldly out in the open. "Then I guess I'd better not fail."

"*That* sounds like a rather good plan." She smiled a good-bye—though it did little to break the concern in her eyes—and hung up. I stared at the black screen for several seconds before slowly shoving it back in my pocket.

"Well," I said eventually. "That sucks."

"Yes," Azriel commented. "But it might well be worth uncovering what lies behind that wall."

"I know." I waved a hand. "I was referring to her confirmation of our time-frame limitations."

He shrugged. "Think of the shorter time frame as a benefit rather than a curse. At least it means we can move on with a life together once we survive it."

"Yeah, but it's the whole 'surviving it' bit that has me worried." I eyed him for a moment. "It's not like you've been overly effusive about the possibility, now, is it?"

"That's because, as you say in this world, I refuse to count my chickens before they hatch."

"Or because you're more intimate with fate's plans than what you're saying, and even you're not sure we'll both survive."

"There is also that possibility," he agreed. "But you can be certain that I will not only do all in my power to ensure you survive, but that I am here to enjoy the on-coming years beside you."

Yeah, but would the fates come to the party as well? That was the question that worried the hell out of me. Especially given that Azriel wasn't giving any ironclad guarantees.

"Because no life, either here or on the fields, ever comes with an ironclad guarantee," he said softly, "sim-ply because life is a series of intersections and alternate pathways. What path you take not only depends on *your* actions and decisions, but also on every action and deci-sion of all those who come into your life—however pe-ripherally."

"Meaning our future lies in the hands of a mad sor-ceress set on unleashing hell on earth, and the blood-sucking disciple of a god getting orgasmic at the thought of ultimate power?" I muttered. "Fabulous *not*, as Amaya would say."

Just kill, Amaya commented. *Fix problem.*

I couldn't help laughing, even as I wished the answer was that simple. I Googled Found Treasures to get the address and realized it was on Therry Street, just near the organics section of the Victoria Market. I raised my gaze to Azriel. "Can you take us there?"

He nodded. "The image of the market is clear enough in your mind to allow transport."

"Good." I grabbed my handbag, then stepped into his waiting arms. "Onward, dear reaper."

He zapped us out of there. Therry Street wasn't all that crowded, thanks to the fact that the market closed at two on Thursdays and it was close to that now. I stepped away from Azriel and scanned the nearby build-ings, looking for building numbers. After a moment I spotted one; Found Treasures was closer to the Elizabeth Street end. We headed there in silence, our shoulders occasionally brushing and the sounds of the stallholders packing up for the day ringing all around us. Normal, everyday sounds in a life that had become far from normal. And in many ways, it was *never* going to be normal again—not only was I in love with a reaper, but I also carried his child.

"What are we going to do once this is over?" I said abruptly.

He glanced at me, one eyebrow raised. "Live and love and raise our child."

"But you're a reaper—a Mijai. You can't walk away from that, can you?"

"No, I can't, especially now, when there is only one portal remaining between hell, the fields, and here."

"So how can you live here and yet be there? You may be an extraordinary being, Azriel, but you cannot be in two places at once."

He half smiled, but there was a seriousness in his eyes that suggested he'd been thinking about this very question for some time. I guess it was pretty typical that it had only *just* occurred to me.

"Being a Mijai simply means that when there is trouble, I will be called away. I am a warrior, and like the soldiers of this world, I will answer the call to arms when it comes."

"So when there is no such call, you can be here?"

His smile grew, crinkling the corners of his bright eyes. "This is where both my Caomh and my son will be—do you really expect me to be anywhere else?"

"Well, you do have a family—"

"Who, aside from my sister's appearance when Jak died, I have not seen in aeons."

"Who," I added, ignoring him, "I would very much like to meet. You once told me that family means everything to reapers, Azriel. I want our son to be a part of not just *my* family, but yours as well."

"Using our son like that," he said, voice even despite

the flash of annoyance in his eyes, "is what I would believe you'd call playing dirty."

"Hey, if it overcomes your stubborn determination to set yourself apart from your family—a decision you made because you were ashamed of your fall from grace more than they were—then it's worth it."

"You have no idea what my family does and doesn't think—"

"Neither do you," I cut in. "But if your family was so ashamed, I very much doubt your sister would have answered your plea for someone to come and collect Jak's soul. Especially if stubbornness runs in the family."

"I can see it running in *our* family," he all but muttered. "And may the fates help me if our son has acquired even a portion of yours, not to mention your determination to stick your nose into the business of others."

I grinned. "Ah, but your business is now my business. That's what being a couple means here on good old Earth." I stopped as we reached a pretty, purple painted sign that said, in a whimsical sort of font, "Found Treasures." The shop itself was a tiny space squeezed in between two larger shops. It had a small window barely two feet wide and an ornate wooden door that was currently open. A gaily colored string curtain hung in the doorway, swaying softly in the slight breeze. "And here we are."

He brushed aside the curtain and ushered me inside. The air in the small shop was rich with the scents of sandalwood—a scent from my childhood, as Mom had used it to help calm the minds of her clients—as well as bergamot and clove, both of which provided protection from negative or harmful forces. In *this* case, however, I doubted they'd be of much help, given we were dealing with the ultimate of negative forces—a dark practitioner.

The shop itself consisted of little more than a cloth-covered round table and several comfortable chairs. The walls were painted in a soothing green but otherwise bare, and the floor was a mix of old rugs and polished floorboards. Again, it very much reminded me of my mother's workroom, and a pang of regret and sorrow ran through me. Her soul might have moved on to be reborn, but—because I was destined to become a dark angel—mine would not. Which meant that I'd never have the chance to see her again—unless, of course, sometime in the future, when my life here had ended and my life as a Mijai had begun, I could find her. Maybe even talk to her.

That wasn't too much to hope for, was it?

Azriel, unsurprisingly, remained mute on *that* particular subject.

The curtain at the far end of the room was pushed aside, and a pretty blond woman in her midthirties entered. Though she gave us a welcoming smile, her brown eyes scanned us both somewhat critically. I very much suspected that she knew in that instant who we were and why we were there. She didn't look the type to miss much.

"And how can I help you this lovely afternoon?" she said, her voice warm and mellow.

"Maggie Stiller?" When she nodded, I smiled and held out my hand. "I'm Risa Jones. I believe Kiandra has been in contact with you about helping me locate the owner of a cuff link."

"Ah yes." She waved a hand at the small table. "Please, be seated."

I did, but Azriel remained standing behind me. Maggie closed and locked the door, slipped an "Open Again Soon" sign in the window, then lit four white candles, each one centered in a corner and surrounded by a series of black stones. Warding stones. That there were so many meant she'd taken Kiandra's warning seriously. As any sensible witch would, I guess.

When she was finally seated opposite me, I said, "Is that going to be enough to protect us?"

She shrugged. "Under normal circumstances, yes, but we are dealing with a dark sorceress, and I daresay she is far more capable in the art of magic than I am. I am a seeker of the lost, not a witch of any true power."

I frowned. "Then why put yourself at risk like this? I'm sure we could—"

"Psychometry is not an everyday skill," she cut in, her expression as gentle as her voice. "And there is no one else in this city who has both the skill *and* the knowledge to at least provide *some* means of protection against any possible attack."

I bit my lip and studied her worriedly. I didn't want to get anyone else either hurt or dead because of this damn quest, but, by the same token, we really *didn't* have another option. If there had been, Kiandra would have given it to us.

Maggie reached across the table and pressed her hand over mine. "This is important, is it not?"

"It could be, but—"

"Then we shall proceed," she cut in again. "Please, give me the cuff link."

I hesitated, then slowly retrieved it from my handbag and placed it in her waiting hand. Her fingers closed around it, and she frowned. "This piece has a very nasty feel to it—though I guess that isn't really surprising given who it may belong to." She rolled it around in her fingers for a minute; then she glanced up at Azriel. "Be on guard. There is undoubtedly a spell on this item, but I cannot sense what type it is. If the wards fail, you will need to protect us all."

Azriel nodded, something I sensed rather than saw. Maggie took a deep breath, then pressed the cuff link between the palms of both hands and closed her eyes. For a long time, nothing seemed to happen. Then she twitched and frowned. "I see . . . many people. Men and women, all different, all the same." Maggie hesitated, her agitation increasing. "Her soul is bitter, dark. I see . . . I see a connection to *you*, one that goes back to your very birth and beyond."

I glanced grimly up at Azriel. *I wonder if that means our sorceress has been connected to Lucian and his plans since before my birth, or whether the cuff link actually belongs to someone I know.* Like Mike, I thought uneasily.

It could be either, he replied. *Perhaps tonight you should ask if he is missing such an item.*

He wouldn't admit it if he were, I said. *And it might just prompt him—or our sorceress, if he is connected—into some form of retaliation. We don't need that right now.*

No, but it would be one way to confirm if he is involved. Valdis could then consume his soul and that would be one less threat against you.

It was a nice thought, but a risk I wasn't sure was worth taking.

"She has many faces, this one," Maggie continued. "But there is one she wears most often."

Again she paused, and fear began to taint the air. Fear and something else. Something that whispered of hell and was awfully familiar.

Ania.

I swore softly. Ania were demons and were usually summoned to perform minor tasks such as harassment or kidnapping, although they apparently weren't above the odd bit of murder, either. We'd come up against them a number of times already on this damn quest, only on each of *those* occasions, they'd been sent by the Raziq to grab me. This was the first time the dark sorceress had resorted to them, though she *had* flung an odd assortment of other demons at us on various other occasions.

In the corners of the room, the air began to stir, waver. Tension wound through my limbs as I reached back and drew Amaya. Her hissing scratched at the edges of my mind, and lilac flames shimmered down the edges of her blade, filling the shadows with an eerie light. I rose, the chair scraping across the wooden boards, a sound that was abnormally loud in the thick silence that filled the room.

"Oh shit," Maggie said abruptly, as all color leeched from her face. "They're coming."

And with that, the Ania hit us.

Chapter 7

"Grab Maggie." Azriel's expression was grim. "Get her into the back room and keep her safe. I will deal with these things."

Maggie needed no further urging. She stood up so suddenly her chair crashed backward; then she ran for the back room. I followed but had barely taken three steps when the air between us began to shimmer and the uneasy sensation of magic crawled across my skin. I paused as a wispy figure appeared, then raised Amaya and brought her down, hard. Her sharp point tore through the center of the emerging demon, and her flames wrapped around its remnants almost lovingly, destroying it even as she fed on it.

Two more Ania appeared and surged toward me. I swept Amaya around in a half circle. The demons scattered, left and right, but as the blade whooshed past the tail of the one on the right, setting it aflame, the one on the left darted forward and seized my sword arm. It snarled, revealing several rows of tiny needle-sharp teeth, then bit down on my arm, drawing blood as it gnawed at my flesh like a dog would a bone.

I swore and battered at the thing with my free hand—an action that was instinctive more than useful, because my fist just went straight through the ethereal creature. Amaya hissed in fury and her flames raced over the hilt of the blade, then across my hand, heading for the demon. Her fiery fingers wrapped around the Ania's body, wrenching it from my flesh even as she burned it to a crisp.

The air behind me began to crawl, the sensation stronger and fouler than before. I swung around, my grip on Amaya slick with the blood pouring down my arm. To the left of Azriel and the three Ania he fought, a dark and dangerous-looking doorway had begun to form.

It was a type of doorway that I'd seen once before, when the Ania had made their very first appearance in my life.

Our dark sorceress *wasn't* intending to kill me or even harm me—even if the Ania had gotten a little too enthusiastic on my arm—she was intending to *snatch* me. Maybe she figured that with Lucian gone the only way she would now have any hope of finding the remaining key was if I were under her full control. There was no other logical reason for her wanting me taken.

More Ania began to appear. Lilac flames dripped from Amaya's point and raced across the wooden floorboards toward them, as if she were eager to wrap the emerging creatures in her heated embrace.

Don't burn this place down like you did that café, I said, as the air behind me stirred, warning of another demon's approach.

Not burn, Amaya muttered, as if offended I'd even suggest such a thing. *Just eat.*

Good. I swung around and swept Amaya through the tail of a retreating Ania. It screamed and darted back, lashing out with claws that were long and vicious looking. I jumped away, but not fast enough, and its talons tore across my shoulder, breaking flesh and drawing blood. I flicked Amaya from my bloody hand to the other and slashed upward. The Ania fled, but this time, *it* wasn't quick enough, and Amaya's dark steel skewered it. The demon screamed again, but the sound abruptly cut off as my sword devoured it.

Another one hit my leg. I swung Amaya downward, but even as I did, the Ania's grip tightened and suddenly I was on my butt and being dragged toward the still-forming doorway.

I cursed and swept Amaya across my legs. The sharp edge of her blade became ethereal where demon-forged steel met flesh, leaving me unharmed even as she slid deep into the wispy heart of the Ania. Once again she consumed it with glee, her steel becoming just a little bit heavier.

Then Azriel was standing in front of me, Valdis screaming her fury as he sliced her through the remaining Ania. They exploded, and a second later, the doorway was gone, sucked back into whatever place it had come from.

He sheathed Valdis, then reached down, gripped my arm, and pulled me upright. "Are you okay?"

"Aside from a few scratches, yes. Are the Ania completely gone?"

"For the moment. I doubt it would be wise to attempt to find the sorceress through that cuff link a second time, however." He pressed his hands against the bloody slashes across my shoulder and the bite marks on my arm. Heat radiated from the epicenter of his touch, and the pain receded as the bleeding stopped and the wound began to heal.

"With that," Maggie said, as she came out from behind the curtain, "I entirely agree."

I glanced at her. "Why didn't the protection stones and spells stop them?"

"Because, as I warned earlier, we are dealing with a dark sorceress. A very canny one, too."

I frowned. "Meaning what?"

"Meaning the spell she placed on that cuff link was a

transport one, and, through it, she circumvented my spells."

"By transporting them directly into the room?"

She nodded. "There are ways to protect oneself against such spells, of course, but neither Kiandra nor I had expected such an extreme method of attack."

"Why is it extreme?" Azriel twined his fingers through mine, squeezing them briefly before releasing me. My wounds—while not completely gone—were little more than a couple of vicious-looking slashes of pink.

"Because it is a spell that severely taxes personal strength. It is very likely your sorceress will be immobilized for the next few hours, at least."

"But wouldn't she have called on dark magic to create her spell? Used blood sacrifices and such?" That was why it was called the dark art, after all.

"Yes, but in any magic there is always a personal price to pay. Dark magic, and dark sorcerers, may draw on forces from without themselves, but they can never totally escape the required fee." Maggie shrugged and held out her hand, palm up. The cuff link gleamed dully in the candlelight. "You had better take this and place it somewhere safe."

I plucked it from her hand warily. "What is the likelihood of the sorceress using this to attack us again?"

"This attack was probably an all-or-nothing event, and I doubt it will be repeated anytime soon."

Relief spun through me. "At least that's something."

"Yes," Maggie said, "but I still wouldn't carry it around with you, as it is entirely possible she could use it to track your location."

"Given we dare not attempt to find her through it again, would it not be better to destroy it?" Azriel said.

Maggie glanced at him. "Ideally, yes, but I would ask that you not do it here, as its destruction will undoubtedly release dark energy, and that is not something I desire in my shop."

He plucked the cuff link from my hand and said, "Then I shall take it onto the fields and destroy it there."

I nodded and glanced back at Maggie. "Thanks for your help, and I'm sorry that we placed you in danger. We didn't think—"

She smiled and waved a hand, effectively cutting me off. "I was forewarned about the dangers, so there is no need to apologize. Good luck with your quest."

"Thanks. I think we'll need it."

Maggie unlocked the door and, as we left, took the sign out of the window. I paused on the pavement and glanced to the left. It would have been nice if the market was open—I could have grabbed some much-needed clothes.

"There are retail shops not far from here, are there not?" Azriel said, ever practical.

"Yes, but it would have been cheaper here." And not only did I *not* want to waste good money on clothes that would only get destroyed by either becoming Aedh or in whatever upcoming battles the fates had planned, but I didn't feel up to fighting the crowds that were undoubtedly there. "But I can't run around in borrowed clothes all day, so down there I will go."

"Will you return to your office once you have secured some fresh clothing?"

"Yes." I squinted up at him. "Why? It shouldn't take that long to destroy one cuff link, should it?"

"It shouldn't, but I am not familiar with dark magic and have no idea what it might involve." He shrugged. "Call me if you need me, or if you feel the slightest inkling of danger."

"I will."

He half disappeared, then paused, his gaze narrowing

as he said, "And don't do anything stupid while I'm away."

I grinned. "Damn, and here I was planning to go offer a certain bitch a prime seat on the express coach to hell."

"I would call that comment sarcastic, except for the fact that you are more than a little capable of such an action if the right buttons were pushed."

I held up my hands. *I promise, no attacking Hunter— or anyone else for that matter—until you get back to hold my hand.*

"Good." And with that, he finally left.

I spun on my heel and headed for Bourke Street and Myer. By the time I'd skimmed quickly through the department store and bought enough clothes to last a few days, then caught a cab back to the café, several hours had past.

Azriel reappeared just as I dumped all my parcels onto my desk. "That cuff link," he said heavily, "proved to be a very difficult item to destroy."

I raised my eyebrows as I turned to face him. "Meaning you couldn't just give it a whack with Valdis?"

"Valdis is very put out by your use of such a term," he said, amused. "She wishes to inform you she is far more refined than that."

Refined, Amaya noted. *Me not.*

I couldn't help grinning. She might not be refined, but she sure as hell was developing a wickedly dry sense of humor. "So how did you get rid of it?"

"In the end, we didn't. I simply dumped it in the one place she's not likely to go looking for it—hell."

"What?" I said. "Why the fuck would you risk opening the last gate just to get rid of a sorcerer's cuff link?"

"I didn't, which is why it took me so long. I waited until it needed to be opened to allow a soul to go through. The reaper escorting said soul was appreciative of the extra protection."

I blinked. "You know," I said slowly, "I hadn't even thought about what losing the first two gates actually *meant* for reapers. All I've really focused on was the fact there was now only one gate standing between us and hell."

"Or, more precisely, one gate and at least several Mijai." Azriel's expression was somber, and with good reason. Mijai numbers had never been huge, but with hell's spawn escaping daily, their resources were being stretched to the breaking point. "In this instance, there was a bigger-than-normal breakout not long before the soul and guide arrived, and the Mijai stationed there were dealing with that."

"And it isn't a situation that will change anytime soon, even if we find the key and spoil the plans of everyone who wants it, is it?" I said. "The remnants might have said they can train reapers to become priests, but I'm thinking that's not going to be a quick process."

"It won't be, which is why I cannot forsake my duties as a Mijai, even to be with you, as much as I might wish. I cannot stand back and watch others fight—and perhaps die—in my place."

A sentiment I'd repeated often enough myself, so I could hardly say anything against it in this case. I glanced at my watch and saw that it was only four in the afternoon. So much had happened since Hunter's phone call this morning that it seemed odd that only eight hours had passed rather than ten or twelve.

"Let us be grateful that it's *not* ten or twelve," Azriel commented, voice grim. "Hunter's deadline is tight enough as it is."

Yes, it was. I grabbed some fresh clothes out of the bags, then said, "I'm off for a shower." I hesitated, then added, with an enticing, hopeful sort of smile, "I don't suppose you want to join me?"

"I would *love* to join you." Amusement and desire

briefly warred for center stage in the bright depths of his eyes. "However, I do not think it wise right now."

"Well, damn," I muttered, even though I really hadn't expected any other answer. "You do realize all these missed opportunities are going on the tab, and I do expect you to pay the bill once all this crap is over with."

"It will be my great pleasure to do so."

"And mine, I would hope."

"Undoubtedly. Now, go, before my desire gets the better of wisdom."

I grinned, spun around, and headed for the shower. Twenty minutes later, feeling a lot fresher and wearing sensible jeans, a long-sleeved T-shirt, and sneakers, I returned to the office—just in time to answer my phone.

"Uncle Rhoan," I said, as his image appeared on the vid-screen. "There's not a problem, is there?"

"Not yet," he replied. "Unless, of course, you've decided to do something daft without consulting me."

"Anyone would think I make a habit of doing dumb things with the way you lot carry on." My voice held an edge that was both amusement and frustration. "I take it you didn't just call to check up on me?"

"No, I didn't, although it is a tempting thought." Humor creased the corners of his bright eyes. "I'm just reporting back with the search results of that phone you handed me."

"Oh good," I said, having completely forgotten about it. I had to wonder whether said forgetfulness was the result of having too much on my plate, or simply pregnancy brain kicking in. I might not be that far along, but from what Mom had said, her brain had pretty much gone to mush for the whole term of her pregnancy.

And she so would, I thought with a stab of sorrow, have loved being a grandmother.

I cleared my throat, ignoring the ache as I added, "Did you find anything useful?"

"The phone belongs to one Harriet Monterrey, and she has several addresses on file."

"One of them undoubtedly an apartment that was blown to smithereens a day or so ago."

Uncle Rhoan gave me one of those long looks. "And how would you know that?"

"Because she tried to blow *us* up, not just the apartment. Monterrey is one of our dark sorceress's aliases."

"Your sorceress seems to have gained a liking for detonating things of late."

She certainly did—and I was seriously hoping it wasn't third time lucky when it came to apartments and bombs. "Well, I guess it's a lot easier than summoning a demon to do your dirty work. Less personal cost involved."

"And has the side benefit of destroying any evidence she might not wish found," he said. "In which case, you had better be careful if you're intending to visit her second address."

"We will." If only because Lauren and Lucian had been one step ahead of us right throughout this damn quest, and even now that Lucian was dead, Lauren still seemed more than capable of guessing our next move.

Which made me wonder whether perhaps there was some other form of *geas* on me. What if Lucian had placed more than one? The charm Ilianna had given me *was* supposed to nullify the strength of any *geas* placed on me, but I'd discovered the hard way that it didn't entirely render them useless. Lucian's attraction spell had still been active when I was in his presence; the charm just meant that I was better able to resist it.

"Where's the second address?" I added.

"In Perth," he said. "Forty-four Gingin Road, Lancelin, to be precise. It's a very exclusive area, so your dark sorceress obviously has some money."

"Obviously, given she also has a beachside property

on the Gold Coast *and* several houses here in Melbourne in rather expensive areas." I hesitated. "I don't suppose there are any traffic or security cams in the area you could hack into, are there?"

"No, but I ran a background check on the house. It's basically been used as a luxury holiday rental for the last couple of years, so it's doubtful there'd be anything of interest there."

"Maybe. Maybe not." After all, our sorceress had a habit of doing the unexpected. And a holiday rental, luxurious or not, could certainly provide a good cover for darker activities. "Did you uncover anything about Monterrey herself?"

"Not a great deal," he said. "The funds from the rental are going into a bank account, but the money hasn't been touched for several years. According to tax records, she's a retiree with a good income stream from investments, there are no outside fines or warrants on her, and she hasn't used her Medicare card to go to the doctor recently."

"Miss Joe Normal, in other words," I said. "She's damn good at setting up and maintaining alternate identities, I tell you."

"I gather Stane is checking her other IDs for you, but you might want to send them along to me, as well," he commented. "Sometimes the Directorate *has* more access to information than a black market racketeer."

His voice was dry, and I grinned. "Yeah, but I don't have to listen to him nagging about keeping safe."

"Getting nagged is a whole lot better than getting dead. Just remember that."

I did remember. I couldn't forget, actually, given I had already died once. And I had no intention of repeating the process anytime soon.

"I'll send a list of our sorceress's other names now, and I promise to call if I intend to do anything daft." I hesitated, thinking about my upcoming dinner with

Mike, then added, "I don't suppose the Directorate has a tracker available that's virtually undetectable—one that I could maybe borrow?"

"There might be," he said, voice noncommittal. "Why?"

"Because I have someone I want to track, and they may or may not be aware of my suspicions of them."

"Is this someone involved with the sorceress and the key hunt?"

"We're not sure, but we did find a minor connection, and at this stage, I think it's better to be cautious than not." Even if I *still* didn't really want to believe Mike could be so convincingly two-faced.

"Then I'll supply the tracker, if you supply the name. I'll run a check on him or her from here."

I hesitated, but it wasn't like I had any other choice. "His name is Michael Judd."

Surprise rippled across Rhoan's expression. "Your investment adviser?"

"And Mom's before me. As I said, the connection might be coincidental, but we nevertheless need to be sure."

"Yes, you do." He paused, glancing away from the vidphone. "Okay, we have several in stock. If you want to ask Azriel to meet me in the foyer in five minutes, I'll hand both the bug and the tracker to him."

"Excellent. Thanks, Uncle Rhoan. I owe you big-time."

"Pay me by keeping yourself alive," he said. "And by calling me the minute—"

"I will," I cut in. "I promise, as I said."

"Good." With that, he hung up.

I shoved my phone back into my purse, then glanced at Azriel. He smiled and said, "Don't do anything untoward while I'm gone."

Once he'd disappeared, I walked over to my computer and Googled the Perth address, then flicked it over from maps to street view. The area, as Rhoan had noted, was definitely upmarket.

Azriel reappeared a few minutes later and handed me a small box. Inside were what appeared to be two skin-colored dots hardly bigger than pinheads, and a small GPS device. "Your uncle said to place one of the dots on Mike's wrist. It is designed to take on the wearer's skin color and once in place will not come off. Nor will he feel its presence."

"And did he say how I'm supposed to get it onto his wrist?"

"He suggested when you were shaking his hand. It has two sides—the side currently visible in the box clings to your finger; then it's simply a matter of pressing that finger against his wrist when clasping his hand."

Which sounded a whole lot easier than it probably would be. I placed the kit on the table, then waved a hand at the satellite image on the computer screen. "Can you get us there using this as a base?"

Azriel looked over my shoulder. "Yes."

"Excellent." I turned, dropped a quick kiss on his lips, and said, "Onward, James."

He rolled his eyes but nevertheless wrapped his arms around me and transported us out of there. Lauren's Lancelin house basically looked like someone had taken a bunch of differently sized white boxes and stacked on them on top of one another. It was only two stories high, but there were lots of different angles and sections thanks to the stacking effect. The windows—at least at the front of the house—were long and thin, and the entrance box was painted dark purple. There was a Mercedes and a BMW parked in front, suggesting the house was occupied.

"It is," Azriel confirmed. "There are five adults and two children within."

I frowned. "I wouldn't think she'd set any traps that her paying guests could accidentally trigger."

"As you noted, our sorceress has a habit of doing the unexpected."

"Meaning we need to get those people out of there before we go in and explore." I squinted up at him. "Could you apply a bit of mental pressure, and get them to leave?"

He studied the house for a moment; then his gaze met mine again. "Done. They are all currently heading for the beach. Security screens will remain down."

"Excellent." I headed down the long driveway and entered the house. It was open plan in design, all white walls, rich wood, and a beautiful glass staircase. The rear of the house was all windows, providing a sweeping view of the beach and the boats dotting the bay beyond it. "Stunning" didn't even begin to describe the place and the view.

But we weren't here for either of those things. I walked around the house, downstairs and up, looking for anything that seemed out of place or strange. There was nothing—not even the slightest whiff of magic. Not until we got into the triple garage, anyway.

I stood in the middle of the vast space, trying to pin down the vague sensation, and, after a moment, spun on my heel and headed for the far corner. Though the outside wall of the place looked solid, electricity nipped at my skin, the sensation not unlike the bite of ants. Something was here.

I glanced at Azriel. "Can you feel anything?"

He shook his head. "But Valdis says there is some kind of doorway present."

Is, Amaya said. *Old, but not dark like others.*

"Meaning it *hasn't* been created by our dark sorceress?"

"Or," Azriel said, "it was created early in her career, before she took the darker path."

"But this house isn't that old."

"No, but perhaps there was a previous dwelling here, and what you feel is little more than a remnant of the magic that protects whatever might still be left of it."

"Maybe." I hadn't thought to ask Uncle Rhoan about the history of the place, and I should have, given Lauren's penchant for passing on properties to one of her other aliases. I squatted and swept a hand across the pristine concrete. Energy skittered across my fingertips, the feel slightly sharper than before, but definitely not dirty or dark. I glanced up at Azriel. "She's shown a liking for hiding things underground—do you think it's possible that she's got another bolt-hole here?"

"There is only one way to find out."

He drew Valdis. I rose and stepped out of the way. "Just do a small hole. One that's just big enough to look through. We don't want the kids staying here falling through anything."

He nodded. Flames flared from Valdis's tip, then split and raced left and right, until they'd formed a circle barely bigger than a small fist. Gray smoke began to billow and the concrete dust teased my nose, making me sneeze. Deeper and deeper the flames bored into the concrete, until suddenly they were through and the concrete ring dropped into a deeper darkness. The flames clung to its side, providing us with shadowed glimpses of what lay below.

I knelt down and peered into the small hole, but Valdis's flames weren't bright enough to lift the darkness all that much. But the air smelled foul and there didn't appear to be any sort of magical surprise waiting for us, as there had been last time.

I looked at Azriel. "Can you sense anything?"

He shook his head. "I do not believe hell creatures wait below."

"Right, then, I'm going in." I raised an eyebrow, waiting for a useless automatic rebuttal, but he surprised me.

"Be careful," he said. "And if you do not wish your clothes destroyed, it might be wise to strip first."

"Ha! I knew there was a reason you didn't object to me going down there. You just want to see me naked."

"Of course. Even if I prefer the song of your soul and your energy, I have been wearing this form long enough now that I've gained a human male's appreciation of the female form." Amusement briefly creased the corners of his eyes, but it faded as he added, tone a touch more serious, "And I *would* stop you from going down there if I thought there was any danger, or if I actually had some location markers that would allow me to go down there instead."

I rose, stripped, and handed him my clothes. Then, drawing Amaya, I ignored his appreciative glance and the heat it stirred and called to the Aedh. The energy came thick and fast, and in a very short space of time, I was little more than particles. I slipped through the hole and down into the darkness. Magic tingled through my being, but its touch was old and distant and didn't particularly feel threatening. If there *was* a spell here, then it was an old one—maybe one that had lost its strength over time.

The darkness was so impregnable I couldn't see anything beyond the puddle of Valdis's flames. I moved around, trying to get some sense of the place. It was only a small chamber by Lauren's standards, and there didn't appear to be any other chambers leading off it.

I moved back to the beacon that was Valdis and, taking a mental breath and warning Amaya to be ready, called to the Aedh once more. A heartbeat later, I was flesh again. Dizziness swept me, but the traditional blinding headache that used to always come with re-forming was little more than a muted, ignorable ache. I was definitely getting better at this whole energy-to-flesh thing.

Nothing, Amaya grumbled. *Shame that.*

Only to your bloodthirsty little self, I said, amused.

Not bloodthirsty, she muttered. *Soul thirsty. Difference.*

I guess there was, in that her thirst had a more permanent ending for her victims. I lifted her blade and her flames flared brighter down her sides, peeling away the heavy cloak of darkness. The chamber was circular and little more than ten feet wide. The magic that I'd sensed earlier clung to the outer walls of the small cavern, but it was no stronger down here than it had been up in the garage. Like previous bolt-holes we'd uncovered, this one had various shelves and storage areas hewn into the earth walls. The bottles and various other witchy-type accoutrements that lined them were heavy with dust and old webs.

Awareness tingled through me as Azriel appeared. He glanced around, then handed me my clothes and said, "This does not appear to have been used for a very long time."

"No." I quickly dressed, then walked across to the nearest shelf and plucked one of the jars from its dusty perch. The glass was so old it was almost opaque, but there was what looked to be hair inside. I undid the lid and tipped the contents out onto the dirt. "But even so, I have no intention of leaving anything here that she might come back and use."

"Might she not sense the destruction of the items?"

"If she was going to sense anything, it would probably be our entry into this place." I shrugged. "I can't imagine she'd sense these bits and pieces being destroyed, because in and of themselves they hold no magic."

"Good."

He moved to the next shelf and began emptying the contents of all the bottles and jars onto the floor, and in a relatively quick time we had a good pile. I shoved Amaya into the middle of them. Her flames crawled over everything and quickly turned them to ash. I swept my foot through the small pile, scattering the remnants, and wished I had some holy water. Spreading it around would have made this place a little bit more inhospitable if she ever *did* come back to it.

"What next?" Azriel asked.

I glanced at the time and swore softly. "Next we go back to the office. I need to get ready for my meeting with Mike."

"I'm glad you stopped calling it a date," he said, as he gathered me close. "That word has the power to annoy me greatly."

I tsked. "Too long in human form for sure."

"Yes," he agreed. "But it does have its benefits. Some of which I intend to explore when and if I get the chance."

"It would seem certain parts of your body are more eager for exploration than others."

"That," he said severely, but with humor dancing in his eyes, "is a function of this body that I have no control over. And, I might add, it is extremely uncomfortable."

I laughed and kissed him. "I do love you, you know."

"I know. I have always known how you felt, even when you yourself were unsure. You cannot lie to your Caomh."

"You can't?" I said, in mock horror. "Damn, there go my plans of hiding future spending sprees in the closet and telling you later I've had them for ages."

He gave me a blank sort of look. "I do not even pretend to understand *that* particular comment."

"Oh, you will, trust me."

His expression remained unsure. I grinned, kissed him again, and said, "Home, James."

A second later we were standing in the middle of the office once again. I pulled away from his embrace somewhat regretfully and started getting ready to meet Mike.

*   *   *

Winter's was a long, skinny restaurant squeezed in between two larger establishments. The walls were rough
brick, the ceilings high and part glass, and there were lots
of old iron tools and sculptures adorning the walls.
Though it had a warm, friendly vibe, I felt anything but
warm as the waitress led me through the main part of the
restaurant and into a more private dining area. This area,
like the main section, was heavy on the brick and metal
decorations, but at the rear of the room was a bank of
sliding glass doors that—while currently closed—opened
out to a small but pretty courtyard. Thankfully, Mike
wasn't the only one in the room—there was another couple sitting in the corner near the doors, though I doubted
they'd be of much help if things started to go downhill.
They didn't seem to be aware of anything but each other.

"Risa," Mike said, rising from the table. "Right on
time, as usual. And looking rather nice, might I add."

He was wearing black, close-fitting pants that rather
looked like breeches, a beautiful emerald green vest, a
white linen shirt, and a black cravat. A double-breasted
waistcoat hung from the back of his chair.

He looked like he'd just stepped out of the Victorian
era—as had, I thought with a chill, the men's clothing I'd
seen hanging in Lauren's wardrobe. It *might* have been
nothing more than coincidence. I mean, Lauren knew
we'd been to her place and had seen those clothes, so if
Mike was involved with her—or, worst-case scenario,
actually *was* her—then surely he wouldn't risk wearing
similar clothes.

"Thanks. And I'm on time because I'm starved." I
clasped his offered hand, suddenly thankful that our relationship was strictly professional despite his apparent
relationship with my mom. I slid my finger to his wrist
and pressed the tracker onto his skin. His grip, I noted
with some distaste, was unusually warm and slightly

moist, but he didn't seem to notice the tracker's transfer and that was good. I just had to hope now that it *had* transferred. I couldn't feel it on my finger, but that wasn't proof, as I hadn't felt it when it was.

He released my hand, then moved around the table, gallantly pulling out my chair and seating me. His closeness had no particular vibes going off, and yet it still unnerved me. I had no idea why.

"I hope the newlyweds in the corner don't bother you," he said, sitting back down opposite. "I did ask Beatrice to book a private room so we could discuss your friend's problem without being overheard, but it appears she ignored me."

"That's okay." I smiled at the waitress as she handed me the menu. "I don't think the newlyweds are worried about anything but each other right now."

"True." He studied the wine list for a moment, then said, "What would you like to drink?"

"Just water, thanks." Even if my wolf constitution did allow me to drink a little alcohol without the risk of harming my child, my damn stomach was churning so badly I probably would have brought it right back up.

"Make that two, thank you." He closed the wine list, handed it to the waitress, then once again turned his full attention to me. There was something unnerving in the way he watched me—there was an intensity, a stillness, that reminded me of a predator about to pounce. "How was your day, my dear?"

Was there just a little too much interest behind that casual question?

I studied him for a minute, seeing lines in his face and shadows under his eyes that I couldn't remember seeing before. Maggie's comment about the drain the Ania attack would have caused ran through the back of my mind and I couldn't help connecting two and two. But was I seeing things—sensing things—simply because I wanted to see them? Because there was some minor part of me that *wanted* them to be there?

If Kiandra's warning was correct—and I had no doubt that it was—then in all honesty I would much rather the person who wasn't what they seemed to be, be Mike than anyone else in my life.

Because everyone else in my life was someone I loved.

"Fine," I said eventually, "but the café is so busy we're thinking about employing several more waitstaff. We're run off our feet during peak hours."

"You have to be careful if you do," he said. "Prime costs are sitting at about sixty-three percent of the total volume of sales. You don't want to run it too much higher, especially if you ever want to sell it in the future."

I raised my eyebrows. "What gave you the idea that I might want to sell it?"

"It happens. Partnerships break up, or it just gets too much." He shrugged. "What happens if you—or indeed, Ilianna—get pregnant? What will you do with the café in that sort of event?"

"The days of a woman giving up her job or her business when she becomes pregnant are long gone."

"Oh, I'm well aware of that." He half shrugged. "It was just a theoretical question."

There was nothing but casual interest in either his voice or his expression, and yet that odd watchfulness was still very much present.

The waitress reappeared, filling our glasses with water, then taking our orders.

"I can't see there'd be any difference to the current situation if either of us did get pregnant," I said, once she'd left. "We'd just hire in someone to take our place. Why?"

"As I said, I was just curious as to whether you'd given it any thought." He produced a small manila folder and handed it to me, then lightly began to tap the table. I wondered whether it was impatience or something else.

"That's all the information I could find on those properties you asked me about," he said. "I believe the bulk of the information has already been shredded."

I looked through the folder. The information wasn't even as detailed as what Stane had told me, though what information it did contain was the same.

I handed the folder back and said, "Would it be possible to talk to either Sands or Macintyre and ask them if they remember anything about the properties in question?"

"Macintyre?" He frowned. "That's the first time I believe you've mentioned someone by that name."

I silently cursed the slip, even as I wondered whether it *was* a slip. "Sorry, I meant Greenfield. He apparently owned one of the properties my friend is interested in."

"Absentmindedness seems to be catching lately." His brief smile appeared warmer than it actually was. "Even I've been struck with the malady. Most inconvenient— though not unexpected, given my age."

"I'd hardly call you old," I said.

"Very gallant of you to say so, even though you must know I'm in my sixties."

He didn't look it—or at least, he hadn't up until tonight. And while his somewhat gaunt and tired expression did add more than a few years on him, it was more his eyes that told of his age. They were a clear gray and not only filled with a vast sense of power but oddly magnetic . . . I felt myself leaning forward and jerked back with a frown. What the fuck was going on? I had no sense of magic, either coming from Mike or in the near vicinity, and surely I would have if some sort of spell was in operation.

I cleared my throat and said, "As I said, if you have contact details for either Sands or Greenfield, I'd really appreciate it."

"If I had such details, you could have them. But they have not been clients of mine for some years now, and I only have these records on the off chance the tax department queries me about them."

"That's unlikely after all this time, isn't it?"

He raised an eyebrow. "As unlikely as either of those two remembering anything about properties they owned so long ago."

Touché, I thought. I took a sip of water, then said, "Do you remember anything about either of them?"

"Nothing much. My dealings with them were strictly business, and I basically only advised them on a couple of transactions before they moved away."

"Any idea where?"

He hesitated. "I believe Sands went to Sydney and Greenfield to the Gold Coast."

Again, he seemed to be watching me just a little too intently. But why would he mention either location if he had something to hide? I took another sip of water and wished I'd never come here. I wasn't any good at this sort of cat-and-mouse game—if that was what was actually happening.

"No wonder you lost contact with them." I shrugged. "I might see if Stane can track them down for me. They might not remember anything, but at least I can say I tried."

"Indeed." He was still tapping his fingers, and the sound was almost as mesmerizing as his eyes had been moments before. "I saw on the news that a converted warehouse in Richmond had been blown apart, and it looked an awful lot like yours—was it?"

I nodded, my unease increasing even though I still had no real idea why. "Unfortunately, yes."

"What on earth happened?"

It was a combination of my demon sword and the backlash of a witch's spell, and it blew the hell out of both my father and *the house*. The words were right on the tip of my tongue, ready to blurt out, but I somehow restrained them. Maybe I was more tired than I thought. Or maybe, I thought, my gaze flicking briefly to his fingers, something else *was* going on.

But if it *was* magic, it was so subtle that I couldn't feel it.

"I believe they're still investigating," I said, a little more abruptly than I should have, "but they suspect a faulty gas pipe."

"Then it was fortunate no one was caught in the blast." He paused. In the brief silence, his rhythmic tapping seemed to echo, a sound that had my nerves crawling. "Though I would have thought a blast strong enough to create such a crater would have at least damaged the houses on either side."

"Obviously, the fates decided it wasn't anyone else's turn to die right then."

"Anyone else's?" He raised an eyebrow. "That's an odd way of putting it. It almost sounds as if someone *did* die."

That's because someone did. Again I had to bite down on the comment. Which was weird. I might think those sorts of things, but I rarely came so close to blurting them out that it was an effort to restrain them.

Except, maybe, when that restraint involved Hunter. Though I could and *did* hold back comments from her, and more easily than I was here. It was almost as if I'd been slipped some sort of truth drug . . . but if I had, when had it happened? The waitress had brought our water in a jug, and I doubted it had been tainted with anything, as she'd used the same jug to fill the newlyweds' glasses.

I frowned, my gaze again going to his fingers. The uneasy sensation that something was happening got stronger. Maybe the tapping had nothing to do with my sudden urge to answer more honestly than I should, but could I take the risk?

"No, no one died, because there was no one in the house at the time." I hesitated, then added, somewhat testily, "I hate to say this, but your finger tapping is getting *damn* annoying."

He glanced down at his hand, his expression surprised. "Sorry, I didn't realize I was doing it."

I stared at him, torn between wanting to believe him and suspecting a lie. His surprise *seemed* genuine, but part of me just wasn't buying it. But that same part was also looking—almost hoping—for evil to be found here rather than somewhere closer to home.

"Sorry, it's just been a shit day. I didn't mean to sound so snappy."

He waved the comment away. "And I didn't mean to be overly inquisitive. I just—" He hesitated and waved his hand again, this time the movement overly dramatic. "I promised your mother to keep an eye on you if anything ever happened to her. I know our relationship is a merely professional one, but I'd still feel remiss if I didn't at least try to keep my word."

I suspected it was said to make me feel bad, and in that, he succeeded. And yet, I still couldn't escape the notion that something was very off—with this situation, and with him.

Azriel? Is there anyone else in this restaurant who seems to be acting oddly? Or anyone who appears overly interested in what might be going on in this room?

There was no reply. Where the warm buzz of Azriel's thoughts usually was, there was only radio silence. I had no sense that anything was wrong—and I surely would have, given that we were now linked body and soul—so that could only mean he was somehow being blocked.

And *that* required magic.

Which meant that either Lauren was near, or Mike was a whole lot more than he ever seemed.

And despite half hoping that he might be the betrayer

in my life, I really *didn't* want to believe it. It didn't matter whether he was simply involved with Lauren or was the shape-shifting sorceress herself; the key problem was, his lies and evil had infiltrated not only *my* life, but my mom's, as well. And in the growing pile of things I could never forgive, *that* would be right up there on the top. .

Am here, Amaya said. *Can eat if wish. No more lies then.*

I hesitated, oddly tempted. But I'd already taken one innocent life; I would not take another. Not until I at least had some *definite* evidence—and the presence of magic in this restaurant wasn't that. So I simply said, *Can you feel the magic?*

Some, she said. *Near.*

Define near.

Near, she repeated. *Not here.*

Which was not at all helpful, although I guess it *did* mean whatever magic was active in this restaurant wasn't actually coming from Mike himself. I reached for my glass again, but as my fingers wrapped around it, Mike caught my wrist, stopping me.

"This is new." His thumb brushed the multicolored ribbon-and-stone tattoo around my right wrist. "And very unusual."

His touch had my skin crawling again, and yet there was nothing inherently wrong with it. It was no longer even moist.

"Yes, it is." I gently tried to pull my hand from his, but his grip only tightened.

"Does it represent anything in particular?" His gaze narrowed as he leaned a little closer to study it. "The ink is unusually vibrant. It almost appears to be real ribbon rather than merely ink."

"That's what you get for going to a good tattooist," I said. "Mike, please let go. You're hurting me."

"My dear girl, I'm so sorry." He released me immediately, but his gaze, when it met mine, was anything but contrite. And the tension I'd sensed earlier was back, only this time it had an almost furious edge. "I've just never seen something so ... intricate before. Whoever designed it for you was very proficient at his or her craft."

"Which is why they get the big money." I smiled at the waitress as she placed our meals on the table, somewhat relieved at the interruption.

When she left, Mike placed his napkin on the table and rose. "If you'll excuse me for a moment, I have to go to the bathroom."

"Your bladder has very inconvenient timing," I said, hoping my relief at getting a brief respite from his presence didn't show.

"That," he said, amusement in his voice, "is also another problem that comes with age. I won't be long."

I nodded and picked up my utensils, tucking into my shepherd's pie as he walked away. But the minute he'd left the room, I scrambled to my feet and all but ran to the door. I peered around the edge of the frame to watch him, torn between wanting him to leave — and therefore prove himself a bad guy — and *not* wanting it to happen.

He didn't leave. He did what he said he was doing — went to the bathroom.

I swung around and hightailed it to the rear of the dining room. The couple glanced at me and smiled but quickly went back to staring adoringly into each other's eyes.

Thankfully, the door out to the small courtyard wasn't locked. I opened it and stepped out. Almost immediately, Azriel appeared, though he was in the left rear corner, squashed between a fountain and a planter box filled with colorful pansies.

"I'm gathering there's some sort of barrier around the café," I said, unable to keep the amusement out of my voice or expression. "And that's why you are where you are."

"Indeed," he said. "And it is a most uncomfortable position."

"It looks it." My smile faded. "What sort of barrier is it?"

"It is similar in feel—although decidedly darker—to the barrier we raised around the building that held both the weapons exhibition and the second key."

Meaning there were undoubtedly wards placed on each corner of this building, because that was the only way to raise such a complete barrier. "Do you think it's worth hunting around to find them? I might be able to displace them."

"No, because whoever placed the wards would undoubtedly have taken into account the location and the possibility of accidental or purposeful displacement." He paused, his gaze narrowing. "I smell something odd on you."

I frowned. "Define odd."

"Odd," he said, almost echoing my sword's response not so long ago. "A scent that wasn't evident when you entered this place. It has an almost otherworldly feel."

"Otherworldly as in magical?"

"Perhaps." His concern raced through me, knife sharp but edged with anger. "Perhaps it would be wise for you to disappear now. The fact there is magic both around this place and on *you* very much suggests that Mike is at least involved with Lauren."

"If he is, then we can't afford to make him suspect we're aware of that," I said. "Lauren undoubtedly has a dozen other identities she could disappear into, and if that happens, we lose her."

Though his expression gave little away, he could no longer keep his feelings from me, and to say he was not happy would be something of an understatement. "You placed the tracker?"

"I did." I hesitated. "If we want to track him, though,

we need some form of transportation. My car was blown up with the house, and he knows my bike too well. Do you think you can convince someone to lend us a car?"

"I shall appropriate one immediately." He paused. "Mike is on the way back."

I blew Azriel a kiss, then scooted back to the table and quickly demolished several mouthfuls so that it would seem as if I'd been eating the whole time he was gone. I glanced up as he sat back down. His expression was less than happy. "Is everything okay?"

He nodded. "Although I'm afraid I may have to cut our dinner a little short. I have another meeting I forgot about."

I raised my eyebrows. Coincidence or truth? And was that "other meeting" a result of a phone call he'd made while in the bathroom? A phone call to Lauren, perhaps? It seemed likely, given that he'd so abruptly left the table after examining the ward on my wrist—and it would certainly explain his expression now.

"You need to get yourself a portable memory device," I said. "You know, a smartphone."

He picked up his knife and fork and began eating. "I do have one; I just prefer *not* to put my life onto a device that could be stolen."

"They're fingerprint secured nowadays," I said. "No one but you can access them." Well, no one but a hacker of high skill. Like Stane, for instance. And maybe *that* was something we needed to do.

He waved the comment away. "I still prefer to rely on my brain, even if I do occasionally forget things of late."

"If you were a woman, I'd ask if you were pregnant." Though the comment was lightly said, I couldn't help but watch his reaction carefully. Because if he *was* Lauren, then he *would* be pregnant. Lucian had been absolutely certain, and I had no reason to doubt him given that a similar conviction with Ilianna had proved true. And though I had no idea how a full-body shift would affect any child she/he might be carrying, Lucian had been well aware of what Lauren was, and he wouldn't have impregnated her if there'd been any risk of a shift damaging or aborting his child.

Mike snorted, the sound somewhat disparaging. And yet, there was something about his reaction that had me frowning—something that didn't quite sit right. Maybe it was just the glimmer of smugness that had flared briefly in his eyes.

"*If* I was female, *and* a lot younger, then that would be a possibility," he said, "because I am certainly not a monk."

"Age is no barrier to pregnancy these days."

"No, but being male *is*." He eyed me severely for a moment. "This is a very odd line of questioning."

I smiled. "I'm not questioning; I was merely having a bit of fun."

"Ah." He glanced at his watch and shook his head. "I really do have to go. Perhaps we can reset this dinner for a later date?"

"Sure. Though I hope you don't mind if I finish my meal first."

"By all means, go ahead." He took his wallet from his pocket and placed some cash on the table. "I am sorry I have to leave so abruptly."

I wasn't. But I smiled and waved a hand. "Don't worry about it, Mike. We'll catch up again when you have a chance."

He nodded and rose, sweeping his coat off the back of the chair, then giving me a slight, old-fashioned bow. "Till next we meet."

I nodded, and he left. I waited until I was sure he wasn't coming back, then reached down into my purse and grabbed the tracking device. Once I'd turned it on, a street map appeared, accompanied by a small red dot that was steadily moving away from the restaurant's position on Smith Street. I scooped up a few more mouthfuls of the delicious pie, then grabbed my bag and headed out the door. Mike was half a block ahead, climbing into his silver Mercedes.

Turn right, Azriel said. *I have acquired a car, but it is parked around the corner from the restaurant.*

I glanced Mike's way again, then headed right. Azriel was standing beside a white Ford Focus.

"Good car choice," I said, as he tossed me the keys. "It's fast, but common enough not to stand out. Who'd you steal it from?"

"I do not steal. I merely borrow."

I grinned as I climbed in and started the car. "So that coffee you acquired from McDonald's for me not so long ago was merely borrowed? Am I supposed to regurgitate it at some point and give it back?"

"Now," he said, his expression severe but amusement dancing in his eyes, "you are just being silly."

"Totally." I checked for traffic, pulled out of the parking spot, then handed him the tracker. "You can direct me."

"A situation I should probably enjoy, given it is the only time you are likely to take direction from me without some form of argument."

My amusement grew. "I don't argue *all* the time."

"No," he agreed. "Just ninety-eight percent of the time. Mike is on the move and is several blocks ahead of us."

I swung onto Smith Street but kept just below the speed limit. With the tracker in place and working, there was no need to get too close. We drove through Collingwood, then made our way onto Hoddle Street, but didn't—as I'd half expected—head toward Mike's office. Instead, he continued on, driving over the Yarra River and onto Punt Road.

"You know," I said into the silence, "I have no idea where Mike actually lives."

Azriel glanced at me. "Why not? Has he not been in your life since you were born?"

"Yes, but I don't believe he's ever mentioned his home address, and I can't remember Mom ever going there. I mean, she may have, but it certainly seemed that he came to our place more than the other way around."

He raised an eyebrow. "Did you not think it strange that he would never mention his living arrangements, given his intimacy with your mother?"

"Now that I think about it, yes. At the time, no. I mean, I didn't even realize he and Mom were intimate until after she'd died." And if anything was strange, then it was *that*. I mean, no child really wants to think about her parents having sex, but Mom had been a werewolf— even if a lab-designed one—and she had a werewolf's sexual nature and outlook. She'd certainly never hidden the existence of other partners during my childhood, so why would she hide the fact she'd been in a long-term relationship with Mike?

She wouldn't, I thought with a chill.

And maybe that meant their relationship *hadn't* been sexual. Maybe it had been nothing more than an avenue of access—to me, to keep an eye on me.

After all, Lucian had obviously known of my creation before he'd been cast back in time by the Raziq, because it certainly *hadn't* been luck that his path had crossed mine. He'd also obviously known that my father had created the keys in such a way that only he, or one of his blood, could find them. So why wouldn't he have placed someone in my life—someone outwardly ordinary—to keep an eye on me? Especially if that someone was well practiced in magic—or, at least, had easy access to someone who was?

It was only when my father had come back into my life that Lucian had enacted his own plans, starting with my mother's murder. He'd believed that without her presence, without her advice, I would be infinitely more vulnerable, and therefore more accepting of his advances. And he'd been right, up until the moment when I'd finally realized there was a lot more going on than just sexual attraction.

Of course, once I'd killed Lucian, I'd cut Lauren's access to me—and therefore the key search. And *that* could certainly explain Mike's attempts to become a bigger part of my life since Mom's death. As my accountant and investment adviser, his contact with me was limited to business meetings. But as a friend of my mother's—a friend who'd supposedly promised her that he'd keep an eye on me—he certainly had more of a chance of doing that.

I briefly scrubbed a hand across my eyes and swore softly. Azriel wrapped his fingers around mine and squeezed gently. "Do not feel bad. The Aedh had centuries to plot. It is not really surprising that we are still unraveling the threads of his treachery."

"Yeah, but if I'd listened to you a bit sooner—"

"We cannot change the past. We can only learn from it and move on."

"Something that's more easily said than done," I commented. Especially when the past involved the two deaths that should never have happened—although one of them certainly wasn't either Lucian's or Lauren's fault.

"Hunter's turn will come," Azriel said.

I glanced at him. "You can't be sure of that. Hell, even the fates aren't sure of that, from what you've said."

"True." He half shrugged. "But there's also karma. And if you've been thinking the fates are a bitch, then you've obviously never met karma."

I raised my eyebrows. "You're saying *that* like karma is a living thing."

"She is as real as the fates, and has very nasty tendencies if you do the wrong thing by her." He paused. "He's turned right onto Pasley Street North. It's two streets up from our current location."

I slowed as I neared the street, and waited for a gap in the oncoming traffic so I could turn. A massive park dominated one side of the street, while on the other, pretty Victorian terraces rubbed shoulders with more modern houses and ugly apartment buildings. The Mercedes had stopped just beyond a bend in the road, and there was no one in it. I slowly cruised past and peered at the house it was parked in front of. It was one of the two-story Victorian terraces, a beautiful white building complete with an original-looking wrought-iron balustrade lining the upper balcony. It was the sort of house that would be worth a fortune, especially in a location like this. Mike was just disappearing inside the front door.

I parked farther up the road, switched off the car, then twisted around to look back at the house. "Can you sense anyone else in there?"

Azriel shook his head. "There is a barrier around the house."

"We seem to be coming up against a few of *those* lately," I muttered. "It's damn frustrating."

"But not surprising, given who we are dealing with. This one is similar in feel to the one around the warehouse that had the hellhounds."

I glanced at him, amused. "That doesn't exactly cut the options down, given we've discovered hellhounds at nearly every warehouse we've been to."

A wry smile touched his lips. "I meant the first warehouse, not the second."

Which was the one the Brindle witches had woven an exception into, allowing Azriel to enter, and also the place that held a secondary barrier within its bowels. We'd know soon enough what that one might be protecting, given that Kiandra now had the witches working on it.

"So *this* barrier is designed to keep out reapers and Aedh, but not human?"

"From the feel of it, yes." He gaze came to mine. "I presume this means you are about to break in?"

I raised an eyebrow. "You say that like we've got another choice."

"There are always other choices, as I believe you have often noted. However, they may take more time than we have; we need to know what goes on in that house *now*, not later. And with the barrier present, it is a task that necessarily falls to you."

"Which doesn't mean you're happy about it," I said.

"No, but then, I *was* assigned this task to protect you."

"No, you were assigned to find the keys. Protecting me was a secondary—even if necessary—part of that task." I leaned over and kissed him. "I won't be long. And I'll be careful."

"Good. But you might want to face-shift, just in case Mike—or whoever else might be in that house—happens to be looking out the window."

"Good idea."

I leaned back, took a couple of deep breaths, then closed my eyes and pictured a face that was very different from mine—a sharper nose, a smattering of freckles across my cheeks, green eyes rather than lilac, and short but curly brown hair.

Then, freezing that image in my mind, I reached for the face-shifting magic. It exploded around me, thick and fierce, a gale-like force that made my muscles tremble and the image waver. I frowned and concentrated harder—easier said than done when the magic was designed to sweep away sensation *and* thought. But the energy responded and my skin began to ripple as bones restructured and my hair shortened and curled.

When the magic faded, I opened my eyes and glanced

in the rearview mirror. The face that stared back at me was not my own. It was always a weird feeling.

I met Azriel's gaze again. "Wish me luck."

"I wish you safety," he said. "Just don't take unnecessary risks while in there."

I grabbed the coat the car's owner had rather conveniently left in the back and threw it on to hide my clothes as I climbed out of the car. While I might no longer look like me, Mike had noted what I'd been wearing and, given that he knew both Mom and I were face shifters, would undoubtedly be suspicious of anyone wearing the exact same clothes.

Tension rolled through me as I walked back to the white terrace, and it took every ounce of willpower I had not to stare up at the windows to see whether there was anyone watching me.

I opened the hip-height wrought-iron gate and stepped onto the bricked pathway that led both to the front door and around to the back of the property. The minute I did, the magic hit me, crawling across my skin like a thousand fireflies, stinging and burning. My skin twitched and crawled, and I had to resist the desire to back out. However unpleasant the sensation was, it *wasn't* actually stopping me. I guess that was something to be thankful for, even if I suddenly *didn't* want to enter this place alone.

I walked on. The farther away from the gate and the barrier I got, the less intense the stinging became. My gaze swept the nearest windows, but I couldn't see anyone watching. If there was an alarm woven into the magic, then it certainly hadn't roused anyone.

Amaya, can you sense any life inside?

Nothing, she said. *Evil only.*

So Mike's not there?

No.

Meaning there had to be some sort of transport device inside the house. *The evil you're sensing—is it magic? Or the creatures-from-hell-type evil?*

She hesitated. *Sure not.*

Fabulous not, as she would say. Still, if we wanted answers, then I had little choice but to continue on—and given that Mike was no longer inside, there was little point in sneaking around. Sometimes, going boldly was the only sensible course of action.

I marched up the steps and over to the door. The only noise coming from inside the house was the steady ticking of a clock. I had no sense of the evil Amaya said was there, but she was more finely tuned to all things hell than I was. I pressed the doorbell; the cheery sound seemed to echo for an abnormally long time but drew no response.

I rang it again, just to be sure, then retreated and followed the path to the rear of the house. Surprisingly, the gate into the backyard wasn't locked, but I paused in the act of opening it and whistled softly, just in case there was something more substantial than magic protecting this place.

No dog came a-running, but I didn't relax. I couldn't, really. We were too close to the endgame now, and I very much doubted the warding-stone barrier would be the only thing protecting this place.

I drew Amaya and held her in front of me, like a shield. Lilac fire crawled down the edges of her steel, but the flames were restrained. She was holding her energy in check until needed.

The rear yard wasn't huge, but there were so many trees and flowering shrubs crowded into the space that it felt like I was entering a different world—one that was cool, green, and rich with many scents. It was a space that very much reminded me of the greenhouse I'd stepped into when I'd used one of Lauren's transport stones and found myself up on the Gold Coast.

Coincidence? I tended to think not.

The rear glass door was locked, and a quick look through it confirmed there was no one inside—or at least no one I could see. I double-checked that none of the neighbors were peering through the curtain of green, watching what I was doing, then shoved Amaya into the small gap between the frame and the door. In very little time, she had sheared through both the ordinary lock and the dead bolt.

I took a deep breath that did little to calm the butterflies going berserko in my stomach, then stepped inside the dark and silent house.

Chapter 8

Like most of these renovated terraces, the rear part of
the house had become one big, open kitchen that also
had plenty of room for a dining area. Amaya's lilac
flames cast a cool light across the white expanse of walls
and kitchen cabinets but oddly gave the polished floorboards a richer, redder glow. I slid my shoes off so my
footsteps didn't echo, then carefully walked on. Beyond
the soft ticking of a clock, the house was silent. But the
still air was rich with a combination of leather and
roses, the smells coming from both the furnishings and
the various floral arrangements dotted around the
room. There was no TV in this room, just a small kitchen
table and a comfortable-looking sofa. Bookcases lined
the wall to my left and were filled with hardcovers—
some fiction, most not. Aside from the flowers, those
books were the only spots of color in this otherwise
white world.

I moved through the kitchen and up a couple of steps
into the more formal dining area. There was a staircase to
the right. I paused at its base, looking upward. There was
a skylight at the top of the stairwell, but the moon hadn't
fully risen yet and there was little light shining through it.
There was no sense of movement or life coming from the
upper floors—and yet, there *was* something up there. I
had no idea what it might be, but my skin crawled with
awareness. Maybe it was the evil Amaya had sensed.

Not, she said. *That ahead.*

Oh. Great. I licked my lips and forced my feet on. The
dining room, like the kitchen-diner, was expensively but
sparsely furnished. In fact, there was very little in the
way of decoration in this place—nothing beyond the furniture and the flower vases, anyway—and certainly nothing that hinted at the personality of the owner. It was
almost a show home—although even show homes generally had a warmer feel than this place.

Beyond the dining room there was a small corridor
and a gorgeous old grandfather clock. There were also
two doors. One was the front door, so I reached for the
doorknob of the other one. But as my fingers touched the
metal, that sense of evil sharpened, its touch old and
oddly putrid. I quickly released the doorknob and backed
away.

What the fuck is in there, Amaya?

Sure not.

I frowned and glanced down at my hand. Though I
couldn't see anything, it felt as if a film of some kind had
crawled from the knob to my skin. It was cold, wet—
even though there was no moisture on my hand—and
oddly reminded me of Mike's grip when I'd shaken his
hand.

Amaya, flame up. When she did so, I added, *I want you
to burn whatever it is I have on my hand.*

I stuck my palm against her blade, and her flames
crawled around my fingertips, their touch light, warm,
and tingly.

After a moment, she said, *Taste foul.*

Is it magic or something else?

Not hell magic. She paused. *Of this place.*

*Meaning the stuff is from Earth, or it's simply not dark
magic?*

Latter. Witch, not blood.

If it was witch magic, did that mean Lauren was nearing the end of her strength limits? All magic had its costs, but the price of blood magic was apparently far higher, and Lauren hadn't exactly been cautious about its use of late.

Is it the same sort of magic that waits in that room?
No.

I frowned at the door for a minute, then realized *I* didn't actually have to go anywhere near the door or whatever magic had been placed on it to find out what lay beyond it. I took a step forward, raised Amaya, and thrust her into the middle of the door. There was a moment of resistance—from the magic rather than the door—then her steel was through.

What can you see now? I asked.

She hesitated. *Evil.*

Care to be a bit more descriptive than that?

Her hesitation was even longer. *Not demon. Not spirit. Of this world but not flesh. Can't eat.*

And that, I thought with amusement, pissed her off greatly, if the tone of her voice was anything to go by. But what were we dealing with? Was it some form of ghost? I'd never feared ghosts, having seen them most of my life, but something held me back from entering that room and confronting this one.

What is it doing?

It waits.

For what? Someone to enter the room or for its master to return and give it instructions? *Is there anything or anyone else in that room besides the ghost?*

No, she said. *Office.*

Meaning there just *might* be something in there worth finding. But to do that, I'd have to confront what might be some sort of vengeful ghost, and I really didn't feel like doing that right now. Besides, though we'd seen Mike enter this place, he obviously wasn't still here. And that meant there *had* to be a set of transport stones around somewhere. Better to find them before I tackled anything else.

I slid Amaya free from the wood and headed for the stairs. I walked up cautiously, my back to the wall, Amaya in one hand and my shoes in the other. Her soft hissing overrode the sound of the clock's ticking, though I think her noise was more frustration that there'd been nothing so far for her to attack than any sense that danger was near.

We reached a landing, but the only thing on this level was a generously sized bathroom. I continued upward, senses alert for even the slightest caress of something out of place or unusual. There was nothing.

And yet there *had* to be something here. Mike hadn't simply disappeared. Creating that sort of magic took time, so either there were transportation stones here somewhere, or he'd gone out the back door, leapt over the back fence, and run away. And I honestly couldn't see him doing *that*.

I reached the final landing. Two doors led off this, and both were partially closed. Eenie, meenie, minie, moe . . .

I stepped forward, raised a foot, and lightly toed the nearest door open. No demons jumped out at us. No vengeful ghosts, and definitely no magic.

It was a bedroom and it ran the entire width of the building. A glass door led out onto the front balcony, but even from here I could see it was securely locked. He hadn't gone out that way—though we would have seen him if he had. The all-encompassing white theme was in residence in this room as well, with the only splash of color coming from the dark wood of the old-fashioned four-poster bed and the large vase of cream and pink lilies and roses sitting on the dressing table.

I swung around and headed for the back bedroom. My skin began to crawl, and the awareness of . . .

something ... was growing. I slowed as I neared the door, listening intently, trying to figure out whether the thing I felt was real or imagined.

Not, Amaya said. *Evil inside.*

I do wish you'd get a bit more descriptive, I mentally muttered. *I mean, are we talking live evil, dead evil, or something in between?*

Live not, she said. *Dead not. Just is.*

Which still wasn't very helpful—but I guess it was hardly fair to blame her.

Will eat if can, she added.

If it attacks, feel free. I took a deep breath, then once again pushed the door with my foot. Tension ran through me as it swung open, and every bit of me was ready to jump back, to react, if anything so much as squeaked the wrong way.

Nothing did.

What stood in the middle of the room was a set of cuneiform stones. They were about six feet tall and roughly four feet wide at their base, and both reached up to a needle-sharp point. Though most of the other stones we'd discovered had been primarily gray in color, these were white—as white as the walls within this house—and their surface was littered with small crystals that Amaya's flames sparked to life, sending rainbow-colored flurries skating through the room. They reminded me of the second set of stones we'd found under the warehouse near Stane's—the ones we'd initially believed had been the sorceress's entry point onto the gray fields.

They even *felt* like those stones. All the others we'd come across had felt ancient and powerful. *These* stones—like the others—were undoubtedly both old *and* potent, but there was also a foulness emanating from them. It was as if they were something that should not exist in this time or place.

I took a step closer. Pinpricks of energy snapped at my skin, drawing blood. I shivered and stepped back. While I had no doubt that Mike had disappeared through this gateway, there was no way in hell I was about to follow him. I might have risked it had it been only my safety I had to worry about, but I was a mom-to-be now, and I wasn't about to jeopardize the health of my son by exposing him to something that felt so . . . unclean.

I retreated to the wall and walked around the stones. I didn't learn much. I didn't understand cuneiform, and I wasn't about to call the one person in my life who did back into the line of fire. I might have promised to call Uncle Quinn if I needed help, but I wasn't about to risk Hunter finding out where they were hiding for something as minor as this.

Which meant that as far as Mike went, we were at a dead end until he showed up again.

I sheathed Amaya, then left the house, making sure that I left everything as I'd found it—everything except the rear-door locks, and there wasn't much I could do about that except hope that no one noticed it.

"So this would appear to confirm that Mike is at least working with the dark sorceress," Azriel said, as I climbed into the car.

"It confirms that both my mother and I are blind fucking fools." I thumped the steering wheel. "Damn it, how could he keep something like that a secret for so long? Mom wasn't an innocent when it came to the arcane— why did she never sense something was wrong until it was altogether too late?"

"The Aedh placed a spell you," Azriel said. "What makes you think they didn't also do the same to your mother?"

"I guess. It's just—" I stopped and shrugged. "I guess I'm just sick of being three steps behind everyone else in this game."

"It's possible Mike is not aware that we suspect him. That will play in our favor."

"Only for as long as it takes him to realize someone broke into his house. He's going to suspect it was us."

"Which may or may not matter to him. He needs you, remember, so if it prompts any sort of action, it's going to be another attempt to ensnare you."

I glanced down at my hand, remembering the some-what slick feel of his initial handshake. "Do you think that's what he was doing in the restaurant?"

"No. I think he was simply trying to uncover both what you knew and what you suspected. I also suspect you will hear from him sooner rather than later, proba-bly with another invitation for dinner."

"Over which he'll try to magic me." I rubbed my wrist and hoped the ribbon bracelet was strong enough to withstand the onslaught of dark magic. "Do you think he's Lauren?"

Azriel raised his eyebrows. "That is a question you should answer, not me. You know him. I don't, nor can I read him."

"I'd like to think he's not, that we couldn't be that gullible." My lips twisted. "But then, I've already had more than enough proof of *that* with Lucian."

"Everyone is entitled to make a mistake," Azriel com-mented sagely. "At least you rectified yours by ridding this world of his presence."

"Yeah, but revenge didn't taste as sweet as I'd hoped."

"It never does." He reached over and squeezed my hand. "Let's dwell on the problems we can do something about, not the ones we can't."

"Good idea. So where the hell do you think Mike might have gone?"

"We know Lauren has at least two warehouse bolt-holes. It is possible that we have not found all that either of those places conceal." He shrugged. "Given the relative ease with which we found that first one, it is entirely possible that she allowed us to find what we did in the hope we would then discard it."

"Then let's head there and see if we can pick up Mike's signal." I started the car and pulled out into the street.

"And if we do? We have no idea whether Mike is merely working for her or if he's our sorceress herself, but either way, I doubt it would be wise to confront either of them in one of her lairs."

"No, but at least we'd finally have a concrete lead." And once the bastard stepped away from protection, well, one way or another, he was ours.

It didn't take us all that long to cut across to the warehouse. I parked in the street behind the building, then glanced down at the tracker Azriel still held. It was deathly quiet.

Mike wasn't here.

"It is still worth checking the building," Azriel said. "The witches are here. If nothing else, we can see how their progress with that second barrier goes."

I nodded, climbed out of the car, and walked around to the front of the building. It wasn't much to look at in its current state—the wind rattled the rusted iron roof and whistled through the small, regularly spaced windows, many of which were broken. Like many of the other buildings in the area, its walls were littered with graffiti and tags, and rubbish lay in drifting piles along its length. But its bones were essentially good, and I couldn't understand why it had lain derelict for so long; it would have made several smashing apartments.

But once again there was an odd, almost watchful stillness about the place. It was a stillness that seemed to affect the immediate surrounds, which were unnervingly quiet. Even the roar of the traffic traveling along nearby Smith Street seemed muted.

I shivered, despite the heat rolling off the man walking so closely beside me. This place had always seemed . . . wrong . . . to me. More so now, perhaps, because I knew what evil its dark interior sheltered.

There were two entrances into the building on West Street. The first one remained heavily padlocked, but the other—a roller door over what had once been a loading bay—was where we'd gotten in previously. Someone had done a rough repair job on the broken section of the door, but the welding didn't look too good and I didn't think it would take more than a kick or two to be rid of it. Which was precisely what I did.

I got down on my hands and knees and squeezed through the small hole. The witches had woven an exception into the magic that warded this place to allow Azriel to enter, but it seemed to have a wash-over effect on me, because this time there was very little in the way of resistance or stinging as I crawled through the small gap. I still felt it, but it wasn't resisting me like it had previously.

I rose and dusted the dirt off my jeans as I scanned the area. The large loading dock and the offices that lined the upper area hadn't changed, and I couldn't smell anything in the air that suggested anyone was in this portion of the building.

Azriel rose and stood beside me. "The witches are still here, but I cannot feel the presence of anyone else."

"I'd normally say that was a good thing, but in this particular case, I'm not sure it is."

"That would depend on what lies behind the hidden door and whether the magic that protects it also interferes with my ability to sense souls." He pressed his fingers against my spine and guided me toward the stairs. "We may yet find either Mike or our sorceress here."

I snorted softly. "Do you really think it's going to be that easy?"

"No, but one can always hope."

We went through the end office—the one the farthest away from the trapdoor Jak and I had fallen through during our first visit—and moved into the deeper darkness of the main warehouse. The roof here soared high above us and was snaked with metal lines and some sort of conveyer system. The windows lining the left side of the room were so thick with dirt that very little outside light seeped in, and on the right side, there were several small, rubbish- and rat-filled offices. The concrete floor was stained with rust lines and thick with grime.

Azriel drew Valdis. Her flames flared across the shadows, making it easier to traverse the space, especially in the end third of the building, where the sludge from the old machines was thickest and as slippery as hell.

I briefly wondered where the ghost of the woman who'd led me to the hidden doorway was. I couldn't sense her presence anywhere near, but maybe she was simply keeping watch now that there was no immediate danger.

We reached the inky wall that protected the stairwell down into the basement. I led Azriel around to the two-foot-square doorway Rozelle had woven into the sorceress's magic and crawled through. Magic immediately hit me, but its feel was clean, pure, caressing my skin rather than attacking me.

The witches were still at work on that door.

I grabbed the metal railing and made my way down to the basement. It was a cavernous space, all concrete, and filled with lines of dust-laden, somewhat rusty metal shelving—all of which were empty. Whatever the inky barrier was protecting, it wasn't *this* particular area.

I led the way through the shelving. Rozelle turned around as we approached. She was tall and pretty and looked all of twenty. Given that most witches didn't usually begin training to be masters—which was what she was doing at the Brindle—until they were at least thirty, she'd either become *very* proficient at a very early age, or she was much older than she looked. I suspected the former, if only because Kiandra had placed a lot of faith in her.

"We're almost through," she said. Though her eyes were bright with excitement, her skin looked pale and the droop in her shoulders suggested weariness. "The spell protecting this entrance is nothing any of us has ever seen before. It's been quite a learning curve unpicking all the interwoven threads."

I glanced past her. Six witches sat within a protection circle in front of the section of wall that held the hidden doorway. The crisp, clear magic that rolled across my senses was emanating from them, but underneath it, I could still feel the caress of the sorceress's dark and oddly dirty magic. But it was an energy that was flickering, fading, fast.

I returned my gaze to Rozelle. "So whatever the magic is protecting, it's something our dark sorceress cares about greatly."

Rozelle nodded. "We suspect it could be her ritual room. There is no other reason for a spell of this intricacy."

"And if it is?"

"We destroy it. She will undoubtedly have other, minor rooms she could use to cast spells, but the loss of this one, situated as it is on a main ley-line intersection, will severely curtail her ability to create major blood magic."

I frowned. "Why? Couldn't she just make another one somewhere else?"

Rozelle shook her head. "Blood magic is a difficult and dangerous art, and it cannot be performed any old where. It would have taken her years to set up her ritual space so that she was secure and well protected from the forces she is summoning."

"If that's the case, why isn't she here, protecting this place with everything she has?"

Rozelle's cheeks dimpled. "Because we are not without some skill ourselves. She has not attacked because, as far as she is aware, this place is as safe and as secure as it ever was."

"Using magic to counter magic. Nice."

"We thought so." She turned to face the circle, her gaze narrowing. "It shouldn't be too long."

"Do you think there will be any sort of spell or trap inside?"

"Possibly. We'll ensure it's safe to enter before anyone does so." She glanced past me. "But in case it *is* protected by something more mundane than a spell, I would have your sword ready, reaper."

Azriel didn't comment, but Valdis's flames flared brighter. Surprisingly, Amaya had nothing to say about being left out of the possible killing spree, but maybe she was merely waiting to see whether there *was* something worth attacking before she started complaining.

In the brief silence, there was a loud crack, and a doorway-sized section of the concrete wall began to shimmer, waver, fading in and out of existence and providing tantalizing glimpses of a rusted metal door. The flickering got faster, more violent, as if the magic that concealed the door was fighting back. Then, with a sigh rather than a bang, it bled away, and the solid metal door was revealed in its entirety.

I instinctively took a step forward, anxious to see what might lie beyond the door, but Rozelle grabbed my hand, stopping me from going any farther.

"Wait," she said. "We're not finished yet."

I took a deep breath and tried to curb the impatience that rattled through me. We were dealing with a dark sorceress's lair, and god knew how many traps might wait inside. But that still didn't stop the need to get in there, to know whether Mike was just a lackey or our shape-shifting sorceress himself.

Though why I was so certain I'd find confirmation inside, I couldn't entirely say. Maybe it was just wishful thinking.

I crossed my arms and watched the witches continue to work on the door. Their magic was sharper than before, holding a knife-edge that bit into my skin without drawing blood—meaning, no doubt, there were even darker spells on the old metal door itself.

Five minutes passed. I shifted my weight from one foot to the other, trying to curb impatience and the growing need to *know*.

Their magic peaks, Azriel said. *It won't be long now.*

As if his comment was a catalyst, the metal door began to groan, to creak. Its metal hinges seemed to get longer and longer, as if there were two opposing forces holding either end, stretching them thinner and thinner.

Then, with an explosive roar, they shattered, firing shards of thin metal through the air. Rozelle ducked, as did I, and the deadly missiles flew over our heads and pinged off the shelving behind us.

As the dust settled, it revealed the metal door lying at a downward angle, suggesting there were steps just beyond the doorway. The candlelit room beyond appeared to be large. Nothing moved within the room. Nothing leapt out at us.

I remained where I was. There might not be hellhounds and whatnot inside that chamber, but if there were candles lit, there might very well be magic.

Two of the six witches sitting within the protection circle rose, chanting softly as they joined hands and stepped onto the first step. The tension running through me ramped up several notches as they gradually disappeared downward, but there was no immediate or obvious response.

After several minutes, the sharp sense of magic eased, and one of the witches reappeared in the doorway.

"It is safe to enter," she said, voice weary. "We have deactivated the remaining spells."

I glanced at Azriel, who raised an eyebrow at my unspoken query, then took the lead, skirting around the witches' protection circle but pausing on the top step. I stopped beside him. This chamber, unlike the others we'd discovered, had not been hewn out of the earth. It was obviously part of the building's fabric, a deep, wide bunker that, like the room behind us, was longer than it was wide. At the far end of the room several large black candles burned, their light barely illuminating the heavy stone table that stood between them. Even from here I could smell the blood, desperation, and fear that clung to the stone like a well-worn cloak.

"Her ritual table," I murmured, trying to ignore the urge to turn around and run, as far as I could, from this place and that table.

"Yes," the second of the two witches said. She tucked her brown hair behind her ear and gave a small grimace. "It will take some time to fully nullify its power, I'm afraid."

I frowned. "You can't just use holy water on it?"

"Oh, we can, and will. That will at least prevent her from using it in the short term. Longer term, however, needs a more careful destruction. We need to ensure this table can never be used again, either by our sorceress or anyone else of her ilk."

My eyebrows rose. "Meaning ritual tables are handed down from one generation to another?"

She nodded. "And each generation enriches the stone with their dark energy. That is why *this* sorceress has been able to do all that she has—this stone is very, very old. You may come farther into the room, reaper," she added. "It is safe enough for now."

Azriel walked down the remaining dozen steps. Valdis's fire cut across the deeper shadows, revealing more metal shelving. Unlike those in the other room, these were filled with earthen jars, glass bottles in just about every hue imaginable, and all sorts of witch tools. But I couldn't see anything in the way of an athame, and there were certainly no chalices, which meant that while this might be her main ritual site, she certainly wasn't keeping her most important ritual items here.

It is possible they were kept in those chests we saw in her Gold Coast home, Azriel commented. *It would make sense to keep her most important tools close and safe.*

I guessed it would. I clattered down the stairs after Azriel and walked across to the nearest shelving unit, my gaze running across the different bowls, jars, and bottles. If Mike was involved in this whole mess—and really, any doubt had now all but disappeared—and had placed a *geas* or some other sort of spell on Mom, then there *would* be something here belonging to her. Hell, there might even be something here belonging to me. We'd already found strands of my hair in one of her other lairs, and I doubted *that* would be her only cache.

As I walked up and down looking at the shelving, Rozelle came down into the room, two heavy-looking canvas bags gripped in her hand. Once she'd reached the base of the stairs, she placed both on the floor and opened one of them, revealing several large bottles of liquid. Holy water. The cleansing of this space was about to begin.

"Will she sense it?" I asked, briefly diverting my attention away from the shelving.

"Not unless she suddenly decides to appear." Rozelle handed one of the bottles to the taller witch. "Though she will sense the destruction of the ritual table when we split it asunder."

"You split it?" I said, surprised.

She nodded. "Once we deactivate the spells that still

protect it, yes. It is the heart of the stone that holds the power; destroying it will render the stone unusable not only for her, but for future generations."

"Good." Especially when it meant there was one less means of dark magic and mayhem in this world.

"Risa," Azriel said. He was studying a row of glass jars on the shelving opposite. "You might want to come and look at these. They have a very familiar resonance."

"Familiar as in me or someone else?"

He glanced at me, expression grim. "Both."

I walked across and stopped beside him. The jars that had caught his interest looked far newer than any of the others that sat nearby. Those were covered in a thick layer of dust and obviously hadn't been touched for years, if not decades. Of the four jars that had caught Azriel's interest, two had a light coating of dust that was smudged in various places, indicating more recent usage. The other two had a heavier coating, but it was nowhere near the thickness of the other jars on the shelf. Unfortunately, the glass was smoky, making it difficult to see the contents.

"The resonance from the recently used jars is an echo of your own," Azriel said. "The other two are reminiscent of your mother."

So she *had* been spelled. There could be no other reason for her resonance to linger in these jars. I blinked away the tears that were both remorse and anger, and glanced at Rozelle. "There's no spell lingering on these things, is there? They're safe to pick up?"

Rozelle nodded, her concentration more on the water line she was creating around the base of the stairs. "The only magic that now resides in this chamber is that within the ritual table."

"Thanks." I plucked the nearest bottle off the shelf and unscrewed the lid.

Inside sat a solitary earring. It was simple in design—

a perfectly circular dark pearl in a gold setting. I couldn't remember ever seeing Mom wearing something like this, but maybe Mike had stolen it when I was little more than a baby. I tipped it out into my palm and for an instant heard an echo of my mother's warm laugh, felt the kiss of lips across my cheek. Impossible, I knew, because she'd long ago moved on.

Not so impossible, Azriel said, mental tone soft. *Not when her resonance lingers.*

And this solitary earring, I realized suddenly, was the only piece of her jewelry I had left. Everything else she'd left me had been stored in the safe at our apartment and was now little more than a sprinkling of dust in a hole filled with ash and destruction.

Yet I couldn't regret my actions and certainly wouldn't have altered them even if I had a chance to do it all again. Mom lived on in my memories and in my heart, not in material things. And she would be the first to call me foolish for mourning the loss of such unimportant things as jewelry.

Still . . .

I closed my fist around the earring, holding on to it fiercely as I reached for the next jar. This one held more personal items—hair, nail clippings, and several other bits and pieces that I couldn't actually guess at. But these sorts of items were all used in placing a *geas* or spell on someone.

I swore softly and handed the jar to Azriel. He shoved Valdis's tip into it, and in very little time, the contents were ash. Mom might be dead, but I still wasn't about to risk leaving the things in that jar here. If it was possible for the Raziq to call me back from the dead, then it was also very possible that Lauren could do the same. She'd been hanging around Lucian long enough to learn at least enough Aedh magic to get herself onto the gray fields without his aid, so heaven only knew what else he'd taught her.

As Azriel placed the jar back on the shelf, I reached for the first of the more recently used ones—and wasn't exactly surprised to find it contained hair, nail clippings, and whatnot. I gave it across to Azriel, then opened the second jar. Silver gleamed back at me from the bottom of it. I frowned, tipped it into my palm, and realized with a sense of shock that it was a baby's bracelet. *My* baby bracelet. I'd seen pictures of it over the years and had eventually asked Mom what had happened to it. She'd shrugged and said she had no idea. And maybe she didn't. Maybe she'd handed it over to Mike at some point and then had been prompted to forget about it.

I stared at it for a moment, then took a deep breath and released it slowly. I couldn't keep it, as much as I might want to. Just as I couldn't keep Mom's earring, no matter how much I might want to. The earrings might not have any sort of spell on them, but they'd been in Lauren's possession for a long time, and I had no idea whether she could trace me through either of them. Better to be safe than sorry. I dangled them into Valdis's flames and watched the silver and pearl slowly disintegrate, until there was nothing left.

I resolutely turned away and inspected the rest of the shelves. I couldn't see anything else of either mine or Mom's.

I glanced at Azriel, and he shook his head. "Which does not mean she has nothing else of yours, just that it is not kept within this ritual room."

I swung around and said to Rozelle, "Would she have more than one ritual room?"

"No." She drew her athame from the second of the bags, then met my gaze. "It takes strength and time for a sorceress to attune such a table to her psyche."

"Does that mean she can't create spells wherever the hell she currently is, or simply that she can't create any major spells?"

"The latter. If the spell involves blood magic, then it must be performed here, on this table. Other magic—and not necessarily minor—she can perform anywhere she can create the appropriate protection circle."

"Damn."

"Indeed." Her smile was grim. "However, the destruction of the table will impinge on both her strength *and* her ability to perform any sort of magic. Which is why we must hasten its destruction."

"Then we'll get out of your way." I hesitated. "You do remember you're dealing with someone capable of taking on any form, don't you?"

Her smile grew, though there was still very little in the way of amusement in it. "Which is why the very first thing we did, before we even attempted to access this room, was create a spell that was not only a barrier against evil, but would reveal the true form of anyone coming into this basement."

"Which won't stop a human type of assassin coming down here and shooting the lot of you."

"It does when we are guarded against all evil—human or otherwise." She half shrugged. "It is not dissimilar to the magic that guards the Brindle."

"Then good luck with the table destruction."

"Luck is not something the Brindle has ever relied on," the taller witch commented. "It is far too fickle a beast."

Well, *that* was certainly true. We headed out of the basement and went back through the warehouse, until we were once again standing outside. I stretched weary limbs, but before I could say anything, my phone rang. The tone told me it was Uncle Rhoan, and my stomach tensed again. Even if he'd said he'd track down what information the Directorate had on Lauren's other aliases, there was something deep within me that said two calls in such a short amount of time could *not* be good.

I dug out my vid-phone, hit the Answer button, then said, voice holding a false note of cheer, "I wasn't expecting to hear from you so soon."

"And I certainly wasn't expecting to call again so soon." His voice was as grim as his expression.

The tension ratcheted up several notches. "I'm gathering there's a problem?"

"You could say that." His expression became grimmer—fiercer—though I hadn't thought that was possible. "Jack's gone missing."

Chapter 9

Surely to god Hunter wouldn't have . . . not to Jack. Not to her own *brother*. I swallowed heavily and said, "What do you mean, he's missing?"

"Missing as in out of contact and untraceable by any known method," Rhoan growled. "Missing as in, we can't find either him *or* his tracer signal fucking *anywhere*."

Holy fuck, she *had*. Which meant she was even *more* insane than I'd figured.

"I'm gathering Hunter has been contacted and asked if she knew where he was?"

"Ringing *her* was the first thing I ordered when it came to my attention he was missing. She doesn't deny that he was with her but says she has no idea where he is now."

Thank god he'd asked someone else to ring her rather than confronting her himself. "And you believe her?"

He snorted. "No, but I have no evidence to the contrary, and I'm not fool enough to make any sort of accusation until I do."

"Is there any security footage anywhere of him? Perhaps coming in or out of her office?"

"They didn't meet in her office; he went to her house. There's no security footage because Hunter had all cameras removed not too long ago."

Meaning this step had been planned for a quite a while—and yet, knowing that didn't make me feel any better. Jack had gone to see Hunter basically because I'd pushed; if he was dead, then in some ways it was my fault.

You cannot take the blame for the actions and choices of others, Azriel said. *Jack's decision to talk to Hunter stemmed from both his desire to keep the Directorate autonomous in the battle he knew was coming and his need to protect both your uncle and the other guardians. Your comments only confirmed what his next course of action should be.*

Yeah, but he might still be alive if he hadn't actually decided to go right away.

Given Hunter's recent cleansing of council members who oppose her, that *is a debatable point.*

I guessed it was. It still didn't make me feel any better, though. I returned my attention to Rhoan. "If Hunter has either killed Jack or simply contained him somewhere to take him out of action, she can't be too far from making her move for total control. And that puts *you* in a very tenuous position."

"A point I am well aware of, believe me."

"Then you're going to do the sensible thing?"

He snorted again. "You ask that, and you've known me how long?"

"I know, but Hunter is a bigger threat—"

"I will do my *job*," he cut in, "and now that Jack has disappeared, that's running the guardian division. The only reason I'm ringing you is to let you know what has happened. Be careful, Ris. If she's done this, she could do anything."

I wasn't the one who needed to be wary. She still needed me to find the key. She didn't need him, other than as a lever to ensure my good behavior.

"Trust me, I'm totally aware of what she's capable of. Just make sure *you* watch *your* back."

"I'm surrounded by people I trust at this very moment. You just make sure you're doing the same. Don't let Azriel leave your side."

"I won't," I said.

"Good," Rhoan said. "Ring me if anything happens."

"I will." I hit the End button and glanced at Azriel. "Do you think it's possible Jack is still alive?"

He hesitated, his eyes narrowing slightly. "I cannot hear his resonance, but that doesn't mean he's dead. It might just mean he's being kept underground, where I cannot sense him."

"I guess we can only hope that's the case." Though I personally feared it wasn't. I thrust a hand through my still-curly hair and added silently, *Do you think it's worth contacting Markel, to see if he knows anything more?*

I doubt Markel would, given he is tasked with following you around. Harry Stanford, however, might be an option.

Except that he'll use Jack's death as a means to entice me into his plot.

It is nevertheless worth talking to him. If someone would have any understanding of Hunter's current moves, it would be her fiercest opponent.

I guess. But to talk to him, I had to go back to the office and get comfortable. It was the only way I could astral travel.

Azriel caught my hand, tugged me into his arms, and a second later we were back in the café's office.

"Fucking *hell*," a familiar voice said. "You could give a person warning when you're going to drop in like that!"

I swung around. Tao stood in the doorway, his brown hair wet, a towel half slung over his right shoulder, and his expression a mix of surprise and amusement. At first glance, little appeared to have outwardly changed since I'd seen him just over nine hours ago; his face was still gaunt, his body rail thin, and heat radiated from him, the force of it so strong that I could feel its caress from where I stood in the middle of the room. But flames no longer burned uncontrolled in his eyes, and the air of desperation that had surrounded him seemed to have fled.

"You're okay," I said, and it was a statement rather than a question.

"I am," he agreed. "How long it will last, I have no idea, but for now, we're good."

We, not I. That was a new and hopeful sign. "What happened?"

"I did what you suggested I do. I went back to the sacred site and talked to the elemental." His brief smile was almost a grimace. "It wasn't easy, but we got there in the end. You were right, Azriel. It doesn't want to die. It just wants to protect the fire that gave it life."

"So you have reached a compromise?" Azriel asked.

"We have. One I think we could both live with."

"And that is?" I prompted, when he didn't immediately go on.

"I have the days. It has the nights."

"What?" I said, surprised. "I would have thought it would be the other way around, given it draws energy from heat and sunlight."

"There may be neither at night, but there *is* the sacred fire. Not only is it the source of the elemental's power, but *it* is also most vulnerable at night. Therefore, we'll be there at night to protect it, and I'll have the days."

"So why are you here now? It's nine thirty *and* night-time."

"I came back here to grab a shower and to leave you a note. I wanted to let you know I was okay—that we were okay. Then I was heading back out."

"To do what?" I said. "I mean, there's nothing up there but wilderness and the fire."

"The elemental doesn't need anything else," he said, expression gentle.

"So when you're up there, the elemental is in control?"

"Yes, but I am not unaware, just as it is not unaware during the day." He lifted a hand. His skin briefly glowed with a deep orange fire. "I can still have a life, Ris, even if it is one that wasn't what I'd quite imagined."

Half a life was better than no life. Or worse, losing yourself forever in the fires of another creature. I walked over and gave him a hug. "Be careful up there, won't you?"

He returned the hug fiercely, then brushed a kiss across the top of my head. "I will. And I'll see you tomorrow."

"Hopefully, yes."

He frowned and stepped back. "And what, precisely, is that supposed to mean?"

I waved a hand. "Nothing. This whole key quest thing is just getting me down."

"If I can help in any way—"

"I know." I squeezed his arm. His peace with the elemental was too new, too fragile, to even *think* about bringing him back into the quest, even if I *had* wanted to.

Which I didn't.

"I have my phone with me, so if I don't answer it immediately, leave a message," he said. "You know I'll be there if I can."

"I know. And thank you." I kissed his cheek. "Go, before the elemental starts getting antsy."

He turned and went. I listened to the sound of his retreating steps, and though part of me rejoiced that he'd found a solution that enabled him to live, part of me also felt like crying. Because nothing was ever going to be the same. The tight-knit group we'd grown up with had fractured, ever so slightly, and it couldn't ever go back to what it was. The events of the last few weeks had changed us all, and not entirely for the better.

"I do hope I'm not included in the 'not entirely better' portion of that thought," Azriel said, amusement in his voice.

"You, reaper," I said, as I turned and headed for the sofa, "generally have a foot in both fields, depending on where my hormones are at the time."

"Then it is your hormones that are the problem, not me."

I kicked off my shoes and lay down. "You're the reason the hormones are going haywire, though."

"Hardly the only reason," he said, the amusement stronger. "It does, after all, take two to make a life, whether in this world or in mine."

"Yeah, but you could have warned me your rockets were such fertile little buggers."

The amusement faded from him. "Do you regret it? The pregnancy, that is?"

I shot him a surprised look. "Hell, *no*. I've always wanted kids. I could have done with the time to get to know you better, but aside from that, no regrets."

"Ah. Good." His relief ran through me, bright and shiny—an indication of just how important my answer had been to him.

"Azriel, you can read my mind. Surely you knew that whatever else I might regret, the pregnancy wasn't one of them."

"One of the side effects of sharing my life force with you is your ability to now shield some portions of your thoughts from me." He gave me a lopsided smile. "Your feeling on the pregnancy was one such thought."

I frowned. "I wasn't doing it intentionally."

"Perhaps not, but it was nevertheless a source of tension for me."

"Well, you should have just *asked*. It's not like you haven't been vocal about all sorts of other things."

"But if I had, I might have received an answer I did not desire. I would rather face ten hordes of demons than the knowledge that you did not want our child."

"You, reaper, are an idiot." I rose, walked across, and

hugged him as fiercely as Tao had me only moments before. Then I stepped back and gave him a somewhat stern look. "The thing is, I not only want this child, but lots of little brothers and sisters for him as well. You'd better start preparing, reaper, because you have a lot of work ahead of you."

"A task I look forward to." He tapped my nose lightly. "And now, you should do what we came here to do." *And let us hope that Markel still watches, not Janice Myer.*

Because if it was Janice, I might have to kill her, as I had Nick Krogan. Just thinking about the possibility had my stomach turning over.

I returned to the sofa, got comfortable, then closed my eyes. In very short time, I was back on the fields. The fates were with us for a change—Markel was our watcher.

He smiled and gave me a somewhat formal bow as I appeared. *I take it you have come here because of Hunter's recent actions.*

So you know about Jack's disappearance?

I am charged with following you astrally, remember. I heard your conversation with your uncle.

Ah. Bugger. *Does that mean you haven't heard anything else on the grapevine?*

The event is only recent, so no. He paused. *I would doubt if even Harry has more knowledge of it, as I would imagine the murder of her brother is something Hunter wouldn't advertise. It would set off too many alarms within the council.*

I snorted softly. *And her recent behavior hasn't been enough to do that?*

He half smiled. *Well, no, because she is a very old vampire, and old vampires tend to have peaks and troughs when it comes to behavior.*

So they're viewing her whole "I will take the keys from hell and rule you all" as nothing more than one of those troughs? Because you and I know it's a lot more than that.

He nodded. *But not all the councillors feel that way; otherwise, Harry would not have contacted you.*

He contacted me because he wanted me to fight Hunter for him, I retorted. *It had nothing to do with the council's desires and everything to do with his own.*

Not just his, Markel said, a slight hint of censure in his mental tones, *but for the good of all. You've seen what she has become. Do you honestly think someone who would kill her own brother—who also happened to be the one person who has had any sort of influence over her in recent years—should be allowed to remain in control, be it on the council or at the Directorate?*

No, I don't, but I also think it's a bit rich to expect me to do what you, Stanford, and a whole other bunch of very old vampires fear to.

Sometimes, life isn't fair. I would have thought you'd have learned that after all that has happened recently.

Oh, I'd learned it, all right—that didn't mean I had to be happy about it. *Is there any way we can uncover whether Jack is alive or not?*

Markel was shaking his head even before I'd finished speaking. *None. If the Directorate and your uncle cannot find any trace of him, then he has surely been destroyed by her.*

Meaning destroyed as in eaten, I thought with a shiver, as she'd eaten the Jorōgumo, the shape-shifting spider spirit who'd foolishly chosen Hunter's lover as one of her victims. I hated to think Jack had died that way—and I hoped like hell that he'd at least had a chance to defend himself. That he'd got in a blow or two and made the bitch pay for her betrayal before she'd consumed him.

My stomach threatened to rise in my throat again. I swallowed heavily and said, *I still think it's worth asking Stanford if he knows anything. There's always a chance— a very small chance—that she's not quite as bloodthirsty or insane as we think.*

I might not actually believe it, but for Jack's sake, I couldn't help hoping for a miracle.

Insanity is something no maenad can escape, Markel said. *The close contact with their god, and the rituals they perform, usually send them over the edge sooner rather than later. Hunter has held on to her sanity centuries more than most, but these last few years have proven even she is not immune to the fate of her sisters.*

I take it, then, that you do not wish to contact Stanford at this present time and actually ask him about Jack?

He raised an eyebrow, expression suddenly amused. *On the contrary, Harry has already been contacted and is on the way.*

That surprised me. I studied him for a moment, then said, *Telepathy?*

Indeed. He paused. *How do you think we reported to Hunter? She is not the type to wait until the end of a shift to hear an update.*

I hadn't actually thought about it. I paused. *That makes Janice Myer something of a threat moving forward.*

She's certainly a threat if you find the key while she is on duty. She will report immediately to Hunter—and if you think Hunter will not take action right away to acquire said key, then you are a fool.

I know she will, which is why everyone I care about—except Rhoan—is somewhere safe.

You're not. Markel's voice was grim. *And she* will come after you the minute you find it. No one else. Just you. And if you think she has no way to counter the presence of your reaper, then you had better think again.*

The only thing that can stop Azriel is magic. And death—and to kill him, she had to catch him unawares—not an easy task given he was well aware of her intentions when it came to him. I hesitated, then asked the question for which I really didn't want confirmation. *Is she capable of that? Aside from the magic her god gives her, that is.*

Hunter is capable of many things, a new voice said. *Including, I suspect, the darker art of magic.*

Harry Stanford appeared to one side of Markel. He was little more than a shadow, though his green eyes once again glowed with an eerie fire. And from what I could see of his expression, he was *not* happy. But that wasn't actually a surprise, given that Hunter was gearing up for a takeover *he* wanted to prevent, and one of the key players in his prevention plan wasn't playing the game.

But you've never seen her actually perform it, have you?

I've never seen her consume someone in a maenad fever, either, but I'm nevertheless aware that she has and does.

Unhappiness and frustration rolled from his shadowed form, rippling the ether surrounding us and washing across my astral skin; the sensation was unpleasant, itchy.

Good point, I said. *What do you know about Jack's disappearance?*

Nothing more than you, at this point. His tone was grim. *But it is worth noting that killing Jack is the one thing we all thought she would never do. If she has, then it is the greatest sign we have that we are no longer dealing with a rational mind.*

What about the rest of the council? How have they reacted?

In general, with disbelief. He shrugged. *But those who would oppose Hunter are already in our camp. This event will not change anyone else's mind.*

Why? Because they fear to cross her?

Generally, yes, Markel said. *And let's be honest here; she* is *worthy of such fear.*

Then surely you can understand my reluctance to get involved in any sort of confrontation with her?

What I understand, Stanford said, tone even grimmer, *is that if you continue as you are—totally unprepared to battle a woman with the force of a god at her back—then you will not only die, but condemn this world to one of darkness and hell.*

He was right. I knew that. But, by the same token, I couldn't help holding on to the fragile—and no doubt futile—hope that somehow I could find the key *and* avoid any sort of confrontation with the bitch.

Have you contacted your ghostly friend? The one who knows how to counter the powers of a maenad?

Just for a moment, Stanford's eyes glowed even more fiercely. Elation, hope—I wasn't sure which, because his expression didn't actually change much.

I have. We were working on the particulars when I was summoned here.

And what, precisely, are the particulars?

As I have said before, to have any hope against her, you must first disconnect her access to her god and his powers.

How will the disconnection help?

If she can't access her god, she can't access the strength and power of the maenad.

I snorted. *Meaning I'd only be confronting a mad ancient vampire capable of performing ordinary magic. What a relief* that *would be.*

Your sarcasm is misplaced, Stanford said, expression annoyed. *You are an Aedh armed with a demon sword, and more than a match under normal circumstances.*

Hunter *wasn't* normal, though. Neither were the circumstances. *So how do you intend to cut her access to her god?*

With magic, of course. He shrugged. *I cannot tell you the details, because I am not magic proficient. It does,*

*however, involve a type of warding shield, similar in style
to what currently guards the Brindle.*

I frowned. *Meaning we have to get her to that location
for it to work?*

Yes.

But won't she sense the magic before she goes in?

*No, because we won't actually enable the magic until
she is within the building.*

I really don't think it'll be that easy—

She wants the key, Markel cut in. *If you have it as bait,
she will come. Believe that, if nothing else.*

I did believe it. I just didn't believe Hunter would walk
willingly *or* unprepared into any sort of trap. I glanced at
Stanford. *Hunter's well aware of your plot to dispose of
her—aren't you afraid you're next on the hit list?*

A smile touched his lips, but the light glittering in his
eyes turned cold, harsh. *She has already made one attempt on my life.*

Markel raised an eyebrow. *When?*

Stanford glanced at him. *At the same time that the
other councillors were assassinated. She sent Cazadors.*

Markel's anger shot across the astral plan, so strong it
felt as if the very foundations of the place were trem-
bling. *She has no right to use the Cazadors as her own
private kill squad.*

*No, but even Cazadors are not immune to the promise
of power. And that is what she offered them, Markel.*

Them. Meaning Hunter had sent more than *one* Cazador after Stanford, and he still beat them. I'd been
right before—Stanford was every bit as dangerous as
Hunter, just in an entirely different way.

You know this for a fact? Markel asked.

Stanford nodded. *I questioned them.*

Who? There was an odd sense of urgency—perhaps
even a touch of . . . not fear, but something close to it—in
that one simple word.

Frances Halberry and Edward Appleton. Stanford paused, his expression sympathetic. *I am sorry.*

Markel briefly closed his eyes. *I would have sworn neither could have been swayed by her.*

Were they your friends? I asked softly.

Markel's gaze met mine. In the dark depths of his eyes, rage burned—a rage that was deep, fierce, and close to uncontrolled. Berserker, I thought with a shiver. Uncle Quinn had mentioned once, long ago, that the berserker mentality was often a result of being a Cazador for too long. And becoming berserker, these days, was a death sentence. I hated the thought of that happening to Markel, because he actually seemed a pretty decent person otherwise.

Yes, he said, voice clipped. *And I cannot believe they would willingly go to their death on the promise of power from a madwoman.*

I didn't say anything. There wasn't really anything I *could* say, as I didn't know his friends. But I certainly knew firsthand that Hunter wasn't above playing dirty if it meant getting what she wanted. It was also a sad fact that the desire for power sometimes struck the most innocuous people.

They were given a clean death, Stanford said softly. *I did that much for them, at least.*

Markel took a deep breath and released it slowly. *Thank you.*

Stanford's gaze returned to me. *Do not be surprised if Hunter contacts you to demand the key be found sooner rather than later. And I would warn your uncle to be wary; she has more support in the Directorate than he imagines.*

He knows that. I hesitated. *How soon will you be ready to move, if needed?*

It will take a few more hours to prepare the wards, Stanford said. *I will arrange to have the address sent to you as soon as we are ready.*

I frowned. *Why not just meet here on the astral plane again?*

Janice Myer takes over the watch in one hour, Markel said. *While I am willing to take her out if absolutely necessary, to do so would alert Hunter of not only where my allegiances lie, but also that her opposition is on the move.*

It is better she believes us caught flat-footed, Stanford said. *Besides, I would not put it past her to place her own people on the plane, watching the watchers.*

I hadn't thought of that possibility. *How do I contact you if something goes wrong or I decide to accept your help?*

Your reaper can always contact either of us, Stanford said. *Myer cannot track him, and as long as you keep your discussions with him in regards to this matter telepathic, no one will be the wiser.*

Fine, I said grimly. *But accepting your help will only be an absolutely last choice.*

Stanford bowed, the movement holding a slightly mocking edge. *I will nevertheless be prepared, as I believe we both know that your last choice is the only choice you actually have.*

With that, he disappeared. I glanced at Markel. *He's an arrogant bastard, isn't he?*

Not arrogant as much as determined that Hunter's shadow will not linger over the council longer than now necessary.

I snorted. *And, of course, he'll just happen to step into her shoes once she's gone.*

If you mean he would assume her position on the council, then no, he wouldn't. Markel's mental tones held a hint of censure. *That can only be done through direct challenge, and he has no intention of doing that.*

No, because he wanted me to do it for him. *Then what happens when she's dead?*

The rules of ascension come into play. If there is more

than one candidate, they will fight, with the survivor tak-
ing Hunter's place. Harry is not old enough to ascend to
her position so would not be in consideration. The censure that had been evident in his voice appeared in his
expression. *Do not judge those you do not know based on*
your experiences with Hunter. Not all vampires—or in-
deed councillors—serve their own interests first and fore-
most. Not even Hunter did that initially.

And that was me told, I thought with amusement. *I'm*
sorry if I misjudged your friend, Markel, but it's kinda
hard not to, given all the contacts I've had with Hunter
and the council have not exactly been great experiences.

He nodded. *And I'm afraid that is likely to continue*
until Hunter is gone and equilibrium restored. In the
meantime, be careful. There are still those within council
ranks who believe the simplest solution to the current sit-
uation would be to kill you.

Isn't that just what I need at this point in time—the
fucking council coming after me rather than the mad-
woman they've left in charge of the whole zoo.

You, Markel said with a smile, *are seen as the easier*
option. You are not, of course, but Hunter has kept them
relatively unaware of that.

Then they are bigger fools than I'd already thought. I
hesitated. *You'd better be careful yourself, Markel. If she*
is the slightest bit aware of your friendship with Stanford,
you may well be next on her hit list.

Of that, I am well aware. But thank you for the con-
cern.

I nodded. *Talk to you later.*

And with that, I returned to my body. As awareness of
my immediate surrounds began to return, I did nothing
more than breathe deep in a vague attempt to wash the
tiredness and the need for sleep from my limbs. But after
several minutes, the rather enticing scent of coffee mingling with the tantalizing aroma of freshly baked bread

invaded my awareness and made my stomach rumble. I opened my eyes and sat up. Azriel leaned against the front of my desk, his arms crossed and amusement in his expression. Beside him, on the desk, was a large mug and the thickest steak sandwich I'd ever seen. My mouth began watering just looking at it.

"You could have told me you'd arranged food," I said, getting up. "I would have stirred faster."

"You needed the rest, however brief, more than you needed the food. Besides, I figured your olfactory senses would kick in sooner rather than later."

"And you were right." I picked up the sandwich and bit into it as I parked my butt on the desk beside his. It was every bit as delicious as it looked.

As much as I dislike the idea, it was wise to ask Stanford to prepare for a possible confrontation. Especially if Hunter is capable of the darker arts.

I'm protected against the darker arts, so that's not so much a concern. I glanced at him as I munched. *You, however, are not.*

It takes a lot of preparation and power to trap a reaper, he said. *But I nevertheless will be cautious.*

Good. I finished the rest of the sandwich in quick order, then licked the remaining juices from my fingers and said, *Do you think Markel was correct that some of the council still considers me a risk?*

Undoubtedly.

Taking me out won't negate Hunter's madness.

No. His mental tones were somewhat grim. *But it is entirely possible that, given she has just murdered the most vocal of her opponents on the council, those who are neither with her nor against her might believe their only option now is to take out the bigger threat in the equation—and that is Hunter gaining control of the hell portal. The easiest way to do that is to kill you.*

I guess. I took a sip of coffee. *Surely Hunter will know that's a possibility, though, and take steps against it.*

Perhaps. Perhaps not. His gaze met mine. *If there is one thing I have learned in my time here on Earth, it is that human thought processes are not logical at the best of times. When someone has stepped onto the field of insanity, determining what they may or may not think or do is beyond even the ability of the fates to guess.*

Meaning we had better watch out for an attack out of left field?

Confusion flickered briefly across his expression. *Left field?*

I grinned. *Yeah, you know, something totally unexpect—*

I cut the explanation off as the phone rang yet again. I pulled it from my pocket and hit the Answer button. Stane's image appeared on the screen, and he looked rather harassed.

I frowned. "What's wrong?"

"Possibly everything," he said. "Or possibly nothing. It's hard to say, but I'm just not liking the feel of things."

"The feel of what?"

"Events." He glanced sideways, his gaze narrowing slightly. "I've lost all power, the streetlights have gone out, and the street itself has become weirdly quiet. Either I'm becoming paranoid, or something is going on."

I glanced at Azriel. "Bunker down. We're coming over."

"Make it—" He hesitated, and his face went white. "Oh fuck."

And with that, the screen went dead.

Chapter 10

Azriel didn't hesitate; he just grabbed my hand and transported us across to Stane's.

We reappeared in the middle of his upstairs living quarters. The place was both dark and silent. Stane's computer bridge was lifeless, and the air thick with the smell of fear and something else, something less tangible and oddly pungent . . .

Vampires, Azriel said, drawing Valdis. Her blue fire lifted the shadows, revealing the vamps standing together near the kitchen. *Six of them.*

It's not vampires I can smell. It was something else. Something that reminded me vaguely of ash and old newspapers, but possessing an oddly foul chemical undertone. It certainly *wasn't* something I'd ever smelled here before. *Where's Stane?*

Close.

Alive?

Yes.

Relief cut through me. At least I hadn't managed to get someone else killed. *Why aren't they attacking? Do you know what they want?*

You, of course.

Then why not attack the minute we appeared? They would have had the advantage. Because until they *did* attack, he couldn't. Reaper rules and all that rubbish.

I don't know.

Neither do I. I drew Amaya and said, "Come on, guys, six vamps against one werewolf—that's a little unfair, don't you think?"

"Not if our actual aim was to draw you out," the tallest of the six said, his voice urbane and rather pleasant. He stepped forward and gave a small, formal bow. "Risa Jones, the high council has overturned their previous position on you. Therefore, I'm afraid, you are now slated to die."

"And they sent only six to do that?" I tsked. "Not very smart of the council."

He raised an eyebrow. "Who said there were only six of us?"

The words had barely left his mouth when Azriel swore, spun, and pulled me roughly to one side. The knives that would have buried themselves in the middle of my back swung past my shoulder and hammered hilt deep in the middle of the nearest wall.

There were three of them behind us, three who for some unknown reason neither Azriel nor I had sensed.

Three who would have taken us out the coward's way.

Rage exploded, rage that was both mine and Amaya's. Damn it, I was fucking *sick* of everyone threatening me, my family, and my friends, and it *would* end now. I *wasn't* helpless. I could fight and protect myself better than most, and it was time people started realizing that.

Take the three cowards out, I said to Azriel. *I'll keep the others occupied.*

I called to the Aedh and disappeared. My actions didn't seem to faze the vampire who'd spoken. In fact, he seemed oddly pleased by them. Unease slithered through me, but I shoved it aside and arrowed toward the group of six.

And saw, too late, the small device in the leader's hand.

He pressed it, even as they all stepped aside to reveal

a large, barrel-shaped container. I had no idea what it was or what it contained, and I definitely had no desire to find out.

But as I swerved away, the thing exploded.

A black cloud of molten ash plumed through the air, sparkling oddly. The thick cloud surrounded me, clung to me, its touch foul and heated.

The five vampires pulled weapons out and aimed them in my direction. I realized in that instant what they'd done—what the cloud was. It made the invisible visible. And while I had no idea whether bullets could harm me in this form, I wasn't about to take the chance. If they knew enough about Aedh to make me visible, then it was highly probable they also knew what would kill me.

Amaya, shield!

Can't! she all but screamed. *Need flesh. Steel.*

I swore and shifted shape, even as they fired the guns. Lilac flames spun around me, but not quite fast enough. One bullet got through, hitting my arm. Pain exploded even as a cold, deep fire began to burn in my flesh. The bastards were armed with *silver bullets*.

As the remaining bullets bounced off Amaya's shield, I surged to my feet and rushed at them.

Kill, Amaya screamed. *Eat must!*

Go for it, I growled, and flung her, as hard as I could, at the tall vamp who'd been the spokesman. She cut through the air, her scream high-pitched and as scary as hell, her flames flaring wide, as if trying to devour all six at the same time.

The vampires scattered. I dove for the nearest one, hitting him at knee height and driving him down. He crashed to the floor with a grunt but nevertheless twisted and started throwing punches. I became Aedh, allowed several blows to pass through my particles, then shoved my fist inside his chest and re-formed enough to grab his heart. Then I squeezed. Hard.

He screamed, twisted, fought.

But there was no fighting my grip. No escape from death.

He collapsed and died, pain etched into his expression and his eyes wide with shock. There was no reaper waiting for him, only an eternity as one of the lost ones.

I shoved away the sliver of remorse, spun around, and re-formed again. I raised a hand and a second later Amaya hit it, her steel heavier but anger still burning in her heart.

There were four of the original six left. As I reappeared, they raised their weapons and fired again. Amaya shielded instantly and the bullets zinged off to various parts of the room, most of them smashing harmlessly into walls but at least one shattering the kitchen window behind me. I flung Amaya again, then became Aedh and darted sideways, coming in at the vampires from the left as Amaya came in from the right.

They scattered, firing randomly. One bullet zipped across the edge of my particles, and red heat spun through me, a warning that silver *did* affect me, even in this form.

I mentally swore, twisted around, and became solid enough to smash a booted foot into the nearest vampire's face. There was enough force in the blow to mash his nose into the back of his head *and* throw him backward. I hit the ground in full flesh at the same time he did, reached a hand out for Amaya, then drove her deep into the vamp's body. Her flames raced over him even as her deep chuckle filled the air. He was dead before he even realized it.

I spun around again and discovered myself at the wrong end of a gun barrel. "It was a good effort," the vampire said softly. "But in the end, for naught."

With that, he fired.

The gun exploded.

Bits of metal went everywhere, cutting him, cutting me. I yelped but nevertheless raised Amaya and shoved her into the vampire's cold heart.

She quickly consumed him, body and soul. I turned, Amaya raised to counter the next threat, but the remaining vampires were dead. I met Azriel's furious gaze. "Did you have anything to do with that gun exploding?"

He shook his head. "From what I caught of his thoughts, something must have been lodged in the barrel."

Luck, it seemed, had finally remembered we existed. I sheathed Amaya, then walked across to where Azriel was standing. The vampire at his feet was still alive, though his arm had been sheared off at the shoulder and his blood spurted across Stane's pristine floor. "Without wanting to sound too bloodthirsty, why have you kept this one alive?"

"Because I intend to use him—or rather, his telepathy skill—to send a message to the remaining councillors."

With that, he squatted beside the vampire and pressed his hands on either side of his head. The vampire's eyes went wide, but other than that, he made no sound. Neither did Azriel. I'd seen him do something similar in the past, when he was reading the lingering memories of dead people, but each of those times, the images had appeared between his hands, as a sort of movie reel on high speed. There were no pictures here, and the vampire wasn't dead. Not yet, anyway.

After a few minutes, Azriel opened his eyes, then, without warning, sliced Valdis across the vampire's neck, severing his head from his body.

Only then did he meet my gaze. His blue eyes glittered with a fire as fierce as anything I'd ever seen. "They have been warned not to attack you again; otherwise, I will decimate their ranks."

I raised my eyebrows; while I had no doubt he would carry through with the threat, it did surprise me that he was willing to go so far. "I didn't think you'd be allowed to do something like that."

"If they order a second attack after being so warned, then yes, I am. The fates' priority right now is both you and that final key. Anything else—even rules that have been in place since the beginning of time and life itself—is secondary."

"Damn, the fates are getting *serious*," I muttered.

"As am I," Azriel growled. "Enough is enough."

"With that, I can wholly agree." I raised a hand to shake some of the dust and soot from my hair but stopped when I caught sight of my fingers. Blood coated them. Blood that had come from inside a chest and an exploding heart.

My stomach rose and I spun, sprinting for the bathroom. I barely made it. When I'd lost absolutely everything I'd only just eaten, I flushed the toilet, then thoroughly washed my hands with soap and hot water. Once there wasn't a scrap of blood to be seen—not even under my fingernails—I grabbed a cup from the shelf above the basin and rinsed out my mouth.

Azriel stood in the doorway, arms crossed and one shoulder resting on the doorframe as he watched me.

"You really need to stop regurgitating everything you eat," he stated eventually. "That is good for neither you nor our child."

"If the bad guys would stop attacking us—and therefore making me do things I'd rather not do to defend myself—then I might have a chance." I glanced in the mirror, realized I was still wearing my fake face, and swiftly changed it back. It didn't actually make my reflection look any better—I was still far too gaunt, and the bags under my eyes had definitely gotten bigger. I sighed and turned away. It wasn't like I could do a whole lot to fix either problem right now. "Did you include Hunter in your telepathic broadcast to the council?"

He hesitated. "I sent it to all those that vampire had access to. Whether Hunter is one of those, I could not say."

"Then I'm going to ring the bitch and tell her what has just happened."

"Do you think that's wise?" he asked. "After all, there is that saying about not prodding a sleeping bear. I think it would apply in this case."

I half smiled. "It normally would, but I think we're better off letting Hunter know about events."

"I doubt that she would be *unaware* of them, given she has Cazadors tracking us astrally."

"Maybe, but I'd still like to impress on her the fact that she needs me alive if she wants the fucking key, so it would be in her best interests to stop the council from sanctioning another attack."

"I do not think it'll make a great deal of difference, but there's no harm in trying."

I reached into my pocket to grab my phone, only to discover it was little more than metal and plastic bits. I swore softly. In the rush to protect myself and fight, I'd forgotten that any electronics not touching skin would be destroyed by the Aedh magic rather than simply dismantled, then put back together.

Stane had a phone, though . . . *Stane.* Fuck. "Have you managed to pinpoint Stane's location yet?"

Azriel shook his head. "As I said, he is near and alive. I suspect, given that I cannot get any true sense of his location, that he might be underground somewhere."

"How can he be underground when we're up on the first floor? The vampires would have come through the ground floor, and there's no other exit."

"That we're aware of. That doesn't mean there isn't another one. Stane is nothing if not clever."

True. And given he dealt on a regular basis with some very shady characters, it wasn't beyond the realm of possibility for him to have some sort of panic room. It would also explain why his phone signal had so suddenly cut off. Cell services were notoriously unreliable when it came to anything underground, like the rail loop, or even sewerage tunnels. Not that I really had firsthand experience of the latter, but if Stane *did* have a bolt-hole, then he undoubtedly also had an escape route out of said bolt-hole. And there were plenty of decommissioned sewer and utilities tunnels running underneath most parts of Melbourne.

I glanced around but couldn't immediately see anything that screamed "hidey-hole"—which was the whole point of a panic room, really. But knowing Stane's love of technology, it was doubtful that he'd be anywhere without some method of knowing what was going on above him.

"Stane?" I said, voice loud. "It's safe to come out if you want to."

There was no immediate response, but after several minutes there was a soft hiss, and part of the floor under his computer desk dropped down an inch and slid to one side. Two hands appeared, and with very little ceremony, Stane hauled himself back into the room.

"Fuck," he said, face red and beaded with sweat. "That was more unpleasant than I remembered."

I raised an eyebrow. "You've used your bolt-hole before?"

"Hell yeah." He grabbed his desk with one hand and pulled himself upright. "You can't play the black market game without occasionally hitting trouble. It's been a few years, though, and I think I might have put on a bit of weight since I had it installed. Things were a little tight."

"Better tight than you getting dead," I said.

"Oh, definitely." He plonked down on his chair, his expression grim. "So what did those bastards want with me?"

"Well, not you, for a start. They wanted *me* and were merely using you as bait."

He glanced at the sprays and puddles of blood that decorated his living area. There were no bodies; even the vampire Azriel had decapitated had disappeared. I very much suspected Valdis's fire had taken care of them while I was in the bathroom puking my guts out.

"It obviously didn't go well for them," Stane commented.

"No." I glanced at the darkened bridge behind him. "How come you haven't got a backup generator installed?"

"Oh, I have, but it only keeps the main computer system going, not the peripherals."

"Peripherals being the light screens and keyboards?"

"No, they're necessary and included. I just did a quick system shutdown when I saw the vamps entering. Didn't want to chance them getting access to my baby."

I snorted softly. He thought more of his computer's safety than he did his own—anyone else would have disappeared into the panic room and let the computer fend for itself. I had no doubt it would take an exceptionally skilled hacker to access Stane's system, even if he *had* left it on and running.

"I think you need to widen the net and include security in the systems it keeps going."

"I think you could be right." He swung around and splayed his fingers across a scanning pad on his desk. A second later, his bridge came back to life. "I guess the big question is, should I expect similar attacks, or will that be the last of it?"

"We don't know," I replied. "Azriel sent a warning to the council, but whether they'll take any notice or not is another question."

"And the would-be queen bee of said council?"

"Is another matter entirely." My voice was grim. "But speaking of her, can I borrow your cell phone?"

"Sure, but why?" He dug his phone out of his pocket and tossed it over.

"Because I need to contact said queen bee."

"Just as well I've enabled the scrambler for all but selected people," he said. "I don't want her getting hold of my number."

"Stane, she's Directorate." I punched in Hunter's number, and Space Invaders began to uniformly march across the screen as the phone connected. I smiled, then added, "She can get any number she wants anytime she wants."

"Not this one, she won't," he said, amused. "When you get off the phone to her, I've got some information you might not want to see."

"Oh, fabulous." Things were obviously about to go from bad to worse—the thought had barely crossed my mind when the Space Invaders disappeared and Hunter came online. As timing went, it was pretty much perfect.

"Risa, dear," she all but purred. "What a lovely surprise it is to see you."

"I'm betting it is," I all but snapped back. "Considering your fellow council members just sent nine of their finest to finish me off."

All amusement fled, and her expression became very, *very* scary. "When did this happen?"

"About fifteen minutes ago. I take it, then, that my astral follower hasn't reported the situation to you yet?"

"No, because *that* was something I did not envisage and, as such, was not in her brief."

Meaning she'd asked for only key-related information to be relayed? If so, I very much suspected it was a situation that would now be rectified. "I'm also gathering the councillors didn't seek your approval or even ask for your opinion of the action?"

"No, they did *not*." And they would pay for that, if the icy, murderous glitter in her eyes was anything to go by. "It is hardly an action I would approve as yet."

As yet. It was a very telling slip of the tongue.

"Well, Azriel sent them a warning not to make another such attempt, but you might want to address the situation yourself." Somehow, I managed to keep most of the anger out of my voice. If there was one thing I was certain of, it was the fact that I *didn't* want her murderous fury aimed at me. I was in trouble enough with Hunter. "After all, you need me alive to find the damn key."

"I'm well aware of what I do and don't need," she snapped. "I will take care of the council. You had best concentrate on finding the keys—especially given you only have ten hours left to produce that second one."

And with that, she hung up. I blew out a breath and tossed the phone back to Stane. "Well, if there are any councillors left after she's done chastising them, I'll be very surprised."

"That would be no great loss, from what I've seen of them," Stane commented. "So that search you wanted on your accountant."

I walked across the room, grabbed a chair, and sat down. I had a bad feeling I didn't want to be standing when Stane told me the search results. "And?"

"And, as I said, it's not good news." He tapped the screen in front of him, then flicked some images across to the screen nearest me. Two were birth certificates, the other a passport document. The name on one of the certificates was Michael Judd; the name on the other two was not.

"Michael Greenfield?" I glanced at Stane. "Are you saying Mike is the missing Michael Greenfield?"

"It would certainly appear that way," Stane said, voice grim. "And if he *is*, he was born in London over a hundred and twenty years ago."

"What?" I stared at him in disbelief. "Mike *can't* be *that* old!"

"If he *is* our shape-shifter," Azriel commented, "then he can make himself appear whatever age he might wish."

"I guess." I frowned. "Although surely the strain of holding so many different forms *and* creating so much magic *should* show."

"The Aedh was his partner in crime, remember, and more than likely responsible for much of the magic used against us," Azriel said. "Besides, did you not note that Mike appeared to have aged somewhat when you met him in that restaurant?"

"Yes." I shrugged and glanced back at Stane. "What makes you think he's Greenfield?"

"Too many coincidences." He tapped Michael Judd's birth certificate. "There's nothing untoward in Judd's records until he hit the age of twenty-four. He took a year off university to 'find himself,' and promptly disappeared for several months."

"That's not exactly unusual," I commented. "Lots of kids have a gap year before going to uni."

"Yeah, but Judd disappeared in the *middle* of his courses. And certainly not all of those who take a year off so completely disappear that they don't use their bank accounts or credit cards for six months."

I raised my eyebrows. "So what happened?"

"His dad was a prominent—and well-connected—businessman, so his disappearance was given widespread publicity. As was his sudden reappearance."

"How did he explain going so completely off the grid?"

"He simply said he was living off the land with a lady friend and didn't need to access any of his accounts."

I glanced at Azriel. "I wonder if the lady friend was our shape-shifting sorceress?"

"It would seem likely," Azriel said. "And I would imagine that six months would provide ample time to learn someone's mannerisms and habits."

"I'd imagine so." I glanced at the date stamped on the passport image and did the math. "His disappearance happened a year and a half after Greenfield came into the country."

"Yes, but the timing gets even more interesting," Stane said. "Six months before Michael Judd went on a walkabout with a mysterious woman, Greenfield become acquainted with one Edward Judd—Michael's father."

He flicked another image across to my screen. Shock rolled through me, and for several seconds I couldn't even speak. All I could do was stare at the screen and the all-too-familiar figure standing with the much younger Mike and two other men I didn't recognize.

"The Aedh," Azriel growled. "More and more I regret my decision not to kill him the very moment I met him."

"More and more I'm regretting the very same thing," I muttered. I glanced back at Stane. "Who is the fourth man in that picture? I take it the one with his arm around Michael's shoulder is Edward Judd?"

Stane nodded. "The article that pic was attached to said Lucian and Judd were partners in an importing business. The other man is, according to this particular newspaper article, James Bentley."

"Who is?"

"The article didn't actually say, so I did a side search on the man. He was a long-term friend of the family and was also Edward's business adviser."

I raised my eyebrows. "Was?"

Stane nodded. "He disappeared not long after Michael Judd's reappearance. His family had him declared dead via a court order nine years later, though his body was never found."

"If he'd known the family for so long, maybe he suspected the Michael that reappeared was not the real deal."

"It's more than possible," Stane agreed. "Especially given Michael was the last person to see James alive."

Considering there was a very good chance Michael Greenfield had become Michael Judd, it was more than possible that not only was he the last person to see James alive, but also the reason he disappeared. "Did the police ever question him?"

"According to the newspaper articles, yes. I tried to track down the official police interview report, but I'm afraid they just don't keep records that far back anymore. Not for people who have been declared dead, anyway."

"When did Greenfield—via Pénombre Manufacturing—purchase that warehouse?"

"Not long after he'd arrived in Australia, apparently."

I frowned. "Why buy it, then not use it? That makes no sense."

"But he was using it," Azriel commented. "He might not have had his dark altar there, but he *was* doing magic in the caverns under that place."

That was certainly true. And, given that, maybe it was also true of other buildings. "Did Greenfield or Pénombre purchase any other buildings?"

Stane smiled. "Pénombre didn't, but Greenfield certainly did." He flicked another image over to my screen. It was a list of about half a dozen locations. "He actually bought more than these, but they've either been sold to legitimate people, or the buildings were razed, apartments built on the land, and then sold."

"Legitimate meaning you've checked them out?" I said.

He nodded. "I'm still in the process with a couple of them, but I can't immediately see or find a link back to any of our sorceress's known identities."

"And Michael Greenfield? Is he still in existence?"

"According to the tax department, yes, though it took some time to track him down, as he hasn't actually filed a return for a few years now."

"Define a few?"

"Eleven years." He grinned. "He's racking up some big fines to the tax man, I can tell you."

They could only fine him if they could find him, and I somehow doubted they ever would. Mike had obviously ditched that persona. I waved a hand at the list of six. "And these?"

"Have all been sold, but most of them have, at one point or another, been in Lauren's hands."

"So definitely a connection." I studied them for a moment, then frowned. "That place out at Altona North— who's that registered to now?"

He glanced at his screen for a second, then said, "A Mrs. Margaret Kendrick."

"A name I've seen before," I said, voice resigned. "Mike had her folder on his desk one time when I visited him. He told me he was just updating her records."

"He keeps paper records?"

I frowned. "Yeah, and I've already told you that."

"Did you? Sorry." He grinned. "Maybe the shock of someone doing it the old-fashioned way just erased it from my memory."

I snorted softly. "I'm gathering the Altona North place is still a working warehouse?"

He nodded. "Kendrick is an importer, and interestingly, many of the companies she uses are the same ones Lucian and Judd used in their import business."

"So we have a likely connection." I glanced at Azriel. "And one possibly worth checking out."

He nodded. "Although it would depend on whether or not we have a workable list of possible key sites. Hunter's deadline approaches far too fast, and we need to concentrate on our main quest rather than be sidetracked by a rogue sorceress."

"That rogue sorceress has already beaten us twice . . ." I stopped and swore. If it was Myer rather than Markel who was currently on watch duty, then I'd just made a very major goof. I mentally crossed my fingers and added silently, *I'd rather make sure she can't get to the final key before we do.*

With Lucian gone, she has no direct line to your activities.

That we know of. I'd still rather ensure she isn't around when we find the next one.

"Weeding down that list of possible locations," Stane said, obviously not noticing the fact I'd cut my sentence off midstream, "is an exasperating experience. The list is now just over fifty possible sites—which may not mean much to someone who can transport instantly, but it's still going to take time to inspect each one, and some of them have pretty fierce security systems installed."

"I can get us past security," Azriel said.

Stane snorted. "Even you wouldn't get past some of the latest motion sensors, my friend. Besides, as you said, you haven't got enough time left to be fucking around."

"But if you cannot contract that list any further, then we have no other choice." Azriel's voice was grim. "There is always the hope that we will find the key in the first half rather than the last."

I snorted. "I think we had our one and only bit of luck when that gun blew up in the vamp's hand."

"What?" Stane said, confusion evident. "Since when did vampires need guns? They have speed and teeth on their side—why would they need anything else?"

"Maybe they thought a bullet would be a faster and more secure method of killing someone who could disappear into smoke." I shrugged. "What about Michael Judd? What did he do once he'd made his reappearance?"

Stane grimaced. "Nothing out of the ordinary. He went back to university but switched courses, doing a master's in finance with a major in accounting."

"What was he doing previously?"

Stane smiled. "An arts degree in media and communication."

"And no one commented on the rather sudden change of plans? I mean, that's kinda a big jump."

"Well, no one in the media commented. By that point, he was old news. We'll never know what his old man might have said, given he died ten years ago."

"Killed?"

"No, it was a regular old heart attack. Nothing suspicious. His estate, though, was left in its entirety to Michael rather than being spread between his wife and other three children. They contested, but it was settled out of court."

No surprise there, given he wouldn't have wanted the matter raising too much of a fuss in the press. I glanced at Azriel. "Why don't we go check out that Altona North place? That gives Stane a little more time to whittle down the list."

"If you wish." He stood and held out a hand. "But after this, we must at least start searching the buildings that are on that list."

"Deal." I placed my hand in Azriel's, then glanced back at Stane. "While your computers are running that list, I'd be connecting the security system up to the generators. Just in case."

"Consider it done." His voice was grim. "I have no intention of going back into that panic room unless absolutely necessary."

"Good." The words were barely out of my mouth when Azriel's magic swirled around me, zipping us across to Altona North. We reappeared in the middle of a road. I blinked and looked around. On the left there was an open field, although in the distance I could see the lights of what looked to be some sort of chemical plant. To the right there were several large warehouses. There were a few cars in the parking lot, which was a surprise given that it was after ten at night. The one we wanted was slightly farther down the road and had a blue two-story office block running across the front of the larger warehouse building. There were lights on in several of the offices, although I couldn't actually see anyone moving about.

"You may not see them," Azriel commented, studying the warehouse intently, "but they are nevertheless there."

"How many? And is one of them our sorceress?"

"Five, and no." He paused, his gaze narrowing. "There is an odd sense of energy toward the rear of the building, however."

I studied that section of the warehouse. I couldn't see anything that appeared out of place, and I certainly wasn't feeling anything that hinted at the presence of magic. "Shall we go investigate?"

"That is what we came here for, is it not?" He drew Valdis, then added, "Follow me."

"You keep saying that," I said, as I fell in step beside him. "I would have thought that by now, you'd have come to accept the impossibility of it ever happening."

"Oh, I accept it." He glanced at me, amusement touching his lips. "But I keep saying it in the hope that *one* day, you *will* actually do the sensible thing."

"I wouldn't hold your breath waiting."

"Perhaps not," he said. "Though it would not matter if I did, because as an energy being, I do not actually have to breathe."

I nudged him lightly with my shoulder. "You'd get bored if I actually *was* sensible."

"*That* is something unlikely to happen, as I can think of many, many things we could do to relieve the onset of boredom."

I grinned. "So can I. And I bet mine would be a whole lot more imaginative than yours."

"That is a bet I would *not* take if I were you." His gaze

went to the office portion of the warehouse. "Two people are about to leave for the night."

I glanced ahead. There were no cars parked along this side of the warehouse, so we were safe from discovery. "And the other three?"

"Working."

"So there's no one in the warehouse at the moment?"

"*That* I'm not so certain of." He touched my elbow, lightly guiding me forward again. "The strange energy is very definitely present at the rear of the building, and I cannot see past it."

I frowned. "So is it magic, or something else?"

He hesitated. "I think it is magic, but it feels fouler— more corrupted—than anything we've come across so far."

Considering we'd come across some pretty foul magic, that was saying something. We cautiously made our way down the driveway. There were two large loading bays down this side of the building, but both roller doors were down and locked. There was also a regular door at the far end of the building, with a wooden bench sitting under a nearby tree and a bin filled with rubbish and cigarette butts to one side of it. Obviously, a retreat for the smokers.

We walked across to the door and Azriel tested the handle. It turned. He glanced at me, one eyebrow raised in surprise, then carefully opened the door and slipped inside. I followed.

There were no lights on in this section of the warehouse and the air felt cool. There was also a feeling of vastness to the darkness; it almost felt as if it were one big, empty space. And yet there were shelves nearby, most of which held stock, if the odd-shaped shadows were anything to go by.

I'm not feeling anyone close by, I said. *And I still can't feel the magic. Where is it?*

Ahead and down.

His fingers clasped mine; then he tugged me forward. Though our steps were whisper quiet, they nevertheless seemed to echo. Or maybe it just seemed that way because of the tension that was beginning to build within me.

Down? Meaning we're dealing with yet another basement?

It would appear our sorceress has a penchant for them.

Well, let's hope this one doesn't contain any nasty surprises.

He glanced over his shoulder, his blue eyes bright in the cover of night. *That is another thing I would not bet on.*

I certainly wasn't. She'd been one step ahead of us all along, so it would be stupid to think that she'd be unprepared when it came to her remaining bolt-holes. She *had* to be aware by now that we'd already destroyed—or otherwise made unusable—at least three of her ceremony and storage sites.

We continued across the vast space. As my eyes got used to the deeper darkness of this place, I realized that most of the shelves held a mix of tableware, home décor, and glassware, from all over the world. Some of the names stamped on the crates I recognized, and they were definitely upmarket. If Margaret Kendrick *was* another identity of Lauren's—or Mike's, given that we had no idea which form or sex our shape-shifter actually preferred—then she was obviously doing rather well. There was a fortune's worth of stock sitting in this warehouse alone.

About three-quarters of the way across the warehouse, Azriel made a sharp turn left. The laden shelving towered above us and made it seem like we were walking through a canyon. Ahead a green exit sign glowed brightly at the top of a single doorway.

I frowned. *That's the rear wall of the warehouse—are we heading back out again?*

I doubt it, given the energy I feel is below, not above-

ground. He stopped at the doorway and lightly pressed his fingertips against the sturdy metal door. Nothing happened. *Be wary. Whatever it is I feel, it lies beyond this door.*

I nodded and drew Amaya. Her hiss was a sound of displeasure. *Draw sooner,* she muttered. *Safer.*

Not when there's nothing attacking, I replied. *Don't tell me you're bored back there, Amaya.*

Not, she replied, somewhat huffily. *Concerned am.*

I grinned and stepped back a little as Azriel raised Valdis and shoved her point into the door's deadlock. With very little fuss, her flames melted both the lock and the bolt, and the door swung silently open.

It looked altogether too much like an invitation for my liking.

The door didn't open to the outside world, but, as Azriel had suspected, into a basement area. The stairs leading down into deeper darkness were concrete, and the air smelled reasonably fresh. But it was too black to be ordinary darkness, even if there was no immediate sense of danger. I certainly couldn't smell anything that represented any sort of threat.

And I can't sense anything because of that foul energy. His expression was grim when his gaze met mine. *This time, you* will *stay behind me.*

I nodded. While I might not be able to feel any threat, the fact that he couldn't was enough to have warning bells ringing. *Be careful. The dark sorceress is aware of what you are, and she's had the time—and no doubt the coaching from Lucian—to work out some way of nullifying your presence.*

I am aware of that. Watch the first step—it is deeper than it looks.

I gripped the cold metal handrail and stepped down into the stairwell. The shadows seemed deeper for some reason, and tension rolled through me. While I wished we could use the swords to light our way, that would only be a warning to whoever—whatever—might lay below that we were coming.

Azriel headed down cautiously. I followed, keeping close to his back, Amaya's mutterings a sharp accompaniment to the gathering sense of expectation.

Azriel reached the final step and paused. I peered over his shoulder. Ahead in the distance light glowed, but it was a strange blue-black color that flickered and danced. *Candlelight.*

Yes. And the energy comes from the room at the end of this hall, as well.

And you still can't sense anything?

No. He glanced at me. *But if there is candlelight, then someone has lit it.*

Maybe. And maybe not. After all, we were dealing with someone who had the capability of making transport stones. Just because she *had* been here didn't mean she still was.

We crept on. The long corridor was narrow, meaning even if I *had* wanted to walk beside him, I couldn't. My grip tightened on Amaya and her background noise ratcheted up. The odd violet-black light continued to dance and flicker, and my skin crawled. I might not be able to sense the energy or magic that Azriel was, but something still felt very wrong.

We reached the open doorway. Azriel stopped, forcing me to do the same. Flames flickered briefly down Valdis's blade, but they were very similar in color to the light that crawled from the room beyond, and almost unnoticeable.

Anything? I asked.

Only the candles. He glanced at me. *Which only makes me suspect something is, indeed, here. Watch our backs.*

I licked my lips and nodded. He stepped into the room, then paused, body tense. Nothing happened. I pressed my back against the wall and followed him in. The room was largish but unlike the other underground chambers we'd discovered, as there was no shelving here, either hewn into the walls or freestanding. There was a table, and markings on the floor I suspected were incantations of some kind, but no pentagram and certainly no altar.

There were, however, two cuneiform stones. They were smaller, darker, than their kin, and had once stood in a square windowless room within a property that had been inhabited by several—now dead—Razan.

At least we now knew where the damn things had gone. But did that mean this space was a recently created one? The etchings on the floor didn't look new, but that didn't mean all that much.

Light flickered in the middle of the room, brighter and fiercer than the candlelight. It disappeared as quickly as it had appeared, but it sent my pulse rate into overdrive. Something was very definitely about to happen, and I really wasn't sure either of us should be here when it did.

Then perhaps you should follow instinct and leave, Azriel said.

We'll never find our sorceress if I give in to the urge to run, I replied, perhaps more tartly than I should have. *Besides, whatever is waiting here, I'm sure it would be better faced with two swords rather than one.*

He didn't comment, but his displeasure echoed through me. We edged farther into the room. Again light flickered, and I realized—with more than a little trepidation—that it was coming from the floor. Or rather, from the etched markings *on* the floor. I paused, watching an oddly dirty beam of light slip through the various markings and race toward the stones. Nothing happened when it reached them. It just disappeared into the middle of them. The stones weren't active, so the light could hardly have traveled

anywhere, but that didn't stop the crawling sense of unease from getting stronger.

Azriel stopped so abruptly I ran into him. He reached
back to steady me, but his concentration was on a spot
several feet ahead of us.

What's wrong? I frowned at the spot, but whatever it
was he was seeing or feeling, I wasn't.

*That foul energy I mentioned? It lies within arm's
length of us.*

What is it doing?

Nothing. It simply sits there. He took one step sideways, his eyes narrowed. *It could be some sort of barrier,
given it forms a protective semicircle around the standing
stones.*

Air stirred, and the hairs along the back of my neck
rose. I shot a glance over my shoulder, but I couldn't see
anything or anyone. But *that* seemed to be a running
theme in this place, at least for me. *Amaya, is there anyone behind us?*

Not. She paused. *Not live, anyway.*

Meaning there's something dead behind us? My grip
on her tightened.

Not dead. Not flesh.

Magic? Demon?

Not certain.

Great. If my demon sword didn't know what the hell
was approaching, what chance did I have? I glanced
back at Azriel. *Maybe you were right. Maybe we should
get the hell out—*

I broke off as the cuneiform stones came to life. Light
flared between them, warm and soft, shimmering softly
in the candlelit darkness.

Someone is using the stones.

And that someone is undoubtedly our sorceress, Azriel
said. *There are no Razan left.*

That we know of. But she was using blood magic to create her own twisted version, remember?

They were little more than programmable killing machines, he bit back. The warm light was getting stronger and sent slivers of light swirling across the darkness, lifting it, revealing more of the barren concrete space. It was bigger than it had seemed.

It doesn't matter who it is, I said. *We can't get to them thanks to the goddamn barrier!*

Then perhaps we should see if we can remove the barrier. As the light between the stones grew brighter, he raised Valdis to shoulder height, then glanced at me. *Step back.*

As I did, he drew Valdis back, then plunged her into the middle of the barrier. For an instant, nothing happened.

Then Valdis screamed, the invisible barrier abruptly came to life, and the room exploded.

Chapter 11

The force of the explosion picked me up and threw me backward. Amaya's flames flared around me, cushioning my fall somewhat and protecting me from the concrete and heat that spewed all around us.

Azriel? I screamed mentally. *Are you okay?*

There was no reply. Panic surged, but there was little I could do until the shrapnel and whatever else was flying around the room had stopped. If there was one thing I *did* know, it was that he'd be madder than hell if I put myself in harm's way just to see if he was okay.

And surely to *god* he had to be. He was a reaper, an energy being, and no easy kill.

But that didn't mean he *couldn't* be killed, and he'd been a lot closer to the explosion than I had.

I took a deep, shuddery breath, but it didn't do a whole lot to ease the fear-based churning in my gut. As the noise, the heat, and the shards of metal and concrete calmed, I ordered Amaya to lower the shield and carefully rose. Dust, thick and heavy, swirled through the large room, making it difficult to breathe, let alone see.

Azriel? I cocked my head sideways, listening intently, trying to catch even the smallest sound. What I did hear was coming from behind us—footsteps, running toward the room. Obviously, the people still working in the offices had heard the explosion.

I swore and took a tentative step forward. Metal

crunched under my feet, the sound like that of old bones. I shivered and hoped it wasn't an omen of some kind.

Azriel, please, answer me. I took another step. Blue flickered through the dusty darkness up ahead—Valdis. Hope surged. If Valdis had survived, then surely Azriel had as well. But as much as I wanted to rush over there, I couldn't. I needed to do something to stop those people from coming in here. I had no idea what other tricks Lauren might have up her sleeve, but I doubted this explosion would be the last of them. I didn't need innocent bystanders getting caught in the middle of a firefight.

So even though it went against every instinct I had, I resolutely turned around, raced back up the stairs, and closed the door. Azriel had destroyed the lock, but there was a heavy old dead bolt near the top of the door, so I slammed that home, then brought Amaya down on the handrail, chopping off a chunk of metal and wedging it under the door. They'd force their way in eventually, but at least I'd bought some time.

I spun and went back down into the dusty darkness. Valdis's light pulsed across the shadows, reminding me oddly of a lighthouse beacon. I hoped like hell it was a beacon that was guiding me toward good news, not bad.

I swallowed heavily, my stomach churning faster and faster the closer I got. I couldn't see anything resembling a dust-covered body, be it alive or dead. I couldn't smell blood or ruined flesh, either, and that was comforting. At the very least, he hadn't been blown into little tiny pieces.

Valdis's light got stronger, angrier. She was lying on the cracked and filthy concrete, the flames flaring down her sides pulsing between blue and red. She was furious, and I can't say I blamed her. I'd be furious, if I wasn't so scared.

I stopped and looked around. The dust was beginning to settle, and Valdis's light was strong enough to lift the thicker shadows. The standing stones were still and dark once more. I had no idea what had activated them, but certainly no one had come through them. But maybe that had never been the point. Maybe all along the barrier had been the trap, and the stones nothing more than a distraction.

It was a trap Azriel had not only sprung, but been ensnared by.

I flexed my fingers, trying to control my fear, trying to think rather than panic. He had to be alive. He couldn't be dead. Not like this.

Is not, Amaya said.

I frowned. *How do you know?*

Sword, she replied. *He dead, she dead.*

I closed my eyes against the rush of relief and tears. Valdis's furious flames might be a good sign, but that didn't mean he'd escaped unscathed. Didn't mean that death might not yet be his fate.

Damn it, he *couldn't* die. I wouldn't let him!

I reached down to grab Valdis, then hesitated and asked, *Amaya, will Valdis mind me picking her up?*

No, she replied. *One you are.*

Meaning me and Azriel, I gathered, not me and Valdis. *Can you speak to her?*

If wish.

Ask her if she knows where Azriel is.

Amaya was silent for a moment, then said, *Know not. Alive is all.*

I grimaced, but I'd guessed it wasn't going to be *that* easy. Not given who undoubtedly had him.

Fear rose again, but I shut it down ruthlessly. Now was *not* the time for panic or fear. If it *was* Lauren who had him—and really, this had her fingerprints all over it, not Hunter's—then it would be for one reason: to either get me to come to her or to hold him as ransom until the key was found.

Either way, she'd be in contact with me sooner rather

than later, and that meant I had better get myself organized and ready to fight.

Because this *would* end.

Lauren, or Mike, or whatever the hell his or her name really was, had caused enough problems and done enough damage. I'd stopped Lucian and I'd fucking stop her, as well.

Something heavy hit the door behind me, the sound echoing loudly in the dusty chamber. I jumped and spun. The door quivered under the impact but held firm. For how much longer I had no idea. I scooped Valdis up, then stalked across to the standing stones. They didn't react to my presence, but then, none of them ever had when I'd been in human form. I hesitated, then reached out and tentatively touched the surface of one of them.

The black stone was cool and slick under my fingertips, but within its heart, energy pulsed, making it seem as if the rock was alive and waiting. And I guess in some ways it was, as that beat was the magic, ready to react.

Stepping through the gateway would be the obvious action if I wanted to find Azriel, but I had no doubt that *that* was precisely what Lauren wanted. Just as I had no doubt that there'd be some sort of trap waiting for me on the other side of this gateway.

The door shuddered under another impact. I bit my lip and glanced over my shoulder. There were serious dents and splits in it now; it wouldn't take too many more blows before it gave way.

I returned my gaze to the stones. It was tempting—so tempting—to throw caution to the wind and step through them. But as much as I wanted to find Azriel and finally kill our sorceress, it would be a stupid course of action. I couldn't risk everything on the chance that I'd somehow be able to defeat Lauren as I was right *now*. Besides, it wasn't just my life I was risking these days, but that of my child.

Lauren had been one step ahead of us all the way; there was no reason to believe she still wasn't. And Mike had seen the charm on my wrist, and no doubt he/she had already found a way to counter it.

I needed advice. I needed a plan. And the only people who could offer that in *this* sort of situation were once again the Brindle witches. But they would also need to know what they were up against. We weren't dealing with just a sorceress capable of blood magic; we were dealing with one who'd been taught the art of Aedh magic. And whether the Brindle witches could even counter it, I had *no* idea.

Another blow hit the door, and this time the small split became a fissure. I thrust Valdis through my shirt to keep her secure and free my hands, then pushed up my sleeves and squatted beside the nearest stone. I took a deep breath that failed to calm the butterflies doing speed laps around my stomach, then wrapped my arms around the stone and heaved upward. The damn thing was lighter than it looked and came away so easily from the concrete that I just about flung it over my shoulders.

I hugged it close, my bare arms against the slick stone, its inner pulse beating against my skin. Moving it away from its twin obviously hadn't done anything to disrupt whatever magic fueled these things.

As the door's hinges began to groan and give way under the force of yet more blows, I called to the Aedh—and hoped like hell the stone would change right along with the rest of me.

It did.

Though it felt damn weird. It was almost as if I had an additional heart, but its pulse was oddly dark and foul in feel. I turned and watched as the door finally gave way and two men entered, one carrying what looked like some sort of ax, without the sharper end. As they glanced around, confusion on their faces, I slipped past them and made my way back through the warehouse and out into the night.

It took me longer than it normally would have to get across to the Brindle. The magic contained within my particles was not only heavy, but also very draining. The lack of strength *might* have been due to my inability to keep food down of late—which meant I was running more on reserves and determination than anything else—but I rather suspected it was more to do with the stone itself. Our sorceress had created these things, at least in part, through her own blood and life force. Maybe the magic sustained itself that way, too. And because I had wrapped it within my particles, it had naturally started draining *me*.

The Brindle finally came into sight. I shifted downward, calling to the Aedh and flowing into human form on the grassy area at the front of the building. I stumbled and hit the ground knees first, my body shaking and my head light. The stone was still clasped tight to my chest, so I released the thing and instantly felt a little better. A little cleaner.

I drew a shuddery breath, then looked up at the Brindle, waiting for someone to come out. I didn't want to cart the stone inside—and seriously doubted I'd be able to, anyway, given the Brindle's restrictions on evil entering its space—but I had no doubt the witches would be aware of my sudden appearance. They would have at least felt the ripple of the stone's foulness across the magic that protected this place.

I had to wait only a second or so before three figures appeared—Ilianna, Zaira, and Kiandra. But as Ilianna took the stairs two at a time and ran toward me, there was something in her face—a light in her eyes—that told me she really *had* become a part of this place. At that moment, I had no doubt that she and Carwyn would come to an agreement and that she and I would never share a house again. We *would* remain close for the rest of our lives, but things could and would never go back to what they were before all this madness began.

I blinked back tears—again, selfish ones, because life itself was all about change, not remaining static—and smiled as she all but slid to a halt in front of me.

"I'm okay," I said swiftly, "despite my somewhat inelegant landing."

"Maybe, but what the fuck is *that*?" She knelt on the other side of the cuneiform stone and tentatively reached out a hand. She didn't touch it, however, but hovered her fingers an inch above the stone.

"It's another of those cuneiform stones."

She frowned. "It's rather small, isn't it? Aren't all the others at least six feet tall?"

"Yes, but don't let its size fool you," I said. "It's as powerful as its taller brethren."

"Do they all feel this damn nasty?"

"Yeah, but then, a very nasty sorceress made them."

"I think 'nasty' is underdescribing the bitch." She pulled her hand away and sat back on her heels. "Why bring it here?"

"Because I wanted to know if the warding bracelet you made me is strong enough to withstand the assault of someone capable of *this* sort of magic." I half shrugged. "I figured if I brought one of them here, you'd have a greater idea of what I face."

"We are well aware of what you face." Kiandra stopped beside Ilianna. "But we can give no guarantee as to whether the wards will withstand the type of magic that burns within that stone. It is a very foul mix of both the magic from this world *and* the other."

I glanced at the stone lying in front of me. "But if it wasn't actually created with blood magic, shouldn't the wards hold up against it? It's only blood magic that's the problem, isn't it?"

"Again, I cannot say." She studied me for a moment, then said, "What has happened?"

I took a deep, somewhat shuddery breath, and said,

voice surprisingly calm, "We walked into a trap. Azriel was taken."

Ilianna sucked in a breath. "Is he . . . ?"

I smiled, but it felt grim. False. "He's okay." Or, at the very least, he was alive. "I'd know if it were otherwise."

"The sorceress using his life as a bargaining chip for the key is not quite what I had envisioned," Kiandra murmured. "I had thought it would be Hunter."

"Our sorceress is nothing if not adaptable." Once again I shoved fear and the need to be doing something—anything—rather than kneeling here calmly discussing logistics and magic back into its box. I couldn't allow fear free, because it could all too swiftly become debilitating. And if I rushed, I could kill everything—everyone—I was trying to save. "And given that everyone else who means anything to me is otherwise protected, I guess he's the logical target."

"But your reaper would not be an easy target to contain," Zaira said. She tucked a hand under Ilianna's elbow and helped her rise. "Creating a cage capable of such a feat should have weakened her."

"*Should* being the operative word there," Kiandra commented, "Remember, she has had access to Aedh craft and spells, and we have no knowledge of the effects *that* will have on human flesh and spirit. It may not leave her anywhere near as debilitated as blood magic."

"True." Zaira's expression was pensive. "Perhaps the only safe way to counter any spells designed to capture or otherwise control your actions would be to somehow *not* be you."

I frowned. "She knows I'm part Aedh. She'd surely take that into account in any magic she aims my way. And given her connection to Lucian, she undoubtedly knows I'm also a face shifter."

"Face shifting is not the answer," Kiandra said. "Any alternate form you may take is still you."

Join, Amaya said. *Then magic not problem.*

I blinked. *What?*

Join, she said again. *Become one. Then not flesh or steel but both.*

My heart began to race. As solutions went, it was a pretty damn good one. There was just one slight problem, and that was Amaya herself. *The last time we became one, you decided you liked being in my body and I had to battle to get you back into the sword.*

Weak you were, she said, somewhat huffily. *Not so now.*

Which isn't actually a guarantee you'll leave when asked.

Can't eat her soul in flesh. The huffy tone was even more pronounced. *And eat will.*

That's one promise I sure as hell hope you'll keep.

Will, she said. *Together we strong.*

Maybe, but it was yet to be seen whether we were stronger than a dark sorceress. Or, indeed, a mad vampire with the power of a god behind her.

"I may have a solution that will work." I glanced at Ilianna. "But I need to find Azriel fast, and I don't want to use the stones to do it."

"No," Kiandra said. "A very well-prepared trap would undoubtedly wait at the other end of them."

"Then *I'll* search for him," Ilianna said. "Wait here while I get my athame."

She turned and ran back to the Brindle. I returned my gaze to Kiandra. "Would destroying this stone have any rebound effect on the sorceress's strength?"

Kiandra hesitated. "Possibly, but it is not something I'd wish to do within the grounds of this place, as we could not guarantee that the evil bound within the stone would be deflected by the Brindle's shields once released."

I frowned. "But you have my father's warding stones in place now—shouldn't they work?"

"Again, possibly, but we are talking about a bastardization of magic from this world *and* the next. I will not risk the lives of all those within these walls on such un-certainty. Not when there are greater perils to be dealt with first."

Like keeping the final gate to hell safe and secure. She might not have said it, but she was certainly thinking it.

"Besides," Zaira added, "it would warn your sorceress that her plans have gone awry. That might not be a wise move if you wish to save your reaper."

"Which is why I came here rather than charging head-first through the stones," I said. "And you have no idea how hard it was to *not* do that."

Zaira gripped my arm and lightly squeezed. "It's not easy to kill a reaper—and the sorceress would be foolish to even *attempt* it before she gained possession of the key. There is time yet."

I took another of those deep, shuddery breaths and released it slowly. "I know. It's just that ... everything that can go wrong has gone wrong so far. I don't want Azriel to join that list."

"That possibility has been there from the beginning," Kiandra said, "and the reaper was more than aware of that fact."

I met her gaze. "That may be true, but it's not exactly comforting right now."

"You must be prepared to fight *hard*, regardless of who or what is at risk," Kiandra said. "Because unless you are, you will lose, and you will take this world down with you."

"I'm more than a little aware of what is at stake," I said, voice grim. "And more than willing to kill both women at the heart of this mess. I just need help to do it."

"I know, and I do not mean to chastise you in any way. It is more a warning. The fights that approach—" She hesitated and half shrugged. "It will, in the end, fall to you alone to end all this, no matter what outside help you might have."

Which was both what I expected and what I feared. That, in the end, it would be just me and Hunter and the fate of the world hanging on the outcome.

Ilianna appeared at the top of the steps, athame in one hand. As she ran toward us, Kiandra added, "I wish you luck, young Risa. Leave the stone where it is—it can hurt no one when separated from its twin. We'll deal with it when all this is over and done, one way or another."

She turned and walked gracefully away. I had an odd feeling I wouldn't see her again, even if I did survive the next nine hours.

Zaira stepped forward and kissed my cheeks. "Good luck," she said softly. "Not that I think you will need it. You have grown in so many ways over these last few weeks, Risa. I truly believe neither Hunter nor the sorceress really understands the force they now face."

I smiled, though it felt tight. "I'd like to think that's true, but I'm afraid they both know altogether *too* much about me. They certainly know all about my weakness."

"But your weaknesses are also your strengths. Had they realized that, I doubt they would have taken the paths they now have."

I frowned. The paths they *now* have? "Does that mean Hunter has a kidnap plot up and running as we speak?"

Because if that *were* the case, then I had better warn Rhoan as soon as I could. He might not be happy about me harping on about the risk he was under, but he *was* the only one she had any hope of getting her grubby little mitts on right now.

Zaira hesitated. "I cannot tell you that for sure. I just know both evils are on very similar paths."

"Fabulous." *Not,* as Amaya would say.

Zaira hugged me briefly again, then turned and followed Kiandra back to the Brindle. Ilianna stopped in front of me and gestured toward the sword shoved through my T-shirt. "Is that Valdis?"

"Yes." I pulled her free and held her out.

Ilianna reached out but didn't immediately take her. "Will she mind?"

"I doubt it. Not if it helps find Azriel."

"Oh. Good." She somewhat tentatively wrapped her fingers around Valdis's hilt. Flames flickered briefly down her bright blade, but otherwise there was little reaction.

Ilianna moved several feet away and placed Valdis at her feet. She raised the athame, holding it forward and slightly to the right of shoulder height. Facing east, she drew a pentacle in the air, then said, "Masters of the Watchtowers of the East, Masters of the Air; I wake and summon you to witness my works and to guard the Circle."

She turned to the south, then west and north, repeating the pentacles and beseeching the masters of fire, water, and earth for their protection. A light wind sprung up, teasing the ends of her hair and tugging lightly at her clothes. Then it died, replaced by a sense of watchfulness.

She sat cross-legged on the ground, placed Valdis across her lap, and began the finding incantation.

I paced. I simply *couldn't* stand still. I needed to be moving, to be doing something, and pacing was better than nothing. It was certainly better than worrying over the fact that I couldn't ring Rhoan right away because the phone was in bits or over what might be happening to Azriel . . . I shoved the thought away. He was alive. For now, that was all that mattered.

I have no idea how much time passed, because I wasn't wearing a watch, but it seemed like hours rather than the ten minutes or so it probably was before Ilianna made a move.

She rose, made a motion with her athame to remove the protection circle, then walked toward me. The night's shadows played across her face and made her look tired and worn; my requests were taking a toll on her, and guilt slithered through me. No more, I promised mentally. She'd done enough for me, and so had the Brindle witches. As Kiandra had said, the fights from now on were mine, and mine alone. It was time to acknowledge that and just get on with it.

Though that *didn't* mean I would walk into any fight unprepared. I wasn't *that* stupid.

"Any success?" I asked, even as I feared the worst.

She smiled and handed me Valdis. "Yes, although he's protected by some very fierce barriers."

"That's not exactly unexpected."

"No." She ran a hand through her hair, pushing it away from her face. It just made the tiredness more evident. "He's at that second warehouse you and Jak found."

Surprise ran through me. I thought they'd be somewhere new rather than someplace we'd been before. But then, I guess it *was* situated on a ley line, which enabled the sorceress to tap into that magic and use it to power her own. She might even be able to siphon the force of the ley-line intersection near Stane's through it.

I shoved Valdis back through the tear in my shirt. "Then that's where we'll head."

"You really shouldn't go alone—"

"There is no other choice," I cut in gently. "Kiandra's right. This is my fight. You've all done what you can to help me, but in the end, I'm the only one who has any chance against them."

And I had to hope that the Brindle's barrier had kept my Cazador watcher out of earshot. Because if it was Myer rather than Markel, then I'd just outed myself to Hunter.

Ilianna stepped forward and wrapped her arms around me, her hug fierce, almost desperate. "Just be careful. Please. I couldn't bear to lose you as well as Tao—"

I pulled away slightly. "Tao's doing fine. He and the fire elemental have come to an agreement. He has to spend his nights up at Macedon, but he'll have the days free."

"Oh, thank *god*," she breathed. "When did you see him?"

"A couple of hours ago. He was just heading back to the sacred site so the elemental can take over."

"That's a good sign, then." She gave me a twisted half smile. "Now I just need you safe, and all will be good in the world again."

"Believe me, I have no plans to become a dark angel just yet." I hugged her again but kept it brief, then pulled away. "You'd better go back inside and get some rest. You look like crap."

She laughed. "There's a case of the pot calling the kettle black, if I ever heard one."

"True. Go. Amaya and I have to prepare ourselves for our meeting with the sorceress."

Her laughter faded, but she didn't say anything, just turned and ran for the Brindle. I had a suspicion she didn't want me to see her fear. Or her tears.

I waited until she'd disappeared inside and the Brindle's grand old doors had closed once more against the night, then drew Amaya. Lilac flames rippled down the sides of her shadowed blade, and her expectant, excited hum began to roll across the outer edges of my mind.

"Let's get this party started," I said, voice grim. "Amaya, become one with me."

For a moment, nothing happened. Then the lilac fire exploded, becoming a minifireball as power surged across the night, the steel, and me with equal ferocity. It was a storm that tore my core apart, then pieced me back together, all within a heartbeat.

Only it was no longer just me in this body, but *we*.

Amaya was once again within me, sharing my flesh and my thoughts, even as we shared powers and abilities. It was a strange, unsettling sensation, but one I was more than happy to put up with if it saved both my butt and Azriel's.

I called to the Aedh. The magic's response was both swifter and more powerful than ever before, and I couldn't help wondering whether the union with a demon spirit had amplified its power. In particle form, we turned and headed for the warehouse as fast as possible. The night blurred around us, and the headlights of the cars and trucks on the streets below were little more than bright streaks of light.

It didn't take us long to reach the old defense site in Maribyrnong, where the second of Lauren's warehouses was located. There were several other similarly old warehouses located along the same section of road, all of them little more than large concrete boxes. There were no cars in this immediate area, and there didn't seem to be anyone moving about.

Which didn't mean there wasn't anyone here.

Azriel was, for starters. Ilianna's finding spells were never wrong, and I seriously doubted Lauren would have been able to move him in the brief time it had taken me to get here. Besides, it took almost as much time and effort to dismantle spells as it did to create them. She'd hardly have set this place up as a trap, then flee the minute I didn't step into it precisely how she'd planned.

We did a quick circle around the building. It was a two-story structure, with small, evenly spaced windows lining both levels. The bottom ones were protected by metal bars, but not the top. I couldn't see anything unusual or out of place, nor could I feel any sort of magic. But I had no doubt that it was here.

We arrowed closer. Tension rolled through us—mine

more fear based, Amaya's filled with the need to rent and tear and consume. She really *was* a bloodthirsty little demon.

Is, she said, her voice echoing weirdly through the mass that was the two of us, *what demons meant to do.*

I guessed it was—and it wasn't like I could complain given that very bloodthirstiness had saved my backside more than once.

As we drew close enough to look through some of the windows, energy began to flicker across my particles. Its touch was unclean but powerful, and warning enough that magic *was* active here. But what, exactly, it was set to do was undoubtedly the question we would soon find an answer to.

I spun around and headed for the rear of the building. When Jak and I had come here, we'd gotten into the warehouse through a window left partially open at the back of the building. We'd left it as we'd found it, so unless Lauren had discovered it was open, it might still be possible to get in that way. If the magic didn't stop us, that was.

The window was still open. I hesitated, then cursed myself for doing so and slipped in through the small gap. Energy crawled across me, pinpricks of power that nipped and stung my particles, but they didn't impede our entry in any way.

But maybe *that* wasn't the intent behind the magic. Maybe it was nothing more than an early warning system. If it was, then Lauren would now undoubtedly be aware of my presence, and *that* meant I had to be more cautious.

I looked around. This room hadn't changed any since the last time I was here. Metal shelving lined the walls, but there was little else except dust. I scooted under the small gap between the door and the concrete floor, then checked out the various rooms on this upper level—all of which were still empty—before making my way downstairs.

The foul bite of magic got stronger. Amaya hissed in annoyance, the sound grating as it echoed through our joined beings. I ignored it and swept around the room, trying to see what traps—if any—Lauren might have left here. Again, there was nothing to see but dust, and it was only the magic that nipped at our particles that told me anything had changed since the last time we were here. There were certainly no obvious signs of magic—no black candles, pentagrams, or other magical accoutrements, and certainly no conventional types of security, like cameras, guards, or demons.

But then, most of the other times we'd been attacked by some form of demon, they hadn't actually appeared until we'd gained flesh form.

I did another run around the inside perimeter, just to be certain I hadn't missed anything obvious—and given my current state of tiredness, that was certainly a possibility. But other than the furniture remnants left in offices that lined the street side of the building, this place was a vast, empty space. Which left only the stairs—or rather, the hole Azriel had created under them when we'd raided this place and discovered the tunnels and caverns our sorceress had created beneath the building.

That was where Lauren was.

That was where Azriel was.

And it was undoubtedly also where any trap would be.

But it wasn't like I had any other choice. Not if I wanted to save Azriel and kill the bitch who held him.

We one, Amaya said. *Magic not stick.*

I hope like hell you're right, my friend, because otherwise we could be in trouble.

Trouble not, she said. *Trust must.*

I did trust her. It was the sorceress I didn't trust.

We went over to the hole and carefully looked down,

every particle tense, ready to run or fight, depending on what happened. Nothing did, but that only made the tension worse, not better. The hole revealed nothing more than a deep well of blackness, and everything was silent, still.

I half thought about dropping down in Aedh form, but that would probably be a move she'd expect. So I edged away from the hole, hunkered down to present less of a target to anything that might attack the minute we appeared, and called to the Aedh again.

The madmen in my head did their usual mad dance around my brain as I regained flesh form, but I had a feeling the lack of food was causing that rather than it being an aftereffect of the change.

I remained where I was, gaze roaming the building's shadowed interior, body tense as we waited for something to happen. The concrete was cold against my knees and the air chill as it caressed my body through the newly created holes in my clothes.

But again, there was no response from the magic I could still feel. There wasn't even any familiar scent in the air. Lauren and Azriel were certainly here, but they *weren't* in the chamber immediately below the perfectly circular hole in the concrete.

My gaze returned to it. There wasn't a doubt in my mind that there was a trap waiting in one of the rooms below, and that we *would* spring it, sooner rather than later. But if Amaya was right, and Lauren *couldn't* spell us when we were combined, then maybe our best chance of beating the bitch was to make her think she *had*.

Amaya, I said, *can your steel still merge with my flesh when you're inside me rather than it?*

Yes, she said. *Steel still connected to us. Magic still within.*

Excellent. *And would it be possible for Valdis to take on a darker shade of steel?*

Yes, she said again. *Sneaky you are.*

I half smiled. *I think it's the company I've been keeping. Can you ask Valdis to take on your coloring?*

Am. She fell silent for a moment; then flames flickered down Valdis's sides, blue at first, then gradually shifting to a darker violet. Her steel went from bright silver to a gray that was almost, but not quite, black.

Best can do, Amaya said. *Shadowed steel hard to copy.*

It'll do. Neither Lauren nor Mike had actually seen Amaya, so they'd only be going on what Lucian might have told them. *Okay, now we need to conceal your blade.*

Hold flat, she said. *Press.*

I rose and pressed her blade against my chest and stomach. Energy stirred, prickling across my skin, its touch heated and clean compared to the foul feel of magic that filled this warehouse.

Harder, Amaya said. *Hurt not.*

I pressed harder. The hilt dug into my skin but, as she'd promised, didn't actually hurt. The prickle of energy increased, and the sword began to disappear. It seeped into my flesh, the sharp tip of the blade the first to merge, but the rest of it soon followed, until my hands were pressing against my chest rather than the hilt of the blade. I could feel it within me—it was a weight that was oddly warm, an energy ready and waiting to be called and used—but it wasn't restricting in any way. I twisted from side to side just to be sure, then smiled and hefted Valdis. Lilac fire rippled down her sides and my smile grew. Lauren would see precisely what she expected to see. Nothing more, nothing less.

Hopefully, it would be enough.

I jumped into the hole and dropped swiftly into the darkness, landing lightly and half-crouched. It was pitch-black and as still as death. There was no sense that anything or anyone was near; even the foul bite of magic seemed to have disappeared.

Anything? I asked Amaya.

Something, she said. *Not here.*

That wasn't really surprising. This chamber had appeared to be little more than a storage area; the place where she'd had her pentagram and where she'd performed her magic had been in one of the chambers that ran off the two tunnels that were accessed from this one. I did destroy that particular pentagram, but I guess for a sorceress of her power, that wouldn't have been much of an impediment.

Could you ask Valdis to provide a little light? The last thing I wanted was to be moving around in this utter ink and stumble into a more conventional trap.

Flames flared brighter down Valdis's sides, half lifting the shadows and lending the rough-hewn walls a faint lilac glow. Nothing appeared to have changed since the last time we'd been here. The few small tables that had been hacked out of the soil and stone were still empty, but the clean spots in the thick grime that had items she'd moved before we'd raided the place were disappearing under yet more dust.

I turned and headed for the first of the two tunnels that led from this room. I chose the one that had held her pentagram, as it was the most likely place for a trap to wait. The tunnel was small and narrow and cut so roughly into the earth that the sharp edges tore at my already shredded clothing and down into skin. Thankfully, it wasn't all that long, and I soon found myself standing in another chamber. This also held empty shelves and tables hewn out of the earth, but there was one major difference here. A very elaborate protection circle had been etched into the stone floor, and the melted remains of black candles sat on each of the four cardinal points.

The twin scents of frankincense and cedar that had been so evident last time had faded greatly, however, as had the sharper, almost caustic aroma that Azriel had said was the scent of hell. My gaze went to the floor; the place where I'd scored the circle that had been etched into the stone—therefore breaking the circle and its ability to protect—had not been fixed. The magic within this room was no longer active.

They weren't here.

I squeezed back through the rough-hewn tunnel, gaining yet more scratches—some of them deep enough to bleed. The sharp scent seemed to fill the air, and somewhere out there in the deeper darkness, evil stirred.

Find, Amaya muttered. *Kill.*

That's the plan. I just hoped it was Lauren's presence I was sensing, and not another of her traps.

The second tunnel was wide enough to walk down normally and led into a chamber as large as the main one. I scanned the floor, but once again there was little more than dirt here. The shelves and tables that had been hacked out of the earth held various dusty items, none of which appeared to have been touched or moved since we were here last.

I frowned and slowly turned around. There was nothing here—nothing that hadn't been here previously. Yet the nip of magic was stronger, indicating we were at least closer to whatever it was Lauren had planned.

So where in hell was she?

There was nothing else in this underground system—no other rooms or tunnels. Or was there? It wasn't like she hadn't concealed entranceways before—she'd certainly done it in the underground system we'd discovered under that warehouse near Stane's.

Amaya?

Something, she said. *Trace not.*

Which wasn't a lot of help. I flexed the fingers on my free hand, though it didn't do a lot to ease the tension that was growing stronger by the moment, then walked across to the wall and pressed my fingers against it. The magic that continued to nip at my skin had no pulse in the warm earth, so I moved on, keeping my fingers against the stone and earth as I slowly moved around the room.

As my touch ran across one of the half-filled shelf slots, energy stirred, the sensation cold and oddly flat. Amaya hissed, the sound filled with excitement as it echoed through me.

Evil, she said. *Down.*

Down?

She didn't answer, instead briefly taking control and forcing me to squat. The cold bite of magic got stronger. I ran my fingers across the space between the shelf and the floor. If this was a doorway, then it was a damn small one. At barely two feet square, there certainly would be little enough room to maneuver, let alone fight.

And that was probably the whole point.

I pressed my hand hard against the cold, flat magic concealed within the wall of earth. It resisted briefly; then, with a slight sucking sound, my hand went through. Damp air briefly caressed my fingertips before I jerked my hand back. There was definitely a tunnel behind the magic, and one I very definitely had to explore, even if every instinct within me screamed to do the exact opposite.

With the butterflies going nutso in my stomach, I took a deep breath, then pushed Valdis through. Her flames crawled away from the touch of the magic, dancing across her hilt, then my hand, before finally extinguishing as I went in after her. As had been the case the last time we'd gone through one of these concealed doorways, it felt like I was crawling through molasses. The magic creating the illusion was thick and syrupy, and its cold tendrils clung to my body, resisting my movements, then releasing me with an odd sucking sound. I shuddered, my skin crawling with horror as I continued to force my way through.

But unlike before, there was no wider tunnel to provide relief. The cold, foul magic played around me, resisting my movements, tearing at my strength and will as I moved deeper into the underground darkness.

Then, with a suddenness that forced a yelp from my throat, the ground gave way and I was falling.

Chapter 12

I landed on my back with a grunt of pain, the sound echoing as I scrambled to my feet. The room in which I'd landed smelled of wet earth and foul magic, and it was so filled with shadows that the light from the candles forming a large circle around me barely made an impact.

I couldn't see but I didn't care. Azriel was here. The connection we shared flared to life, bright and fierce, even if somewhat constrained. I couldn't hear him—whatever magic caged him obviously restricted our ability to communicate—but given the circumstances, that was probably a good thing. He'd no doubt be furious about me walking—or, more accurately, falling—into Lauren's trap.

Fire rippled down Valdis's sides, lilac flames that briefly glowed a fierce and bloody red. Her steel quivered in my grip and tugged lightly to the left, as if eager to be free and moving. But until I knew for certain where both Azriel and Lauren were, I couldn't release her. Our demon swords might be able to move of their own will, but I didn't need Lauren realizing that.

"Well, well, well," an all-too-familiar voice said. "Look what the trap just dropped into our laps."

I swung around, Valdis raised high. Her lilac flames burned through the shadows and revealed the evil that hid beneath them.

Lauren stood twenty feet away. She was a tall, full-bodied—almost matronly—woman, with angular features and dark hair cut close to her head. Her nose was large and Roman, and it gave her an arrogant air. But it was her eyes that sent shivers skating across my skin. It wasn't so much that they were a blue so pale it was almost impossible to separate the iris from the white, but that, in this place, they glowed with a fire that was cold, cruel, and very definitely otherworldly.

But then, this was a woman who had willingly handed herself into the hands of hell—and then walked free.

"I have to say," she drawled, voice coolly amused, "while I did not really expect you to be so foolish as to step into the transport stones, I certainly *wasn't* expecting your capture to be this easy *or* this fast."

"It was only easy because I wished it to be," I said. "Where's Azriel?"

She raised an eyebrow and made a slight motion with her hand. In the shadows that lingered to the left of where I stood, torches appeared, their flames a bright and unnatural blue.

Azriel was caged. Literally.

It was a metal structure that resembled a fancy birdcage, but the steel was silver and glowed with an unhealthy green-yellow light. At the top of the cage there was an odd sort of haze that swirled in a lazy circle and, every now and again, sent a pulse of brown down the metal. Even from where I stood, the foulness of those pulses was evident.

Azriel sat crossed-legged in the middle of the cage's base. He looked very relaxed, almost serene. But then, he *was* a master of concealing his thoughts and emotions, and I knew him well enough now to understand that the blanker his expression, the more he was trying to conceal.

In this case, he was furious. Murderously so.

At me, as much as at Lauren.

I switched Valdis from my right hand to my left and

saw his gaze narrow slightly. Tension, anger, and perhaps a glimmer of understanding briefly rolled through the connection between us, but the brown haze pulsed and the connection was shut down again.

I frowned and returned my gaze to our sorceress. "What do you want, Lauren?" I hesitated, then added, "Or should that be Mike? Or even Harriet? What name do you *actually* prefer?"

She raised an eyebrow. "You can call me whatever you wish. I don't care, because none of those names are mine."

"So what *is* your name? And do you actually own a face of your own? Or has it been so long since you've worn it that you've forgotten?"

"I forget *nothing*."

As she spoke, her skin began to ripple and move, rather resembling putty that was being pushed and prodded and remolded by invisible hands. Even though I was a face shifter myself, even though I'd seen Mom transform more than once, there was something quite revolting about the way Lauren shifted. When she'd finished, the woman who stood in front of me had thickset, almost manly shoulders, a thin face still dominated by a large, almost regal-looking nose, and short, colorless hair. It wasn't white, wasn't gray, wasn't anything, really. Much the same could be said of her skin. It was almost as if she were an unwashed canvas, waiting for the arrival of paint. Even her eyes held so little in the way of color that her pupils seemed to be drowning in a sea of white.

I couldn't help the shudder that ran through me, and a thin, humorless smile touched her lips. The shift magic crawled across her body again and, after a few moments, it was Mike who stood in front of me.

"Does this form make you feel more at ease?" he said, his voice almost mocking. "It is certainly the one with which I am most familiar these days, given the length of time I have held it."

Amaya began to hiss, the sound fierce and angry as it echoed from my lips. I clenched my fingers against Valdis's hilt and resisted the urge to throw her at the mocking figure in front of me.

Kill must, Amaya muttered. *Taste her we will.*

Yeah, but first we have to find out what sort of circle surrounds us, I snapped back. *So behave yourself until we actually* can *attack her. We don't need to tip her off that all is not as it seems.*

Her muttering continued, the sound echoing through my mind. But she didn't attempt to wrest control from me and, for the moment, seemed content to do as I asked.

"Actually," I said. "Your current form does nothing more than increase my rage. I *will* kill you for all your years of deceit, you know. Mom deserved better than that."

He laughed. The familiar sound itched at my skin and only made the determination to kill him stronger. "Your mother was a means to an end. And, may I point out, a jolly good fuck."

My grip on Valdis became so tight my knuckles practically glowed. He laughed again. "Go on, throw it. You know you want to."

"Actually," I somehow managed to reply, "what I want is to thrust my hand into your chest, to watch the fear grow on your face as my fingers wrap around your heart, and then squeeze tight. I want to watch the pain grow, I want to taste your fear, and I want to watch the life bleed from your body. And then I want to rest content in the knowledge that you will never move on and never be reborn."

He raised an eyebrow, expression still mocking. "It is always good to have ambitions, even if you will never see them come to fruition."

He made a flicking motion with his hand, and the candles surrounding me shivered and danced. Magic settled around me, thick and cloak heavy. My knees buckled briefly under its weight, but I locked them tight and remained upright.

His gaze narrowed slightly. "Release the sword, Risa."

My grip on Valdis tightened. I actually did *want* to release her, because until I did, she couldn't make her way toward Azriel. But I also couldn't seem too eager.

"Go fuck yourself, Mike."

He made another motion with his hand. "Release the sword. *Now.*"

The weight of the magic increased. This time, I allowed my knees to buckle. They hit the cavern's stone floor hard, and pain slithered through me—something I was more aware of than truly felt.

"Sorry, but my previous response still applies," I said through gritted teeth.

"This stubbornness obviously comes from your father. Your mother was certainly far more pliable."

My mother had *trusted* him—and for that alone I would kill him. But I held the words back and kept my spine straight against the continuing force of magic.

He made another motion with his hand. "Release it."

I made a show of fighting the order—although it *wasn't* all show. The magic was so damn heavy it felt like a ton of bricks was settling around my shoulders. My muscles were screaming and sweat poured down my face and bowing spine.

Enough was enough.

I flung Valdis toward Azriel as hard as I could. She landed on the stone halfway between me and him and slid several feet closer.

"Well done," Mike said, his voice losing its edge of command. "Although if you have any hopes of the reaper being able to reach your weapon, I can assure you that will *not* be the case. His cage is, I'm afraid, rather more than it seems."

I licked my lips, my body still quivering under the weight of the magic. "Meaning what?"

"Meaning, it has been specifically designed with dark angels in mind. The steel contains him, and the mist drains him." His smile was edged with satisfaction. "He will die, slowly but surely, unless you do precisely what I ask."

Which explained the bouts of dizziness I'd been getting. It wasn't the lack of food; it was Azriel drawing on my strength. I glanced at him, suddenly worried. We might not be able to communicate, but he obviously sensed my concern and minutely shook his head. He was okay for the moment. Relief flooded me.

I took a deep, quivery breath and returned my attention to our sorceress. "Trouble is, he's going to die even *if* I do what you want. Or do you honestly expect me to believe you're going to leave either of us alive once you have the final key?"

"Oh, I have no intention of killing you, my dear. I did, after all, promise your mother to look after you, and I do actually prefer to keep my promises if it's at all possible. It's bad karma to do otherwise."

I snorted softly. "I think you're well past the point of worrying about karma."

"That is more than possible, given once I have the final key in my possession, the kingdom of hell is mine to fully control. Karma will be of little concern once *that* happens."

"If you think karma and the fates will idly sit back and watch you destroy two worlds," Azriel said, his voice as flat as his expression, and all the more scary because of it. Or it would be to the sane, and I had a suspicion Lauren or Mike or whatever the hell his/her real name was had passed that point long ago. "Then you have very little understanding of the forces you seek to control."

Mike glanced at him. "Given the lack of intervention

by either party so far, I think I'm justified in believing they no longer care what happens in my world or yours."

"And in that, you'd also be wrong," I said, drawing his attention back to me. The last thing we needed right now was him noticing that Valdis had slid several feet closer to the cage that bound Azriel. "But *that* is beside the point. If you don't intend to kill us, what do you intend? Because we both know that only death will put an end to our attempts to stop you."

He raised an eyebrow. "Oh, death is your outcome; have no doubt of that. But it will not come from my hand—not directly. Rather, the magic of this place will restrain and drain you both, until there is nothing left of either of you but memories and regret."

I suspected it wouldn't take us all that long to reach that point—not if the cold cruelty in his eyes was anything to go by. God, why hadn't I seen what this man truly was before now?

Why hadn't Mom?

It was a question I was never going to get an answer to. Mom had moved on and, in many ways, that was precisely what I had to do. There was no point in dwelling on what-ifs; all that mattered now was stopping this bastard.

"But we have not reached that point yet," he continued. "We have a key to find first."

"Sorry, but there's nothing you can say or do that will make me hand that damn key over to you when I get it."

"And that is where you are yet again wrong." He walked toward me, his strides long and assured. "Just as Lucian taught me how to cage and kill a dark angel, so, too, did he teach me how to control the mind of someone like you."

Lucian. It seemed we were never going to be free of that bastard's shadow. "I blew him to little tiny pieces, you know. I fully intend to do the same to you."

Mike laughed, but it was a short, sharp sound of anger. "Oh, I know very well what you did to him. It is only the promise to your mother that controls the dark urge to inflict the same on you."

So he was more than happy to destroy two worlds in his attempt for domination of all, but unwilling to break something as fragile as a promise? How in hell did that make any sense? It didn't, at least to the sane mind—and that *wasn't* what we were dealing with here.

He stopped directly in front of me. Only two feet and the weight of the magic separated us, but it might as well have been a mile. I could barely move, let alone do so with any sort of speed. And even if I could, there was still the circle of candles to contend with. It was undoubtedly some form of barrier—he wouldn't be standing so confidently close otherwise—and until it was down, I had no choice but to bide my time.

Waiting, Amaya growled. *Sucks.*

Amusement ran through me, but it quickly died as Mike raised his hands. Power surged across the night and the candles shivered in response. A heartbeat later, a muddy yellow arc of lightning shot from one candle to the next, until all of them were connected by that thin sliver.

This wasn't blood magic.

This was Aedh.

Doubt crept through me. Amaya might be confident that our joining forces would negate any magic designed to control me, but I still wasn't so sure. But it wasn't like I had any other option now. I mentally crossed my fingers and said, "Lucian was running his own game; if you think he'd hand over the means of controlling *him* as much as me, then you are a fool."

"Which I'm not, and neither was he."

His reply was absent. He was still weaving his magic, and the thrust of it was beginning to burn around me.

Through me. Its touch was unclean and made me want to scratch—something I couldn't do because the weight of magic was so fierce I was barely able to remain on my hands and knees. Moving one hand would tip the balance and have me face-planting into the stone.

"Which doesn't negate the fact that Lucian trusted no one." I risked a quick glance toward Azriel. Valdis was almost within his reach. "Not after my father's betrayal of him."

"He trusted me. He loved me."

I snorted. "Now I *know* you're crazy. Lucian was *Aedh*. They're incapable of loving anyone or anything other than their own schemes and plans."

Anger flared in Mike's pale eyes and found an echo in the sudden tightening of the magic that pressed down on me. I grunted under the force of it and my arms began to shake. I had to hope that whatever spell he was forming would be done sooner rather than later. I didn't want to end up getting squashed flat against the stone, and right now that was a very real possibility.

Movement caught my eye; it was short, sharp, and gone in a nanosecond. I glanced in Azriel's direction. He sat still and calm in the middle of his cage, his face as impassive as ever. But his eyes glowed with a fierceness that was frightening, and the force of his fury was such that even with our connection shut down, I could feel the burn of it. He wanted action. He wanted revenge. He could do neither until the cage around him had been destroyed.

Valdis no longer sat on the stones in front of the cage.

Relief ran through me, but it was tempered by the fact that we were a long way from being safe yet. But at least now that he was armed, Azriel had a fighting chance of survival.

"Which only proves how very little you knew about him."

Mike's sudden comment made me jump. I returned my attention and tried to shake my head. Even that was restricted. "I knew Lucian well enough to understand he was a megalomaniac whose desires far outstripped his abilities. He was an apprentice, not a master, Mike. What he taught you was nothing compared to what my father has taught me."

He snorted and made more grand gestures. The sickly colored lightning grew stronger, and fingers of power shot toward me. I tried to edge away from them, but the weight bearing down on me forbade any sort of movement. The tension within me grew, as did Amaya's howling. Her need to taste his soul was becoming so fierce it beat through my blood and made me hunger. I was still in control, but I had to wonder for how long.

"Your father only came into your life when he needed the keys found," Mike said. "Do not try to bluff, dear Risa. You are not very good at it. Now, please, be quiet. I need to concentrate."

"Oh good. I'll keep talking, then."

Again anger flashed, and again the weight pressing down on me increased. I hissed as sweat began to drip off my chin and splashed down onto the stone beneath me.

"Sorry, Mike," I said, my voice little more than a harsh whisper—and even that was a goddamn effort. "But if you expect me to give up so fucking easily, then you really don't know me, despite all those years you spent worming your way into both Mom's life and mine."

"You really *are* getting annoying," Mike growled, then added, the note of command back in his voice, "and you *will* be quiet."

I fell silent, though not because his magic forced me to do so. The weight of it might be making it hard to remain on my hands and knees—hell, it was becoming difficult to even think and breathe—but it hadn't yet gained the power to force me to obey. I hoped that was a sign

Amaya was right, that our joining would negate whatever spell he was about to weave around us.

He began to murmur, but the language wasn't one I was familiar with. I wondered if it was Aedh, wondered what the hell Lucian was thinking, giving a madman access to *that* sort of power. But then, he'd obviously foreseen his own death, if not the method—his begetting children on both Lauren and Ilianna was evidence enough of that—and maybe this was his last throw of the dice. A means of getting what he wanted through someone else.

Someone who carried his child.

I wondered whether Mike—Lauren—had been aware of that fact before I'd mentioned it. His vehement denial had been believable, but I remembered the odd glimmer that could have been smugness, or even satisfaction.

So perhaps Mike *did* know. Perhaps he was hoping for a son or daughter who—as half Aedh—would be far more powerful than he could ever hope to be.

It was a scary thought.

The lightning began to flicker and moan, the sound haunting, tortured. Something began to form in the sickly light that surged between the candles, something that was at first featureless and formless, but gradually gained shape, until it became vaguely humanoid.

Soul, Amaya growled.

I frowned. A soul? Why would Mike be calling a soul into existence?

From hell, she said. *Control it he can.*

Realization dawned. He was going to insert the soul into *me*. Fuck! *Is there any way to stop it?*

The last thing I wanted was that foul creature getting anywhere near me, let alone becoming part of me. Besides, this wasn't the sort of spell I'd been expecting, and I had no desire to find out whether we'd be able to combat it.

Can devour, she said. *But inside it must be.*

But if it gets inside, won't it gain control?

Only if stronger than two, she said. *Will shield.*

It was a risk. A *huge* risk. I glanced at Azriel; though his face remained impassive, the muscle along his jaw ticked and there was real fear in his eyes. He knew what this thing was, knew what it could do, and that made me even more frightened.

Then shield. And I mentally crossed everything I had that this would work.

Power surged through me, and just for a moment, my skin seemed to glow a rich, violet hue. Thankfully, Mike didn't appear to notice. His chanting reached a peak, then stopped, and the following silence was filled with eerie expectation.

"I am sorry to have to do this, my dear," he said, sounding anything but, "but I cannot risk allowing you to walk free from this place without some means of controlling you."

I met his gaze and had no doubt the hate I felt was evident in my expression.

He raised an eyebrow and added, "And *that* is why. You would kill me—or, at least, destroy the key before you ever gave it to me. Unfortunately, because of the wards you now wear, I cannot spell you, which forces my hand somewhat. But don't worry, it won't consume you, not entirely. You will merely be a passenger in your own body. It won't even be *that* painful."

Like *fuck* it wouldn't. But once again I bit back the comment. Amaya had no such restraint, but at least she kept it internal.

The soul broke away from the lightning and drifted toward me. I tried to edge away from it, but my hands and knees were locked to the stone thanks to the weight still pressing down on me. All I could do was watch as the gossamer wisp raised an almost fingerless hand and ran it down my face.

It felt like I was being caressed by fire and brimstone. It felt like hell itself.

A scream rose in my throat, but I somehow clamped down on it. I couldn't scream; it would warn Mike that his spells weren't working as well as he thought. The soul's touch moved on. My skin crawled in horror and the sweat that beaded my body froze in place—which would have seemed odd except for the fact that everyone's version of hell was different. For some it was icy, for some it was heat, and for others it was an endless pit of torture and pain. Perhaps this soul was trying a combination of all three to see which affected me the most.

It continued to flow over me until its fragile form covered me entirely. I wanted to twist and scream and swat it away—wanted to feel the steel of my sword in my hands and watch it destroy whatever life this thing had— but I did none of those things. The barrier was still in place, as was the weight of magic against my body. Until both of them were gone, I couldn't react.

No matter what happened, no matter how bad it got.

Mike was adept at both blood magic and Aedh and could bring the force of both against us. Besides, I had no idea just what that cage would do to Azriel if I revealed my hand too soon.

My one chance—*Azriel's* one chance—was surprise.

The soul began to seep into my skin. The sensation was unlike anything I'd ever experienced, and the horror increased, making me gag.

But as the soul leached into me, the lilac fire that was both Amaya and her sword came to life within. It latched onto the flimsy filaments, preventing them from going deeper into my body even as it consumed and destroyed them. The soul began to moan and twist, an eerie sound that echoed both through me and through the cavern itself. But it couldn't get away. My sword—and the demon that controlled it—ensured that.

But the conjured soul was merely an appetizer. The real meal still stood before us.

And *he* was smiling in satisfaction. No doubt he'd mistaken the soul's dying moans for my capitulation. I didn't move, didn't react in any way, trying to make it seem like the life within me was gone and that his conjured soul was now in residence—or, at the very least, in control.

After several minutes, he made a quick, chopping motion with one hand and said something I didn't quite catch, and the weight abruptly lifted from my shoulders. Excitement stirred, mine and Amaya's, but we didn't move. The endgame was close, but the candles still stood between us and ultimate victory.

"Rise, dear Risa," he said, making an up motion with his hand.

Slowly, stiffly, I obeyed. My legs were decidedly unsteady, and I wasn't sure whether it was due to the sudden release from the weight or the fact that Azriel was still drawing on my strength.

Either way, unsteadiness wasn't something I needed, given that when we moved, we'd have to do so fast. I took several slow, deep breaths and flexed fingers itching with the need to feel steel and blood on them.

His expression was a mix of satisfaction and amusement. "I can see you in there, Risa. The hate"—he paused and tsked—"no one so young should feel such an emotion so deeply. It is not good for the soul."

Eat him, Amaya muttered. *Good for* my *soul.*

Just consume him slowly, I bit back. *The bastard deserves pain. Lots of pain.*

Then blow apart not, she said. *Can't eat bits.*

Oh, I wouldn't be blowing him apart. He didn't deserve to die *that* quickly.

Now think like demon. Better.

I snorted internally and continued to meet Mike's gaze. After a moment, he walked to the left, moving around the circle until he was out of my immediate sight. My shoulder blades itched with awareness as he paused behind me, but I didn't dare move in any way. He grunted, then walked on, until he reappeared on my right side.

"Right," he said, stopping where he'd started. "This is how it works. You will find the key, Risa; the soul will monitor and control your actions, stopping anything that might be detrimental to the search. The minute you discover it, you will be brought back here."

I remained mute, though it was the hardest thing I'd *ever* had to do.

He smiled and continued. "Of course, I cannot afford to have the search take forever, so please *do* remember that the cage will continue to drain your reaper until you return with the key." He half shrugged. "I believe he has, oh, maybe three or four hours before the situation becomes critical."

Amaya screamed in fury, the sound so loud inside my head it felt like she was physically stabbing my brain. My eyes watered and a tear began to roll down my cheek.

"Now, now," Mike murmured, "it won't be that bad. Not if you hurry."

Bastard, I silently intoned. Bastard, bastard, *bastard*!

"The exit lies to your right." He made another motion with his hand. Light flared across the shadows to my right, revealing an archway roughly cut into the cavern's stone wall. "It will take you to an old munitions tunnel that was missed when this estate was being changed from a military base, and into the industrial estate itself. You will immediately begin the search for the key and will not stop until you find it. Is that clear? Nod if that is clear."

I nodded. His satisfied smile grew. God, I so wanted to smash it away . . .

"Then let's get this show under way."

Yes, let's, Amaya all but purred. *Sword ready.*

Even as she spoke, energy stirred, a heat that pressed

against my skin, eager to get out. She was back in her sword and ready to go, and it took every ounce of will I had not to move, to remain where I was, still and silent. Mike raised both hands and began to chant. One by one, the candles in the circle that contained me went out, until there was absolutely nothing standing between me and him.

Now, I said, and leapt forward.

The sword materialized from my body and leapt into my hand. Mike's eyes went wide, but he had no time and no chance to react. Amaya flamed, fierce and bright, quickly encasing him in a cage through which no magic could get in or out. And best of all, my hand was in his chest, my fingers around his heart.

Just as I'd promised.

I stopped, my face so close to his that I could feel the foul rasp of his breath against my cheeks. Sweat was beginning to bead his forehead, but there was fury in his eyes and incantations on his lips. I waited and watched as the realization dawned that *my* cage had rendered him as helpless as I'd been only moments before. The incantation became swearing. But he didn't plead for his life, and there was hard light in his pale eyes.

"Kill me," he spat, "and you kill the reaper."

"Actually, no," I replied evenly. "You see, that sword you had me throw away was his, not mine, and a reaper's sword is designed to protect its master against all manner of evil. Including, I'm afraid, the sort of magic you've conjured with that cage."

"My life force is all that holds this place together." The slightest hint of desperation had begun to creep into his gaze. "Destroy me, and the whole cavern will fall in on you."

"That," I said, "is a chance I'm willing to take. Amaya?"

She chuckled softly, the sound so filled with menace even I shivered. Fingers of flame began to tease and slap his skin, and his whole body shuddered under the impact. With every touch she tasted him, drawing his soul into her, piece by tiny piece. And all the while, my grip on his heart slowly tightened, until his expression was one of horror and he was screaming in pain.

It was enough.

As much as I'd sworn to kill him as slowly as possible, the taste of revenge had suddenly become sour.

End it, I ordered Amaya, even as I clenched my fist and shattered his heart, killing him in an instant.

He was dead—and his soul fully devoured—before he even hit the cavern's floor.

I half turned to see if Azriel was okay, but a powerful explosion rocked the cavern and blew me off my feet. I hit the ground hard and tumbled ass over tit several times before coming to a halt on my back.

But as I stared up at the ceiling, fighting to catch my breath and desperate to know whether Azriel was okay, I realized the ceiling was *moving*.

This whole place was collapsing, just as Mike had promised.

Chapter 13

"Azriel?" I screamed, both physically and mentally. "Are you okay?"

There was no answer. And though I could no longer feel the barrier that had prevented us from communicating before, I couldn't feel *him*, either. Either he was out cold or he was dead.

Fear surged and I scrambled to my feet. The air was thick with dust and debris, making it almost impossible to see. Damn it, he couldn't be dead! Not now. Not before we'd had some chance of a life together.

Amaya, can you sense him or Valdis?

I didn't actually wait for her answer, but dashed across the cavern, heading for the place where the cage had been. Stones began to shudder around me, the chunks getting bigger and bigger.

Something, she said. Her flames flared to life again, this time forming an umbrella that protected my head from everything that was crashing down around us. *Right go.*

I swerved that way, leapt over a boulder that landed heavily enough to make the ground quiver, and ran on. Somewhere ahead in the dust and the confusion, blue glimmered. It was little more than a flicker, feeble and not bright, but it had hope surging. If Valdis was still aflame, then surely Azriel was alive.

The rain of dirt and stone was getting heavier, and overhead, huge fissures were forming. The whole place was getting ready to collapse. We had to be out of here before that happened. I scrambled over rocks, my gaze not leaving the flickering flame, hoping against hope that he wasn't hurt, that he'd just been knocked unconscious.

Finally, I saw him. He was lying on his side, his face bloody and bruised, and a myriad of cuts over his torso. Thankfully, none of the wounds appeared particularly deep, and his limbs—though covered by dirt and rubble—didn't look to be injured in any way.

I dropped to my knees beside him and roughly pinched his grimy cheek. We had no time for finesse; we had to get out of here before we were buried.

"Azriel," I shouted. "You have to wake up!"

There was no response. Frustration and fear swirled through me. I took a shuddery breath, then brushed the hair and dust from his eyes with a bloody hand and saw the large lump on his forehead. He'd been knocked out cold.

Something cracked high overhead. I glanced up sharply and watched a fissure form in the stone overhead, then move, with ever-increasing speed, toward the center of the cavern. The ragged fingers of several other fissures were also reaching toward the center; when they all met, the whole place would cave in.

I swore and grabbed Valdis, then dragged Azriel into a sitting position and hugged him close. We couldn't wait for him to wake; we had to get out of here. *Now.*

I called to the Aedh. The magic surged around us, thick and fast, tearing us apart even as the rain of dirt and stone grew fiercer.

In particle form, I arrowed for the archway and tunnel Mike had pointed out. Though I desperately wanted to get out of here as fast as I could, the dust cut visibility down to practically zero, and the stones—while they couldn't actually hurt me in particle form—could and did impact, and it made moving through them fucking unpleasant.

Another crack echoed loudly, and a heartbeat later

there was a huge *whoomph* of noise as half the cavern disintegrated. It fell with such force that the wind of it battered me, sending my particles tumbling for several yards. I eventually controlled it, but the air was now so thick with dust I literally couldn't see.

I spun around, uncertain where I was in relation to the door. Panic surged, but I forced it down. *Amaya, have you any idea where the fucking exit is?*

Left, she said. *Can feel fresh air.*

I was glad she could, because I couldn't. I went left, as fast as I was able. But carrying Azriel was taking its toll on my body and my strength, and I didn't have a whole lot of it to spare in the first place.

Bigger chunks of ceiling were beginning to rain all around us, and the nearby walls were beginning to crack as well. I swore and tried to go faster. But it felt as if I were swimming through a sea of molasses, and any sort of speed was just impossible.

Close, Amaya said. *Try harder.*

Like I wasn't already giving it all I had? There was nothing left in the tank. There really *wasn't.* Every particle was burning, and I very much suspected that if I didn't get out of this cavern and find somewhere safe to shift shape, instinct would kick in and the choice would be taken out of my hands.

An archway appeared out of the gloom, but its sides were cracked and beginning to fall apart, and the whole upper section of the arch looked in imminent danger of collapse—and, in fact, did, just as I went through it.

The falling stones tore through me, and pain was a wave that threatened to overwhelm me. I kept going, needing to put as much space between me and the fragmenting cavern as was possible before my strength inevitably gave out.

The tunnel, like all the other ones in this place, had been hewn out of the earth and possessed sharp edges that tore into my particles every time I brushed against its walls—which happened a lot. Behind me, an odd rumbling began to override the noise of the falling stones, getting louder and louder, until it almost sounded like a freight train was bearing down on top of me. The walls of the tunnel began to vibrate under the force of it, and it felt like the whole world was about to come down on top of me.

Then it did.

Air slapped me, sending me tumbling yet again as a rolling wave of stones and dust and debris began to fill the tunnel. I had little choice but to roll along with it, simply because I didn't have the speed to outrun it.

After what seemed like an interminably long time, the force of the wave began to ease, until it was only the wash of dust that accompanied me through the tunnel. It was at that point that my strength gave out.

The Aedh magic crawled across my skin and slowly shifted both me and Azriel back into flesh form. We crashed to the grimy floor as one, his body pressed against my back and taking the brunt of the fall. I rolled off him but for several minutes could do nothing more than suck in air and thank the fates, the gods, and whoever else might be listening for letting us survive.

We might still have Hunter ahead of us, but we'd at least survived two of our three major adversaries, and that was far further than I'd ever thought we'd get.

You need to have more faith in your own strength, came the somewhat weak comment.

Relief surged. I twisted around and flung myself into Azriel's arms. "You're okay," I said, kissing his cheeks, his nose, his lips, all in rapid succession. "Thank *god* you're okay."

He laughed softly and wrapped his arms around me, the fierceness of his grip belying the wash of weakness I could still feel in him. "You just spent five minutes thanking everyone imaginable for our survival, and yet you sound both relieved and surprised to hear me speak."

"Surviving is one thing. Surviving *intact* and relatively unhurt is another." I paused and pulled back a little. "You are unhurt, aren't you?"

He nodded. "Weaker than sin, but yes, unhurt."

"Thank god," I said again. I ran a finger down his cheek, creating a clean spot. "What actually happened to you and the cage when I killed Mike?"

"The cage exploded and would undoubtedly have killed me had I not had the protection of Valdis." He smiled and kissed my fingertip. "That was a very clever move on your part."

"I couldn't think of any other way of getting both Amaya and Valdis inside whatever trap Mike had waiting." I shrugged. "I'm just glad it worked out as well as it did."

"So am I." He kissed my finger again, then released me and pushed—somewhat gingerly—into a sitting position. "Valdis protected me from the worst of the explosion, but the force of it basically shredded her net and blew us both across the cavern. I'm not sure what I hit my head on, but the first thing I remember after that was waking to your weight landing on top of me."

I lightly slapped his arm. "You say that like I weigh a ton."

He smiled. "In my current condition, a feather would feel like a ton."

My amusement fled. "How badly did that cage drain you?"

He shrugged. "It is nothing that I can't recover from."

"That's not exactly answering my question, you know."

"I know. Shall we return to the office, or the room we have acquired at the Langham?"

"My clothes are all at the café, but if you need to recharge, we'd better head to the Langham. It's more private."

"I do not think we should run the risk of recharging given we are little more than seven hours away from Hunter's deadline."

"Which is precisely why we can't run the risk of *not* regaining our strength," I said crossly. "Hunter will be the hardest of them all to defeat, and who knows if she'll actually wait until eight in the morning anyway."

And if it is Myer who watches us astrally rather than Markel, you just gave the game away, Azriel said.

Hunter is undoubtedly aware of the fact that I have no plans to actually give her the key. I half shrugged. *Myer will become a problem when we actually find the key. We can't let her—or Hunter—know what we plan to do with it.*

His gaze sharpened. *We know what you're going to do with it—give it to the reapers for safekeeping.*

Which was undoubtedly a sensible move except for the fact that it was never safe for something of such power to be held entirely in one space . . . My thoughts stalled. *That was* what Kiandra's warning—that safety lies in four—had meant. If we wanted to be safe, then the key had to be broken into four pieces, with each piece being guarded separately from the others. While the Raziq were no longer a problem, there were still plenty of dark forces left in this world *and* the next that might yet discover the existence of the key and attempt to find it. But if it was split, and no one but myself and Azriel knew where all four pieces were, there was a greater chance that its existence would be forgotten.

And it is possibly an action the fates might live with, Azriel said.

It's not like they've got any other choice, given I'm the only one who can find it. I pushed to my feet. The tunnel wobbled around me for a bit, and I flung out a hand, pressing it against the rough wall to steady myself.

Oh, they have plenty of choices, and plenty of means of getting what they want. His tone was grim. *Let's just hope it doesn't come to that.*

I didn't say anything, mainly because there really wasn't anything I *could* actually say. I offered him a hand. His fingers clasped mind and I hauled him upright, though it was touch and go for a moment whether we'd both remain upright or not.

"You're right," he muttered. "We cannot proceed with our strength levels this low."

"Finally, the reaper agrees with something I say. Have you got enough strength left to get us out of here?"

He hesitated. "Perhaps."

"Then let's head to the room at the Langham first. At least we can recharge and shower."

He nodded, tugged me further into his embrace, and got us out of there.

Two hours later, recharged, freshly showered, and wrapped in one of the Langham's thick, comfy bathrobes, I made myself coffee, then moved across the room to stand at the window beside Azriel. Melbourne stretched before me, bright and beautiful at night. We were two steps closer to making that beauty safe from the shadow of hell; all we had to do now was find a key and beat a bitch with a god on her side.

I drank some coffee, then said, "We need to go see Stane. Hopefully he's had some success in pinning down the list of possible locations."

"Yes." Azriel's gaze met mine. "I would suggest, however, we retrieve some clothes for you first."

A smile tugged at my lips as I struck a pose. "You don't think he'd appreciate my current attire?"

"I think he'd appreciate it entirely too much, and that is the problem."

I laughed, then rose and dropped a quick kiss on his lips. "I do like it when you get all human on me. But Stane is a look-only guy—at least when it comes to me."

"I am well aware of that. I was merely stating the fact that in *this* form, I have no desire to share."

I raised my eyebrows. "Meaning in energy form, you do?"

He smiled. "Yes and no. To reapers, the music of the soul is a beautiful thing to behold, and it is something we share with all those close to us. It isn't a sexual thing—as nakedness very often is here on Earth. It is—" He hesitated, frowning. "I cannot really define what it is, or what it means to us. But we do not have music or art or anything along those lines in my world. There is no need when there is the music of a soul."

"*That* is a very beautiful sentiment."

He raised an eyebrow. "You sound surprised."

"Well, I may have seen you guys for most of my life, but I actually grew up reading all the regular myths and stories about angels, reapers, and demons. Let's just say that none of you are really what I was expecting."

"And that, I assume, is a good thing."

"A very good thing, given I'm now carrying a reaper's child." I glanced at the clock near the bed and sighed softly. "I guess we'd better get this show on the road. Hunter's deadline is getting altogether too fucking close."

"Indeed." He tugged me close, and a second later we were standing in the middle of my office at the café. Once I was dressed, I picked up the phone and rang Stane. It might have been easier to simply go there, but if he hadn't pinned down the list, there was little point.

"Hey," he said, his smile cheerful despite the deep rings of tiredness under his eyes. "I've been trying to contact you."

"Sorry, been busy fighting evil, and all that."

"With anyone else, that statement would be funny." He half smiled. "I've managed to pin the list down to fifteen possibilities. I doubt I'm going to get any closer than that."

"Fifteen is a hell of a lot better than the thousand or so we initially had," I said.

He nodded. "Some of them are fairly heavily secured, though, so you're going to have to be careful."

"Bypassing security is the least of my problems right now."

"Maybe, but I just happen to have gotten my hands on a couple of e-bombs."

"You can explain what the hell they might be when we get there. We're coming in direct, so don't have a heart attack when we appear out of nowhere." I hesitated. "And I sincerely hope you've got those additional security screens up and running."

"Don't worry, I have no desire to be vampire bait in the near future."

Neither did I, but it would undoubtedly be a possibility if we weren't very careful. "See you soon, then."

I hung up, then finished my coffee and stepped into Azriel's arms. A heartbeat later we were standing in the middle of Stane's living area.

He swung around and handed me a somewhat scruffy-looking phone. "Seeing you haven't got one at the moment, I took the trouble of finding my old one. It's loaded up with the list of addresses."

"Thanks." I quickly found the list and brought it up onto the screen. "Some of these places I've never even *heard* of."

"Which is a problem given I cannot transport us to places you have no clear image of," Azriel commented.

"There *is* a thing called Google," Stane said. "It'll provide pictures aplenty."

I raised my eyebrows. "You keep your discarded phones active?"

"Well, no. But when you can hack as well as I can, activating an old phone isn't actually a problem."

I snorted. "You are a very sneaky but very handy person to know."

"That I am." He swung around, picked up a small

black device, then tossed it to me. "And this should take care of any security you might encounter."

I looked at it somewhat dubiously. It was rather innocuous looking for something with such a deadly-sounding name. "I'm gathering this is your e-bomb?"

He nodded. "Or, as they're more officially known, an electromagnetic pulse weapon. This one is a small-scale version, but very handy if you want only a particular building taken out rather than a whole city."

I blinked. "They can take out whole cities?"

"Well, not this one, obviously, but the larger versions, yes."

"How?" This thing was no bigger than a golf ball and looked a whole lot less dangerous, so how could it possibly have the power to take out a building's entire security system?

"By overwhelming electronic circuitry with an intense electromagnetic field. It basically fries circuits and renders them useless."

"Wow." I studied the smooth black ball for a moment, then said, "It is reusable?"

"No, but I do I have three of them for you, and that should cover the more secure places. You'll just have to figure out a way to take care of whatever security the other places might have."

"How do I set it off?"

"There's a small indent at the top. Press that down, toss it into the room, and let it do its stuff."

I found the indent and nodded. "It won't hurt people?"

"Unless they have a pacemaker, no."

He handed me a small but well-padded bag. Inside it were the other two e-bombs. I added mine to them, then tied the bag to a loop on my jeans. "Thanks for this."

"What's the good of having a black marketeer for a friend if he can't sometimes help you out with the good stuff?" His grin was wicked. "Anything else you need? Laser cannons, invisibility shields, fighter jets?"

I blinked. "You are kidding, aren't you?"

His grin only grew, leaving me totally uncertain. I cleared my throat and added, "All I want now is for you to keep the security screens up and running for the next twenty-four hours."

He waved my concerns aside. "Trust me, not even a gnat will get into this place without me knowing about it. And I have no intention of going anywhere until you give the all clear."

"What about a gnat armed with an e-bomb?"

"My shields are shielded against such a possibility."

"Good." I looked down at the first address on the list. I didn't know the street, but I'd been to Foster itself and was familiar enough with the place that Azriel could at least get us there.

I glanced at him, and within a matter of seconds we were standing in the middle of Foster's small and rather empty Main Street. The address was listed as the Foster and District Historical Society and didn't actually give a street number. But Foster wasn't a huge town, so it couldn't be too far.

And it wasn't.

The historical society center was a collection of beautiful old buildings, including a post office, an old school building, several cottages, and a jail, and while both the post office and the old school bore old coats of arms, neither of them registered on the internal radar. They weren't the key in disguise.

But I guess that wasn't really that surprising. After all, why would the fates make it easy for us?

"They are believers in the old adage, the harder the tasks, the more you appreciate surviving them," Azriel commented.

"That may be the case, but they still don't have to

keep shoveling the shit on." I Googled the next address and brought up some pics. "And giving us *one* little break isn't going to kill them."

"We are still alive," he said, voice somber. "I do not believe we should be asking for anything more than that."

I flicked the phone around so he could see the pictures of our next destination. "If it comes down to a choice between survival and getting shit dumped on us, I totally agree with you. But they're the ones who allowed this situation to get so out of control. It'd be nice if they gave the people who are trying to fix their mess more than just survival."

"I do not believe the fates agree with your sentiments."

Obviously, given they weren't heaping on the help. We zipped across to the next location, a little town called Heyfield, but while the building—a pub with the name of O'Brien's—did bear a coat of arms, it was Irish rather than Australian.

Our next destination was a prison near Sale and was obviously one of the places that Stane had meant when he'd mentioned high security. There was no way I was about to set off an e-bomb in such a place and let all manner of criminals loose, so I became Aedh and checked the place out that way. There was more than one coat of arms within the perimeter of the prison, as it was a government-run facility, but none of them were situated upside down or wrong way around, as my father's hint had suggested.

Locations four, five, and six also proved to be useless.

"This is getting depressing," I said, as we appeared on the center dividing strip of another town's—this one called Yarram—main street.

"At least we now only have eight more locations to check out," Azriel said. "That is far better than the fifteen we started out with. And are there not two possibilities in this town?"

I glanced down at the list and saw that he was right.

"The first one is the post office." I glanced over the road, looking for a street number. "It's further down the road, by the look of it."

He caught my hand and tugged me forward. Though it was not yet dawn, lights were on at the bakery and the delicious aroma of freshly cooked pastries and breads filled the air. My stomach rumbled, despite the fact that I'd eaten a full meal not that long ago.

"I can go acquire some, if you wish," Azriel said.

I laughed. "Thanks, but no. And you're going to have to get out of the habit of acquiring things. I have plenty of money to buy what I wish, and besides, I can't imagine either the fates or your reaper bosses would look too kindly on you stealing."

"You may be right in the long term," he agreed. "But for the moment, if it relates to keeping you safe and/or in good health, they will turn a blind eye."

So they could turn a blind eye but couldn't lift a finger to help? "I think they've got their priorities screwed."

"Possible." He stopped as we reached a beautiful old redbrick and white concrete building. "I believe this is the building we seek."

My gaze scanned the terrace that fronted the building. Two archways framed the square main entrance to the building, and on the left-hand side of these, there was a royal crest with the letters "ER" on them—once again, not what we were looking for. I pulled my hand from Azriel's and walked up the steps. Postboxes lined the left-hand wall and an old sash window dominated the right. The door, however, was modern and clear glass. I peered inside. It was pretty much your typical country post office, with not only postal facilities, but sundry other items like cards, gifts, and various office items for sale. What I couldn't see was a coat of arms. I became Aedh and slipped inside anyway, just to be certain.

"Off to the next one?" Azriel said, as I reappeared next to him.

I nodded and glanced at the address. "It should be at the end of the next block."

We headed down that way. With the night so still and quiet, and the stars bright in the sky, it would have been easy to forget what we were here for, to pretend that we were nothing more than lovers out for an early-morning stroll.

As we neared the building, energy slithered across my skin—a caress so light it barely brushed the hairs on my arm. But the Dušan stirred in my flesh and I stopped abruptly. The key was near.

Remember we have a watcher, Azriel said, and tugged me forward again. *You cannot give her any hint that we may have found the key's location.*

He was right; we couldn't. I forced myself to keep the same slow pace even as my gaze scanned the nearest buildings. The building we were just passing was an old weatherboard home that had been turned into a pizza place, and then there was a small Mazda garage. The building beyond that was a large two-story structure that was painted a pale green and looked to be a mix of residential and commercial, with stairs leading to the upper floor nearest us, and a café at the far end.

The closer we got, the stronger the wash of energy became. Excitement and dread began to pulse through my body. We needed to find the key, to keep it safe from Hunter, and we couldn't do one without jeopardizing the other.

I fought the fierce draw of the key's closeness and slowed my steps as we reached the old building. I had to make a show of looking around for our watcher's sake. The Dušan's movements were growing stronger, and her head snaked up from my skin and stared upward. Knowing that the last two times she'd done something like this, she'd actually been telling me where the key was, I had no doubt it lay on the floor above us. But I couldn't go straight there. I had to play the game first.

Azriel tugged me on. As we passed the last arch of the

residential section and moved on to the café, the Dušan snaked around, her tiny claws digging into my flesh, as if in frustration.

I know, I know, and I wondered even as I said it whether she could hear me. I still had no idea.

Given she should not even be able to move or lift herself from your skin on this plane, Azriel said, *it is entirely possible she could also understand even if she cannot communicate.*

Why can *she move here on Earth? Your Dušan can't— can it?*

No, it cannot. He mentally shrugged. *Perhaps it is a result of your mixed ancestry, and the fact that you have always been not only sensitive to the elements of my world, but the more arcane arts here on Earth as well.*

I made a show of looking through the café's large windows. There were a number of tables scattered through the room, all decorated with checkered tablecloths in pale green and white and small vases of flowers, and along one wall there were a number of comfortable-looking sofas for those who wanted to relax a bit more.

"No crests inside," I said, even as I mentally added, *But it's not like I can perform magic, so why would being sensitive to it matter?*

I do not know. Dušan are not something reapers have ever been gifted with, so I am not overly familiar with what they may or may not be capable of. He mentally shrugged. *But it is more than possible that—given your father was responsible for their creation—he endowed your Dušan with an ability to interact with this world.*

Maybe. I walked on toward the intersection and the end of the building. The Dušan's claws were digging deeper and beginning to sting. She was *not* happy we were moving away from the key. *Why do you think my father gave you a Dušan if it's not customary for reapers to have them?*

Again, I do not know. Your father's motives were never easy to understand at the best of times. Perhaps he merely wished to ensure the Mijai sent to protect you had the best possible chance of doing so.

He couldn't have known you'd be the one, though.

Couldn't he? He paused at the end of the building and looked down the side street. The building stretched before us, longer than it was wide. We turned the corner and continued on. *Reapers and Aedh—even rebel Aedh—were not unknown to each other before this event. It is entirely possible he was aware that the most likely candidate to protect you would be a Mijai who not only had a dark and bloody past, but who was already familiar with this plane.*

I guessed that did make sense. After all, he'd had me because he'd obviously known that he would need the help of blood kin to find the keys. It was entirely possible he'd also foreseen that Azriel would be assigned to keep me safe until they were found.

Smaller windows dotted this side of the building. I made a show of looking in each of them, but I really wasn't paying much attention to what each actually revealed.

"Right," I said, as we reached the end of the building. "Nothing there, so we'd better check the first floor. Is there anyone inside?"

Azriel's gaze momentarily narrowed. "There are two people in the bedroom of the front apartment. I can use their memories to gain access."

"Do it."

A second later we were inside the building. I stepped away from Azriel and looked around. We were in a largish combined living and kitchen area and there were several rooms leading off it. One was obviously the bedroom, given that someone within was snoring very loudly, and the other was a bathroom.

Can you keep the occupants asleep? I asked, glancing at Azriel.

He nodded. *They will not wake until after we leave.*

Excellent. The Dušan was pointing toward the apartment's middle front window. Given that there wasn't a crest or coat of arms to be seen anywhere near it, it had to be outside, on the building itself.

Which meant we had to make more of a show of looking around. We might be doing nothing more than wasting time when we didn't have a lot of it to waste, but we also just might be saving ourselves a lot of grief. Hunter couldn't know we'd found the key. Not until we were ready to confront her.

I checked out all the rooms, then finally walked across to the middle sash window and lifted it. There was no veranda along this portion of the building, so I leaned out as far as I dared and looked up. There was some sort of crest or shield at the top of the building, but I couldn't make out what it was from here. Not that I really needed to. The energy pulsing from it stung my skin almost as sharply as the Dušan's claws. I called to the Aedh, slipped out the window, and headed up.

It was very definitely an Australian coat of arms, but not the one that was in use today. This one was very old, with the positions of the emu and the kangaroo reversed, and the shield holding images of a sailing ship, a sheaf of wheat, a sheep, and an anchor—images I guess were meant to represent both our origins and the two industries that had helped Australia grow.

I materialized a couple of fingers on my right hand and brushed them over the whole coat of arms warily. Energy bit me, sharp and dark in feel.

The shield portion of the coat of arms was the key.

I pulled my hand away and went back through the window.

"That's not it," I said, forcing an edge of disappointment into my voice. "This is *really* starting to piss me off."

"Shall we move on to the next one?" Azriel asked, then silently added, *We cannot risk leaving it there too long, just in case your ploy fails.*

I know. But we can't retrieve it until we do something about Myer. I wearily rubbed the bridge of my nose. I was beginning to get a headache, and it was no doubt entirely due to tension. Out loud, I added, "I need a coffee. Why don't we head back to the café, and resume this in half an hour?"

The only way to deal with her might be to kill her. "Hunter's deadline is little more than two hours away—"

I don't want to kill her. It was somewhat weird to have a conversation on two very different levels. "I know. But if I drop with exhaustion, that isn't going to find the key, either."

"She may not see it that way." *And there is little other choice.*

"Right now, I'm beyond fucking caring. I need coffee." I hesitated, then glanced around the room and said, "And if you're listening, Myer, feel free to mention my sentiments. I'm beyond caring about *that*, too."

There was no response—but given she was on the astral plane rather than *this* one, that was no surprise. I returned my gaze to Azriel.

"Baiting Hunter, even via our watcher, is not a wise idea."

"Yeah, well, she can't fucking kill me until we find the key, and if she kills anyone else, she'll never get it." I glanced over my shoulder. "And you can tell her that, too, if you like."

"Enough, Risa." *If Hunter has killed her brother, she is well beyond any sort of reasoning. Do not goad her into an action everyone will regret.*

I sighed and stepped into his arms. *Fair enough.* "Home, James."

He whisked us back to the café. I headed downstairs

and made myself the largest mug of coffee I could find, then helped myself to some chocolate mousse cake and went back upstairs.

So, Myer, I said, as I plonked down on my office chair and munched on the cake.

Azriel moved across to the window and stared out. *As I said, I really don't think there are many options.*

And I really don't want to kill her if I can avoid it. I paused to take a sip of coffee. *What if I knock her unconscious and bind her? From what Markel said when I killed Krogan, I think wherever they're astrally traveling from, it's a place only they access.*

It is a very dangerous ploy.

I know, but I really don't want to have too much blood on my hands at the end of all this, Azriel. Not when it's the likes of Krogan and Myer, who are really only doing their job.

I can understand the desire, but in war, there is sometimes little other choice.

We aren't at war, I wanted to say, but the fact of the matter was, we were battling dark forces who wanted to either destroy this world or control it, and if that wasn't war, then what was? I finished my cake and licked the mousse from my fingers. *The only trouble is, to know where her physical body is I'm going to have to astral travel, and she'll suspect something is wrong the minute I step onto the plane.*

Can you not travel from where you are? It would be less obvious.

I can try.

Then do so. And be fast, in case she becomes aware of what is happening.

I drank some coffee, then put my mug on the table and closed my eyes. There was no time for finesse, no time to find calm and inner peace. I quickly went through the process that would take me onto the astral plane, and

in very little time felt the pull of my soul as it came away
from my body.

I immediately imagined myself standing in front of
Myer's physical body, and even as I pulled fully free
from my flesh, the plane blurred around me; then I found
myself in a small, dark room. Myer was short and dark
haired, with muscular arms and scars down one side of
her face. She lay on one of half a dozen beds that were
in the room, none of the others of which was occupied.

I glanced around, the tension running through me re-
flected in the vibrations beginning to roll across the
nearby plane, creating an odd sort of thunder. I flexed
imaginary fingers, trying to calm down, yet knowing I
couldn't stay here long. Myer was far more adept at astral traveling than me and might just realize something
odd was happening back at the café. If she decided to
travel to wherever I now was, the shit would really hit
the astral fan.

I spotted a heavy-looking metal door and imagined
myself on the other side of it. In the blink of an eye I was.
There was a security checkpoint in this room, complete
with iris and body scanners, and a guard armed to the
teeth. They weren't taking any chances with the safety of
their travelers—which made me wonder how in the hell
Markel had gotten rid of Krogan's body.

I moved on, past the scanners, following the shadowed corridor. I couldn't travel in Aedh form to this
place if I didn't actually know where in Melbourne it was
located.

The corridor led to a series of other rooms containing
beds, some of them occupied, some of them not. I
frowned, confusion growing, and moved on. I came to a
lobby, saw a directory on the wall above the call button,
and felt like swearing.

I was at the Directorate.

Which made sense, I guess. It was the safest place to

conduct such journeys, given it would take an army to break into this building.

I wasn't an army, but break in I would have to. I imagined myself back in my body and shuddered, gasping in pain, as the force of my return hit like a club.

I took several gulps of coffee, which hit my stomach and threatened to come right back up again, then swung around to face Azriel.

That area of the Directorate is unlikely to be shielded against astral travelers given that is its purpose, he said, *so it is unlikely they would be guarded against your Aedh form.*

It's unlikely they'd be warded against Aedh anyway. Before all this crap started, no one was even really aware such protection was necessary.

Yes, but the Directorate are *now aware, and no doubt will be working to solve the problem. How do you wish to play this?*

I glanced at the time, thinking fast. Dawn would soon be upon us, and with it came the countdown to Hunter's deadline. But there was another deadline approaching, one we could use to our advantage. "You need to go report to Aunt Riley. The last thing I need is for her to come out of hiding and present the perfect target to Hunter."

"Your aunt is cannier than that."

"I know, but I still don't want to take the risk."

"And you? What will you do while I am gone?"

I hesitated. "I might go to Stane's and see if there's any way he can hack into the security of the remaining properties. If we can use their camera systems to look around, it might stop us wasting so much time."

"If that were possible, I think he would have done it."

I shrugged. "It's still worth a shot. Shall I meet you there?"

"Do." Silently, he added, *Not. If you are unable to sub-*

due Myer, then we have a brief window of opportunity in which to grab the key and take it to safety.

Then where will we meet? The first place she'll look is back here.

He hesitated. *It will take you too long to travel in Aedh form to the key's location, so meet me at the Aedh's apartment building and we shall go from there.*

I raised my eyebrows. *Why there?*

Because it is close, and also a place they will not immediately think of. Aloud, he added, "Be safe."

I nodded, finished my coffee, then called to the Aedh. In particle form, I sped from the café and arrowed not toward the Directorate but to a hardware store, where I bought rope and duct tape. Only then did I continue on toward the Directorate. And every bit of me was crossed that we'd guessed right, that the Directorate hadn't yet had the time to form any sort of defense against energy beings.

The green glass building came into sight. I slipped down to the pavement level but didn't immediately enter, waiting impatiently for someone else to do so. As they walked through the bristling array of scanners, I went in with them.

No alarms went off.

Relief slithered through me, but it was tempered by the fact that I hadn't reached my destination just yet. I continued on to the stairwell, slipping in under the door, then swirling down the stairs until I reached the floor that held the astral traveling room. I retraced my steps, flowed over the guard, and entered the room where Myer slept. It was still otherwise empty.

I moved across to where she lay, then imagined Amaya in one hand, the tape and the rope in the other, and called to the Aedh.

The minute my feet hit the floor, alarms went off.

Chapter 14

There were fucking sensors in the *floor*.

The moment I'd regained flesh, I set the damn things off. And as soon as they went off, Myer began to wake. I flipped Amaya and swung her as hard as I could. Even half-groggy and still suffering the aftereffects of her swift return to her body, Myer was fast. She threw herself sideways, and the blow that should have smacked her across the jaw and knocked her out hit her temple instead. She came up fast, murder in her gray eyes.

Amaya, flame and contain, I yelped, even as I reached for the Aedh magic.

A ball of lilac erupted from the sword's side and shot toward Myer. She swore and dove away, but there was no escaping Amaya's cage. As the door behind me began to beep, Amaya's flames flashed around Myer and pinned her to the spot. In half-flesh, half-Aedh form, I moved over.

"I'm sorry," I said, "but it was either this or kill you, and I really don't want to do the latter."

And with that, I raised Amaya and knocked Myer out. As she dropped limply to the floor, the door crashed open and the security guard all but fell into the room. I became full Aedh and flowed past him as he ran for the unconscious Myer.

I made my way through the halls of the Directorate and up the stairwell to the lobby. Once I was out in the street, I shot down Collins Street, heading for Lucian's grand old apartment building. Thankfully, there still weren't any workmen on the site, but I guess that was not surprising given he'd only recently died and it was doubtful his will had even been read yet.

Azriel was waiting inside the almost finished lobby, out of sight from those walking by on the pavement. I became flesh, tugged my clothing back into some sort of order, and said, "We haven't got much time. I knocked Myer unconscious but I have no idea if she managed to get a message off to Hunter or not."

"Then we need to go."

He caught my hand, and a second later we were standing on the rooftop of the pale green building that held the key. I pulled my fingers from his and ran to the raised edge. The coat of arms was positioned in what looked like a circle that had had its top section lopped off. Sitting on top of this flatter bit was a rising sun, but it was easy enough to lean past this bit of ornamentation to get to the shield. Energy flickered across the shield as I reached for it, as if acknowledging my presence. It was dark and unclean in its feel, snapping at my fingers.

The Dušan crawled from my flesh, leaving just its tail wrapped around my wrist, gripped the bottom of the shield with tiny claws, and pulled it free. It swung around and crawled back, the shield seeming to shrink in its grip.

I grabbed it from the Dušan before she reached my flesh, suddenly fearful she was going to leach it into my skin. The last thing I needed was the key to hell sitting right alongside the two charms that had become permanent tattoos on my wrists thanks to the Dušan. She hissed, looking annoyed as she returned to her usual position on my left wrist.

The shield was little more than palm sized, but oddly heavy. I heaved it over my head, brought it down on the concrete edge, and smashed it into four uneven chunks.

I tossed one to Azriel. "You keep that one safe. I'll give one to Tao up in the sacred site, then take the third bit to the remnants."

He didn't look happy. "And the fourth?"

"I'll need something to offer Hunter. Once we kill her, we'll decide where it should go."

He nodded, half disappeared, then hesitated and said, "Be careful. It is likely Hunter now knows of your attack on Myer, and she will not react well."

"I know—which is why I won't be going back to the café or anywhere else familiar."

"Good. I'll come to you, so wait for me before you do anything Hunter related." He disappeared.

I glanced down at the three remaining pieces of key. I couldn't hold them all, simply because I needed to keep one hand free in case I had to draw Amaya. And while concrete *should* change with me, the key was actually metal. The concrete was just a disguise it wore in this world. And *that* meant it might have to touch skin. I bit my lip, debating the merits of bra versus tucking them into the back of my jeans, and went for the latter simply because my bras had a tendency to be shredded by the Aedh shift.

I called to the Aedh and, in particle form, took to the sky. With as much speed as I could muster, I headed for Mount Macedon and the old sacred site that was now Tao's home—at least for the evenings.

Dawn was beginning to creep pink fingers through the night sky as I arrived. I swept down to ground level and changed form but landed rather ungainly and half fell onto one knee. I grunted in pain but thrust upright, ignoring the dizziness threatening to topple me again as I ran for the old wrought-iron gates that guarded this place. As before, they were padlocked, the lock ancient and heavy, and the chain as thick as my arm. I swerved left and headed for the old chain fence that disappeared into the darkness to either side of the main gate. I leapt up, grabbed the top of the fence, and dropped, somewhat inelegantly, to the ground on the other side. My fingers brushed the dirt as I steadied myself and scanned the shadow-filled landscape around.

"Tao?" I said. "I need to talk to you."

There was no reply. But then, if he was still in elemental form, he wouldn't be able to. I bit my lip for a moment, tension slithering through me, aware that time was slipping from my grasp and the longer I stood here, the more time Hunter had to bait her traps.

I swore and forced my feet forward, following the faint path through the trees and the darkness. Shapes loomed through the shadows—small buildings that smelled of smoke and ancient magic, as well as various lichen- and moss-covered stony figures that, even at night, seemed to cast long shadows. I shivered, shoved my imagination back in its box, and strode on.

The path meandered its way through the trees, sometimes widening into broader clearings but generally remaining little more than a goat track. The wind lifted my hair from the nape of my neck and smelled faintly of decomposing forest matter, eucalyptus, and the musk of kangaroo.

But the farther I walked into the mountain's heart, the stronger another scent became—wolf and magic and fire, all weirdly combined.

"Tao?"

My voice seemed abnormally loud in the silence. An odd sort of tension began to slither through the trees, and the forest somehow seemed more alert.

I slowed my steps and proceeded more cautiously. Ahead, through the trees, light danced, a fierce orange glow that sent sparks cascading into the air and filled the rising dawn with the raw aroma of burning green wood.

It was the witch fire—the fire from which the elemental had come, and what Tao now had to help protect.

The glow of the fire grew stronger, until its warmth and electricity rode the air. The flames moved and danced in a manner that almost seemed to suggest awareness—as if there were still beings inside of it, ready to come out given the right incantation. And maybe there were—maybe that was why the elemental was so determined to protect this place and this fire. He had kin within the flames.

I paused on the edge of the clearing and looked around. The clearing appeared empty of everything but the fire.

"Tao, I really need your help. If you're here, please come talk to me. Or even just listen, if you're in elemental form."

My words seemed to echo softly in the still morning air. After a moment, one edge of the fire seemed to pull away from the other; then it rose. The elemental swung around, its faceless form seeming to contemplate me for several seconds. Then its fiery form began to contract in on itself, until what stood before me was flesh and blood, not fire.

I heaved a sigh of relief and walked toward him, but he held out a hand, stopping me. "Wait. Don't approach the fire, because the elemental is not trusting of anyone being near it and might just attack to protect it."

I stopped immediately and waited for him to come to me. Then I threw my arms around him and gave him a fierce hug. "I'm so glad you and the elemental appear to have worked things out."

"Yeah, so am I." He returned the hug briefly, then stepped back, his gaze scanning mine. "What's this about you needing help?"

I produced one of the small, ragged pieces of concrete. This bit had the anchor on it, though one edge had been snapped off. "I want you and the elemental to guard this."

He frowned and took it from me, turning it over for

several minutes before meeting my gaze again. "And why would you want this broken bit of concrete guarded?"

"Because it may be concrete here on Earth, but on the gray fields it's actually one-quarter of the final key to the gates of heaven and hell."

"Oh fuck, you *found* it?"

"Yeah, and we beat every other bastard to it, too. Of course, now the trick is going to be keeping it safe."

"And one part of that is hiding the bits in different locations. Good idea." He ran a finger over the raised anchor part of the shield, then added softly, "I can feel the magic in it, you know. It feels like the fire, but sharper, almost cleaner."

And yet it had felt foul to me. But then, the elemental owed its existence to dark magic, so it was logical he would be sensitive to its presence — even if the source of that dark magic was Aedh rather than human.

"Can you keep it safe? We can't allow anyone to access it, Tao, not ever."

"Then I have the perfect place." He spun on his heel and walked back to the fire. The closer he got, the more the fire responded, until it seemed to be dancing in eager anticipation. He stopped and held out the small section of shield. Fingers of flame reached out from the body of the flame and wrapped lovingly around both the key and his arms. An odd sort of smile creased his features, and just for a moment, flames rolled across his flesh. Then the fingers retreated, taking the key with them. Tao spun around and walked back. The fires still glowed in eyes.

"No one will take it from the flames," he said. "And if they destroy the fire, they destroy any hope they have of accessing it."

"Thank you." I hesitated, then added, "Both of you."

He smiled. "The elemental says it is happy we both have a reason to keep the flames going. What is your next move?"

"I've got to hide the rest of the key."

"And Hunter?"

I grimaced. "Will be murderous, to say the least, when she discovers what I've done. It might be wise for you to hang around here today, just to be safe."

"I doubt—"

"Tao, it's not just Hunter we have to worry about right now. The council attacked Stane; I don't want to chance them having a go at you, too."

Alarm spread across his features. "He's okay?"

"Yes, and he's added extra security that he assured me a gnat couldn't get through. But you're a juicier target, so please, stay here. It's just for one day. It's all going to be over with, one way or another, by tomorrow."

His expression, if anything, grew more alarmed. "Fuck, Risa, if you need help—"

I squeezed his arm. "I know, and I appreciate it, but this is my fight."

"And Azriel's, I would hope."

"Considering he's basically glued to my side, that goes without saying." I rose on my toes and kissed him. "I'll see you tomorrow."

"I fucking hope so."

I did, too. Resolutely, I turned around and retraced my steps. Once I was back over the fence, I walked over to the gate and sat cross-legged on the ground, pressing my back against the sturdy metal structure. The magic that protected both the gate and this place ran up my spine and seemed to cocoon me. Hopefully, it would also protect me, because I was about to step onto the gray fields, and that meant leaving my body totally without protection. If Hunter had any suspicion that I might have come here, then I could be in big trouble.

Of course, I could—and probably should—have asked Tao to guard me. But he and the elemental's truce was still relatively new, and I didn't want to do anything to jeopardize that. Asking him to walk away from the fire the elemental was desperate to protect might just throw their truce into turmoil. I'd rather risk my own safety than do that.

I took a deep breath and released it slowly, trying to calm the tension running through me. I might as well have tried damming a river with a feather. The Dušan stirred to life as I fought for calm; then her tail flicked out and wrapped itself around the small chunks of concrete I held in my hand. Ensuring, I realized, that the key was transported to the gray fields with us.

Awareness of everything around me began to fade. Ilianna's charm flared to life, and a heartbeat later, my psyche pulled free from my body and stepped onto the gray fields. The key was in my hand, and this time it *was* a key—an old-fashioned metal latchkey, or the broken end parts of it, anyway.

The Dušan unraveled her tail from my hand, then exploded into being, her energy flowing through me as her serpentine form gained flesh and shape. She swirled around me, the wind of her body buffeting mine as her sharp ebony gaze scanned the fields around us. There was no sign of concern in her movements, however, no sense that danger was near. The Raziq were gone, and while I had no doubt there were other dangers in this place that I knew nothing about, right now they were not my concern.

I headed for the temple grounds, moving as fast as I could in this place, and yet aware that it wasn't fast enough, that time was passing. And I had a horrible feeling that back in my own world, events were beginning to escalate.

It was tempting—so damn tempting—to exit out of here. But we'd fought long and hard—had shared blood and tears and lost friends—to gain this key, and I couldn't walk away from the chance of keeping it safe.

No matter what the cost.

I hit the temple grounds but didn't stop, moving on to the section that held the living quarters. The Dušan peeled away from my side as I did so, unable to enter this particular area. The ethereal and surreal buildings disappeared, replaced by a honeycombed tunnel along which ran various oddly shaped doors. Some glowed; some did not. I ran along the corridor until I reached the odd-shaped door that led into the rooms that had been both my father's and Lucian's. I pressed my palm into the middle of the door and it reacted instantly, emitting a warm, nonthreatening light that briefly scanned my hand.

The door clicked open. The room beyond was large and circular in shape, with ghostly honeycombed walls defining its area. There was no furniture or adornments — or nothing that I recognized as such. It felt empty, and yet there was an odd sense of expectation.

That is because those who gave it warmth are now dead, and she who will inhabit it in the future is not yet born.

I jumped and spun, Amaya instantly in my hand even as recognition stirred. It was the remnant who'd stopped Malin. Though I still couldn't see him, his presence hovered near the still-open door.

Sorry, I said, lowering my sword. *You scared me.*

In this place, there are certainly things that should be feared, but I am not one of them. He paused. *What is your purpose here?*

I found the key. I raised one piece of it. *And I want to store it in this room, if the magic that protects it from all but invited guests is still active.*

For as long as there are those who carry the bloodline of either Hieu or his chrání are alive, this room will remain in existence.

Hieu or his chrání — my father and Lucian. Which meant . . . me, my son, and Ilianna's daughter. *So I can leave this key here?*

You may. No reaper, soul, or even the darkest practitioner can enter this place. Not without some link back to those who created it.

Good. I spun around, walked to the center of the room, and deposited the key on the floor. I stared at it for a moment, oddly uneasy about leaving it simply sitting there, ready to be picked up by anyone who happened by. No one *could*, but that was beside the point. So I imagined a cage around it, one that was as strong and as ethereal as the temples themselves.

An orb-like filament of light formed around it, linked to the floor by a fiber no thicker than a hair. The key sat within it and seemed to emit a muted, brassy gold light.

I turned around and walked back to the door. The remnant retreated, allowing me to exit. The door closed softly behind me. I knew it would be a long time before it was opened again.

Now, I said, as I retraced my steps through the honeycomb hallway, *I must return home.*

And the piece of key you still hold?

Is bait for a monster we need to bring down.

And after?

I don't know. The only thing I'm certain about right now is the need to keep the pieces separate. I returned to the main temple area; the Dušan swirled around me, her movements impatient, eager. And yet there was nothing here to fight.

Not here, the remnant agreed. *She is eager to fight the foe in your world.*

She can't help me with that.

Normally, I would agree, but there is a magic and a presence in this one I have not sensed before. It might provide a solution to the problem you face.

Meaning she can be active in my world? A tiny sliver of hope burst through me. The Dušan was one hell of a weapon to have in your corner.

I cannot say yes or no, because I am not familiar with the magic that created this one. I merely suggest it is a possibility given the right motivation. Good luck, young Aedh.

The right motivation? What the hell does that mean?

The remnant didn't answer, mainly because he was already gone. I sighed in frustration and returned to my body. I woke with a start but didn't immediately move, keeping my eyes closed as I listened to the call of birds and the whisper of the wind, trying to find any sense of change, or danger.

No one was near. Not even Azriel.

I pushed upright. The remaining bit of key had shifted position and was now digging into one butt cheek. I moved it to a more comfortable spot, then began to pace. The sun was on the rise and it made me acutely aware that time was passing, that Hunter's deadline was drawing uncomfortably close.

But would her deadline even matter now that we'd made such a blatant attack on one of her Cazadors? She'd have to know the only reason we'd do something like that would be to prevent her from knowing the key's location.

Familiar energy slithered across my skin. As I spun around, Azriel appeared. "You took longer than I thought you would."

"Yes." His expression was less than pleased. "The fates were decidedly unhappy about your decision to split the key. I was forced to defend it."

"Oh." My gaze scanned him. He looked whole and unhurt, which was something of a relief given the sudden suspicion that when he said "defend it," he meant physically rather than verbally. "And?"

"They're still not pleased, but they do see certain advantages in the current situation. Which, they assure me, is still tenuous."

"Oh, fabulous."

"Yes." He crossed his arms and glanced at the nearby gateway. "You were successful?"

I nodded. "But I have a bad feeling about Hunter."

"With reason, if what the fates implied is anything to go by."

The tension running within me ramped up to another level. If the fates were saying that, then Hunter was on the move. I flexed my fingers and resisted the urge to scream in frustration. It wouldn't help. It wouldn't even make me feel better.

"We need to contact Markel and Stanford and see if they've had any luck fashioning a means to stop Hunter." I hesitated. "Are you able to find either of them via their life force?"

He hesitated, his gaze narrowing slightly. Then he nodded. "I've located Stanford."

"And can you take us to him?"

He hesitated again. Our connection came to life and, just for an instant, I saw what he was seeing—a rather old-fashioned living room, complete with roaring log fire and antique furniture. He was tapping into Stanford's memories.

"Something I can only do from this distance because I have met the man and am familiar with the song of his soul." Azriel held out a hand. "Let us go."

A heartbeat later we were standing in the middle of the room I'd just seen. Stanford leaned against the smoke-stained wooden mantel, contemplating the flames, but the moment we appeared, he spun, teeth bared and eyes promising death. Then recognition hit and he immediately composed himself, although his canines were a little slower in retracting.

"I do apologize for my reaction," he said. "But given the events of the last twenty-three hours, it is, perhaps, somewhat understandable."

"If you think the last twenty-three hours have been

tough on you," I replied grimly, "then you should try standing an hour or two in *my* shoes."

"I would not trade positions with you for all the wealth and power in the world," he said, the amusement in his voice at odds with the shadows that remained in his eyes. "Particularly at the moment. Hunter, as you may suspect, is less than happy."

"Which is why I'm here. How did you do getting those wards developed?"

"Ah," he said. "There has been a minor problem in that area."

"You had better *not* be telling me that you can't build the wards and break Hunter's connection with her god." I took a step forward, Amaya suddenly in my hand and screaming for blood. Azriel touched my shoulder, though I wasn't entirely sure whether he was calming me or himself with the contact, given that I could feel the rush of his anger through my mind.

Stanford looked somewhat taken aback. "It is one thing to hear tales of your sword, quite another to actually see and *hear* her."

"The wards," I said, through somewhat gritted teeth. God, if this bastard didn't come through after everything he'd promised, Amaya might just get the blood she was screaming for.

He held up his hands. "Please, let me explain."

I waved a hand in silent invitation. He smiled, though it was a little less than gracious.

"The wards we talked about would be of little use in the current situation. Hunter is marshaling all those who support her, and she plans both murder and war."

"War? Against who?" I asked, confused. "She's already taken out the most vocal of those who oppose her."

"The most vocal, yes, but certainly not all her opposition. I and many others still live, and it is against us she plans her war. It cannot come to that."

No, it could not, if only because a war between the fractional sections of the vampire community could never be good for the rest of us. Hunter certainly wouldn't care about the collateral damage she'd cause, not in her current state of mind, anyway.

"So what has this got to do with your inability to produce the wards?"

"It's not a matter of inability; it's a matter of practicality." He began to pace. "Hunter is undoubtedly aware of our moves, as we are of hers. I have no doubt that she is now using Cazador travelers to track us, as we have been using them to track her. While this place is warded against astral interference of any kind, many other places are not. Nor is there such a thing as personal wards against travelers spying on you." His gaze flashed to mine. "As you well know. She will also suspect that I have been in contact with you—"

"If she suspected that," I cut in, "she would have warned me against it. She hasn't." Not since warning me against talking to Stanford after I'd interviewed him during the investigation into her lover's murder.

"Which does not preclude the possibility of awareness," he snapped. Then he grimaced. "Sorry, but Hunter has not lived this long by being caught unprepared. Hence the problem with the wards—she will never, in this current climate, agree to meet you at some location over which she has no control."

"But that's an easy solve—we simply agree to her location but in my time frame, thereby giving you time to set up the wards."

He snorted. "And you think she wouldn't already have such a location well guarded? Surely you are not that naive."

Maybe not naive but overly hopeful given the situation and whom we faced? Yeah, I was that. "So what you're basically saying is that despite all the promises you made, I'm on my fucking own?"

"No, I am *not* saying that." There was a dangerous edge to his voice. One that suggested he wasn't all that different from Hunter. And yet Markel stood by him, and while I didn't know Markel all that well, either, my instincts leaned toward trusting him.

Whether those instincts could be relied upon in this instance remained to be seen.

"Then what *are* you saying?" *Because we're running out of time here,* I wanted to add, but I somehow managed to restrain the urge. He was just as aware as I was of the time frame, and I certainly didn't want that fierce and angry light in his eyes to get any stronger. Stanford was a former Cazador; it was also possible that he'd either been a berserker or come close to it.

The latter, Azriel said. *He would not be standing here otherwise.*

Because the council killed berserkers. Still, did I want to help someone who walked such a fine line between sanity and madness gain control of the council?

If it helps us defeat Hunter and gives us a chance for a life together, then we have little other choice.

True. I returned my attention to Stanford as he said, "Markel is again following you astrally—"

"Why?" I cut in again. "Surely Hunter would suspect he's working for the opposition?"

"She probably does, but in this case it does not matter. He is not following you officially, but rather from the safety of a location even I am unaware of. Once Hunter contacts you—which should not be long given your attack on Myer—he will contact me with the location of the meeting, and we will move in to nullify Hunter's forces the instant you and the reaper are within the building."

"Great, except for the fact that it's not going to help with the whole 'line to her god' problem with Hunter."

"No, but this will." He strode across the room and picked up a small, dusty-looking box from a side table. Inside, sitting on plush red velvet, was a simple black-stone knife. Its blade was rough-hewn and connected to the haft by simple rope, but edges of the actual blade looked razor-sharp and it glinted softly in the room's half-light.

"How is an old knife going to help in this situation? She's not going to let me get close enough to stab her, and I doubt if this thing was designed to be thrown."

"It isn't." He took the knife from the box almost reverently. "It is designed to be used in close combat. It is also the means with which you will break Hunter's connection to her god."

I glanced down at the knife in his hands. It certainly didn't look *that* powerful. "How?"

"Ah," he said. "That's the rub. I'm afraid it takes both the blood of the user and the blood of the foe to activate the magic within the weapon. Only then can it sever celestial contact."

Of course there'd be a clause like that. I mean, why would it actually be easy? Nothing else in this whole fucking drama had been, after all.

"So I slice myself, then stab her," I said, trying not to ignore the fear that rose at the mere thought of having to get that close to the mad bitch. "The trouble is, she's unlikely to let me enter the building with any sort of weapon."

Which may apply to our swords, as well, Azriel said. *She will be aware of their capabilities.*

"*That,* I'm afraid, is a problem you will have to sort out," Stanford said. "I have provided the means with which you can nullify her power, as promised, and I will take out whatever force she has protecting the building. But until you sever her connection to her god, I can do nothing more."

"Why not?" I stared at him, looking for fear and, unsurprisingly, finding nothing. If he wasn't afraid of Hunter, why would he not openly confront her?

"Because many others in recent times have tried to take her out and failed. I will not waste my life, or the lives of others, on a battle that will ultimately prove fruitless." His expression was grim but determined. "Sometimes what is needed to take out a being with godly powers is another being with such powers."

"But I'm not—"

"Human," Stanford cut in. "You never have been; now you are even less so. And you have weapons at your disposal that we here on Earth can only dream of."

He glanced at Azriel as he said that. And yet I knew, as Azriel knew, that this battle was always destined to be between me and Hunter. That he, in the end, could not and would not deal the final blow.

All we had to do was somehow survive to get to that point.

I took a deep breath and released it slowly. As usual, it didn't do a whole lot to ease the tension in me. I held out a hand. "I guess you'd better give me the knife, then."

He held it out, haft first. The minute my fingers touched it, the Dušan reacted, swirling down my fingers, then wrapping her entire body around the small blade. Stanford released it immediately and watched, expression closed, as the Dušan retreated to my flesh and once again became little more than a tattoo on my arm—only this time it was one that was entwined around an ancient-looking knife.

I guess *that* was one way to solve the problem of getting additional weaponry into whatever location Hunter chose. I doubted she'd paid all that much attention to my tattoos, especially given that I now had a number of them thanks to the Dušan.

"I would suggest you ring Hunter as soon as you can," Stanford said. "But you cannot do so from this place, in case she has the call traced. And if you wish to remain free, I would not return to your café, either, as she undoubtedly has the place watched."

I nodded and glanced at Azriel. "What about Aunt Riley's place? It's well enough protected and not an obvious place for us to be."

He nodded and held out his hand. As I placed mine in his, I glanced back at Stanford. "You had better hold up your end of the deal, or there will be hell to pay."

He placed a hand on his heart. "I vow on the life of my creator, I will do all that I promised—and more if possible—to help you in this quest."

I nodded. Three seconds later we were standing in the warm and spacious surrounds that was Aunt Riley's living area. The phone I'd borrowed from Stane was once again in bits, thanks to the fact that I'd become Aedh without actually thinking about it, so I walked into Rhoan and Liander's suite of rooms, knowing that the phone lines in there had permanent scramblers on them. It was amazing the things you could learn when you were a nosy kid gifted with the ability to become little more than matter. I'm sure I heard more than one state secret over the years, even if I couldn't remember them.

I hit the Speaker button and started dialing Hunter's number. But before I could finish, energy surged across my senses.

Something—or someone—was coming into the house.

Azriel and I swung as one, swords raised and spitting fire. Then I realized whose energy it was and lowered Amaya as I walked back into the living room.

But I didn't relax.

If Uncle Quinn was coming back here, then something had to be wrong. He and Aunt Riley had promised to keep away, to keep safe, and they weren't people who went back on their word.

They re-formed near the kitchen. Riley immediately swung around, her expression wild, dangerous, and fear filled.

My stomach clenched. There could be only one reason for a reaction as fierce as this from her. Rhoan. *Please, god, no . . .*

But her very next words confirmed my fears.

"Have you heard from Hunter?"

I shook my head, afraid to speak in case my violently churning stomach took the opportunity to make its presence felt.

"Why?" Azriel's hand cupped my elbow, as if ready to support me if my knees gave way.

"Because Rhoan's disappeared. The bitch has him."

Chapter 15

I didn't bother asking whether she was sure. She was his twin, and their connection was as strong as anything Azriel and I shared. I swore and rubbed my eyes wearily. I should have warned him. Should have called him the minute I'd thought about it. But I'd given other things priority, and now he was in Hunter's hands.

"Is he . . . ?" I couldn't get the rest of the sentence out. Couldn't ask if he was still alive.

Although if he was dead, Riley wouldn't be standing here spitting fire. She'd be tracking Hunter down, determined to kill her.

I had to stop that. *Had* to.

"He's okay," Riley and Azriel said together. Riley flashed him a narrowed look. "Can you tell me where he is? I have a general idea of location, but pinning it down is somewhat fuzzy. It's as if there's some sort of field around him that's redirecting our connection."

"Given we believe Hunter is capable of magic, that is more than possible." My voice sounded hoarse, and I still wasn't entirely sure my stomach was going to stay where it was supposed to. This was my fault. If anything happened to Rhoan . . .

"This is not your fault," Quinn said softly. "You undoubtedly made the risks as clear to him as you did us. He chose to remain."

"Yeah, but—"

"No buts, no guilt," Riley said. "Just action. You need to contact Hunter."

It *was* the next logical step. I spun on my heel, walked back to Rhoan's room, and once again hit the Speaker button before dialing Hunter's number.

She didn't take all that long to answer. "Hunter," she said, voice cool and ultrapolite. "How may I help you?"

"You can fucking tell me what you've done with Rhoan," I replied, unable to help either the language or the edge of anger in my voice.

"Risa," she murmured, voice deceptively mild. "I was just about to contact you."

I wasn't using a vid-phone and I couldn't actually see her, but it didn't matter. It was almost as if she'd reached down the phone lines, wrapped her fingers around my neck, and squeezed tight. It was all I could do to remain on the line, to *not* run.

"Forget the fake niceties," I somehow managed to spit, "and just answer the damn question."

"The damn question," she said, tone still as polite as before despite the menace that continued to wash over me, "will be answered in my own good time. Meanwhile, you might want to explain your attempt at murdering my Cazador."

"If I'd wanted her dead, she would be," I said. "Where's Rhoan?"

"He's tucked away somewhere nice and safe. Consider him a bond against your good behavior."

"Such a bond will only work if he's alive," I said. "What guarantee do I have that he is? Or, if he is, that he'll remain that way?"

"You have my word—"

"I'm sorry, but I'm not inclined to trust the word of a woman who would murder her own brother."

I felt Riley start and glanced at her. Her face had lost much of its color. *Jack's dead?* she mouthed.

"We believe so," Azriel murmured. "I cannot find the resonance of his soul, and death is the most logical reason for that."

"Oh dear *god*," she whispered.

I knew she was thinking—as I'd been thinking—that someone who would kill her only living relative wouldn't blink twice when it came to killing one of the best guardians the Directorate had ever produced. Rhoan would be just one more bloody blot on her road to ultimate control.

"Jack," Hunter said, voice even quieter and all the more frightening because of it, "was foolish enough to go up against me—"

"No," I cut in. "He merely intended to warn you against using the Directorate in your mad scheme to rule the world."

"You were not there, so do *not* tell me what was said and done between us." There was something in her voice that went beyond mere viciousness, something that was almost otherworldly, and it had me wondering uneasily if her connection with her god had just come online. "He was warned, long ago, never to go up against me because it would go ill against him. He ignored that warning."

"Because he cared about the organization you started and he helped run."

"I was his sister. His *older* sister. He owned me homage and obedience."

It was a statement that showed just how far she'd stepped away from the sanity barrier. "He owed you nothing—not if you were about to destroy everything you and he had spent centuries building."

She snorted. "As creator, it was mine to do with what I wished. He knew that, just as he knew the consequences of going against me."

There was nothing I could say to that. Nothing that was going to get through to her. Jack's death was a great loss to the Directorate, but many more good men and women would lose their lives—both within the Directorate and without—if Hunter wasn't stopped.

"But we digress," she continued. "I gather, given your attack on Janice Myer, that you have found the key, and right on time, too."

"Yes."

"Then why the attack on Myer?"

I snorted. "Because I didn't believe you'd actually let me retrieve it without attempting to snatch it from under my grasp. I had no intentions of losing control of another key."

"And yet you *will* lose control of it; otherwise, Rhoan Jenson will die."

I clenched my fingers but otherwise didn't respond to the threat. "When and where do you want to meet?"

"You may bring it to me here, at my office."

Her *office*? At the Directorate? My gaze shot to Azriel's. That was the one location neither of us had expected—and the one place where she certainly had the odds on her side.

"What, no smart reply? Have I finally rendered you speechless?" Hunter paused, and a stronger hint of amusement crept into her voice as she added, "What about you, dear Riley? I'm gathering you're there, fuming away in the background?"

"That I am," Riley growled, "and you had better not hurt my brother—"

"My dear *former* guardian," Hunter said, a patronizing edge in her voice, "I am more than aware of your capabilities thanks to your years under my employ, but you have no idea about mine. Please control your temper, or I might just end your brother's life for the fun of it."

The anger that exploded from Riley was so fierce that it knocked me back a step or two. And yet, somehow, she controlled it.

"Do *not* hurt my brother," she said softly, and for the first time in a long time, I saw the guardian in her. It was every bit as scary as the change that happened in Rhoan. "As my former boss, you also know that I keep my promises. And if Rhoan dies, then there is nothing—in this world or the next—that will stop my vengeance."

"Oh, I believe a threat or two to your children might just do that," Hunter drawled. "Do not play this game, Riley. You have far more to lose than me."

Riley opened her mouth to reply, but I held up a hand, stopping her. "Let's stop the threats and concentrate on what actually matters right now."

"Good idea," Hunter said. "I want the key. *Now.*"

"No. Not until I know Rhoan is safe."

She snorted. "I'm hardly likely to release Jenson before I get the key."

"And I'm hardly likely to give you the key, given you then have no reason to release Rhoan. Sorry, but I trust you as little as you appear to trust me."

I could almost see her smile. It wasn't a particularly nice smile. "Undoubtedly true. The only difference is, I'm willing to destroy not only Rhoan Jenson, but everyone and everything else you might hold dear until I get what I want. You, I'm afraid, cannot say the same."

No, I couldn't. But I'd be more than happy to destroy *her*. Only trouble was, that wasn't going to be easy, either. If the bitch was inviting me to her place, then it could only mean it was protected against all comers—human, nonhuman, and possibly even those not from this world.

"What about a compromise?"

"Not a word I'm all that familiar with, but I'm willing to listen."

Eat this one, Amaya muttered. *Enjoy will.*

Eat her slow, I growled back. *I want it painful.*

Slow good, she replied. *Slow fun.*

"I'll come to your damn office," I said, batting away

delicious visions of Amaya slowly devouring Hunter. "And you'll tell me where Rhoan is. Once he is safe, I hand over the key."

"Just like that?" Hunter drawled. "Somehow, I very much doubt it."

"Oh, you can have the damn thing," I said. "But it won't be of any use to you. You can't get onto the gray fields, and the temple guardians will certainly never allow you to pass through their grounds, let alone access the gates. So yeah, have the key, for all the fucking good it will do you."

Her amusement seemed to swim around me, thick and savage. "Oh, how little you understand me. Did not the sorceress you defeated only very recently make a perfectly usable gateway? I am more than willing to wait the length of time it takes for my people to figure out its complexities. As for the key—the mere threat of it is, for now, enough."

"Then you have nothing to lose by agreeing to my terms."

She didn't immediately answer, but I had no doubt she was using the time to mentally order more of her people into the protection of her office. She wasn't the type to take chances.

But the numbers didn't matter. Getting into her office—the one place she obviously felt safe—did. Every instinct I had was now telling me it was the only way I was ever going to get close enough to use the knife Stanford had given me.

"Fine," she murmured. "We shall do it your way, for the moment. I expect to see you in five minutes, or I will ensure there aren't enough pieces of Rhoan Jenson left for his loving sister to bury."

There was a long, deep growl from behind me. Hunter laughed and hung up. I hit the End button and glanced at Riley. She was clenching and unclenching her hands, but very little of that emotion showed in her face. How she was remaining so controlled, I had no idea.

"I will kill that bitch once Rhoan is free—"

"No," I snapped, "that's *my* job. *Your* job is to get your brother out from whatever trap Hunter has laid around him, then get safe."

Her gray eyes became little more than icy slits. "I will not—"

"Riley, enough." Quinn gently squeezed her arm as he glanced at me. "You cannot do this alone. I have known Hunter for a very long time, and for all the knowledge you have gained over the past few months, for all the strength, skill, and heart Azriel has, neither of you will defeat her."

"When she is connected to her god, that is undoubtedly true." My brief smile was grim. "We know what we're doing. We know what we face. You *have* to trust us. You have to let us go; you have to let us do the task the fates have given us, without interference of any kind."

His gaze flicked from me to Azriel, and it lingered long enough to make me wonder if some sort of communication was happening between them.

"So be it," he said eventually. "But be warned. It is said that Hunter's true lair in the Directorate lies not on the top floor, but in hidden recesses deep underground— and that it is so well protected, not even ghosts can get in—or get out."

Then *that* was probably where Jack had been killed. And I wondered whether I'd find his ghost there.

Riley swung around to face Quinn, her expression a mix of surprise and anger. "You cannot be serious—"

"There are some things that simply *have* to be. This, my love, is one of them."

"But—" She glanced at Azriel for a moment. "What did you say to him?"

"That we are at a crossroads," he replied. "What path our futures take very much depends on all our actions over the next hour."

Her face paled. It was a threat of death. She knew it; I knew it. Whose death was now the question—and one we would all get an answer to soon enough.

"Look, we don't have the time to stand here and argue." I tugged off the ring I'd gotten from Rhoan and offered it to her. "Please, just get Rhoan out from whatever net Hunter has around him, and let us deal with her."

"It would appear that I have little other choice." She accepted the ring, then stepped forward and gave me a fierce hug. "Don't let Hunter win. I want to be a grandmother; I want to spoil your son as rotten as I did his mother."

Tears filled my eyes. I blinked them rapidly away, pulled from her grasp, and held out my hand to Azriel. Three seconds later, we were standing outside the Directorate. I raised my gaze, studying the upper levels of the green-glass building. Somewhere up there was Hunter's office. Or at least the public face of it.

This was it. This was the endgame.

I spun, wrapped my arms around Azriel's neck, and kissed him fiercely.

"Just in case," I said.

He didn't reply. He didn't need to. I could feel his emotions flow through the inner reaches of my soul, and they were even more turbulent than my own.

After all, he knew in full the paths that lay before us, thanks to the fates.

I swung back around and marched into the Directorate's foyer. The security guard glanced up as we entered, and an odd sort of expression—one that was part fear, part pity—crossed his face before he managed to compose himself.

"Risa Jones, I believe," he said, voice neutral.

"That I am," I replied. "I'm here to see Director Hunter."

"She is expecting you." He glanced at Azriel. "I'm afraid you'll have to hand in your weapons."

Azriel crossed his arms and simply said, "No."

The guard blinked. "I'm sorry, but I have been ordered not—"

"I will not relinquish my sword," Azriel said, "but even if I did, it would do Hunter no good, as the sword has a mind of its own and will follow me into her lair regardless. And heaven help those who try to stop her."

The guard hesitated, and an odd sort of blankness came into his eyes. Communicating with the boss, I realized. Obviously, Hunter had stacked the decks with *her* people, rather than people who were loyal to the Directorate itself.

Life returned to the guard's eyes. "You've been cleared to carry within the building." He paused to hand us both a pass. "Please use elevator five—it will take you express up to the director's suites."

"Thank you."

I turned and headed for the elevator. Number five opened as we approached, but my steps slowed as I was hit with a vision of the doors closing and the elevator plunging to unknown depths, killing us both. It would certainly be the easy option when it came to getting the key.

"Hunter knows I can transport us both out in such an event." Azriel's fingers lightly pressed against my spine, urging me on. "And she is so arrogantly sure of her own superiority that she would prefer to kill us herself rather than employ a third-party means of doing so."

"If she was so sure of defeating us, she wouldn't be meeting us in one of the securest buildings in Melbourne."

I swiped the pass across the scanner. The doors closed

and the elevator rose rather than dropped. Relief still swam through me. Azriel might have been certain of this outcome, but Hunter never did the expected. I wouldn't have been surprised if she *had* chosen the smashing-elevator option.

I watched the numbers climb on the softly lit floor-level indicator above the doorway, and with each level that passed, my tension grew. When the elevator finally stopped on the tenth floor, I was wound up so tight it felt like the slightest touch would shatter me.

I licked my lips and forced my feet forward as the doors opened. Azriel was at my back, his calm exterior belying the tension and readiness within him. Once in the foyer, I paused and glanced around, wanting to get an idea of the layout before I went any farther. The only way on or off this floor was via the elevator we'd used. Where the other elevator doors should have been there was solid concrete, and directly in front of us was a reinforced security area that practically bristled with all sorts of scanners and weapons. Hunter was taking no chances. There was also no fire exit, and apparently no bathrooms. Hunter, old vampire or not, still had to use the loo like the rest of us, but if she was this paranoid about her safety in a place that was filled with guardians, then it would make sense that she'd have a private bathroom.

The guard beyond the security barrier had one hand on a rather nasty-looking weapon as we approached. He nodded his head toward the scanners. I stepped through first, stopped when he motioned me to do so, and watched as several lights, some blue, some red, scanned me. No alarms or lights went off. I was motioned through into what looked like a glass cage and held there while Azriel went through the scanning process. Again no alarms sounded.

"Weapons in the box," the guard said, shoving a clear plastic container into our little cell.

"I will not relinquish my sword, and Hunter is well aware of this fact. And," he added, glancing up at the discreetly placed camera in one corner, "she would be well advised to stop playing these games or I will simply transport into her chambers and kill her. I care nothing for Rhoan Jenson's safety myself, remember."

The guard's eyebrows rose, but before he could say anything, a light flashed; then Hunter said, voice cool and amused, "Let them in, Walter, swords and all."

He pressed a button and one section of the glass cell retracted. The walls and ceiling had been covered with thick but plush soundproofing, and it gave the corridor an ominous, almost forbidding feel.

"Second door on the right," he said.

We moved forward. Our footsteps made no sound; in fact, the only sound to be heard in this place was the squeak of the guard's chair as he settled back into position, and my somewhat rapid breathing.

The second door slightly clicked open as we neared it. I wouldn't have been surprised if some black-hooded creature suddenly appeared and bade us entry into hell itself, but imagination and reality were two different beasts. There was no one at the door, or even in the large conference room beyond it.

"Welcome to my humble home away from home," Hunter said, her voice coming from everywhere and yet nowhere. I looked around for speakers but couldn't immediately find them; nor could I find any cameras. They had to be hidden in the walls. "I am glad to see that you are punctual. Or rather, Jenson will undoubtedly be glad that you are punctual."

"Enough with the word games," I said, keeping my voice even. I wished I could so easily control the tension. "Tell me where he is and how to free him from whatever trap you may have wrapped around him."

"As you wish. There is, however, one small

complication—*you* can't rescue him." The amusement in Hunter's voice was stronger. "And it is the reason I have allowed your lover to keep his sword. You see, the magic that secures Jenson can only be bypassed by a full-energy being such as your reaper. Your uncle, as a half-breed, will only succeed in killing both Jenson and himself if he undertakes the rescue attempt."

"Meaning Azriel has to make the choice—me or my uncle." I wasn't surprised, because I'd suspected all along it would come down to me and Hunter, but that didn't mean I wasn't pissed off.

"Precisely," Hunter all but purred. "And we all know what your decision will be given what such a death would do to his sister."

In that she was right. "Where is he?"

"In a secure depot just outside Melbourne." She gave us the address. "I suggest you go, reaper. Jenson's situation is somewhat precarious."

She didn't explain what she meant, and I didn't ask. I simply swung around and gave Azriel a hug. *Be careful. This barrier might well be set to kill both you and Rhoan.*

Undoubtedly, he replied, unfazed. *But your uncle and aunt are already on the way to that location, and between the three of us, we shall unpick the trap. Then I will return to help you.*

She won't let you return. I forced myself to step away from him, though all I wanted to do was cling tight. I'd see him again. I had to believe that, if nothing else.

She will undoubtedly ban me from her offices, but she is not in her office. She is deep underground, where she believes she is safe from me.

And she is. You can't track a soul underground unless they are due for death.

Perhaps, but I can find you. Out loud, he added, "Hunter, if anything happens to her, my vengeance will be brutal."

"Reaper, we both know that murder is beyond the realm of your charter here on Earth, so do not—"

"It has nothing to do with my orders and everything to do with desire. Trust me, neither your flesh nor your soul will enjoy the spoils of your kill for long if you decide to take that path."

And with that warning lingering in the air, he left.

Hunter's laugh was low and soft. "I never knew reapers could be so overly dramatic. But then, he *has* been associating with you for a while now." The huge double doors on the other side of the room silently began to open. "Risa, please, do come in."

Said the spider to the fly. I flexed my fingers and resisted the urge to draw Amaya. Hunter hadn't actually mentioned her yet, and I wasn't about to remind her— though I very much doubted she'd actually *forgotten* her.

I walked around the table and warily entered the large room beyond it. A large black desk dominated the room, with several comfortable-looking chairs in front of it and a wall of windows behind it. There was very little else in the room; no wall art and nothing personal.

Hunter, as Azriel had said, wasn't here.

"What game are you playing now, Director?" I stopped in the middle of the room and looked around. Though there didn't appear to be any other exits, there obviously had to be. Whether they were concealed by magic or simply brilliant workmanship was the question.

Magic here, Amaya said. *Active not.*

I frowned. If there was magic here, why wasn't it active? What was she waiting for?

Even as those questions crossed my mind, Hunter said, "I've just received word that your reaper, Quinn, and Riley have all appeared at the depot. Time to ensure none of them can interfere with our little tête-à-tête."

Energy surged through the room, a short, sharp caress that was both electronic and magical in feel.

Now active, Amaya said, rather unnecessarily.

"I'm afraid it's just you and me now. The barrier that is now in place will repel any sort of energy being entry. Unfortunately for you, it will also prevent your becoming Aedh." Hunter's tones were smug. "Please, come on down to my true office, and let's discuss this key matter."

"More than happy to," I said easily, despite the fact that I wanted to flee so badly that the Aedh magic surged unasked, causing my extremities to fade in and out of being without actually progressing to a full change.

"Excellent." There was a slight hiss of air—like that of an airlock being released. Then one section of the wall moved forward and slid to the left, while a second door stepped back and retreated to the right. Beyond it was a small black elevator. "The elevator will bring you down to me. Oh, I believe you have an invisible sword—leave it behind. And I want to hear it hitting the floor—no faking."

"No." Silently, I added, *Amaya, make a lot of noise but remain invisible, and get into my flesh, fast.*

And then I crossed mental fingers that Myer *hadn't* reported this trick to Hunter.

She sighed. "Do I really have to kill your aunt and uncle?"

"Fine," I said, through gritted teeth. I made a show of drawing Amaya from her sheath, then released her. She hit the ground hard, her steel tip smacking against the leg of the nearby chair, the sound ringing across the silence. But almost immediately, she bounced up to my chest. I crossed my arms, holding her in place as her steel melted into my body and became one with me once more.

"Excellent," Hunter purred. "Now the key. Hold it up so I can be sure you have it."

I reached behind me, pulled out the key fragment, then held it up. I had no idea where the camera actually was, but I had no doubt Hunter could see the sharp bit of concrete.

"That," she said, "is not quite what I was expecting."

"It's a piece of the shield on a coat of arms," I said. "It *is* the key."

"Of course, I only have your word on that."

"Ask Myer what was at the last location before I attacked her. She'll confirm we were inspecting a coat of arms."

Hunter was silent for a moment, then said, "Very well, please proceed into the elevator."

I did so. The twin doors closed with a hiss, and darkness settled like a cloak around me. I had no doubt it was meant to unnerve me—and in that, it was succeeding. But in the utter blackness, the Dušan shifted the knife, her sharp nails digging into my skin as she slithered up my arm, around my shoulder, then down my spine. As the elevator began its descent, the knife's cold stone pressed against my skin and the Dušan's tail whipped back and forth.

Both knife and serpent were ready to fight.

As the elevator dropped, so, too, did the temperature. The air became heavier, laden with the scents of earth and foul water. Hunter's lair really *was* deep underground.

The elevator finally slowed, bouncing slightly as it stopped. The doors hissed open but didn't really reveal anything. The ink was as dark outside as it was inside. I flared my nostrils, drawing in the scents of this place. A fresh mix of jasmine, bergamot, and sandalwood lingered in the air. Hunter was here.

"A little light wouldn't go astray," I said, not immediately moving from the elevator. "We wouldn't want me tripping over and losing the key, now, would we?"

"Oh, decidedly not."

Her reply was dry, but she nevertheless switched on a light. It threw out a cold blue glow that barely made a dent against the deeper shadows of the place, but it at least revealed the flagstone flooring beyond the elevator as well as several worn leather sofas. Hunter herself remained hidden, though her scent was coming from the left. Which probably meant she was actually standing to my right.

I stepped into the room, then stopped. The light barely touched my toes, leaving the elevator behind me wrapped in darkness—but only for a moment. The doors soon closed and the elevator left. Trapped, I thought, as my heart accelerated and pinpricks of sweat broke out across my skin. Never a good thing when faced with a vampire, let alone *this* vampire.

Kill bitch, Amaya said, ever practical, *solve problem.*

"Now," said bitch continued, "deposit the key on that coffee table."

Her voice was coming from the thick darkness beyond the small, slightly raised seating area. I could vaguely see the outline of a desk, but given the shadows, there was no hope I'd ever see her. This darkness was her friend, not mine.

Can lift, Amaya said.

Not yet.

Amaya muttered something I didn't quite catch, although I didn't really have to understand it to know she was not happy with the delay. She wanted to fight, to destroy; it was a sentiment that was apparently echoed by the Dušan, if the ever-increasing force and speed of her lashing tail were anything to go by. Only trouble was, Hunter's hearing might be sharp enough to pick up the slight slap of flesh against flesh.

But even as that thought crossed my mind, the tail movement stopped. It was the first clear indication I'd had that the Dušan *could* understand me.

Dušan, I think it's time for you to leave my skin if you can. Hide in the shadows near her, but don't do anything until I say.

The Dušan immediately slithered down my left leg, its

sharp little claws making my muscles twitch with fleeting pain. Then it was gone, skittering away into the deeper shadows that hid Hunter.

"You won't get this key until I get confirmation that Rhoan is safe."

"Dear girl," Hunter said, voice condescending, "you are down here alone, without any of your protections. Do you really think you can survive my wrath for more than the second or two it will take me to retrieve the key from your cold, dead grasp?"

"A second or two is all I need to destroy the key and ensure you never get your nasty little mitts on it. Are *you* willing to take that chance?"

She seemed to consider me for a moment, as if weighing whether I was bluffing or not, but it was something I felt rather than saw.

"Fair enough," she said eventually. "We will play it your way for now."

There was a faint click; then brightness flared across the darkness, catching me by surprise. I blinked rapidly, and my pulse rate accelerated yet again when I realized that I was seeing a security screen—one that was split into four panels, two of them showing an unfamiliar building and lobby area, and the other two revealing very familiar figures. Quinn and Riley were in one, guarding what looked like a pile of bodies, and Azriel in the other, approaching a slowly rotating sphere of blue light.

I watched, heart in my mouth, as Azriel walked around the sphere, inspecting it. When he'd returned to his starting point, he touched it with his fingertips. Blue light crawled across his hand but didn't appear to hurt him. After another moment, he stepped into it.

I think I stopped breathing, and time seemed to drag.

Then he reappeared, and with him was Rhoan— bloody, beaten, but very much alive.

Relief shuddered through me, and just for a second,

my legs felt weak and my knees gave way. Somehow, I managed to stay upright.

"Right," Hunter said, her attention fully on me again—something I could tell by the wash of animosity and satisfaction oozing from her. "Rhoan is safe, as is your precious reaper. Give me the key."

"They're not out of that building yet."

"No, and they won't get out of it unless you give me the key. *Now*," she added, when I didn't move. "Or have you forgotten I can still blow them all to smithereens?"

"Then take it." I held out the hand that held the key and silently screamed, *Azriel, you need to get out of there—now! Hunter has the place rigged to blow.*

I had no idea whether he could hear me; certainly there didn't seem to be any sudden awareness of danger in his or Rhoan's actions. I wanted to scream at the screen, tell him to get his ass moving, but I did nothing, just watched, as the two men moved out of camera range, then reappeared in the next screen.

Hunter stepped forward, out of the shadows. Her gaze was on the shard of concrete rather than on me, so I carefully reached back with my free hand and wrapped my fingers around the knife. The stone blade pressed lightly against my palm; it would take only the slightest pressure for it to slice into my skin.

Dušan, be ready. You, too, Amaya.

Her excitement raced through the back reaches of my mind, sharp and eager to kill.

Hunter's fingers hovered above mine for a moment; then she carefully picked up the concrete shard. "I can indeed feel the weight of magic within it. It is a powerful thing." Then her gaze rose to mine. "And more the fool you are for trusting that once I had this in my grasp, I would keep my word."

The words were barely out of her mouth when the images on the monitor behind her exploded into flame.

Chapter 16

I screamed and reacted instinctively, clenching my fist and swinging as hard as I could at Hunter's smug face. But even as I did so, Amaya's voice cut through the panic.

Not dead! Safe they are!

My blow didn't land. Instead, it was caught in a vise-like grip and held firm. I didn't fight her hold; I just glared at her.

Are you sure?

Valdis contact. Reaper comes.

Which didn't mean he could actually get *in*. Even so, relief flooded me for the second time that night. But I couldn't let it show. Hunter had to believe *I* believed everyone I cared about was now dead.

Hunter's grip began to tighten against mine, and her sharp claws sliced into my skin. Blood welled. Anticipation and hunger flared in her eyes, but a similar sense of anticipation echoed through me. She'd just provided the perfect cover.

My grip tightened on the blade at my back. It sliced into my palm and was met by a rush of blood. The sweet metallic scent grew stronger in the air, but I doubted Hunter was aware of this secondary source. She was too intent on crushing my hand, too aware of the blood that dripped in fat splashes down onto the paving stones between us.

"I'll kill you for that," I growled.

Her smile was slow and lazy. "Oh, you most certainly are welcome to *try*. But remember what I am; remember that what I did to the—"

I plunged the stone blade into her stomach, and the rest of her sentence became a screech that was both fury and pain. She flung me backward so forcefully that I literally sailed through the air for several feet before crashing onto my back and sliding to a halt hard up against the elevator doors.

I scrambled to my feet, Amaya out of my body and in my hands. But even as I did so, light flared across the shadows—a fierce white light that was nigh on blinding. I raised my hand against it, battling to see what was going on, where Hunter was.

After a moment, I realized the light was coming from *her*.

Or rather, from the wound in her stomach.

Tendrils of brightness flowed from the knife's entry point and entwined around her, their movement getting fiercer, angrier, as they flowed up her body, then continued on, as if reaching for the very distant heavens. But they disappeared long before they even reached the roof of this cavern.

She wasn't moving, wasn't doing much of anything. The light held her immobile; now was the perfect time to attack—

Not, Amaya said. *Light force of her god leaving. It still protects.*

And wasn't *that* typical of this whole sorry episode. I shifted my grip on Amaya and stalked closer. I might not be able to attack the bitch until the power of her god left her body, but I sure as *hell* could do so the second it *had*.

Dušan, when she moves, strike.

I stopped several feet away from her. She might be immobilized, but she was totally aware of what was happening. Her eyes were thin black strips that promised death, and her fury washed over me in heated waves. I shuddered. Even without the force of her god, Hunter was *not* going to go down easy.

Get ready to both shield and attack, Amaya.

Flames flickered brightly down her sides, and her need to kill became so fierce I could almost taste the bitterness of Hunter's blood on her steel.

The brightness of the tendrils began to fade. The tension running through me ramped up another notch, until my whole body seemed to be humming with it.

Then I realized it *was* humming—and that it was Amaya's energy flowing through me.

Together we strong, she said. *Together we taste her blood.*

The light blinked out. Hunter howled—a sound that was fury and grief and utter, *utter* madness combined—and launched at me, claws and teeth elongating. I dodged and swung Amaya, but Hunter was too fast and the blow skimmed past her side and did no damage.

Amaya chuckled, the sound low and savage. Hunter disappeared into shadows.

Flame, I said, and Amaya immediately did. Fire exploded from her, leaping high, tearing away the shadows and revealing the vastness of Hunter's den.

Revealing the laser held in her hand, aimed straight at my heart.

Shield, I screamed, even as I dove away.

Can't! Flame or shield, not both!

I hit the ground and rolled. Blue light followed me, slicing into the flagstones and across my left boot. The smell of burned leather and flesh seared the air. I bit back a scream and scrambled to my feet, forcing myself to run despite the fire in my foot. The laser nipped at my heels, threatening limb loss if I so much as stumbled.

I flung Amaya and called to the Aedh. The magic surged, and just for a moment, my legs and arms became little more than particles. Then the magic fell away and I was flesh again. Hunter hadn't been lying—her shields were stopping me from becoming full Aedh.

Dušan, grab her!

Amaya arrowed toward Hunter. The laser shifted, hitting her. Lilac flames flared against blue light, and though Amaya slowed, she didn't appear hurt by the laser's hit.

Then Hunter went down, confusion briefly replacing the fury and madness in her expression.

While she might not have expected the Dušan's presence, her surprise certainly didn't dull her reactions.

I scrambled forward, as fast as I was able, as vampire and Dušan twisted and fought each other. Again blue light flared. The Dušan hissed and slithered away. Hunter scrambled to her feet, her movements little more than a blur as she launched herself at me. Amaya thundered back into my hand and I swung her, hard. Hunter hissed and deviated at the last moment, coming in under the blow. Her foot smashed into my kneecap and thrust me backward. Pain, white-hot, hit, but I somehow managed to remain upright. She came at me again, movements little more than a blur. That I could even see her was a miracle, and I had no doubt that it was all due to Amaya's presence in my mind.

I waited until the last minute, until I could see the bloody glimmer of hate in her eyes, then raised Amaya. Black steel met sharp claws, and blood spurted as two fingertips plopped to the flagstones.

Lilac slithered in from behind her and wrapped around her legs. Hunter hit the floor face-first, but her hiss was more a sound of fury than one of pain. She made an odd motion with a bloodied left hand, then twisted around and grabbed the Dušan with her right, forcing the laser into its mouth. I swung Amaya before she could fire, aiming for her head. She ducked and the blow sailed over her head, but it at least forced her to release the Dušan. It slithered away again.

Flames leapt from Amaya's steel and anchored onto Hunter's flesh, flickering and dancing in eager anticipation as Amaya began to feed on her soul.

Hunter either didn't know what was happening or didn't care. She jumped upright and ran, which was so out of character I swung around instead of giving chase.

Twelve other vampires were now in the room. Hunter certainly *wasn't* taking any chances. If ever there was a time for Azriel to appear . . .

Can't, Amaya spat. *Magic stop.*

Meaning it was just me and her, as I'd always feared it would be. *Fine,* I thought, resolutely. *Let's have at these vamps first.*

And with that, I attacked. Or rather, *we* attacked. Because the minute I moved, Amaya surged fully into my mind, and together we became a killing machine.

Everything became a blur. We weaved, dodged, blocked. Attacked, retreated, parried. There was pain and blood and screams, and I really couldn't have said whether they were mine or whether they belonged to the vampires we slowly but surely decimated.

But in the end, the sheer force of numbers overwhelmed us.

I went down in a bloody tangle of arms and legs. Teeth tore at me, fingernails sliced into me, and all I could smell was blood and fear and rancid vampire.

Flame can, Amaya said. She sounded as weary as I felt, no surprise given that we'd undoubtedly been drawing on each other's strength.

No, I said. *We have one chance left. Hunter thinks she's won. We have to play with that.*

Could cost.

Yes, it could. But if blood and pain were the price I had to pay to kill Hunter, then pay them I would.

"Enough!" Hunter's voice rang out across the din of growling, angry vampires. "She is *mine*."

I was dragged unceremoniously to my feet. Blood poured down my face, blocking my vision, but I didn't need to see Hunter to know she was closing in. I could smell her. Smell the rancidness of her.

It was new, that smell.

Or maybe it was merely what remained after the strength of her god had left her.

The soft sound of her steps stopped. I waited, body thrumming with pain. Pain that I had no doubt was about to get far worse.

"Drop your sword, Risa."

No! Amaya screamed, even as my fingers tightened instinctively around her.

"Drop it, or I will be forced to chop your hand off."

Behave, Amaya. Don't react just yet. I released my fingers. The vampire on my left took her from me and flung her away. She shadowed immediately, but her metal clanged as she hit the stone and bounced. She hissed in displeasure, but it was a sound only I heard.

And only I knew that she was already on her way back to me.

Hunter smiled, all teeth and nastiness. "And now, you will pay for this." She raised her left hand with its two missing fingers; she was gripping a thin, sharp knife. "Flesh for flesh seems only fair, after all."

The trouble was, the blade was aimed not at my hands or even my heart, but at my stomach.

At my child.

Time seemed to slow to a crawl.

I screamed and twisted and fought, cursed and kicked, only to be pinned down even harder. My screams were echoed by another, the source far from human. Flames shot from Amaya's steel and arrowed toward us, but they were never going to get here in time.

Then, from out of nowhere sprung the Dušan. It chomped down on Hunter's wrist, consuming flesh and steel in one large gulp, then twisted around, lashing its body around Hunter, binding her completely.

I gave her guards no time to react. I called to the Aedh, pulled my particles free from their grip, then dropped and flung out a hand. Amaya hit it almost immediately, and in one smooth motion, I swung her around in a circle, severing the legs of both vampires. As Amaya's flames crawled over both of them and began to consume their souls, I rolled out from under their dropping bodies and killed the third vampire. A quick check told me there were no more.

Now it really *was* just me and Hunter.

I pushed to my feet and somewhat unsteadily walked back to her.

She bared her teeth and hissed at me, but there was nothing she could do. The power of her god had departed, and she was just a very old, very powerful vampire whose blood was pulsing out onto the stones at my feet, draining her strength with every second that went by.

"This is for Jak," I said, and gutted her.

Then, as her stomach split and her insides began to leak out, I swung Amaya again and beheaded her.

The Dušan unwound itself from her, allowing her body to slump to the floor. As the Dušan crawled back into my flesh, steam began to rise from Hunter's body. Her soul, rising.

"Do not think I'm going to let you off that easily, Hunter," I said, and stabbed Amaya through the wispy heart of her.

Amaya's chuckle was fierce and savage as she almost lovingly consumed Hunter's soul.

Evil this one, she murmured. *Full for many months.*

I half laughed, but the sound disintegrated into a sob as weakness washed over me and I dropped to my knees.

Ten seconds later I was pulled into arms that were warm
and strong and shaking with relief.

I wrapped my arms around Azriel's neck and somehow murmured, "Dingdong, the bitch is dead."

After that, I knew no more.

Epilogue

"I really do *not* like the idea of you moving all the way up here." Riley crossed her arms, every bit of her body bristling with indignation.

"It'll take you less than an hour to get here," I said, voice mild as I maneuvered down onto the picnic blanket. My back was aching but my stomach was so damn large these days I made whales look positively svelte. It made doing *anything* extremely awkward.

Not everything, Azriel commented, amused.

I snorted softly and shot him a look. He was standing close by, ready to offer a hand if needed. I didn't need it, not in this instance. Barrel belly or not, I was determined *not* to lean on him too much for help. It was that whole stubbornness thing I was famous for raising its ugly head again.

I wasn't thinking about sex, reaper.

No, I was. His amusement grew. *Have I told you how utterly irresistible you are when you're fat and round with my child?*

A hundred times a day, I said dryly, *but I'm getting a little tired of the word "fat."*

Rotund?

Worse.

Portly?

No.

Amply proportioned?

I picked up a twig and tossed it at him. His laughter ran through me, warm and teasing.

"That's an hour I could be spending with my grandson," Riley grumbled, oblivious to the fact that there was a whole other level of conversation happening. She dropped beside me. "You're sure you wouldn't reconsider the warehouse near our place? It'd make a truly stunning home."

"So will this—if it ever gets finished."

"If you'd bought the warehouse, I could have been there every day to hassle them along."

I grinned and twined my hand through hers. While it hadn't taken us all that long to find and buy this acreage up in the Macedon hills, it *had* taken months—and months—to get council approval for our uniquely designed, rough-hewn residences. I did not want to go through all that red tape again—especially now, with the birth of our son so close. Besides, I wanted him to grow up in the clean, fresh air of the mountains rather than in the city.

"How's Uncle Rhoan coping with being the boss of the guardian division?"

She snorted. "He says he hates it, but he's always loved a challenge. And with the Cazadors on his side, helping him clean out Hunter's factions, I think we'll soon see a very different—and ultimately more efficient—Directorate." Her gaze met mine, gray eyes glittering silver in the morning sunshine. "That was a very shrewd move on your part, suggesting he appoint Markel second in charge. They make a good—and dangerous—team."

"All I did was ask a favor. Rhoan's the one who deserves the congrats. He took the chance on him, not me."

And I was grateful he had, however dubious he might have been at the time. Markel certainly deserved the opportunity to be something other than just another Cazador lost to the berserker bloodlust.

And while neither he nor Stanford might have had as much of a place in the final battle with Hunter as either they or I had hoped, Stanford had, at least, helped steer the high council away from seeking retribution for Hunter's death. For that, I was grateful.

Movement caught my eye. I glanced around as Quinn and Tao emerged from the thick forest and sauntered down the hill. The rather large tree trunk they were carrying between them might have been a twig for all the effort they were showing.

"There's something very satisfying about watching men building a house," Riley murmured, her gaze following Quinn. "Maybe we need to buy some land up this way and build one of our own."

"Good idea." I reached for one of the sandwiches. "It means my babysitter is that much closer."

She grinned. "And you think I'd mind?"

"Not in the least." I paused, watching as Quinn and Tao positioned the log onto the plane saw. Behind them was the roofed framework of three large pavilions—separate living quarters for me and Azriel, Ilianna and Mirri, as well as Simi, Tao's new partner, and the woman he'd initially been afraid to go on another date with because of the elemental. She, when it had become obvious he'd had no intentions of taking their relationship any further than the one date, had taken matters into her own hands. She was definitely a woman who knew exactly what she wanted, and she'd fit in rather nicely to our little group. Both Ilianna and Tao would be living here only part-time; Ilianna had recommitted herself to working at the Brindle—which was where the last piece of the key now resided. Tao—in elemental form—was still spending his nights up at the nearby sacred site.

It didn't matter. I'd once feared, with everything that had happened and our home destroyed, that our relationship could never be the same. And, in some respects, that was true. It wasn't the same, but it *was* stronger. And I hadn't thought that could be possible.

For the moment, everything was good. Hell, even Amaya had stopped grumbling about the lack of action over recent months.

Time yet, she muttered. *Demons still there.*

Yes, they were, unfortunately. And we still had only the one gate between us and hell. Azriel was very much involved in hunting down the demons who broke through into his world and ours, as would Amaya and I be once my son was born. I was a Mijai in waiting; my job now was to protect *this* world.

"You know," I said, watching the two men ready the log for cutting into planks, "I'm really glad the professionals are coming back tomorrow. At the rate these two are working, this child will be going to school before everything is actually finished."

Riley laughed and bounced up again. "I shall go motivate them."

Azriel sat down beside me as she ran down the hill. I leaned against him and smiled. As I did, I felt my water break. Excitement and fear stirred within me. "Have I told you lately how glad I am you came into my life?"

"Not recently, no." He considered me for a moment, a slight frown creasing his features. "Why?"

"Because you need to hear it before I go into full labor and start swearing at you for causing me pain."

He blinked. "Is it normal for women of this world to swear at their partners at an event as beautiful as the birth of their child?"

"You try squeezing a melon out of your penis and see how it feels."

"I do not believe that would be at all pleasant, even if it were possible." He paused again, and this time his excitement surged, just about blowing my senses apart. "Did you just say *before* you go into full labor?"

I smiled. "I did."

"Does that mean—" He trailed off, his expression a priceless mix of hope, excitement, uncertainty, and love.

"It does indeed."

He jumped to his feet. "Shall I let the others know? Should we get you to the hospital?"

I laughed and caught his hand. "We have plenty of time yet."

And we did. We had all the time in the world to build our family and grow old together.

The fates had assured us both of that.

Don't miss the first novel in the Souls of Fire
series by Keri Arthur,

FIREBORN

Now available from Signet Select

All of us dream.

Some of us even have pleasant dreams.

My dreams might have been few and far between, but
they were never, ever pleasant. But worse than that, they
always came true.

Over the course of my many lifetimes, I'd tried to interfere, to alter fate's path and prevent the death I'd seen, but
I'd learned the hard way that there were often serious consequences for both the victim and myself.

Which was why the flesh down my spine was twisted and
marred. I'd pulled a kid from a burning car, saving her life
but leaving us both disfigured. Fire may be mine to control
and devour, but there'd been too many witnesses and I'd
dared not use my powers. It had taken me months to heal,
and I'd sworn—yet again—to stop interfering and simply
let fate take her natural course. But here I was, out on the
streets in the cold, dead hours of the night, trying to keep
warm as I waited in the shadows for the man who was
slated to die this night.

Because he wasn't just *a* man. He was the man I'd once
loved.

I shifted my weight from one foot to the other and tried to keep warm in the confines of the abandoned factory's doorway. Why anyone would even come out by choice on a night like this was beyond me. Melbourne was a great city, but her winters could be hell, and right now it was cold enough to freeze the balls off a mutt—not that there were any mutts about at this particular hour. They apparently had more sense.

The breeze whisked around the parts of my face not protected by my scarf, freezing my skin and making it feel like I was breathing ice.

Of course, I *did* have other ways to keep warm. I was a phoenix—a spirit born from the ashes of flame—and fire was both my heritage and my soul. But even if I couldn't sense anyone close by, I was reluctant to flame. Vampires and werewolves might have outed themselves during the peak of Hollywood's love affair with all things paranormal, but the rest of us preferred to remain hidden. Humanity on the whole might have taken the existence of weres and vamps better than any of us had expected, but there were still far too many who believed nonhumans provided an unacceptable risk to their existence. Even on crappy nights like this, it wasn't unusual to have hunting parties roaming the streets, looking for easy paranormal targets. While my kind rarely provided any sort of threat, I wasn't human, and that made me as much a target for their hate as vamps and weres.

Even the man who'd once claimed to love me was not immune to such hate.

Pain stirred, distant and ghostly, but never, ever forgotten, no matter how hard I tried. Samuel Turner had made it all too clear what he thought of my "type." Five years might have passed, but I doubted time would have changed his view that the only good monster was a dead one.

And yet here I was, attempting to save his stupid ass.

The roar of a car engine rode across the silence. For a moment the dream raised its head, and I saw again the flashes of metal out of the car window, the red-cloaked faces, the blood and brain matter dripping down brick as Sam's lifeless body slumped to the wet pavement. My stomach heaved and I closed my eyes, sucking in air and fighting the feeling of inevitability.

Death would *not* claim his soul tonight.

I wouldn't let her.

Against the distant roar of that engine came the sound of steady steps from the left of the intersection up ahead. He was walking toward the corner and the death that awaited him there.

I stepped out of the shadows. The glow of the streetlights did little to break up the night, leaving the surrounding buildings to darkness and imagination. The ever-growing rumble of the car approaching from the right didn't quite drown out the steady sound of footsteps, but perhaps it only seemed that way because I was so attuned to it. To what was about to happen.

I walked forward, avoiding the puddles of light and keeping to the darker shadows. The air was thick with the growing sense of doom and the rising ice of hell.

Death waited on the other side of the street, her dark rags billowing and her face impassive.

The growling of the car's engine swept closer. Lights broke across the darkness, the twin beams of brightness spotlighting the graffiti that colored an otherwise bleak and unforgiving cityscape.

This area of Brooklyn was Melbourne's dirty little secret, one definitely *not* mentioned in the flashy advertising that hailed the city as the "it" holiday destination. It was a mix of heavy industrial and run-down tenements, and it housed the underbelly of society—the dregs, the forgotten, the dangerous. Over the past few years, it had become so bad that the wise avoided it and the newspapers had given up reporting about it. Hell, even the cops feared to tread the streets alone here. These days they did little more than patrol the perimeter in a vague attempt to stop the violence from spilling over into neighboring areas.

So why the hell was Sam right here in the middle of Brooklyn's dark heart?

I had no idea and, right now, with Death so close, it hardly mattered.

I neared the fatal intersection and time slowed to a crawl. A deadly, dangerous crawl.

The Commodore's black nose eased into the intersection from the right. Windows slid down smoothly, and the long black barrels of the rifles I'd seen in my dream appeared. Behind them, half-hidden in the darkness of the car's interior, red hoods billowed.

Be fast, my inner voice whispered, *or die.*

Death stepped forward, eager to claim her soul. I took a deep, shuddering breath and flexed my fingers.

Sam appeared past the end of the building and stepped toward the place of his death. The air recoiled as the bullets were fired. There was no sound. *Silencers.*

I lunged forward, grabbed his arm, and yanked him hard enough sideways to unbalance us both. Something sliced across my upper arm, and pain flared as I hit the pavement. My breath whooshed loudly from my lungs, but it didn't cover the sound of the unworldly scream of anger. Knowing what was coming, I desperately twisted around, flames erupting from my fingertips. They met the sweeping, icy scythe of Death, melting it before it could reach my flesh. Then they melted *her,* sending her back to the frigid realms of hell.

The car screeched to a halt farther down the street, the sound echoing sharply across the darkness. I scrambled to my feet. The danger wasn't over yet. He could still die, and we needed to get out of here—*fast.* I spun, only to find myself facing a gun.

"What the—" Blue eyes met mine and recognition flashed. "Red! What the *fuck* are you doing here?"

There was no warmth in his voice, despite the use of my nickname.

"In case it has escaped your notice," I snapped, trying to concentrate on the danger and the need to be gone rather than on how good he damn well looked, "someone just tried to blow your brains out—although it *is* debatable whether you actually have brains. Now move, because they haven't finished yet."

He opened his mouth, as ready as ever to argue, then glanced past me. The weapon shifted fractionally, and he pulled the trigger. As the bullet burned past my ear, I twisted around. A red-cloaked body lay on the ground five feet away, the hood no longer covering his features. His face was gaunt, emaciated, and there was a thick black scar on his right cheek that ended in a hook. It looked like Death's scythe.

The footsteps coming toward us at rapid speed said there were another four to deal with. Sam's hand clamped my wrist; then he was pulling me forward.

"We won't outrun them," I said, even as we tried to do just that.

"I know." Sam's voice was grim. Dark.

Sexy.

I batted the thought away and risked another glance over my shoulder. They'd rounded the corner and were now so close I could see their gaunt features, their scars, and the red of their eyes.

Fear shuddered through me. Whatever these things were, they *weren't* human.

"We need somewhere to hide." I scanned the buildings around us somewhat desperately. Broken windows, shattered brickwork, and rot abounded. Nothing offered the sort of fortress we so desperately needed right now.

"I *know*." He yanked me to the right, just about pulling my arm out of the socket in the process. We pounded down a small lane that smelled of piss and decay, our footsteps echoing across the night. It was a sound that spoke of desperation.

The red cloaks were quiet. Eerily quiet.

A metal door appeared out of the shadows. Sam paused long enough to fling it open, then thrust me inside and followed, slamming the door shut and then shoving home several thick bolts.

Just in time.

Something hit the other side of the door, the force of it enough to dent the metal and make me jump back in fright. Fire flicked across my fingertips, an instinctive reaction I quickly doused as Sam turned around.

"*That* won't help." His voice was grim, but it still held echoes of the distaste that had dominated his tone all those years ago. "We need to get upstairs. *Now,*" he added, as the door shuddered under another impact.

He brushed past me and disappeared into the gloom of the cavernous building. I unraveled the scarf from around my face and hastily followed. "What the hell are those things? And why do they want to kill you?"

"Long story." He reached a grimy set of stairs and took them two at a time. The metal groaned under his weight, but the sound was smothered by another hit to the door. This time, something broke.

"Hurry," he added rather unnecessarily.

I galloped after him, my feet barely even hitting the metal. We ran down a corridor, stirring the dust that clung to everything until the air was thick and difficult to breathe. From downstairs came a metallic crash—the door coming off its hinges and smashing to the concrete.

They were in. They were coming.

Fear leapt up my throat, and this time the flames that danced across my fingertips would not be quenched. The red-gold flickers lit the darkness, lending the decay and dirt that surrounded us an odd sort of warmth.

Sam went through another doorway and hit a switch on

the way through. Light flooded the space, revealing a long, rectangular room. In the left corner, as far away from the door as possible, was a rudimentary living area. Hanging from the ceiling on thick metal cables was a ring of lights that bathed the space in surreal violet light.

"Don't tell me you live here," I said as I followed Sam across the room.

He snorted. "No. This is merely a safe house. One of five we have in this area."

The problems in this area were obviously far worse than anyone was admitting if cops now needed safe houses. Or maybe it was simply a development linked to the appearance of the red cloaks. Certainly I hadn't come across anything like them before, and I'd been around for centuries. "Will the UV lighting stop those things?"

He glanced at me. "You can see that?"

"Yes." I said it tartly, my gaze on his, searching for the distaste and the hate. Seeing neither. "I'm not human, remember?"

He grunted and looked away. Hurt stirred again, the embers refusing to die, even five years down the track.

"UV stops them." He paused, then added, "Most of the time."

"Oh, that's a comfort," I muttered, the flames across my fingers dousing as I thrust a hand through my hair. "What the hell are they, then? Vampires? They're the only nonhumans I can think of affected by UV."

And they certainly hadn't *looked* like vampires. Most vamps tended to look and act human, except for the necessity to drink blood and avoid sunlight. None that I'd met had red eyes or weird scars on their cheeks—not even the psycho ones who killed for the pure pleasure of it.

"They're a type of vampire."

He pulled out a rack filled with crossbows, shotguns, and machine pistols from under the bed, then waved a hand toward it, silently offering me one of the weapons. I hesitated, then shook my head. I had my own weapon, and it was more powerful than any bullet.

"You'll regret it."

But he shrugged and began to load shells into a pump-action shotgun. There was little other sound. The red cloaks might be on their way up, but they remained eerily quiet.

I rubbed my arms, felt the sticky warmth, and glanced down. The red cloak's bullet had done little more than wing me, but it bled profusely. If they *were* a type of vampire, then the wound—or rather the blood—would call to them.

"That blood might call to more than just those red cloaks," he added, obviously noticing my actions. "There're some bandages in the drawer of the table holding the coffeepot. Use them."

I walked over to the drawer. "I doubt there's anything worse than those red cloaks out on the streets at the moment."

He glanced at me, expression unreadable. "Then you'd be wrong."

I frowned, but opened the drawer and found a tube of antiseptic along with the bandages. As medical kits went, it was pretty basic, but I guess it was better than nothing. I applied both, then moved to stand in the middle of the UV circle, close enough to Sam that his aftershave—a rich mix of woody, earthy scents and musk—teased my nostrils and stirred memories to life. I thrust them away and crossed my arms.

"How can these things be a type of vampire?" I asked, voice a little sharper than necessary. "Either you are or you aren't. There's not really an in-between state, unless you're in the process of turning from human to vamp."

And those things in the cloaks were neither dead *nor* turning.

"It's a long story," he said. "And one I'd rather not go into right now."

"Then at least tell me what they're called."

"We've nicknamed them red cloaks. What they call themselves is anyone's guess." His shoulder brushed mine as he turned, and a tremor ran down my body. I hadn't felt this man's touch for five years, but my senses remembered it. Remembered the joy it had once given me.

"So why are they after you?"

His short, sharp laugh sent a shiver down my spine. It was the sound of a man who'd seen too much, been through too much, and it made me wonder just what the hell had happened to him in the last five years.

"They hunt me because I've vowed to kill as many of the bastards as I can."

The chance to ask any more questions was temporarily cut off as the red cloaks ran through the door. They were so damn fast that they were halfway across the room before Sam could even get a shot off. I took a step back, my fingers aflame, the yellow-white light flaring oddly against the violet.

The front one ran at Sam with outstretched fingers, revealing nails that were grotesque talons ready to rip and tear. The red cloak hit the UV light, and instantly his skin began to blacken and burn. The stench was horrific, clogging the air and making my stomach churn, but he didn't seem to notice, let alone care. He just kept on running.

The others were close behind.

Sam fired. The bullet hit the center of the first red cloak's forehead, and the back of his head exploded, spraying those behind him with flesh and bone and brain matter.

He fell. The others leapt over him, their skin aflame and not caring one damn bit.

Which was obviously why Sam had said my own flame wouldn't help.

He fired again. Another red cloak went down. He tried to fire a third time, but the creature was too close, too fast. It battered him aside and kept on running.

It wanted *me*, not Sam. As I'd feared, the blood was calling to them.

I backpedaled fast, raised my hands, and released my fire. A maelstrom of heat rose before me, hitting the creature hard, briefly halting his progress and adding to the flames already consuming him.

My backside hit wood. The table. As the creature pushed through the flames, I scrambled over the top of it, then thrust it into the creature's gut. He screamed, the sound one of frustration rather than pain, and clawed at the air, trying to strike me with arms that dripped flames and flesh onto the surface of the table.

The *wooden* table.

As another shot boomed across the stinking, burning darkness, I lunged for the nearest table leg. I gripped it tight, then heaved with all my might. I might be only five foot four, but I wasn't human and I had a whole lot of strength behind me. The leg sheared free—and just in time.

The creature leapt at me. I twisted around and swung the leg with all my might. It smashed into the creature's head, caving in his side and battering him back across the table.

A final gunshot rang out, and the rest of the creature's head went spraying across the darkness. His body hit the concrete with a splat and slid past the glow of the UV, burning brightly in the deeper shadows crowding the room beyond.

I scrambled upright and held the leg at the ready. But there were no more fiery forms left to fight. We were safe.

For several seconds I did nothing more than stare at the remnants still being consumed by the UV's fire. The rank, bitter smell turned my stomach, and the air was thick with the smoke of them. Soon there was little left other than ash, and even that broke down into nothingness.

I lowered my hands and turned my gaze to the man I'd come here to rescue. "What the hell is going on here, Sam?"

He put the safety on the gun, then tossed it on the bed and stalked toward me. "Did they bite you? Scratch you?"

I frowned. "No—"

He grabbed my arms, his skin so cool against mine. It hadn't always been that way. Once, his flesh had matched mine for heat and urgency, especially when we were making love— I stopped the thought in its tracks. It never paid to live in the past. I knew that from long experience.

"Are you sure?" He turned my hands over and then grabbed my face with his oh-so-cool fingers, turning it one way and then another. There was concern in the blue of his eyes. Fear, even.

For *me*.

It made that stupid part of me deep inside want to dance, and *that* annoyed me even more than his nonanswers.

"I'm fine." I jerked away from his touch and stepped back. "But you really need to tell me what the hell is going on here."

He snorted and spun away, walking across to the coffee-maker. He poured two cups without asking, then walked back and handed the chip-free one to me.

"This, I'm afraid, has become the epicenter of hell on earth." His voice was as grim as his expression.

"Which is about as far from an answer as you can get," I snapped, then took a sip of coffee. I hated coffee—especially when it was thick and bitter—and he knew that. But he didn't seem to care and, right then, neither did I. I just needed something warm to ease the growing chill from my flesh. The immediate danger to Sam might be over, but there was still something *very* wrong. With this situation, and with this man. "What the hell were those things if not vampires?"

He studied me for a moment, his expression closed. "Officially they're known as the red plague, but, as I said, we call them red cloaks. They're humans infected by a virus nicknamed Crimson Death. It can be transmitted via a scratch or a bite."

"So if they wound you, you become just like them?"

A bleak darkness I didn't understand stirred through the depths of his blue eyes. "If you're human or vampire, yes."

I frowned. "Why just humans and vampires? Why not other races?"

"It may *yet* affect other races. There are some shifters who seem to be immune as long as they change shape immediately after being wounded, but this doesn't hold true in all cases. More than that?" He shrugged. "The virus is too new to be really certain of anything."

Which certainly explained why he'd examined me so quickly for wounds. Although given I could take fire form and literally burn away any drug or virus in my system, it was doubtful *this* virus would have any effect.

"So you've been assigned to some sort of task force to hunt down and kill these things?"

Again he shrugged. "Something like that."

Annoyance swirled, but I shoved it back down. It wouldn't get me anywhere—he'd always been something of a closed shop when it came to his work as a detective. I guess that was one thing that *hadn't* changed. "Is this virus a natural development or a lab-born one?"

"Lab born."

"Who in their right mind would want to create this sort of virus?"

"They didn't mean to create it. It's a by-product of sorts." He took a sip of his coffee, his gaze still on mine. There was little in it to give away what he was thinking, but it oddly reminded me of the look vampires got when they were holding themselves under tight control. He added, "They were actually trying to pin down the enzymes that turn human flesh into vampire and make them immortal."

"Why the hell would anyone want to be immortal? Or near immortal? It sucks. Just ask the vampires."

A smile, brief and bitter, twisted his features. "Humankind has a long history in chasing immortality. I doubt the testimony of vampires—many of whom are unbelievably rich thanks to that near immortality—would convince them otherwise."

"More fool them," I muttered. Living forever had its drawbacks. As did rebirth, which was basically what vampires went through to become near immortal. But then, humans rarely considered the side effects when they chased a dream.

I took another drink of coffee and shuddered at the tarlike aftertaste. How long had this stuff been brewing? I walked across to the small sink and dumped the remainder of it down the drain, then turned to face him again. "How did this virus get loose? This sort of research would have been top secret, and that usually comes with strict operational conditions."

"It did. Does. Unfortunately, one scientist decided to test a promising serum on himself after what appeared to be successful trials on lab rats. No one realized what he'd done until *after* he went crazy and, by that time, the genie was out of the bottle."

And on the streets, obviously. "How come there's been no public warning about this? Surely people have a right to know—"

"Yeah, great idea," he cut in harshly. "Warn the general population a virus that turns people into insane, vampirelike beings has been unleashed. Can you imagine the hysteria that would cause?"

And I guess it wouldn't do a whole lot of good to the image of actual vampires, either. It would also, no doubt, lead to an influx of recruits to the many gangs dedicated to wiping the stain of nonhumanity from Earth.

I studied him for a moment. For all the information he was giving me, I had an odd sense that he wasn't telling me everything. "The red cloaks who were chasing you acted as one, and with a purpose. That speaks of a hive-type mentality rather than insanity to me."

He shrugged. "The virus doesn't *always* lead to insanity, and not everyone who is infected actually survives. Those who do, do so with varying degrees of change and sanity."

I frowned. "How widespread is this virus? Because if tonight is any example, there's more than just a *few* surviving it."

"About sixty percent of those infected die. So far, the virus is mostly confined to this area. We suspect there's about one hundred or so cloaks."

Which to me sounded like a serious outbreak. It also explained the patrols around this area. They weren't keeping the peace—they were keeping people *out* and the red cloaks *in*. "And everyone who survives the virus is infectious?"

"Yes."

It was just one word, but it was said with such bitterness and anger that my eyebrows rose. "Did someone close to you get infected? Is that why you swore to hunt them all down?"

He smiled, but it wasn't a pleasant thing to behold. Far from it. "You could say that. Remember my brother?"

I remembered him, all right—he wasn't only the first child his mom had been able to carry to full term after a long series of miscarriages, but the firstborn *son*. And, as such, had never really been denied anything. He'd grown up accustomed to getting what he wanted, and I'd barely even begun my relationship with Sam when he'd decided what he wanted was *me*. He certainly hadn't been happy about being rejected. Sam, as far as I knew, was not aware that his older brother had tried to seduce me, although there had been a definite cooling in their relationship afterward.

"Of course I remember Luke—but what has he got to do with anything?"

"He was one of the first victims of a red cloak attack in Brooklyn."

If he'd been living in Brooklyn, it could only mean he'd truly immersed himself in the life of criminality he'd been dabbling with when I'd known him.

"Oh god. I'm sorry, Sam. Is he okay? Did he survive?" I

half reached out to touch his arm, then stilled the motion when I saw the bitter anger in his expression. It was aimed at himself rather than at me, and it all but screamed comfort was *not* something he wanted right now.

"Luke survived the virus, but his sanity didn't." The fury in Sam's eyes grew, but it was entwined with guilt and a deeper, darker emotion I couldn't define. But it was one that scared the hell out of me. "I was the one who took him down, Red."

No wonder he seemed surrounded by a haze of darkness and dangerous emotion—he'd been forced to shoot his own damn *brother*. "Sam, I'm sorry."

This time I *did* touch his arm, but he shook it off violently. "Don't be. He's far better off dead than—" He cut the rest of the sentence off and half shrugged. Like it didn't matter, when it obviously did.

"When did all this happen?"

"A little over a year ago."

And he'd changed greatly in that year, I thought, though I suspected the cause was far more than just the stress of Luke's death. "How the hell could something like this be kept a secret for so damn long?"

"Trust me, you wouldn't want to know."

A chill went through me. It wasn't so much the words, but the way he said them and the flatness in his eyes. I had no doubt those words were a warning of death, but even so, I couldn't help saying, "And what, exactly, does that mean?"

"It means you tell no one about tonight, or it could have disastrous consequences. For you and for them."

And there it was, I thought bitterly. Fate's kick in the gut. When would I ever learn to stop interfering with the natural course of events?

Sam stalked over to the bed, placing the shotgun in its slot and then picking up a regulation .40-caliber Glock semiauto pistol—a partner to the one he already carried. "We need to get out of here."

"But I want to know—"

I stopped as his gaze pinned me and, with sudden, sad clarity, I realized there was very little left of the man I'd known in those rich blue depths. Only shadows and bitterness. I might have saved him tonight, but the reality was I'd been about twelve months too late. This was nothing more than a replica. He might look the same, he might smell the same, but he held none of the fierce joy of life that had once called to me like flame to a moth. This man's world had become one of ashes and darkness, and it was not a place where I wanted to linger.

"Let's go," he said.

"Don't bother, Sam."

He briefly looked confused. It was the second real expression I'd seen—the first being that moment of surprise when he'd realized who'd saved him. "What do you mean?"

I walked across to him. Ashes or not, he still resembled the man I'd never get over—not in this lifetime, anyway—and it was hard not to lean into him. Hard not to give in to the desire to kiss him good-bye, just one more time.

"I'm one of them, remember?" Bitterness crept into my voice. "One of the monsters. And I'm more than capable of looking after myself."

He snorted softly, the sound harsh. "Not in this damn area, and maybe not against the—"

"I got in here without harm," I cut in, voice as cold as his, "and I'll damn well get out the same way."

"Fine." He stepped aside and waved me forward with the barrel of the gun. "Be my guest."

I looked at him for a moment longer, then walked toward the door. But as I neared it, I hesitated and turned around. "I don't know what has happened to you, Sam Turner, but I'm mighty glad you're no longer in my life."

And with that lie lingering in the air, I left him to his bitterness and shadows and went home.